2005

(1)

February 19, 2005

To Wed a Scandalous Spy

St. Martin's Paperbacks Titles
by Celeste Bradley

The Spy

The Impostor

The Pretender

The Charmer

To Wed a Scandalous Spy

Book One in the Royal Four series

Celeste Bradley

For my darling Grace,
who always looks closely at life.

Acknowledgments

Thank you to all the usual suspects!
How can I ever make it up to you?

Every ruler needs a few men he can count on to
tell him the truth
—whether he wants to hear it or not.

Created in the time of the Normans, when King William the Conqueror found himself overrun with "advisors" more concerned with their own agendas than with the good of the whole, the Quatre Royale were selected from the King's own boyhood friends. Lords all, and bound by loyalty rather than selfish motives, these four men took on the names of ruthless predators while acting as the Quatre, keeping their lives and identities separate from their true roles . . .

. . . to act as the shield of deceit and the sword of truth in the name of the King.

Courageous as the Lion
Deadly as the Cobra
Vigilant as the Falcon
Clever as the Fox

The appointment is for life—the commitment absolute. Bonds of family, friends and even love become as insubstantial as a dream when each hand-selected apprentice takes the seat of the master. All else is merely pretense, kept for the sake of secrecy and anonymity. For it is true that the iron bars of duty cage the hearts and souls of . . .

. . . THE ROYAL FOUR.

1

Another day, another suitor carried off in pieces.

Willa Trent sighed as she bent to pluck a stone from the country lane. Poor Timothy, so young to be scarred for life. He'd been so brave about it all.

"Don't fret, Miss Willa," he'd said. "I'm sure to be up and walking in no time." And he'd smiled at her even while his leg was being splinted and his bleeding head was wrapped.

Well, no more. From now on, the affliction would be hers to bear alone. Not that it had ever harmed her directly, but then, if a future of lonely spinsterhood wasn't harm, what was?

She drew a deep breath. That was the past—this morning counted as past, didn't it?—and she had never been one to waste today on yesterday. Just as her dream of seeing something of the world had never come true, so her dream of belonging in a family of her own seemed as though it would never come true. She was sure that in time she would adjust.

Not that she was disheartened or anything of the sort, but she had decided to spend the rest of the day on her own, away from both the sympathy and the smirks of the villagers. With a sigh, Willa left the lane and returned to the field beyond the hedge. As usual, she was cheered by the hues of the evening sky and the green of the rolling Northamptonshire fields.

Which hid the despicable small secrets she was determined to uncover today. It was not yet hunting and trapping season, and she had just found another nasty saw-toothed trap near a clear-running beck. All she needed to do was trigger it before doing her best to smash it with a rock.

Willa closed one eye, just as she had been instructed to by the young boy who had lent her the slingshot. Unfortunately, little Seth wasn't here now, so she couldn't ask him which eye. She shrugged. One eye was no doubt as good as another. Aiming for the precise center of the round, flat trigger of the rusted poacher's trap, she pulled back the strap of the slingshot as far as possible and let go.

Grim anticipation rose from deep within Nathaniel Stonewell, Earl of Reardon, as he urged his gelding to an ever-increasing pace down the Northamptonshire road. He was close behind his quarry now. Blunt took one stride for every two of Sir Foster's lesser mount, ruthlessly eating up the distance between them.

This afternoon Nathaniel had paused in his pursuit to water Blunt at a coaching inn, only to learn that a man matching Foster's description had passed through mere hours before. Since then, Nathaniel had kept Blunt to a punishing pace that only the greathearted thoroughbred could match. Night would fall soon, and Nathaniel had great hopes of catching up to Foster when the traitor took his rest in the village that Nathaniel had been informed lay shortly ahead.

Nathaniel's eyes narrowed against the wind created by

Blunt's gallop and he rose in the stirrups, riding as lightly as a jockey, or at least as lightly as a man of his size could ride. So close . . .

Foster was a greedy coward but a cunning one nonetheless. If the last free member of the traitorous Knights of Fleur made it to the teeming streets of London, it would take an army to ferret him out. Nathaniel didn't want an army's help.

He wanted Foster for his very own. For the betrayal of England, Foster must pay. For the loss of everything Nathaniel had ever held dear?

For that, Foster would pay at Nathaniel's hands.

A political cartoon had unintentionally revealed Nathaniel's involvement with the French sympathizers, the Knights of the Lily. Of course, Nathaniel had infiltrated the group on behalf of the Crown, but the public could hardly be informed of that. In the end, this misconception had been useful in keeping the leader's son, the apparently innocent Louis Wadsworth, free of public taint or scandal. This was not normally a concern of the Royal Four, but the Wadsworth munitions factory had been considered vital to the production of arms for the war with Napoleon.

So the elder, and now conveniently dead, Edward Wadsworth had been declared a hero for exposing the traitors, Nathaniel among them. Being a scandalous traitor was the perfect cover for Nathaniel's true position as a secret power in the government.

Nevertheless, it was bloody painful to watch his treasured reputation shatter like crockery on the cobbles. Nathaniel's personal honor was the armature of his nature, the very framework about which he lived his life. Now, the people of his acquaintance—some of them good, honest folk whose opinion he valued—would sooner seat a card-cheat at their table than the infamous Lord Reardon.

Your reputation is little enough sacrifice for your country, he reminded himself.

Another voice from the past, Lord Liverpool's voice, echoed the thought: *How can you claim willingness to sacrifice your very life if you aren't willing to give up something less tangible as well?*

The Prime Minister had been quite correct of course. Nathaniel had been utterly willing to take the title of traitor to protect the interests of England. Willing and most able.

That didn't mean he had to like it.

It was the Prime Minister's opinion that not only was Nathaniel's disgrace royally convenient, but it also provided a marvelously devious cover for the Cobra.

After all, who would suspect that the man known far and wide as Lord Treason in fact was a member of the elite and untouchable secret order known as the Royal Four?

Yes, it was all very convenient and desirable—and the least he could do for his country. It was marvelous how his "exposure" and subsequent shunning by Society at large had left him with so much time to attend to those little matters deemed of interest by the Four.

Like Sir Lucian Foster—an active, if somewhat cowardly, member of the Knights of the Lily during the latest contretemps who had fled the country before he could be apprehended. Now he was back on British soil.

The Knights of the Lily were dead and it was unlikely that they would ever rise again, but Foster was a loose end that Nathaniel, for one, wanted tied neatly away. Preferably with a noose.

Nathaniel's family had denounced him. His countrymen hated him. He was known far and wide as Lord Treason. He had paid his price. Now it was Foster's turn.

A grim, predatory smile crossed Nathaniel's lips as he bent his head farther into Blunt's whipping mane and urged the gelding to even higher speed.

I have you, you bastard.
That is, he did until all hell broke loose.

The curious thing about slingshots, Willa discovered, was that they rarely shot straight. Or perhaps that had been the wrong eye, after all.

The pebble in the sling took off in quite a different direction from the gaping-jawed trap at which she had aimed. Willa took some pride in its speed until she realized she had missed.

The stone shot straight toward the road, piercing the thick hedge in its way with a mere whisper and a snap.

Thunk. The stone hit something hollow. *Crack.* That sounded like the snapping of a branch. *Thud.* Something hollow hit the road, she was sure of it. *Buzz.* Buzz? Insects? Angry insects, from the ferocity of the hum.

No one was on the lane, she told herself. Likely nothing would—

The thunder of racing hooves cut the evening air even as she had the thought.

Neigh!

Oh no. Not *neigh!*

There came another high equine scream and a startled curse. Next were thudding hoofbeats and the sound of something much more solid hitting the ground.

Then ominous quiet.

Willa ran after her missile, following its beeline path. Torn from a stem, a single leaf drifted from the bushes between her and the road.

Willa squirmed through the hedgerow with no regard for her gown or her hair. Not that her pins were still in place after her evening's romp in the fields. She'd been gone from home since Timothy had been carried off to the doctor in the next village, and her hair was some the worse for it.

She popped through the hedge to see a heap of something lying in the lane. Tiptoeing closer, she strained to
see what it was. Oh dear. The something heavy that had
fallen was a man. A very large man.

"Ouch," she murmured. She knelt and pushed back the
overlong fair hair that covered his face.

The view was only half-reassuring. He was a youngish
man, so she needn't feel as though she had thrown someone's grandpapa off his horse. He was also a good deal
more delicious than any grandpapa she had ever seen.

If Adonis had owned perfectly chiseled cheekbones
and sculpted sensuous lips, he *might* have been nearly as
handsome as the man in the lane. He looked like a fallen
archangel with a bump on his temple. Willa reached for
some more images of perfection to compare the man to,
but frankly, her imagination fell short. He was, quite simply, devastating. She felt something twist just a little below her belly at the fellow's masculine perfection.

Still, he was quite pale and definitely unconscious.
That was no doubt due to the large rock embedded in the
dust of the lane whereupon his head lay.

Only a few feet away lay the shattered remains of the
hornets' nest. Several furious insects still clambered over
their ruined home, but the majority of them must have
taken off after the poor horse.

Willa bit her lip. It was a huge nest. She stood and
peered apprehensively down the lane toward the village.
The hornets wouldn't leave the nest undefended for long.
Willa snapped her skirts to shoo the remnants of the nest
from circling her hem. Already they were showing interest in the two humans in their vicinity. The man must be
removed before the majority of the insects returned.

Squatting next to the man once more, Willa gave him
a gentle poke on his upper arm.

"Please wake up, sir." It was much like poking a rock.

She poked a bit harder, but there was no response. Willa took hold of the man's coat with two hands and tugged.

"Oh . . . my." Gasping, she let loose. He hadn't moved an inch. "You are rather well grown."

Willa was already quite tired from her eventful day, and her back ached at the thought of moving such a big parcel. Then, taking a deep breath, she drew upon her natural optimism. Perhaps she simply needed a better grip.

Gingerly, she picked up his arm and slid her hands down to grasp his wrist. It was a large wrist and an even larger hand. Willa could scarcely wrap her own fingers around it. Backing up until his arm was outstretched, she gave a mighty heave.

The man flipped neatly over and Willa landed on her bottom in the dust. Well. That had done very little good, but it had given her an idea. She would roll him from harm's way.

A bit gingerly, since she was quite unused to touching another person's . . . person, Willa stretched the gentleman's limbs straight up and down, like a child about to roll down a grassy hill. Then, crouching behind him, she put her shoulder into it and flipped him onto his face.

"Oh dear. I am sorry." Well, it couldn't be helped. Best to get it done quickly, before he suffocated.

Again she flipped him, and again. With a great deal of unladylike grunting and perspiration, not to mention all the fascinating things that she learned about male physiology in the process, Willa maneuvered the man to lie in the grassy channel beneath the hedge.

Flopping him onto his back for the last time, with a groan, Willa found herself half-lying across his chest, breathing heavily. What a great fellow he was.

How very tiring.

Willa blew back an errant strand of hair. It had come entirely undone during her exertions. As she pulled it back

to retie the ribbon, she examined her victim by the last
dim trace of sunlight.

His face was all romantic lines and sensual strength.
His golden hair was thick and much too long, but she
rather liked the way it fell past his jaw. His unshaven face
bristled with just a touch of golden-brown beard.

All in all, a somewhat lawless specimen. It made her
wonder if he was something of a rebel. His collar was
plain but fine, his cravat simply tied, elegant but not fop-
pish in the least.

His face was also rather dusty after all that rolling.
Willa pulled out her handkerchief and moistened a corner
of it with her tongue. Moira would have conniptions if
she knew, but no one was around to see Willa do such a
common thing and she couldn't bear to see her fellow so
rumpled.

Gently wiping his cheeks and brow, she wondered who
he was and from whence he'd come. If she didn't know
him, then he didn't live nearby. Derryton was well-known
for its fine ale locally, but it wasn't really on the way to
anywhere from anywhere, so few truly exotic travelers
journeyed through it.

His breath came evenly on her face and his heart beat
in regular time next to her ribs. Willa had some experience with injuries—at any rate with witnessing them. He
didn't seem to be in any immediate danger from his fall.

Nevertheless, she ought to fetch help for him soon.
She lifted her head slowly to peer through the grass at the
broken nest. It was now so covered with angry hornets that
the nest itself was hidden beneath restless winged bodies.
She could feel the concerted buzzing vibrate through the
very ground. Yet more were coming to land with every
passing moment.

It was a sobering sight. Hornets in such numbers could
be dangerous indeed. Slowly, projecting harmlessness with

every fiber of her being, Willa sank back down next to her
latest victim. *"Vespa crabro,"* she explained to him in a
whisper. "The common hornet. Really quite docile and
pretty . . . normally." She listened to the furious drone just a
few feet away.

"Unless the nest is disturbed, of course," she continued, her words a mere breath on his unconscious ear. "I'd
describe that nest as quite disturbed. Ruined even. But
don't feel too badly, for with the passing of summer they
would have only lived a few months more at most."

She heaved a weary sigh and settled more comfortably
into the tall grass. "We merely need to stay quite still and
wait. They'll settle down at dusk and I will fetch you
some help from Derryton."

Dusk was not far away. In fact, one could hardly call
it day anymore, the way the blue twilight was taking over
the sky. It was getting chill as well, a sure sign that the
mist would rise. Excellent. The chill would slow the hornets' defensive fervor and the mist would confuse them
yet more.

Then she would fetch help. She sighed. There was
bound to be a row when she did. And she was so terribly
tired of being the cause of uproar.

Oh, she knew they all loved her, but the horrid thing
about being an orphan raised by an entire village was that
everyone felt quite free to criticize one. And they did.

Bad enough that she had stayed out so late, but to have
caused such an accident when she ought to have been safe
by the hearth? She'd never hear the end of it.

No one would be mollified by her reason that it had
taken all evening to find the traps laid by old Mr. Pratt
and trigger them with the sling she'd borrowed. She'd
told John that she was only going to seek out the last of
the ripe wild currants.

Her guardian didn't approve of poaching, but he didn't

think it was Willa's place to stop it. Of course, it also
wasn't her place to fell innocent strangers on the lane.

Perhaps if her handsome fellow came walking into the
village under his own power, there would be less of a
ruckus over her latest escapade. She craned her neck to
gaze hopefully into his face.

No such chance. He was most assuredly not in walking
condition. Resting her chin on one fist, she gazed at him.
She had never been so near a man, especially one so fine.

None of the men she knew would come close to her,
fond of her as they might be. Not a one of them would so
much as give her a kiss, not after what happened to poor
Wesley Moss. And now, with Timothy, her reputation
would no doubt spread far beyond.

Why, she might go all the rest of her days without being kissed. Since this man was already unconscious, she
may as well take advantage of a unique opportunity.

She leaned over him again, given courage by the growing darkness. He smelled wonderful, like spice and horse
and a heady scent she didn't have a name for but that she
responded to anyway.

Taking another deep breath, Willa fancied she could
smell adventure on him. This was a man who had smelled
the scents of the world, she would wager. He'd breathed in
exotic scents like those of the dusty streets of Cairo or the
perfumed salons of Vienna.

He might even now be on his way to London. This
road didn't go there, but Willa knew that it eventually met
a greater road south of Derryton, although she had never
been that far. Imagine, London!

Willa shook her head. She was being silly. Yet simply
the way the man's lips had felt under her fingertips made
her all breathless and fairly dying of curiosity.

No one was about. No one would ever, ever know.

Sliding slowly up her fellow's chest in a fashion that

made her catch her breath in a whole new way, Willa hesitated. Was it wrong to kiss someone without his permission? Timothy had very politely asked her first. Not that it had done him any good, what with the broken bones and all.

"Would you mind terribly if I kissed you?"

Well, she could quite truthfully report that there was no protest. After running the tip of her tongue over her lips, Willa pressed them to her handsome fellow's mouth.

It was lovely, to be sure, but somehow not what she was expecting. With a disappointed sigh, she slid off his chest and lay low in the grass beside him.

He was terribly untidy, with his coat twisted about and his limbs splayed. If she left and someone else discovered him like this, he'd likely be embarrassed by his disarray. Not to mention that settling him would provide an excuse for her to touch him once more.

By the time she'd gotten him rearranged to her satisfaction, she was out of breath again. Wasn't it odd how touching a hard thigh or a large, roughened hand could take one's very air? Perhaps she should stop touching him if she wanted to ease her breathing.

Leaning on her elbows and tipping her head back, Willa contemplated the growing dusk. She could leave him as soon as the hornets settled. She would go before long, for he had not woken yet, and that was not a good sign.

Just as soon as the hornets settled . . .

2

The chamber tucked away in a tower of Westminster Palace would scarcely interest the offhand observer, for it was simply a round room whose curved walls were punctuated at intervals by arched panels portraying absurdly idyllic country scenes, frescoed by a nameless artist of a previous century. The colors were dimmed by soot and careless housekeeping, giving the plump peasantry depicted there a grimy quality. Not that anyone noticed.

In the center of the room, beneath a not exquisite chandelier, stood a single round table with four chairs placed equidistant from each other. The chairs were very nearly identical in design, but for slight differences in the fanciful carvings adorning the wooden chair backs. Amid the much overdone greenery depicted there, one could, if one looked carefully, discern a different set of eyes carved into each design.

One pair of eyes seemed rather reptilian. Another set reminded one of the watchful gaze of a raptor. There were the unmistakable slanting eyes of a fox on yet another seat, and the last depicted the heavy brow and deep-set eyes of a lion.

The Royal Four had convened.

Or at any rate, the Royal Two. Present today were only half of the four members of the most select and exclusive of gentlemen's clubs, a handpicked group who secretly advised the Prime Minister and the Crown—four brilliant, principled men with such a depth of honor and commitment to England that no amount of power and promises could sway their conviction.

They even abandoned names and rank within their secret circle. No "Lord This" or "Earl of That." Here there was only the Fox, the Falcon, the Lion, and the Cobra.

At the moment, the Lion and the Falcon were at hand. Due to circumstances beyond their control, the Fox and the Cobra were not.

The Fox had a fairly acceptable excuse. The elderly statesman was on his deathbed, after all, being nursed by his lovely, much-younger wife.

The Cobra had no such defense, being merely halfway across the country attending to a matter of national security. Yet the Falcon and the Lion carefully avoided any breath of censure against the Cobra. When they did speak of him, their voices dropped slightly lower to a more sympathetic register.

At the moment, the Lion had his feet up on the ancient central table and the front legs of his chair off the floor. He was a big man, blond and powerful. One only had to look at him to visualize a far-flung Viking traveler chatting up a Norman lady long centuries ago. The Lion quite by chance resembled his title, for the Four were chosen not on looks but on keen intelligence, nearly royal ancestry, and deathless loyalty.

However, there was no denying he did look like a great cat as he lounged in his chair. The Lion yawned mightily. His cheroot sent a spiral of smoke into the arching heights of the chamber.

"Must you smoke that in here?" The Falcon grimaced.

The Falcon looked nothing like his namesake, unless one counted the intense intelligence behind his sharp eyes. He was tall and lean against the Lion's breadth, but no less powerful in his presence. "Can you not wait until we recess?"

The Lion blew an irreverent gust of smoke his way. "Won't taste as good later. Forbidden fruit is all the sweeter."

The Falcon was unimpressed by this argument. "The Fox would have a cat fit if he were here. He holds these chambers nearly sacred."

The Lion shrugged. "I don't see why. It's simply four rather ugly walls and a grotty old table that I wouldn't allow my dog to eat off." Nonetheless, he pulled his feet in and sat forward to stub out his cigar in a waiting saucer. "We could meet in a public house, for all it matters. It is the office that is sacred, not the chamber. Not even the man who holds the office, apparently."

They both went silent for a moment, mourning the loss that their comrade had suffered. Not that they wouldn't have done the same—given up all that they treasured for England and the Crown. In that silence, however, echoed the fervent wish they might never be asked to.

"So has this meeting come to order or not?" The Lion pulled his chair into a more dignified position.

"We two are it tonight, I fear," said the Falcon. "After contacting the Fox and the Cobra, I informed them that the Liars found documents in the safe of a certain Lord Maywell. These, when decoded, led us to believe that Sir Foster was returning from his self-imposed exile—"

The Lion grunted. "That's one way of putting it. I prefer 'hiding out under his rock like the cowardly traitorous slug he is.' "

The Falcon looked sourly at him. "May I continue?"

The Lion waved a hand magnanimously and the Falcon

resumed. "I informed them that Foster is expected to arrive in London shortly with something—we have no concrete information on what it is yet—that Maywell felt would be very damaging to the Crown."

The Falcon tapped the document he'd laid on the table. "I have here the missive from the Fox in response, brought by fast courier."

The Lion reached into his coat. "And I have the same from the Cobra."

The Falcon nodded, then glanced down at his own document. "The Fox relates that he is still of the opinion that our first priority ought to be the trailing of the traitor. The Liar's Club should continue their investigation into the identity of the Voice of Society and how it seems to know a bit too much about their covert activities. We have higher concerns."

"It's just as well. I don't think the Cobra will ever entirely trust the Liars." The Lion unfolded his document. "The Cobra has already begun tracing Foster's path from the town where he landed, but he also reminds us that we are still investigating the possibility that there is someone pulling the strings of the French espionage in England, someone that might very well be an influential member of Society."

"Is the Prime Minister still hoping to dig that name out of Louis Wadsworth?"

The Lion nodded. "Liverpool is letting Wadsworth stew in the Tower at the moment."

The Falcon did not quite smile. "Ruing his greedy ways, I hope. Imagine selling faulty arms to the British government on behalf of the French!"

The Lion scowled. "He got paid twice, the bastard."

"Considering his present position, I'd say he's still collecting on that ill-considered plan," the Falcon said.

The Falcon and the Lion put their cohorts' messages

down at their respective places at the table, in effect making it look as if the two had just stepped out of the meeting for a moment.

The Falcon leaned back in his chair. "I concur with the Cobra's plan. First Sir Foster, then the Voice. I believe that the traitor will lead us to this puppetmaster."

The Lion nodded. "I concur as well. The Cobra has insisted on personally taking the Foster mission, since he has previous acquaintance with the traitor."

"Meaning his ill-fated entry into the Knights of Fleur, I assume. It was a good idea to crack them by joining."

The Lion nodded. "It is to the Cobra's credit that he insisted on taking the fire for the royal arse when things went to hell."

The Falcon shook his head ruefully. "Can you imagine being painted with that brush for the rest of your life?"

The Lion let out a gust. "Sometimes I have nightmares that it is I."

The moment of sympathy stretched on. Then the two men visibly shook off the pall.

"Well, I suppose that brings us to our close." The Falcon stood and gave his waistcoat a single precise tug. The Lion, who tended to be perpetually rumpled, didn't bother.

"I hear you're going to be married," the Falcon said as they moved toward the door. "May I offer my congratulations?"

"Thank you. She's a lovely girl, well brought up and demure. She'll make a fine Lady Greenleigh someday."

The Falcon slid his companion a look. "Is it a love match, then?"

The Lion wasn't fooled by the casual tone. "Have no fear. I won't fall in love and reveal all our secrets on the pillows. She's merely an attractive girl who will breed me an heir." He dug for another cheroot in his coat pocket. "You should consider marrying. It could only improve your cover, you know. You're beginning to be far too in-triguing a mystery to the eligible ladies in town."

The Falcon sent him a long-suffering look. "I'd rather not, thank you. The Falcon's responsibilities do not make for a good husband. Why would I want to do that to an in-nocent woman?"

The Lion looked thoughtful. "Why indeed?"

"Do you suppose the Cobra will ever marry?"

The Lion shook his head. "I'd say 'tis doubtful. After all, what self-respecting woman would tie herself to a publicly branded traitor?" He reached for the latch of the ancient oak door. "Poor bastard."

Someone was stomping on Nathaniel's head. They'd been stomping for hours, apparently, since every thud of Nathaniel's brain had the bruised feeling of long acquain-tance.

He tried to roll his head away from the pain, only to be transfixed by a spike of pure agony through his skull. His eyes shot open in response, then slammed shut against the bright dawn.

Dawn?

Nathaniel tried to raise both hands to his aching head, but only one hand would obey him. The other was cold and numb and pinned by an immovable weight.

Exquisitely alert now, he remained still as he assessed the possibilities. He was lying on his back, pinned by one arm, with a splitting head, outdoors in the morning dew.

None of this was good.

It was no longer today. It was now tomorrow. Frustra-tion roiled through Nathaniel when he realized that Foster was lost to him. The man was traveling hard. He would be far ahead by now.

At the moment, however, there was no sound near him

but the chirping of birds, the chuckling of a beck of some kind, and soft, kittenish snoring. Opening one eye, out of both slyness and anticipated pain, Nathaniel was able to see that he lay in the shelter of a hedge, on a bank of grass, by a road.

There was no sign of immediate danger. The trickling water was somewhere off to his left. The snoring was coming from the vicinity of his chest.

By stretching his neck and angling his head, Nathaniel could see a mop of untidy brown hair and one delicate hand that lay on his waistcoat, half slipped inside. Well, he'd woken to worse things in his life.

He cleared his throat. "I beg your pardon," he said softly, "but we seem to be sleeping together."

The person lying upon him gave a drowsy snort and snuggled deeper into his armpit.

" 'Tis very flattering, to be sure, and you snore quite prettily, but would you mind very much giving back my arm?"

Still no response. Carefully laying his head back on the ground, for he wouldn't want it to break, Nathaniel forced his deadened muscles to move and rocked the sleeper farther onto his chest. Pulling his arm free from beneath the weight, he hissed as feeling began to flood back into his flesh.

Then he gently rolled his companion to the ground on her—yes, most definitely her—back. She was very pliant and went without protest. He went up on one elbow and leaned over her.

"Miss?" Gingerly, Nathaniel brushed his knuckles across her cheek. Her skin was warm and very soft.

She stirred and stretched away from him in a sensual arch, her sleeves sliding up white arms to show dimpled elbows. Lips working sleepily, she sighed, then slowly opened wide blue eyes the distinctive deep color of twilight and blinked at her surroundings.

She smiled at him. "Hello."

Her voice was husky with sleep. Very pleasant, actually, but Nathaniel was in no mood to be pleased.

"Who are you?" he asked with a frown.

She yawned delicately behind her hand. "I am Willa Trent. And you are?" She gazed up at him from her position on the ground with her sable hair spreading across the grass, and suddenly Nathaniel was reminded of waking up with a woman after a rousing night of . . .

"I am Nathaniel Stonewell." Cautiously he left off his title. "Do you know why we are lying here?"

She nodded and smiled proudly. "I saved your life last night."

Last night? Nathaniel lay back on the ground beside the girl. His skull was pounding and his body ached from head to toe. Hissing in pain, he held his brain together with both hands. After the whirling slowed and the throbbing eased, he found he could speak again.

"What happened?" It couldn't have been Foster. Except that, of course, no security was unbreakable. Foster might very well have known someone was after him. He could have doubled back—

She made a slight humming sound beneath her breath. "Well . . . there was a rock."

Nathaniel blinked. "A rock."

"Yes." She hesitated. "In the lane."

"A rock in the lane." The girl was perhaps not very bright.

"Yes. And you fell on it."

Nathaniel took a long breath. "From my horse?"

She looked away. "One would assume."

Nathaniel's mind felt fuddled. Probing his skull, he found a likely knot over his left ear. Having fallen by the roadside with a sore head and no horse in sight, he would normally assume he'd been thrown from the saddle. Unlikely but not entirely impossible.

That still didn't explain the girl.

"All right, girl. Explain."

"I did. You fell from your horse onto the rock."

But her eyes slid away from his and Nathaniel began to suspect there was more to it than that.

"Well, we must get you to the village." Picking herself up from the grass, the girl began industriously brushing at herself.

Despite his headache and his mounting suspicions, Nathaniel watched with some interest as her actions created fascinating vibrations throughout her generous anatomy. Then she began brushing at him with proprietary bustle. Nathaniel took to his feet to avoid her ministrations, which jostled his broken head, only to find her brushing at his backside.

"You are terribly dusty," she said. "It simply won't do."

Nathaniel caught at her hands and clasped them tightly between his. "I would prefer that you not."

Her hands felt like captive birds in his grasp, but the rest of her went very still. Slowly, her candid blue gaze rose from their entwined hands to meet his eyes. Then she nervously licked her full lips with a tiny flick of her tongue.

A minor portion of Nathaniel's mind noticed the damp shine of those lips and responded accordingly. The rest of his thoughts were centered on how exactly he had come to be horseless on this dusty country lane.

The girl seemed harmless, but this would not be the first time he had seen an innocent used by traitors. Nor would it be the first time he'd seen treason housed in a harmless form.

"*Miss Willie!*"

Nathaniel started at the deep voice that boomed down

the lane. Whirling so quickly that his head throbbed anew, Nathaniel automatically dropped into a defensive crouch.

Not that it would do any good. He'd be hard put to defeat the oncoming bloke on a good day, much less when he could scarcely focus his eyes. The man was enormous, as broad as two oxen. Or maybe Nathaniel was simply seeing double. The man was also roughly dressed, and by the way he addressed the girl, Nathaniel thought he might be a servant or perhaps merely a respectful member of her community.

So she was local. A simple, country woman helping a felled stranger by the roadside.

A respectable woman? She was well-spoken and obviously educated. Her blue gaze was innocent and guileless. She was unmistakably of the gentry.

Distant alarms began to go off in Nathaniel's thudding brain.

The man lumbered closer. "Miss Willie! We ain't been half-worried about you. When you didn't come home, we thought you'd been stolen from us."

The giant swept past Nathaniel, and the wind of his passing was nearly enough to send Nathaniel to his knees.

"That's all right. I'll trounce you in a moment," muttered Nathaniel, shaking his head to clear it. Staggering slightly, he turned to see the man swallow one of "Miss Willie's" hands in his massive paw.

"You mustn't worry us like that, miss. You know I'm a nervous sort, I am."

The man blinked sad eyes at the girl, who patted his cheek consolingly.

"I'm quite well, as you can see, John. There is no call to fret. I am safe and sound. I spent the night with Mr. Stonewell."

Nathaniel choked. "Well, now, ah . . . that is to say—"

The giant turned to blink his beagle eyes at Nathaniel. "Spent the night?"

Oh, damn. "Well, perhaps . . ."

"And you, sir, be you well?"

What? Nathaniel nodded cautiously. "Well enough."

For an instant the big man looked as though he would cry. Then his face twisted in a grimace that didn't bode well for Nathaniel.

When the man began to swing at him, Nathaniel prepared himself for pain, but all the blow cost him was his balance as the giant clapped him on the back. As Nathaniel staggered, the man turned around to bellow down the lane at the sturdy woman hurrying toward them.

"Did you hear that, Mrs. Smith? The whole blessed night. And hardly a scratch on him!"

The full import of Nathaniel's situation came over him for the first time since he had awoken with the strange woman in his arms—a woman he'd spent the entire night with, an innocent, apparently decent young woman of the sort that was worried about when she went missing.

An ordinary man might look for a way out, a knothole through which to escape. An ordinary man might simply mount his horse and ride away from such a vast misunderstanding, leaving the woman behind to survive the scandal as best she could.

Nathaniel was not an ordinary man.

Drawing a deep breath that only made the pounding in his head worse, Nathaniel turned to Miss Willa Trent and bowed deeply. "Miss Trent, would you do me the supreme honor of giving me your hand in marriage?"

Willa blinked at the man for a long moment. Mr. Nathaniel Stonewell remained in the bow, his hand calmly held out to her, while John, her guardian, waited with his face nearly purple from lack of breath and Moira, John's wife, hurried up with tears of joy already starting up in her eyes.

Only last evening Willa had told herself to be resigned to spinsterhood. Now a fine, handsome gentleman stood before her, begging for her hand.

He'd been kind when he woke her. And patient when he questioned her, even when she was trying very hard not to answer. Oh, he was so handsome, with the morning sun glinting in his mussed fair hair. . . .

As if in a dream, Willa watched herself slowly put out her hand and slip it into his. "Yes," she heard her voice say, "I will."

Nathaniel was seated at a rough table in the Derryton coaching inn with a mighty bucket of ale foaming before him and the enormous son of the enormous innkeeper at his side.

The young man—Dick? Or was it Dan?—had been with him for the past hour as he'd been introduced to the entire village, as Mr. Stonewell, of course. At every turn he'd been met by faces wreathed in smiles and grateful handclasps. Everyone seemed in favor of the match, from the chandler, to the baker, to the grinning cooper who was even now hammering together an archway on the green where the vows were to take place.

Apparently something unfortunate had happened to the tiny village church recently—which incident had sparked a few snickers and reassuring comments in the vein of "Don't worry, sir. She'll outgrow it soon enough."

Nathaniel tried very hard not to think about the struc-ture on the green and its uncanny resemblance to a gal-lows as he gently questioned the village folk about Foster. He learned little of importance—only that "a right toff" had stayed the night at the coaching inn, had never left the inn, not even to join the search for the missing girl, but had left before dawn that morning on the road south.

Derryton was not on the way from Foster's landing point at Crestford to London by any stretch of the imagination. In fact, Foster's route was most curious. Nathaniel had followed him here to far Northamptonshire, north and west of Crestford and most decidedly far north of London, without a clue where the man was headed.

Perhaps Foster was choosing to remain on the back roads to avoid recognition. His face was nearly as recognizable as Nathaniel's, for they'd appeared together in the infamous political cartoon "Fleur and Her Followers."

Derryton itself seemed unlikely to have been Foster's destination. The village was healthy but not bustling, an attractive example of a thousand other such hamlets adorning the roads of England.

An entirely ordinary town, this Derryton. Except for the girl. The innkeeper's son was oddly reticent on some topics but was willing to discuss the unusual Miss Trent.

As it turned out, she was the de facto ward of the innkeeper and a former lady's maid.

Apparently, the girl's father and mother had died of fever several years ago. Young Willa had been left with no perceptible relatives, and the entire village had taken the girl in at the age of twelve.

All around Nathaniel, said villagers now bustled. The innkeeper's wife tripped by with a smile on her face and her arms full of yellowed fabric. Despite the early hour, pints were raised again and again to congratulate the "happy couple." As mundane a setting as Nathaniel had ever seen.

No, Nathaniel decided that Foster must have simply wanted a night in a soft bed and a pint of good ale on his journey. With a suppressed groan, Nathaniel rolled his head from side to side to ease the pounding. Nathaniel's own bed had been a grassy ditch, and the pint of ale, though tempting, must be refused. He was on duty.

The Royal Four were always on duty.

To be chosen as the Cobra was a distinction beyond price, and Nathaniel was honored to be thus entrusted with the fate of the nation, whether others knew it or not. The Four had been in place since the days of William the Conqueror and, through judicious influence and watchfulness, had steered England into the empire it currently was.

The nutty scent of the ale wafted under Nathaniel's nose. It smelled delicious. Sadly, he put it aside. He was the Cobra. He was *not* the man his father thought him, not the light-minded wastrel he'd made pains to be regarded as.

He was a man above greed, above politics, above self.

And unfortunately, above ale, although he had never longed more for a pint. His head pounded unmercifully, his bones ached from his fall, and his life was about to change forever.

Again.

Today was his wedding day and he was to wed a stranger.

"But he is a stranger to me! Do you genuinely expect me to wed him *today*—"

The rest of Willa's protest was cut off as John Smith's wife, Moira, drew the elderly wedding gown over her head. Apparently they did expect her to. The old silk smelled of benzene and dust. Willa sneezed twice as soon as her head popped out.

They stood in Moira and John's room, for in Willa's room her possessions were being packed with lightning speed.

"There now, miss," Moira said soothingly. "He's a fine

fellow. I can tell by the cut of him. He might even be as high as a lord. John says his horse is an expensive beast, and those boots were made special for him on Bond Street, mark my words. I've been to London, you'll remember. I know about these things."

Willa didn't bother to remind Moira that her journey had been over twenty years ago and had lasted mere weeks. Even that little excursion was more than Willa had ever traveled, at least since she had come to Derryton as an infant on that same trek.

Besides, Moira had been dining out on that story all these years, and in the woman's mind London had become a mystical place of gold-paved streets and confectioner shops on every corner. Surely it was even more fascinating than that.

"But he could be anyone! A . . . a highwayman, or even a gypsy!"

"Pish-posh. He's a fine and handsome gentleman. He knows his duty and he's willing to do right. Honorable, that one is. That means he's perfect for you. You're no common village lass, don't forget. You're as much a lady as any in London, by my way of thinking. Your dear mum certainly was. And didn't she look a treat in this gown?"

Moira sniffled as she tugged the dress into place, and Willa regretted bringing up sad memories. Her mother *had* been a lady, no doubt about it, and Moira her loyal lady's maid until her death.

The gown fit perfectly. Willa narrowed her eyes at her own image in the wavy mirror. Her mother had a been a slender lady, elegantly petite of bust and bottom. Quite the opposite of Willa herself. "Moira, how is it that the dress fits perfectly?"

Moira busied herself with the folds of the skirts. "Oh, I let it out three years ago when I thought William Beckham might be the one."

"Oh yes. Wills. Do you think he's regained the hearing in his left ear?"

"I'm sure he has, pet," Moira said soothingly. "After all, it was a trifling explosion—hardly more than a Chinese rocket going off."

"I do hope so," Willa said sincerely. "One should always be cautious with black powder. After all, I would never have set his gift next to the stove if I'd known it was flammable."

Moira finished doing the many tiny buttons up the back of the gown. "There now." She smiled over Willa's shoulder at her in the mirror. "All ready for your groom."

Her groom. Her husband. "But Moira, a man off the road?"

"Well, he was good enough to spend the night lying beside, wasn't he?" Moira put a fist on each wide hip and glared at Willa. "You mind me, miss! You're fortunate no one in this village would speak against you, or your reputation would be in ruins sure enough! Even so, it's a fair thing you never kissed him!"

Willa didn't answer that one, but obviously her blush spoke for her, because Moira's scowl turned to open-mouthed shock. The woman rushed to the window and threw open the shutter.

"James Cooper, aren't you finished with that archway yet? And where's that vicar from Edgeton?"

There was a pause in the hammering and James Cooper's voice drifted up from the square. "John should be back with him by noon, missus. You want I should skip the benches?"

"Mercy, yes. We'd best get this done spot-on!"

She turned back to Willa and gave a disapproving shake of her head. "You mind me, miss. The man spent the night with you and lived to tell the tale. Wed him and bed him and be quick about it. I have just the thing for that."

Moira led Willa to where a wisp of fine lawn hung from a hook behind the door. The dainty concoction of lace and gossamer fabric was in odd contrast to the rustic room, with its homemade bed frame and chest and worn rag rug on the floor.

Moira held the scant thing up proudly, displaying it on her wide front.

Willa gaped. "Moira! Oh, gracious, you don't mean for me to wear *that*."

"And what's wrong with it? It's white, it's long, and it covers you neck to toe."

"Except that it might as well be invisible!"

"Well, no one ever said a bride had to wear a flour sack, now did they?" Moira handed it to Willa.

Since that was the undeniable truth, Willa didn't bother to protest any further. "Where did it come from?"

"I purchased it off a gypsy peddler a while back, when it looked like that Donovan boy might survive long enough to crack the question."

"Oh yes. Poor Sam." Goodness, that had been two years back. "Have you seen his mother lately?"

"A few Sundays ago. She told me he's married now and they're all hoping he'll still be able to father a child."

Willa shook her head sadly. "Such a pity. He was very sweet. But one can never be too careful around a cider press."

Moira gave her a pointed look. "You don't want this man to come to the same end, now do you?"

"Oh, Moira, you know the same thing never happens twice."

"No, as far as I can see, it just keeps getting worse."

Willa stroked the fine fabric in her hands. It was so sheer, she could see her fingernails through it. "But to bed him? I scarcely know his name, let alone love him!"

Moira sighed and her expression softened. "You've

been reading too many romantic stories, my girl. Love comes after. I've told you that time and again. You pick yourself a likely fellow, you make your mind up, and you marry."

"But you love John. I know you do."

"That I do, but I've had twenty years to know him, and find out what a fine man he is. Not that he doesn't have his bad side. I've not had a good night's sleep in two decades sharing a bed with that great lout and his snores." The fondness in her voice belied her complaint. "But, for the most part, a man is what you make of him."

Willa was none too sure of that. "Still, perhaps he won't mind waiting a bit for the bedding part. I certainly don't, and I have been waiting all my life."

Moira frowned again. "Miss Willa, you know very well that poor man's life is in danger every minute you delay. The only way to break that jinx is to get yourself wedded and bedded. If you don't do it now . . ."

Her voice trailing off warningly, Moira gave Willa a significant look and sailed out of the room.

After her guardian and best friend left, Willa sank to the bed and leaned her cheek against the bedpost. Marry a stranger or likely never marry at all, that's what Moira had meant.

The older Willa got, the fewer the young men who gazed her way. Not because she was losing her looks but because word was getting out about the dangers of taking a fancy to the "Mishap Miss" of Derryton village.

3

A half hour later, Willa peered through her mother's veil at the gathering of villagers before her. Yes, they were all there, from the baker's wife to the cooper's daughter. Every woman from the village stood facing Willa on the other side of the square. Behind them stood the men, shuffling shamefaced and uncomfortable, but there all the same.

Willa let her gaze travel over every beloved face, every pair of callused helping hands. These people were her only family in the world, really. She loved them all.

The traitors.

"I can't believe you would do this to me. What would Mama say?" muttered Willa.

"She'd say high time. Now smile, miss."

With a loving peck to Willa's cheek and a reproving pinch to her arm, Moira gave her a push toward the archway where four men waited. The twin sons of John and Moira, the vicar from Edgeton, and the man called Nathaniel Stonewell.

Clutching her fistful of garden flowers, Willa walked toward them, the traditional hesitant pace of the bride suddenly making a great deal of sense.

Who wouldn't hesitate to take such a step? For the rest of her life she would be in the hands of this man whom she didn't even know.

True, they were large and shapely hands. True, he was a good-looking fellow and well-spoken. Actually, it entered Willa's mind that she may have made a fortunate shot with that sling after all.

That is, as long as he didn't murder her in her sleep or sell her to some Arabian sheikh.

Worse yet, what if he *snored*?

Standing in the center of the green, Nathaniel tried not to chafe at the delay in his mission. This was a momentous day in his life, no matter the randomness of the marriage. The noon sun shone down on the picturesque village square, birds chirped a lively tune from the trees, and chubby village children ran laughing in circles around the archway. A lovely day for a wedding, actually. Nathaniel was simply having trouble believing it was his own.

Then all eyes turned to the figure in satin coming down the lawn. A pretty picture indeed. The little miss from the lane washed up nicely, in her fresh country way.

He was marrying.

Of course, it was an entirely illegal union, especially for someone of his station. No banns had been read, no delicate negotiations of dowry and inheritance enacted, no chance for those who might protest to do so.

A village cleric and a garden bouquet might be binding enough for the common folk of Derryton village, who needed very little other than their word to unite them, but since the Marriage Act was passed more than fifty years ago, no peer could legally wed in England without weeks of bloody rigmarole. An impromptu country exchange of vows was considered little more than a betrothal, a rural "jumping over the broomstick" tradition.

Not that he had any intention of refuting the union.

He'd inadvertently ruined a respectable young woman—
more than she yet realized—and he knew his duty. He
would wed her as soon as they arrived in London and all
had been arranged.

He simply didn't think now was a good time to inform
her of that. She was unwilling enough to leave, he could
see. Traveling with a sniffling "bride" was preferable, and
likely faster, than traveling with a reluctant, possibly rebellious woman who could not possibly wish to tie herself to "Lord Treason" once she learned the truth.

He'd allowed this to happen. Therefore, it was his
place to conclude it with as little harm done to the woman
as possible. The best solution would be to return to London, where his money, if not his social standing, would
facilitate the necessary legal maneuverings to finalize this
strange union.

He had merely to get there—bride in tow, apparently—
to repair this. After all, it wasn't as if such a scandal as
marrying outside his class would shock anyone among the
ton. He could likely marry an orangutan ape from the
Royal Menagerie and people would merely nod sagely and
say they'd always known he was a bad one.

People other than the inhabitants of Derryton. In fact,
there had been a shocking lack of interest in questioning
his particulars. And what of the teenage giant who never
seemed to leave his presence? *Companion? Or keeper?*

He'd been too preoccupied with Foster, Nathaniel realized. Instead, he ought to have been questioning the village about why they couldn't wait to wed their allegedly
beloved daughter to a complete stranger.

Was there something wrong with the girl? She might
be tragically mad or shamelessly promiscuous. So far,
Nathaniel had noticed that while she might be considered
a bit odd, he'd seen no sign of real madness. Looking at
her now as she walked up the makeshift aisle, her hands

trembling so that petals were falling from her garden bouquet like pink snow, Nathaniel had trouble believing that the latter was the case. She looked as fair and innocent as any bride ever had. His bride—one he never thought he'd have.

Nathaniel cleared his throat against an unexpected lump. Truly, it was a lovely day for a wedding.

The vicar made no pretense of drawing out the ceremony. In fact, he raced through it as if someone had paid extra for speed. "If ye discern any impediment to be lawfully joined in matrimony, do ye now confess it?" The words came so fast they were slurred together. How curious.

A whisper came. "Pardon me, sir, but do you snore?"

His concentration thrown, Nathaniel peered down at the lace-covered head below his chin. She wasn't looking at him, but her head was cocked in such a way that she was clearly waiting for an answer.

Snore? The very idea. "Absolutely not!" he whispered into the lace where he thought her ear might be.

"Thank you." She gestured for the clergyman to continue.

As the man rattled on, Nathaniel decided to withhold judgment on the madness question. After all, one never knew.

"Sir? Wilt thou?"

The giant poked Nathaniel. "*I will!*" the younger man hissed.

Nathaniel inhaled deeply. There was no help for it. "I will."

"Have thee a ring?" the vicar asked.

A ring. He'd forgotten in his need to search for Foster. He ought to have remembered—but really what did it matter? He shook his head sharply. At his motion, Miss

Trent snatched back the hand she'd half-extended to him as part of the ceremony.

The vicar cleared his throat to cover the awkwardness of the moment. "Then I now pronounce thee man and wife!" The vicar snapped his book shut, and the villagers burst into applause all around them. Loud, prolonged, enthusiastic applause.

That could mean nothing good.

Tentatively, Nathaniel reached out to lift the veil from his bride's face. She peered out at him from the lace, blinking like a plump and rosy angel.

The vicar tapped a fingertip on the holy book. "Aren't ye going to kiss the bride?"

Willa stood back as Dick and Dan carried her packs into the stable with a careless knock of the contents against the door frame and tossed them negligently on the straw.

Willa put her hands on her hips. "Be gentle, lads. My parents' books are in those."

The two giant young men hung their heads like errant schoolboys before her. She sighed. "Now, I know you don't like this any more than I do, but we simply have to make the best of it."

Dick toed the floor with one giant boot. "Are you happy to be leaving us, Willie?" Dan didn't say anything, but then he never did if he had Dick to speak for him.

Willa sighed and took a massive paw in each of her own hands. Such babies they were, for all their size. She'd been their elder sister for more than twelve years now, but it never ceased to amaze her.

"You know I love you lads. I'd never leave you if I didn't have to, but a woman must follow her husband. If he leaves, then so must I."

"But who's going to look out for you, Willie, and bash them that's too forward and such?"

Willa frowned. "My husband will protect me." She hoped.

As one, they all turned to look at the man saddling the mighty gelding. He looked up as if he felt their combined gaze, and his eyes grew a bit wild, as if he would like nothing better than to disappear at that moment. Fortunately, Dick still shadowed him, just in case.

Dan jiggled impatiently. "Do you know what he is yet, Willie?" The two looked at her expectantly.

Willa pursed her lips and gazed at her new husband with her head tilted. "What is he? Hmm."

The game was one she'd taught the boys, one that her own naturalist parents had taught her. One matched up a person with the sort of wildlife he or she represented to the world. After all, every kind of creature had characteristics one could count on when predicting its behavior. A hound would chase anything that ran. A magpie would steal anything bright.

It was nothing but a silly parlor game, but a game that Willa had found useful more than once.

As for her new husband . . . well, she was fairly sure Nathaniel Stonewell was more than he seemed.

A gentleman with sun-browned skin and callused hands. A traveling man, wearing clothes fine enough for any dandy, but that were subdued and road worn, as if what he wore meant nothing to him. A man who rode an expensive horse yet cared for it himself rather than allowing the stable boy to do so.

An interesting conundrum indeed. Fortunately, Willa loved nothing more than researching particulars.

Thinking of research brought her parents to mind and the days that the three of them had spent wandering the fields. A wisp of memory, a mere shadow of its former self, swept across Willa's mind, bringing a longing to go back to a world where there was no problem that could not be solved by a moment in her mother's lap.

Willa's mother was laughing, skirts tucked high, wielding a net and a beaker as she waded in a beck. Willa couldn't bring up much more than that laughter tinkling over the music of the beck and the way the dappled light had gleamed off her mother's shining hair.

Both Willa's mother and father had been amateur naturalists, more interested in the creatures of the world than the people. They had cared nothing for Society and had fled London to live in the nature they loved so well. Derryton had absorbed them with the good humor and tolerance that a prosperous village could afford.

Then the fever had swept the village, and it was too late. Too late for talks of womanhood and the mysteries of men. Too late for trousseaus and bridal confidences. Too late to have her mother when she needed her the most.

A wave of intense loneliness came over Willa. Indulging in one hearty sigh before addressing herself to the problem once more, Willa contemplated the man she would be sleeping beside for the rest of her life.

What a very odd thought that was. And perhaps not an entirely unpleasant one. After all, she was a healthy girl with an appreciation for a finely crafted male. It was her dearest wish to be married to someone kind and honorable, to have children, to have family of her own again.

This particular male certainly seemed well put together. It occurred to her that the point could use some investigation. They were married, after all. Willa approached him, applying a bright smile to her face and making sure she blocked the stable door, just in case.

"Do you not care to have something to eat, Husband?" The entire village was at the wedding breakfast still. If the congratulations were not so heartfelt, Willa might have taken offense at the great degree of celebration going on.

Mr. Nathaniel Stonewell slid her a wary glance, then shook his head and turned back to his horse. Encouraged, Willa let out a breath. "Well, you should. We set an excellent table. Everyone in Derryton is there, waiting to congratulate you. It is a very nice village, and everyone here looks out for one another."

Although having every soul know one's business, down to the last embarrassing detail, could sometimes be bothersome. But Willa didn't say that out loud.

He didn't respond, only brushed his horse with increasingly long and powerful strokes. How frustrating. Heaven save her from another inarticulate male.

Still, she did enjoy watching his shoulders move under his shirt as he worked the currycomb. They rippled and bulged with every movement. Delightful. Willa blinked away her reverie and brought herself back to the task at hand. Discovering Nathaniel Stonewell's intentions.

"Where are you from, sir? Are you—are we traveling far?"

Once, just once, Willa would love to travel far, far away from Derryton and the simple life of following the seasons and minding the earth. Perhaps see some new places, since everything more than ten miles away would be new to her.

Nathaniel Stonewell still hadn't answered. The brush strokes were becoming rather short and quick now, but still quite forceful. The motion made his body flex even more quickly, and Willa couldn't help the way her eyes traveled down to his snugly fitted trousers.

Heavens. What a view.

"Miss Willa! Good, you're here already."

Willa turned away from the captivating sight of Nathaniel Stonewell's flexing buttocks to see Moira pushing the stable door wide. John came through, another overstuffed packsack on his shoulder. He tossed it to the ground as if it were a mere feather pillow, but it landed with a solid thump that drew even Nathaniel Stonewell's attention.

"Careful, you great lout! Them's Willie's wedding gifts. Bad enough that Dan here mucked up her packing. Made a right mess, he did."

"No, mum! Her room was already—"

"Nonsense," Moira scolded. "Shame on you, blamin' Willie, and her bein' as neat as a pin!"

Dusting her hands with satisfaction, Moira turned to Willa. "You're all packed up, pet, right down to your mum's Bible."

Willa blinked. With dawning dismay, she realized that within minutes she would be heading out into the world with a strange man.

"But . . . a few more hours—" Or days. Months, even!

"You're a married woman now, and you go with your man." Moira dusted her hands on her apron.

But to simply leave, like this . . .

Willa turned to seek help from the boys, but they only reddened and backed away. Nathaniel Stonewell could help her, she thought. All he had to do was say that they would stay in Derryton, just for a little while.

She shot him an imploring look, only to find that he was already loading the first sack onto his horse. Dick handed him the other one, and just like that, Willa Trent no longer lived in Derryton.

But she wasn't Willa Trent anymore, was she? Now she was Willa Stonewell. Fighting down the hurt caused by the village's obvious hurry to see her gone, Willa blinked back her tears and marched to her bedchamber.

There she reached under the bed to remove a loose floorboard, for the first time in years caring not at all if anyone saw her secret hiding place. She pulled from it a tiny ivory cameo of her mother as a young woman, a yellowing handkerchief of fine Valencia lace, and a flat silk-wrapped parcel that she tucked swiftly into her bodice.

The wallet contained a love letter from her father to her mother, her grandfather's diary, and something that only Moira knew about—the record of Willa's birth.

Applying the brush to Blunt with more force than strictly necessary, Nathaniel could honestly admit that things were not going as planned. This was an unusual experience for him. Even his disgrace and subsequent shunning had been carefully orchestrated and considered. Rarely in his existence had he been presented with the sheer capriciousness of fate he now faced.

He was married.

There was one bright spot, unworthy thought that it was. Nathaniel smiled slightly as he pictured his mother's reaction. In truth, he could not wait to see her face.

His reverie was interrupted by the tapping of an impatient finger upon his shoulder. He turned to find the innkeeper's wife standing behind him, her fists planted on wide hips, her face a study in maternal protectiveness.

"You listen to me, Mr. Stonewell," she said without preamble. "Our Willie has friends and family here. One letter—one *whisper*—telling us you made her unhappy, well, I'll be cookin' up *your* eggs in my frying pan, if you get my meaning."

Her meaning was more than clear. Nathaniel resisted covering his privates protectively, although he did take a casual step back behind the safety of Blunt's broad rear.

"I assure you, madam, I have no intention of abusing Miss Trent in any way." It wasn't until the woman blinked suspiciously at his reassurance that Nathaniel realized he'd referred to the girl as "Miss."

Dear lord, was he really supposed to think of her as his *wife*?

As Willa strode back into the stable, she saw Dan tearfully saddling a sturdy pony and Moira standing with Nathaniel Stonewell, speaking in a low voice and poking him in the chest with one finger for emphasis.

"Not that one." Mr. Stonewell strode to where Dan stood with the pony. "I need to travel at speed." He looked around the stable. "What about that one?" He indicated an expensive mare. It was the horse kept in the inn stable by one of the prosperous shopkeepers of Derryton. Willa waited for John to correct Mr. Stonewell, but to her surprise, the horse was bought and paid for in the blink of an eye, price seemingly no object.

Apparently Mr. Stonewell got what Mr. Stonewell wanted.

"I am ready to leave," announced Willa haughtily. Her chill melted when all four members of the Smith family rushed to her and wrapped her in a warm embrace.

"You are all so dear. I shall miss you terribly." Willa patted and murmured, reassured and comforted, until the men peeled themselves off the clutch and left the stable, still sniffling.

Willa and Moira faced each other in silence for a moment. How did one say good-bye to someone who was mother, sister, and best friend?

"What did you say to him?" It wasn't what Willa wanted to say, but it was what came out.

Moira gave a serene madonna smile. "I told him that if he didn't treat you like glass, I'd feed him his own balls for breakfast."

Shocked, Willa clapped one hand over her mouth, then spoiled her righteous stance with an undeniable snicker. "Oh, Moira, how shall I ever do without you?"

"You'll do fine, miss. You've got a sharp mind and a good heart." She leaned closer. "Just you remember one thing. . . ."

"What?" Willa whispered.

"Feed 'im good and bed 'im better, and he'll never stray."

Willa laughed again. "You sound as if you speak of a hound."

"Willie, my girl—my own, as much as any daughter could be—men are the greatest hounds ever to walk the good earth." Moira wrapped her in one last hug. "Now you go and see the world, Miss Willa, like you've always wanted."

Tears came into Willa's eyes in earnest as she realized that Moira, at least, wasn't trying to get rid of her but only trying to set her on the path of her dreams. She mounted her mare and followed her husband out of the stable yard with a last wave to the villagers gathered there to see her off.

The path of her dreams, she told herself. She was finally on the path of her dreams.

4

Nathaniel had been married for several hours now and he certainly didn't feel any different. He was still on Blunt, although their pace was frustratingly slower than yesterday. He was still on the road after Foster, only without a chance in hell of catching the man before he got to London.

He was still the Cobra, still reviled in public as Lord Treason, still hell-bent on seeing the last of the Knights of the Lily put to the noose.

Only now the Cobra had a headache. In his more charitable moments, Nathaniel knew the ache in his skull came from his fall. In every other excruciating moment, he was positive the pounding in his head was caused by the endless chatter coming from behind him. It seemed he'd become quite accustomed to the silence of his isolation. Furthermore, it seemed his companion had never encountered a topic of conversation she didn't like.

"If you look to your left," she was currently saying, "you'll spy the droppings of an owl beneath that elm. Of course, the nest will be nowhere near here, for that would only attract other predators. I once found an entire set of bones of a snake in the droppings of an owl. I made Moira a necklace from the vertebrae, but the string broke on the first wearing and the bones were lost—at least that was what Moira claimed at the time. I do think she might have been a bit squeamish about it. I suppose I can understand why now, but when I was a child I thought the bones very lovely. . . ."

At first he'd attempted to respond politely, although it scarcely seemed necessary. Then for a time he'd simply nodded occasionally. Now he was riding a length ahead, wishing he had a woolen muffler to wrap about his ears.

All right. He was married, there was no denying that. He traveled with a bride and all the trappings for a cottage of their own. No doubt the girl thought that was precisely where they were headed. A little hearth and a large family.

Alas, a life such as that wasn't for him. To carry on his ignominy, to have his children labeled with his infamous name, was unacceptable. His legacy of disgrace would end with him.

As for a wife, perhaps he could find a place for her, a place where she would not be before him to tempt him with the life he could never have.

Unfortunately, there was no time to look into that now. He was on his way to fulfill the duty he couldn't refuse, and this mess of a marriage would just have to wait until he had done what he could for the Royal Four.

It was past twilight when he and Willa approached an inn. They had been on the road for several hours—too few by Nathaniel's calculation, but he couldn't ask more from a woman, sturdy country sort or not.

Fortunately, she was no frail hothouse flower. She'd not stopped talking for one moment of their journey, of course, but Nathaniel had to admit that not one single one of her comments had been a complaint.

Willa shifted uncomfortably. The sidesaddle she rode

was not her own and the horse was unfamiliar and inclined to be skittish. Each time the mare started, it threw off Willa's precarious balance.

The mare had finally settled, her freshness wearing off as they rode through the countryside. Willa would have thought the scenery monotonous if not for her enjoyment of the fact that she had never seen that particular hedgerow before, nor that singularly constructed stone wall.

Still, as the evening waned, the glow of novelty had worn off the landscape much as the comfort had worn off her saddle.

By the time the Idiot Male had declared that it was time to stop for the night, Willa was beginning to gather her mad. It had been a full day since the ceremony—she still had trouble thinking of it as her wedding—and the man in front of her had yet to say an entire sentence to her.

When the Unholy Beast finally halted his gelding after turning into a circular drive that led to an inn, Willa fell out of her saddle as quickly as she could unhook her knee from the pommel.

The ground came up too quickly and she staggered. Her fingers dug into the mare's mane so tightly for balance that she grunted and stepped on Willa's toe.

"Get off!"

A large male hand pushed at the snowy hide an inch from Willa's face and the horse moved off. Willa felt her legs dissolve like sugar in water and slowly sank to the grass.

A pair of dusty boots appeared before her. "Are you unwell?"

She cast a blinding smile up at the silhouette of the man against the glow of the inn's windows. "Of course not. How ridiculous. A mere eight hours in a saddle when I've scarcely ridden in years? Why would I be unwell?

I am only a tiny bit tired. Nothing to worry about at all. I'll be up and about as soon as I remember how to walk."

"Oh, did you misplace your knees? I saw them by the roadside a mile back. Didn't know you needed them." A large hand entered her field of vision and waited, palm up, for hers.

Slowly, Willa placed her own into it. The heat from his hand seared directly through the leather of Willa's riding glove and sank into her skin. Her new husband was very warm, and very large. She rightfully ought to be wary of him, but when his fingers wrapped around hers, Willa could quite honestly say that she had never felt so safe in all her life.

A tremble of another kind went through her. Not fear. No, this was something altogether different and altogether more interesting. He pulled her to her feet with ease and took her arm to help her to a bench near the inn's front door.

"Rest here for a moment while I seek out a stableman," he said. "I don't think they anticipated any arrivals this late in the evening." He strode off a few steps, then turned to look at her over his shoulder. His hat was off and the glow from behind Willa glanced off his fair hair. If she was not mistaken, his lips quirked slightly. "Perhaps your knees will find their way home while I'm gone."

He strode off and Willa's mouth dropped open. Humor? From the Hell-Husband? And rather fresh humor at that, for it was most improper of him to refer to any part of her anatomy hidden by her skirts.

Amazing. Apparently, she had wasted her entire day hating a perfectly nice man. Oh well, one should always keep one's practice up. He could turn out to be not-so-nice, after all.

By dint of gradually stretching one leg, then the next, Willa was able to feel her feet once more. At the other side of the yard she saw the stable doors open and a fellow emerge with a lantern to take the mounts.

Nathaniel tossed the stable boy a coin and turned back to the inn. The establishment was nothing special, but it was convenient and, more important to Nathaniel, would not be populated by the upper crust of Society. To be truthful, it likely wouldn't be populated by the middle crust, either, from the looks of it.

All the better. Such a place would not demand names or answers to questions that Nathaniel didn't yet feel up to providing. Even if the folk therein had heard of Lord Treason—and likely they had—they wouldn't know him on sight.

Miss Trent was on her feet when he got to her, evidently much recovered. When he took her arm and guided her into the inn, she was hardly limping at all. Good. He'd been remiss to make her ride so far the first day.

She would have to ride even farther tomorrow. If he could put her on a coach for London tomorrow, he would, but he was unwilling to send her alone. She was an inexperienced, sheltered creature. He'd sooner throw a lamb to the wolves.

Not that marrying him wasn't damage enough.

He showed her the two items of their luggage he'd retained from their gear, the remainder of which would spend the night in the stable with the mounts. "Will you need anything other than this for the night?"

She shook her head. He gestured her on before him into the inn. The taproom of the inn was empty, which was a relief. The fewer people he saw, the less chance of being recognized, even in this rough place. With its thatched roof, huge beams, and stone floor, it could as easily have existed two centuries past as now.

The burly innkeeper nodded, his face impassive as he polished tankards at the tap.

"Be ye needing a room for the night?"

"Yes, thank you, and one for my . . . companion." Nathaniel simply couldn't seem to wrap his tongue around the word *wife* yet.

The man's expression changed. He slid his eyes to Miss Trent, who was craning her head to look about the common inn room as if it were a palace chamber. The innkeeper said nothing, but the knowing disdain in his eyes spoke volumes.

Nathaniel's protective hackles rose. "On second thought, we will share a chamber," he ordered. "Your largest chamber."

Miss Trent brought her attention back to the conversation at that. She shot a questioning look at Nathaniel, who shrugged. He pulled the innkeeper aside for a brief sotto voce discussion. Then Nathaniel grabbed their sacks, tossed them over his shoulder, and tilted his head at the stairs. He went up them without waiting for her.

Willa hesitated at the foot of the stairs. Despite Mr. Stonewell's interesting attributes she was in no hurry to begin her wedding night.

The burly man came and went, bringing items to and from the kitchen.

He kept his gaze openly on her while he moved about the room, sweeping so idly that it could be nothing but a pretense.

Well, then. Yes. Definitely time to follow Nathaniel. Willa shot up the stairs, feeling the man's eyes on her back all the way up.

Mr. Stonewell stood at the top of the stairs against the candlelight, looming just a bit. Willa swallowed. Big scary man downstairs, big semiscary man upstairs. Decisions, decisions.

"Aren't you coming to bed?"

· · ·

Miss Trent stood apparently frozen there on the middle step, watching him. Her eyes were as wide as twin blue moons in the meager candlelight.

What was the matter with the girl? When he'd realized she wasn't right behind him he'd thought she might have ducked out to the necessary. He'd waited, just a moment, before remembering the innkeeper's assumption.

"I really think it would be best if you stayed with me at all times, miss—ah, Willa," he said gently. She didn't respond. If he was not mistaken, she was actually holding her breath. Why? What had he—

Aren't you coming to bed?

Ah. He cleared his throat. "I did not mean—" He stopped. There was no real hope of clearing that one up here in the hallway. He stepped back and bowed, gesturing toward the open door of the room. "Your chamber awaits, milady," he said grimly.

She lifted one foot to the next step, then hesitated again. "*My* chamber? Don't you mean ours? I am your wife."

Well, actually, no, not really. Something else best not discussed in the hall. "I will take the floor," he assured her.

For some reason, she did not seem as relieved by that as he would have thought. She sent him a peevish glance and stomped the rest of the way up the stairs, sweeping past him—if he was not severely mistaken—with a decided sniff.

What had he done this time?

He followed her to their rough room and shut the door, closing them in together.

Willa started at the turn of the key in the lock. She shivered. The room was chill, of course. This was not a true haven of hospitality like John and Moira's inn. No one had come up before them to light the hearth or to warm between the sheets with a pan full of hot coals, something Willa had done many times for guests in the past.

She knelt to the hearth to do it herself with the tinder-box supplied on the mantle. Mr. Stonewell peered over her shoulder to see what she was doing. "Here, now. I'll take care of that."

"Already done," Willa said cheerfully, and it was. Within seconds she'd struck the steel against the flint, creating sparks to drop onto the tinder beneath where the meager coals sat on the grate. She stood, dusting her hands. "It won't warm up in here for hours, unfortunately."

She turned to see Mr. Stonewell gazing at her strangely. "What is the matter?"

He blinked. "Nothing at all. I simply don't know many women who can start their own fire."

Willa snorted. "Then I daresay you must not know many women." She stepped to one side, hoping he'd take the hint and move away so she could get past. He didn't, only remained there, gazing at her as if he were seeing her for the first time.

Suddenly Willa became very aware of the fact that she was alone with the handsome—albeit slightly odd—Mr. Stonewell. Alone, in an inn room, with her husband on her wedding night.

Wed him and bed him. Moira's voice seemed very far away and long ago. That had sounded so simple, if a bit daunting, this morning. Well, she'd wedded him. Cross that one off.

Abruptly he seemed to become aware that he was blocking her way. He stepped back, then turned swiftly to pull their packsacks into the dim circle of light from the single tallow candle provided by the inn.

"What were you speaking to the innkeeper about, downstairs?" she asked him. Not that she was curious—except that she always did seem to be curious—only she wanted him to speak to her, to have conversation, to ease the way the room seemed to be shrinking around them. "Is there something of which I should know?" She put one fist on her hip. "Are you ever going to answer me?"

He gave her a brief glance. "No."

An answer at last! "Wait—which question are you answering?"

He went still for a moment, then shook his head with a rueful twist to his sensual lips. "You choose for me. I've lost track again." He bent to take some items from his bag, then swung it into the corner. All very interesting, and Willa did so enjoy watching her new husband in motion—especially all that bending over—

He stepped away and she followed, for some reason compelled to make him speak to her. Her foot trod on something on the floor where he'd been sorting through his things. A small packet, wrapped in a simple handkerchief. Willa picked it up and unrolled the linen to drop a thick gold ring into her hand. "What is this?" she asked, holding it out to him.

Nathaniel reached automatically, then went very still when the ring dropped into his waiting palm. It was heavier than he remembered, but that was somehow appropriate. The Reardon crest had been carved into the old gold in the days of knights and tourneys, when the title of Marquis of Reardon was first created by a grateful king and the ring given by the royal hand itself. The stone had been reset a few times through the intervening centuries, so last spring Nathaniel had felt no qualms replacing the inferior emerald that had previously occupied the setting.

The large stone was a fine ruby, cut and polished in

Vienna by the finest jewel smiths in the world. He knew because he'd chosen the stone himself. His former fiancée, Daphne, loved rubies, though they reminded Nathaniel of blood. Now the ruby simply reminded him of all that he had freely given up yet still mourned.

His mission fired within him anew. Downstairs he'd taken the innkeeper aside for a moment to ask if he'd seen Foster. The man grudgingly had affirmed that Foster had indeed passed this way. The traitor was an entire day ahead now.

Oddly, Nathaniel had not truly expected Foster to take this route. Nathaniel had diverged to the south road in order to reach London all the faster and deal with his unfortunate marital situation. He'd hardly dared hope that Foster would be traveling the same road.

And why? Why had Foster also turned suddenly hard toward London? At great speed as well, according to what the innkeeper had said. Nathaniel's fingers tightened unknowingly on the ring in his palm, until he felt the gold edges pressing deeply into his skin. He eased his grip enough to display the ruby in the candle's glow once again.

Willa seemed fascinated. She reached to stroke the insignia worked into the shoulder. "Is that a boar? And a sword? What does that mean?"

"Not a bloody thing." Not anymore.

She pulled her hand back and Nathaniel cursed his harsh words. But how could he explain the fresh loss he felt just looking at the damned thing? The grief welled within him again, the destruction of his honor and with it all his private dreams. With a swift motion, he pulled back his fist to throw the ring into the fire.

"No!" Willa reached out to stop him but halted when she saw his bleak face. Nathaniel seemed almost sinister, lit spookily as he was by the flickering fire.

Yet he stopped. With a curse, he shoved the ring back to the bottom of his pack.

"You'll sleep there," he said brusquely, indicating the bed. "I'll spread a blanket before the fire."

Then he stalked to the door.

"Wait!" Willa suddenly didn't mind his presence. Suddenly the strange shoddy room seemed more dangerous without him. "Where are you going? May I come with you?"

He stopped with his hand on the door. "To the necessary. And no, I'd rather you didn't."

She subsided, blushing. "Oh. No, of course. That would be—"

He seemed to relent a bit. "I'll be no more than a moment. Turn the key after I leave if you wish."

He was being kind again and she was being silly. "I shall be fine," she said gamely. "I'm of age to spend ten minutes in a room alone."

He only nodded shortly and left her. Willa dutifully restrained herself from locking him out. Instead, she spent those suddenly precious moments getting herself ready for bed. A quick swish in the chill water kept in the pitcher on the washstand and into her wedding night gown.

Just in case. So far Mr. Stonewell didn't seem inclined to claim his marital rights, but that didn't mean she shouldn't expect something of the sort from him.

The sheer fabric did nothing to keep her from chill and the hearth was only beginning to glow, so Willa slid beneath the thin coverlet on the bed.

She had to admit a feeling of relief that she needn't share it with anyone. With nothing more than a stretch and a yawn, she felt herself slipping gratefully away into sleep. She hoped Mr. Nathaniel Stonewell would be as comfortable as she was.

Just before she slid completely off, a single thought crossed her mind.

This morning, when she'd offered him her hand during the wedding . . .

He'd said he had no ring.

5

Wrapped in his blanket on the hard plank floor before the fire, Nathaniel wasn't able to rest. It was always worse at night, feeling the weight of his disgrace, the pain of his lost honor excruciatingly memorable in the dark and the quiet.

Without the busy noise of his day with Miss Trent—Willa—in the quiet his mind began to willfully recount what he had lost. His father disdained him. His family rejected him. His engagement had been dissolved.

Well, that had turned up a twist, hadn't it? He had a wife at last but, like Peter, Peter Pumpkin-Eater, couldn't keep her.

The isolation only bit more deeply in the sprightly company of the woman. She simply made him think all the more about what he could never allow himself to have.

Finally, he slept.

Willa slept restlessly despite her exhaustion. She'd not slept anywhere but her own bed for twelve years. To be sure, her own bed was finer than this one, but still, one would assume that a long day of equestrian exertion would leave one inclined to sleep.

As she lay there, staring at the cracking plaster ceiling yet again, a soft, low snore emerged from the blanket across the room.

"I just knew it," Willa muttered.

She sat up and glared in Mr. Stonewell's direction. One bare, muscular arm was the only thing visible, outflung as it was. The snore subsided after its single foray into the room, but the damage was done. Willa was thinking about what Mr. Stonewell was wearing beneath that blanket.

She tried to lie back down and erase that wicked thought from her mind.

No. Not effective at all.

After a moment of indecision, Willa left her bed and padded silently across the room. If he woke up, she would simply say that she was tending the coals. She knelt next to him and peered into his face. He truly was extraordinarily handsome. She'd often been told she was pretty herself, but Willa had the uneasy feeling that Mr. Stonewell's looks were quite another degree of attractiveness.

He still smelled good, except that now Moira's homemade soap was added in the mix. Willa didn't mind. It made him smell a bit like home, as well.

Was the rest of him as fine as his face? She couldn't bear not knowing. With two fingers, Willa lifted the covers and peeked down the length of Nathaniel Stonewell. The nightshirt went quite properly past his knees, but she could still see muscled, naked, hairy calves and square, naked, hairy feet.

"Goodness," whispered Willa. "What big feet you have."

She didn't live over a tavern for nothing. Willa knew a bit more about life than either Moira or John suspected. If one sat at an open window on a summer's night, one could hear all sorts of conversations from the tavern window just below. One of those conversations had once touched upon the correlation between the size of a man's feet and the size of his . . . parts.

It seemed a little indecent to be peeking at Nathaniel's naked body parts, but Willa couldn't resist lifting the loose placket at the front of the nightshirt and peering down his wide, naked, hairy chest.

It was a handsome chest, plated with firm, powerful muscles even in his lax state. She could see a little line of light brown hair trailing down his flat, hard belly. Now where did that go? Lifting the shirt a bit higher, she peeked lower—

Oh . . . my.

Clamping her eyes shut, she flipped his collar back to his chin and shot back to her own bed. No, she definitely shouldn't have been looking at big, naked, hairy . . . parts. Bad Willa.

But definitely intrigued, curious, slightly mystified Willa. What she had seen and what she ought to do about it was surely a puzzle.

Oh, she had a vague idea. She lived over an ale room, after all. Yet those accounts had usually assumed male willingness. But if he wasn't going to do his share, could it even happen? How did that work? Various incomplete images came to mind. *Oh my.*

Suddenly the room was on its way to being stifling. Willa dropped the blanket from her shoulders with relief. No point in hiding from a man who didn't even know she was in the room.

To be truthful, Willa liked watching him sleep, at least since he had stopped snoring. He was terribly handsome, especially now that he had been cleaned up a bit. Lying back down on her cot, she willed herself to sleep once more. She was hoping she'd dream about what she'd seen. . . .

. . .

Nathaniel was dreaming. He dreamed he rested on a vast lush mantle, surrounded by satin and velvet. The air was warm and fragrant, and he heard the soft lilt of music.

Peace. Comfort. Ease. He felt as though he were finally home.

Gradually, he became aware of the rising dawn and the hard floor beneath his shoulder and hip, but still the velvety warmth remained.

It was lovely, but it was just a dream. In a moment, he would wake entirely and the sweet comfort he was feeling would disappear, as dreams always did.

Inhaling deeply, he shifted, burying his face into a fragrant pillow of silken hair and sliding his hand up Willa's warm belly to cup her satiny breast.

"Oh, bloody *hell*!" Flinging himself away from her, Nathaniel stumbled to his feet. Willa gave a feminine little grunt and rolled into the warm spot his body had left in the blankets.

Daylight peeked through the clumsy shutters that were hung over the window.

With a rush, the memories flooded back into his mind. He remembered the girl, the innkeeper, and the twin giants with their casual sympathy and their never-ending vigilance.

Oh, bloody hell.

Then came the memory of the wedding ceremony. His wedding ceremony. Witnesses, white lace, and all.

Oh, bloody *hell*.

Willa got up on her elbows on the mattress and blinked vigorously to wake herself up. Then she rolled her head to rid herself of the crick in her neck. Goodness, she felt as though she had rested on a rock all night.

It wasn't until her bleary vision cleared enough to see

the man stalking about the room that Willa remembered that she was now a married woman.

"Hello, Husband," she chirped brightly.

He turned to her, evidently about to speak. Instead, his eyes widened with astonishment.

Curious as to why, Willa looked down at herself. She still wore the gossamer scrap of lawn that Moira had given her. Blushing a bit, she shyly returned her husband's gaze.

She wiggled uncomfortably, feeling very exposed in the light of day. His eyes bulged at the motion, and hope began to stir in Willa.

"I wore it especially for you. Do you like it?"

For a moment, Nathaniel didn't take the words in. He was too busy staring at the appetizing sight before him. Huge dark eyes looked at him from the midst of a cloud of tumbled hair that trailed down to white shoulders and the beginnings of succulent round breasts.

She wore only a sheer white nightgown with no sleeves and a scooped neckline that did nothing to hide the mouthwatering shadow of her cleavage. The night rail did nothing to hide anything at all.

Moreover, her excuse for a nightdress gaped open all down its laced front, and somehow Nathaniel knew that he himself had done the unlacing.

"Hellfire! How did you get here?"

Willa looked around as if surprised herself by her location. "I don't remember. I think I was cold."

Nathaniel gestured wildly to her gown. "Well, close that up or you'll be colder yet!"

Jerking at her gown, Willa glared at him. "Well, that I didn't do!" Standing to face him, Willa planted a fist on each hip. Unfortunately, she also released her hold on the front of her nightdress, and Nathaniel could see everything from the valley between her breasts to her navel.

It was very distracting.

"What are you looking at?" she demanded, then looked down. Quickly wrapping it shut, she frowned at him. Her chin went high. "I'm going to get dressed now," she said grandly, hardly faltering at all. Her blush gave lie to her poise, however.

With that, Willa strode across the room to the splintery screen provided in the corner. She never looked back to see Nathaniel standing in the circle of morning sunlight, smiling his first smile in a very long time.

The road had widened considerably since Derryton and they had passed through a number of entertaining-looking villages on their way, but at the moment the view held little more than fields bound by stone walls, and sheep.

Since this was nothing that Willa had not seen every day of her life, she cleared her throat and tried once more to talk to her husband.

"If you are embarrassed about being too incapacitated last night to bed me, rest assured that I am willing to try again tonight," she called helpfully.

Then again, she'd heard men were sensitive on this subject.

"Not that I am in any hurry or anything. No pressure at all."

Nothing. Not a nod, not a word.

"I am sure that when you are feeling better, you'll have no trouble performing your duties."

Still no response. This would never do. She took a deep breath and increased her strength of voice. She had marvelous strength of voice, since she often needed to make herself heard over the din of the taproom.

"I apologize for disturbing your contemplation of the dust on the road, but I must know. It truly is quite necessary that you are capable, you see. You *are* able to perform, are you not?"

There. He had to have heard that. The folk from miles around should have heard that.

Nathaniel reined in his gelding and his temper at the same time. Twisting in the saddle, he watched as the she-demon from hell rode up beside him. "I hardly think my ability to perform is a topic for discussion on the open road," he said frostily.

Despite his scowl, she brightened. "Well, I want to know. I have asked you a great number of questions these past two days, and you have answered none of them."

Now that was an understatement. Nathaniel had lost count of her interrogations somewhere after a hundred. "What an odd creature you are."

"I know. But I fear you must answer this one, for your own safety."

"My safety depends upon it?" Nathaniel tilted his head. "Well, in that case, I have never had any difficulty 'performing'—if sufficiently interested." That should close that rather unnecessary subject. He turned to ride on.

The mare hurried again. "Are you?"

He was not going to turn around. "Am I what?"

"Are you sufficiently interested?" Her tone was conversational. "In me?"

Nathaniel stopped again and turned to look at her. "You are *so* odd."

"You repeat yourself. My mother said that only people with no imagination settle for repeating themselves."

"I shall endeavor to improve. You are *incredibly* odd."

"Yes, I believe we have established that. It isn't my fault, you know. I'm an orphan."

"Ah, that explains all." Nathaniel gave his gelding a subtle nudge to speed his walk slightly. Surely she would grow weary of shouting over a distance.

The dainty clip-clop of the trotting mare came up next to his gelding, but Nathaniel refused to acknowledge it.

"It won't work to ignore me. It never does."

Nathaniel heaved a great sigh, although he despised sighing on principle. "No, I don't suppose it does. What was it that you asked?"

"Are you sufficiently interested in copulating with me?" *Copulating? Where did she get that word?* "No."

Silence. Nathaniel couldn't believe it. He stole a look sideways, only to make sure she wasn't dead or some such. She still breathed, but there was such a look of concentration on her face that Nathaniel began to fear in earnest.

"I am considered attractive enough in Derryton. I've had no end of suitors, you realize. None as attractive as you, of course, although you are well on your way to being a bit pretty for my taste."

"I am not pretty!" Damn, she was doing it again. Nathaniel took a deep breath and held it for the count of ten. Then another, for the count of twenty. His mood eased and he began to hope she'd finished—

"I shall have to cut my hair, then," she said thoughtfully.

Nathaniel was beginning to see why the village had been so eager to get rid of Willa. The girl was as mad as a caged cat. Nathaniel edged his horse to the side, just in case she carried any concealed weapons.

"How's that?" he asked, keeping his tone mild.

"I shall cut my hair and wear trousers to entice you, since you prefer boys."

That tore it.

In one deadly motion, Nathaniel leaped from his horse and scraped the little snip off her mount. Holding her tightly, he bent her over his arm despite her squeak of dismay.

"I do *not* prefer boys," he growled into her startled

face, then kissed her half-open mouth before she could say one more maddening word.

I'm going to catch fire. Her heart jumped through her ribs. Kisses were *much* better with cooperation.

It was all new tastes and sensations and hot breath. It was strange and invasive and intimate.

It was marvelous. Wrapping her arms around his neck, Willa threw her whole spirit into returning the kiss.

His lips were hard and forceful at first, his beard stubble coarse against her face. He drove his tongue into her repeatedly, startling her and exciting her, and chewed roughly on her lips.

Then his mouth softened and gentled, and his angry grip turned to a caressing embrace, until Willa began to shiver from the pangs of arousal that shot through her.

When his mouth left hers to bury itself in her neck, she gasped but couldn't slow down her racing breaths. All she could taste and feel was him.

His hard hands slid to her backside and pressed her close to his harder body. Pressure built within Willa, until she feared bursting from it. She rubbed restlessly against him, trying to combat that hungry ache that consumed her, that ache to be touched all over.

"Wildflower . . . ," he murmured into her neck, his breath hot on her skin.

"Oh, Nathaniel," she sighed.

Nathaniel came to himself with a jolt and sprang away from the girl in his arms. Breathing hard, he backed away from her as if she were venomous. What was he doing? He had only meant to prove his point, and to shut her up for a moment.

How had she aroused him so completely and mindlessly that he had nearly taken her on the dusty road?

Nathaniel turned away from temptation and shoved his hands through his hair. He still found himself attuned to her, aware of her halting breath and shuffling feet. He heard her go back to her horse and the squeak of leather as she struggled back into the saddle. She gave an offended sniff. Then, when he didn't respond, a louder, more emphatic, furious sniff.

Still he didn't turn. He had to think.

The last thing his convoluted life needed was the further complication of a wife and family. He still wasn't quite sure how the wife had happened, but if he kept on the way he was headed, there would be family indeed.

It was only the intimacy of traveling together, surely. Only his solitude weighing heavily on his desires. Once in London, he could put her in the farthest chamber of Reardon House and keep his distance until the time came to send her off.

Until then, for the good of both of them, he had to stay well away from the diabolical little minx who would be his wife.

Thinking back on his overwhelming response to her untutored kiss, Nathaniel had to admit that might be easier said than done.

As he mounted Blunt once more, Nathaniel hoped that at least his instant of madness had made her angry enough to keep her own distance.

6

Unfortunately, her resentment didn't seem to last, and Willa was back to her normal chatterbox self by noon. However, it didn't bother Nathaniel so much today. With her forthright manner and her odd Willa-esque insights into life, she was actually rather refreshing company.

"Are there many bookshops in London?" she asked at one of their infrequent rests.

"A few," Nathaniel said drily. He had avoided most of her questions again today, but what could be the harm of answering this one?

"I've read every book in Derryton many times, except for Dulcie Mason's copy of *The Housekeeper's Exploration of the Uses of Vinegar.* I could only read through it twice."

"All of two times?" Nathaniel was impressed. He couldn't imagine reading the title twice without falling asleep.

"Whenever someone from Derryton traveled, they would always bring back a book for me," she said, her fondness for her far-reaching family evident in her tone. "Of course, since some of them don't read themselves, this did make for rather unpredictable variety. Of all, my favorites were my parents' collection. Have you read Linnaeus?" she asked eagerly.

"A bit," Nathaniel replied, startled. Carolus Linnaeus was a bit deep for a country miss, for the naturalist's works had yet to be translated from Latin into English as far as Nathaniel knew. It seemed she was indeed a well-educated country miss!

"My mother did so love Linnaeus," Willa commented. " 'The flower's leaves . . . serve as bridal beds'," she quoted rapturously. "Really, I find it so much more satisfying than mere romantic poetry, don't you? All that 'heavenly bosoms kissed by moonlight and dew' rot simply leaves me cold," she said matter-of-factly.

Nathaniel nearly choked. What the devil had she been reading? "Well. . . ."

Thankfully, she didn't wait for him to reply.

"I'm glad I'm not angry anymore," she said cheerfully. "It's a lovely diversion once in a while, but so tiring."

Nathaniel looked away. He'd made a right fool of himself. "About that—"

She nodded. "Yes, well, you can see why I was too busy hating you to talk."

"You hate me?" Nathaniel couldn't believe it bothered him, but it did.

"Oh, not anymore! After all, none of this is your fault, is it?"

"It isn't your fault, either," he said.

"Well—" Abruptly she turned from him and pushed the mare into a fast trot. "Aren't we making wonderful time today?" she called back over her shoulder.

Nathaniel knew guilt when he saw it. Blunt caught up easily at a nudge from Nathaniel's heels. "Willa? What really happened that evening in the lane?"

She edged away, still chattering. "Such good weather for traveling—"

Nathaniel reached for the mare's rein and pulled both horses to a stop. "I'd like for you to stand still and answer my question this time."

"Oh, I'd really rather not."

"*Willa!*"

"Don't puff up at me. I am not afraid of cobras."

Cobras? Nathaniel blinked. "Wh—what? Why would you say something like that?"

Willa pursed her lips. "You'll think me odd."

Nathaniel put one hand over his heart. "I promise, my opinion of you will not change."

She hesitated, looking askance at his phrasing. Then she shrugged. "Oh, very well. It is merely a game I play. People can be difficult to understand sometimes. I find it easier to predict how they will behave if I decipher what sort of wild creature they resemble. For instance, Moira could be compared to a brown bear."

Since Nathaniel had experienced Moira's burly protectiveness firsthand, it seemed like a good match to him. A game? Could this truly be all there was to her deadly accuracy? "So you find me snakelike?" If the matter turned out to be a silly jest, he might take the time to be insulted.

"Oh, don't take offense! If you understood snakes, you'd like them very much, I'm sure."

"But Willa," he said quietly. "Why a cobra?"

"Oh, a number of reasons!" She began counting on her fingers. "Cobras are really quite shy, and don't like to be disturbed. When they are disturbed, they put on a great show of ferocity, raising their hoods and weaving about, but it's really mostly show. They only strike when they must." She smiled hesitantly at him. "Like you."

"I'm not poisonous," Nathaniel reminded her, although a voice inside reminded him that his disgrace might very well be contagious.

She shrugged. "I did not say it was a perfect concept."

"I have never 'puffed up' at you—until now, anyway."
Nathaniel wasn't too happy about her astuteness. Who
would have thought a curvaceous country miss could have
such a keen mind? If that was truly all there was to this.

Willa sighed. " 'Tis only a game," she said slowly, as if
to a simpleton.

Nathaniel scowled. "So you have decided that I am a
cobra. What difference does that make?"

"No, not just any cobra. A king cobra. *Naja hannah.*
I have a book that describes them very well. They live in
India. They are very large and handsome, but are the
shyest of them all. They will retreat from a child."

Lovely. Now I'm a cowardly snake. "Enough. You were
going to explain how I ended up on the side of the lane, unconscious."

"I'd rather talk about snakes."

"Willa."

She huffed. "Oh, very well. It is commonly considered
a fact, not only in Derryton and Edgeton but in all our surrounding farms and communities, that I am jinxed."

Hell. And here he'd thought her sophisticated. She was
just a superstitious country miss, after all. "You don't believe in such nonsense, do you?"

"I wish it were nonsense. I wish it were some silly
story, but most of all I wish it were about someone else."

Nathaniel rubbed the back of his neck. "So you believe
you are jinxed?"

"Some would say I *am* the jinx."

Ha. More like the "minx." "Who would say that?"

She ticked off one finger. "Wesley Moss, for example."

Nathaniel dug deep for patience. "Willa, would you
kindly just tell me everything, so I don't have to pull it
from you word by word. You believe you have bad luck?"

"Oh no, I have marvelous luck. I am always the first

one to find berries in the spring, and my cakes never fall. It is only my suitors."

"Such as this Wesley Moss?"

"Yes, poor Wesley was one of my more famous incidents. Of course, that may be because he actually went so far as to kiss me. Or to try to."

"So what happened to him? Did this terrible jinx smite him dead?" Nathaniel smirked.

Willa shook her head quite seriously. "No, thank goodness, although it was close. But he regained consciousness after only a few weeks, and I hear he is now able to walk again."

Nathaniel was appalled. "What did you do to him?"

"*I* did nothing. It is not my fault that he fell into the millstream. I was only trying to push him back. He should never have let his feet get tangled in my knitting like that."

"So he was injured when he fell into a stream?"

"Oh no, he only got a wetting from the stream. It was the waterwheel of the mill that did him in."

"He fell under the wheel?"

"Not right away. That was after the footbridge crumbled under him as he tried to climb out."

"The footbridge?" Good God, maybe she *was* jinxed.

"Yes, when he caught the big stick I threw to him to help him out of the water. Or rather, tried to catch it. He should never have let go of the side of the mill."

"No, of course not. How careless of him," said Nathaniel faintly. The story of Wesley Moss made him feel as though he had narrowly escaped his own death on the road today at midday.

"Well, there you are. Jinxed."

Nathaniel was confused. What did this have to do with waking up by the side of the lane?

"So, you threw a stick at me?"

"Oh no." Willa shook her head earnestly. "I never throw sticks anymore. In your case it was a stone. I was attempting to spring a poacher's trap before some dear hedgehog lost his life. My stone hit a hornets' nest. Which fell before your horse. But it wasn't intended. The slingshot was defective."

Nathaniel felt something wild and vaguely familiar and a bit frightening bubbling up inside him. He clenched his jaw and waited the episode out with grim determination. When he was quite sure he would *not* laugh, he put the horses to a brisk walking pace and handed Willa back her reins.

She seemed relieved that he wasn't angry about the slingshot. He was far too bemused to be angry. What kind of woman waited by the road to bag a husband like a rabbit? He hoped the method didn't catch on.

They rode in silence for over a mile before Nathaniel realized that something was odd. Silence? It was certainly a relief, but after another mile, his unease began to grow.

After the third mile, he couldn't stand it anymore. He pulled Blunt nose to nose with the mare. They shared a whuffling greeting, which was more than he got from Miss Trent. Finally, he turned to her abruptly. "What is wrong?"

Willa only looked at him. He eyed her suspiciously. Something was up. "Why aren't you talking? You never stop talking."

She shrugged.

"Are you ill?"

She shook her head. *No.*

"Are you angry? Have I offended you?" He felt uneasy, looking back on his behavior. "Why won't you speak?"

She grinned at him.

"Willa?"

"Being on the receiving end of the silent treatment makes the questions come all by themselves, doesn't it?"

She had tricked him. Quite neatly, too. Nathaniel could only stare at her, mouth open. This time he couldn't help himself. He laughed, a single rusty bark.

Now it was Willa's turn to stare.

She pointed at him. "You laughed. I heard you. Don't deny it."

Nathaniel scowled at her. "And now you are very pleased with yourself, aren't you?"

"Indeed." Her expression was smug. "If I had paper and ink, I should record this event for history. They shall declare it a holiday someday, no doubt."

"Keep that up, Willa, and you'll find a spider in your sheets come morning."

"I like spiders," she said staunchly, but then she wrinkled her nose. "Although I prefer them to stay out of doors. You wouldn't, would you? Were you one of those awful boys, full of pranks and wickedness?"

"Nothing so interesting, I'm afraid. I was a sullen little sod, envious of my father's attentions and spoiled to boot."

She considered him for a long moment. "Who did your father love better than you? Your brother?"

"I have no brother. Only a foundling boy that my father schooled and encouraged. A poor, hungry boy off the streets—and I was jealous of him. Can you imagine?" He snorted. "I told you I was spiteful."

Willa smiled. "I can understand that. I shouldn't have liked sharing my parents' love with a stranger, I think. What was the boy's name? If I am bound to hate him for you, then I hope he has a properly poisonous name. Percival? Mortimer?"

"I don't hate him." Nathaniel turned his face away. "And his name is Simon."

Simon, who had rescued five-year-old Nathaniel from kidnappers and had been rewarded with an education and the respect of Nathaniel's stepfather, Randolph.

Simon, the son Randolph had always wanted. Simon, who could not be used as a weapon in the staged battle that was Randolph's marriage to Nathaniel's mother. Simon, the heir who had no title bestowed upon him, no estate to learn the responsibility of, no family, and no ties—Simon was the perfect answer to carry on after Randolph.

Even Nathaniel could understand that. Nathaniel the man, at any rate. Nathaniel the boy had tried so hard to win his stepfather's love and respect, to make him forget that Nathaniel wasn't really his son, to forget that he had no father of his own. . . .

Abruptly he kicked Blunt into a canter, away from Willa. She was doing it again. It was uncanny. And unwelcome.

Willa watched him go, mourning the simple moment of friendship that had so quickly soured. Getting to know Nathaniel Stonewell was like peering through chinks in a stone wall. Only glimpses, lovely winning hints that were all too brief. Why couldn't he just talk to her? His secretiveness was fair to driving her mad with frustrated curiosity.

Regardless, if he wanted to give her the silent treatment, then he should expect to receive the *un*silent treatment. Perhaps an hour or two on the virtues of good communication? Then she would tell him about every single individual in Derryton.

And their dogs.

Happily, Willa settled into the saddle for a nice long chat. Nathaniel was going to wish he were dead.

"Please, God, kill me now," Nathaniel begged under his breath.

If Napoleon had aimed Willa at Europe, Bonaparte would currently be sitting on the British throne. She was relentless, cruel, and unyielding.

For hours she had regaled Nathaniel with tales of village life, from naming the most accomplished belchers in order of importance to dividing the village babies up by degrees of nappy rash.

For the last hour, Nathaniel had longed for death or deafness, whichever might come first.

"Now," she was currently saying. "The only man in Derryton to ever lose a toe was old Mr. Malcolm Beddleby, who never would use a chamber pot. He claimed they were unsanitary. Summer or winter, day or night, Mr. Beddleby would make his way to the outhouse. One January night, after a large meal of stewed mutton with prunes, Mr. Beddleby found himself—"

They crested a low hill and saw a village up ahead. "We'll stop there for the night!" Nathaniel interrupted desperately.

The inn here was large and fine. Nathaniel decided to pay for the largest room they had. Perhaps the space would be enough to dispel the sexual thrumming that began within him whenever they were too close. At this point, he didn't even want to be alone with her in a barn!

No, that brought to mind lying in a bed of sweet-smelling hay, unlacing that nightdress while fully awake, fully aroused, fully—

Blunt whinnied and shook his bridle impatiently, obviously tired of waiting to be led to the water trough. Willa was way ahead of them, standing with her mare at the trough and surreptitiously rubbing at her rear.

He laughed helplessly for a moment, leaning against Blunt's solid neck. She was so unaffected yet so quick-minded. In truth, he found the combination of intelligence and natural forthrightness rather devastating. She was nothing like any other woman he'd ever met.

He knew a few excellent ladies, of course. They were, quite unfortunately, married to his friends. Other than those few, no woman in England would currently bother to spit on him if he were on fire.

So perhaps it was merely the lack of any female companionship lately that made Willa seem rather special. After all, she wasn't precisely beautiful—and he'd always preferred beautiful—although she did possess a great deal of innate attractiveness. And a bloody good figure. The stuff of dreams, or at least the stuff of his dreams.

He ruthlessly pulled his mind off that path.

She was quite mad of course. Country living had doubtless driven her round the bend, for she talked more than any three women put together, whether or not he made any sign of listening.

The worst thing was, he found himself being interested in Willa's stories, and that was surely a bad sign.

She walked back to him, unsuccessfully hiding a limp that made her skirts swing a bit sideways across the cobbles. Her hem was stained and her face was dusty from travel. There was a spot of horse slobber on one sleeve and she had one hand pressing to the small of her back.

Still, she smiled cheerfully at him. "Would you like me to water Blunt for you, darling?"

That was the other thing. All day she had been tossing out these endearments. "Darling." "Beloved." "Dear husband."

And, bizarrely enough, "biscuit."

"Willa, I really just prefer to be called Nathaniel."

She shrugged. "Very well, but you started it."

"I did not!"

"You did so. On the road, at midday. You called me 'wildflower.' "

"I—" Had he? He was rather uncomfortably sure that he had. "Well, at any rate, it isn't necessary to use endearments."

"Of course it isn't. That isn't why people do it. They do it to show that they care for one another. But if you like, I won't call you anything but Nathaniel."

"Very well then." He turned away to tend the horses.

"That will be fine, Nathaniel. Thank you, Nathaniel. I'll be in the inn, Nathaniel."

Nathaniel halted in his tracks and inhaled deeply for a moment. The calming technique had always worked for him while he was in the thick of political negotiations, so he didn't understand why it failed him now. Except that there was no defense against a creature from hell.

From hell? Damn, she probably ran the place.

Cold water was the only answer. He considered sticking his head in the trough. If he was really fortunate, he might be allowed to drown.

Willa was very proud of the fact that she managed to wait until Nathaniel had turned the corner to the stables before she succumbed to laughter.

Willa had already gone to their room, but Nathaniel stayed below in the taproom to speak to the innkeeper over a pint of ale.

"He's a small, thin man, older than me. A gentleman . . . of sorts."

The innkeeper rubbed the white stubble on his round jowls. "There was a fellow come through. Yesterday noon it was. He didn't stay, just swapped horses. I remember because he paid too much for the new horse and his old one was near dead, he pushed it so hard. I told the missus that there was a man with more than money at stake."

Only his neck. Nathaniel thanked the man and paid well for the ale. "Lovely stuff," he assured the innkeeper.

As Nathaniel walked away, he heard the man mutter,

"Don't know how he can tell how lovely it is. Didn't drink a drop."

Foster was a day and a half ahead. Nathaniel's last wisp of hope that he would not lose the man in London had vanished. Damnation, the traitor was in the city already!

Scowling, Nathaniel mounted the stairs two at a time. The moment he got Willa to Reardon House tomorrow, he would be able to concentrate completely on finding Foster again. Damn, to have him slip through his fingers when he'd been so close—

He opened the door and strode in, in no mood for Willa's fey humor now. "We'll leave before dawn—"

He stopped short with his words unfinished. There, in the candlelight, sitting primly on the bed with her hair falling down around her, was one *very* naked Willa.

"Are you ready to copulate with me now?"

7

Willa tried very hard not to shiver, but inside she was most definitely shaking. Not so much from cold but from mingled fear and anticipation.

Oddly, she wasn't sure if she was more afraid of being rejected or accepted. It had taken some determination to make this offer after the episode on the road this afternoon, but then, a part of her was greatly looking forward to more of that sensuous adventure.

And since he obviously hadn't liked the nightgown, she had gone a bit further this time. She ruthlessly kept her mind far away from the word *naked*. After all, her tresses were quite long.

He looked at once grim and flabbergasted, standing there at the rim of the candlelight with his lips still parted from speaking and his fair hair mussed from travel. He looked like a slightly gob-smacked highwayman.

Her gaze fell slightly, curiously, to the front of his trousers. The precopulation phenomenon was happening again. She could see him change before her eyes, the same change she had felt when he had pressed her close to him on the road this afternoon.

It was an intriguing spectacle, but an intimidating one

as well. Willa knew a great deal about animal reproduction, and she was sure that people weren't far different.

So even with him restrained by his clothing, the prospect of his . . . well, his endowment . . . it was a bit unnerving.

By sheer will, she raised her gaze to his face, searching for some clue to his response to her. Would he follow his obvious instincts? Or would he walk away again? She didn't know him well enough to predict.

Part of her wanted him to refuse; she couldn't deny it. As curious as she was over the process, there was a little voice within her that cried over the lack of feeling of it all.

The silence slowed time, interrupted only by the crackling fire.

Biting her lip, Willa waited.

She was from hell. Nathaniel was sure of it.

Where else could spawn a creature so maddening yet so tempting? And she *was* tempting. She drew him like a starving wolf to her plenty.

He couldn't take his gaze from her delicious curves outlined by firelight. It glazed her flesh with hot golden tones on one side, while the other was kissed with cool darkness.

He ached. She was more than sex, although that was definitely there. She was longing and lust. Lust for her flesh, yes, but worse was the dangerous wicked longing for a little warmth.

No. Unfair to her, unfair to his mission. He must remember who he was.

While he could still hold that thought in his head, he shrugged from his coat and threw it at her. "Cover yourself!" Hell, he was barking again. He closed his eyes against the sight of her startled face. "Please," he added gruffly.

He heard the rustle of fabric and dared to look once more. She was standing with her back to him, and the coat mercifully covered her to her knees. She turned, and Nathaniel realized that his coat truly wasn't going to do the job.

Although the black frock coat hung shapeless and concealing over most of her body, the shorter front hem stopped high above her knees. In the candlelight, her skin shone whiter than the linen. Plump and smooth, her legs were gleaming curve and mysterious hollow. Nathaniel's mouth watered at the sight.

She bent quickly to gather up the coverlet and cover herself further, but it was too late. The sweet ripeness of Willa's thighs was burned into Nathaniel's memory. His groin pulsed in response, his erection promising to be towering and of dismaying longevity.

She was eyeing him a bit sideways, but there was no denying that she was looking.

Quickly Nathaniel pulled up the packsack to hide behind, before her eyes traveled farther and she saw what she had done to him.

"Turn your back," he ordered.

"Why don't *you* turn *your* back, since I am the one who must search my things for a gown?"

"Fine," he snapped, and thrust another bag at her. He turned around and closed his eyes. The darkness behind his closed lids was soothing. He was exhausted; he'd not bothered to eat properly on this mission, and he had spent two days fighting the nauseating effect of a blow to the head, not to mention fighting the erratic effect of far too much Willa.

He had only known her for a short time, and already she was driving him as mad as she was. Nathaniel never knew if he wanted to strangle her or ravage her, and the strain was beginning to get to him.

Everything would be better in the morning. After a
good night's rest, sleeping far across the fire from the she-
demon, he could start a new day. Resolving to keep his
carnal thoughts in line, he turned. She was sitting up in
the bed, tucked into the covers, with her flannel nightdress clearly visible, since it was tied tightly all the way
up to her neck.

She still looked entirely delectable.

He could have her body now, that was obvious. She
thought he would be her husband, clearly, and only wanted
what any bride would expect. The throbbing in his groin
urged him to do just that. He could walk over to her right
now and satisfy himself, although he doubted once would
do it.

He could tangle them within the blankets until sunrise
and not get enough. He could ride her every half hour
until they reached their destination, and she would freely
grant him his "husbandly rights," believing herself bonded
to an ordinary man.

For now.

Then they would arrive in London and all would be revealed. And when tales were told, she would leave. Anyone would. He had the proof of that. After all, when his
own family had declared him outcast, what should he expect from an accidental bride?

Resolution flooded him once more, driving back the
tide of longing triggered by Willa's offer. Gratefully
Nathaniel sank into the cold comfort of his duty. So instead of yearning, what came out next had more the tone
of lack of interest.

"You test me to no avail, Willa. I have no intention of
consummating this marriage now." *Or ever.* Picking up
the poker, he strode past her to build up the flames.

Now Willa really did want to push him into the fire.
Except that somehow she couldn't. There was something

so sad about Nathaniel, something in his eyes that made
her think he expected nothing from anyone but pain.

How frustrating. And until Willa figured out the com-
plex clockwork that was her new husband she was, no
doubt, in for more mysterious changes of mood. Really,
and men claimed women were changeable!

Huffing with impatience, Willa pulled the covers higher,
her natural modesty returning tenfold. Still, she was never
one to give up once she'd set her mind on something. "I
don't know why you refuse me, sir, but I must warn you—"

He didn't look up. "We don't even know one another,
Willa. We should make this decision after . . . after some
time has passed."

"If you live that long," she muttered.

"What?" Now he turned his head and frowned at her.

"Moira is of the firm opinion that the jinx won't lift
until I'm wedded and bedded—"

He looked back at the coals. "Oh, are you talking that
jinx nonsense again?"

"Ask Wesley Moss if it is nonsense! Or Timothy
Sealy!"

"Timothy who?"

"Carriage accident. A little matter of a flaming handkerchief and a runaway horse. *Not* my fault."

He bent his head to rub it with one palm. "Ah, of
course not."

"At any rate, you should not dismiss this danger."

Nathaniel didn't smile, but his tension relaxed somewhat. "Willa, if I promise that I will be careful, will you
promise to stop trying to get me to . . ."

"Copulate?"

"Let's not use that particular word. Let us say 'make
love.' "

His voice when he said the words deepened ever so
slightly, although she didn't think it intentional. This time

Willa did shiver on the outside. The odd thing was, just hearing it made her want to do it.

With him.

Now.

"Willa? Can you agree to that?"

"What?" She blinked. "Oh well, if you insist. Just let me know when you want me." Absently she turned her back to him and flopped down onto her pillow.

Nathaniel didn't think she saw the effect her choice of words had on him. He hoped not. It would never do for her to realize how very much he did want her.

It was better this way. And maybe if he kept telling himself that, his rebellious body would believe him. Moving to make his own bed before the fire, Nathaniel had to admit that there was something agreeable about having someone else around. For the first time since his disgrace, he didn't feel quite so alone.

Off in London, in a seedy room that cost more than it was worth for no questions to be asked, hid a man with a great deal more to lose than money. Slow-burning panic crawled through the man's belly like worms.

Events were not going as planned. Nothing had gone as planned since that damned political cartoon had come out. His future had once been rosy. Success, public respect, and wealth, more wealth than most men ever saw . . .

He'd been so close. And now, nothing.

Worse than nothing, for there were people with expectations of him. People who were not inclined to listen to excuses.

He had not acquired the item. Or the girl.

She'd disappeared, according to what he'd heard. Someone else had gotten to her first; he was sure of it.

Girls didn't simply disappear from their home villages on a whim.

His collar choked him. He raised a hand to loosen it, only to find it loosened already. His hand shook before his vision. He shut his eyes and reached for control.

There was still time.

Nathaniel ran his hand down Willa's soft naked belly to the brunette curls nestled between her round white thighs. She sighed and writhed against him, begging for more. He caught her hands and held them gently above her head with his other hand. She breathed a soft sob, willing and trembling at his hands.

He teased her until she quivered. Then he stroked his fingers boldly within. She was wet and hot within, her flesh blossoming at his daring invasion. She gasped aloud and he covered her mouth with his in a deep wet kiss, swallowing her cries as he drove her onward with deep strokes and the pressure of his thumb upon her clitoris. She writhed in his arms, helpless against his wicked assault, her will taken by the pleasure he was causing her.

Breathlessly she begged, "Please . . . oh, Nathaniel . . . oh, please."

He sucked a tight pink nipple deep into his mouth and pressed his thumb more quickly. She arched violently, then came pulsing around his touch.

With a start, Nathaniel realized where he was.

Oh no.

Not again.

By force of will, Nathaniel jerked himself completely awake, ready to leap away from the woman who had invaded his bed once more.

There was no one there.

Nathaniel froze, then looked wildly around the room. It was very late, and the fire had died to embers in the hearth. If she wasn't in his bed, then where was she?

She slept in her own bed across the room, precisely where she belonged. Curled tightly in her blanket with only a few stray locks of hair emerging from where her head was supposed to be.

Relief swept Nathaniel. Then alarm.

He had no business dreaming such dark things about Willa. He'd pinioned her hands; he'd handled her forcefully. That . . . he wasn't that sort. At least, he hadn't been. Once upon a time, he'd been a lazy, playful lover, with no impulse to *possess* a woman's body that way.

Especially not Willa. He would never touch her that way and shouldn't even want to. And he didn't. He was simply . . . in need of a good rogering, that was all. He hadn't had a woman in far too long.

Dreams were just dreams, after all. A man at his level of sexual deprivation would naturally begin to dream a bit. After all, he'd not touched a woman since becoming engaged to Daphne last year. Of course, since his engagement ended, there weren't too many woman willing to receive his touch.

Excepting Willa. Nathaniel's imagination grabbed him by the nape of his neck and dragged him back to that moment on the road. Full lips parted in lust. Sweet white flesh that was his for the taking.

Hot, trembling, wanting Willa.

He manfully freed himself from fantasy's grip. Willa was simply the only woman about. And she was attractive, in her ample dairymaid way.

She was no Daphne, of course. There were few women in the world as beautiful as Daphne. Daphne was a goddess.

Tiny and elegant, ruthlessly fashionable, with the refined features of an alabaster masterpiece.

There was a woman to dream about. Of course, he had no business dreaming of Daphne, either. She was as lost to him as the loftiness of his name.

As she should be. He'd broken the engagement himself, although it was publicly assumed she had done it. Loyal fiancée that she was, Daphne had at first claimed she didn't wish to be released from their obligation. However, Nathaniel couldn't allow her to be dragged down with him, and eventually she'd seen the merit in his insistence.

Yet, loyal as she'd protested herself to be, she'd believed the rumors. "In time," she'd said gravely, "I believe I might eventually forgive your mistake."

He wondered where Daphne was now. A lady so lovely and well-bred as Miss Daphne Danville likely had suitors galore, if not a new fiancé already.

The curious thing was, though he and Daphne had been intended for each other since childhood, he didn't miss her at all.

Nathaniel rose and shook out his blanket. Stepping quietly to the bed, he draped the blanket over Willa and tucked it in beneath her feet.

Her body began to relax into the added warmth immediately. Within moments, she had shifted her death grip on her blanket and allowed herself to come up for air.

Still, only a pert nose and a stubborn chin showed. Nathaniel silently added more coals to the hearth. It would likely be stifling by morning, but he didn't like the idea of her shivering all night.

Pulling his coat off its peg, Nathaniel draped it around himself and settled back down on his makeshift bed. It had only been a dream.

Nothing more.

• • •

The next morning, Willa gathered up the things they'd taken into the inn and packed the bags one last time. Nathaniel had brusquely informed her that they would be reaching his home in London tonight.

She ought to be excited about seeing London, but Nathaniel's cool manner had her preoccupied. He was obviously none too pleased with her after last night. Honestly, one would think most men would be thankful for such an obliging bride!

Willa had always taken pride in her even temper. After all, a jinx was enough to endure, without a reputation as a shrew on top of it. But Mr. Nathaniel Stonewell was fair to driving her mad with his changeable heart. The escalating edginess she was feeling didn't help.

For a moment, she watched the dust motes dance in the morning sunlight streaming in through the windows, until the image of Nathaniel's beautiful body imposed itself on her vision. He didn't have to be anywhere near her for her knees to weaken and her breath to come fast. Heavens, he'd had that effect on her from the first, even while unconscious.

Was she just an animal then, to be so driven by her physical impulses?

Thinking of the warring flashes of desolation and laughter she saw in his eyes and the unutterable loneliness on his face when he thought she wasn't looking, Willa had to admit that there was more to her longing for Nathaniel than the perfection of his form.

He needed her. As desperately as she needed him. He just didn't know it yet.

The question was, how was she to bear her growing desirous feelings until he figured it out?

Wrapping both arms about the baggage, she carried it

downstairs and out to the yard where Nathaniel stood with their mounts. He took it with a nod of thanks but didn't meet her eyes.

Irritation flared once more. "You're welcome. Oh, do stop," she gushed. "No need for such a display. It was nothing, nothing at all."

Willa walked away, but her sarcasm stuck with Nathaniel.

It *was* nothing. Just a simple sharing of the load, nothing that he wouldn't expect of any man sharing the journey with him. It occurred to Nathaniel that he knew of no other women who would stand up and shoulder the load of travel as Willa did.

He knew the pace he was setting was hard on her and that she was unused to riding much, but other than a few acid comments on her lack of knees, she had scarcely complained.

True, she had also knocked him unconscious and trapped him into marriage, deafened him with her chatter, and nearly driven him mad with her importuning to "copulate," but in general she was a very satisfactory traveling companion.

Mounting much more easily than she had done the first day, Willa settled into the saddle and turned her mare toward the road. "Shall we be off then?" she asked coolly.

Nathaniel mounted Blunt and nudged him to follow the mare. Willa was right to distance herself from him. Cool and formal was definitely the appropriate manner.

So why wasn't he happier about it?

As the morning progressed, the landscape became more and more familiar to him. Gone were the utilitarian farms of Northamptonshire. They were now in the more fashionable Buckinghamshire, playground of the wealthy and useless. Just the way he used to be.

There was a pasture where he had ridden a race against

his host's thoroughbred. There, a small lake known for its good shooting. Soon they would pass through Wakefield, a town where his family had often stopped on the way from Reardon to London for the Season. It was a sizable place, grown prosperous as the best place to halt before the last leg of the journey to London.

With a deep breath, Nathaniel decided it was time to come out of hiding. There was no doubt in his mind that someone in this town would recognize him. If he and Willa were lucky, things wouldn't get too ugly before they managed to get back on the road. Lord Treason's presence anywhere tended to create scenes. After all, his purpose was to ferret out the slippery Sir Foster. He couldn't do that hiding in the hedgerows.

However, it would not be fair to Willa to take her into London unprepared. When they stopped at midday to water the horses, he would tell her everything.

8

Silently Willa cut the bread and portioned out the meal of cheese and cold meat that Nathaniel had purchased this morning from the inn. She felt prickly and off-center, her nerves tightening by the moment. The morning had passed in silence but for the clopping of the horses' hooves. Would he never speak?

When he did, would she want to hear what he had to say? She had offered herself to him twice now, and he had refused her.

"Willa . . . ," began Nathaniel, but he stopped when she raised her eyes to his. She was astonished to see that he appeared to be as ill at ease and unsure as she was.

"I—" He stopped, then began again, more firmly. "There are some particulars about me that you remain ignorant of."

That was an understatement. She didn't say anything, however. He seemed to be having enough trouble finishing a sentence without interruption.

"My name, as you know, is Nathaniel Stonewell." He raised his gaze to hers, his green eyes boring into her blue. "What you don't know is my title. I am the Earl of Reardon."

Willa blinked. She certainly couldn't have predicted that revelation.

Nathaniel rushed on. "I wasn't born to it, since my father—who died when I was but a few years old—was only the nephew of the Earl and he was a much younger son at that. Through a serious of rather freakish events, the other heirs died off in quick succession and I became Lord Reardon when I was but a boy."

"I see," she said slowly, since he seemed to be waiting for a response. "How . . . nice."

"You shouldn't feel intimidated by my title, now that you know," he assured her.

She didn't smile, given that he was being so sincere with his permission. "I won't," she promised with equal gravity.

"So you see wherein lies our problem," he said, spreading his hands. "We aren't actually wed."

Willa thought about it for a long moment. "My apologies, but no. I don't see."

"Peers cannot legally marry in spontaneous country ceremonies like a blacksmith or a farmer," he explained gently. "There are laws requiring that we post our intention for three Sundays first, to allow anyone with property or title claims, or even previous marriages, to come forward." He shrugged. "There are dowries to be discussed, lines of maternal inheritance to be assured, endless negotiations. . . ."

Oh, heavens—was that all he was worried about? Willa sat forward, her chin on her hands. "Do I get another proposal of marriage? The first one wasn't really up to snuff."

Nathaniel took a deep breath. "Yes, well. I wasn't feeling my best."

He went to one knee before her in a quick, fluid motion. "Miss Trent, will you be my wife?" he said quickly.

She sighed. "It's a good thing I'm ruined, for that was truly a stinker. You couldn't tempt a cat from a brook with a proposal like that."

He was beginning to look impatient. "Oh, very well," she said. "I accept."

He returned to his seat, obviously thinking she was being unnecessarily tongue-in-cheek. Willa sighed. Oh well. A proposal was just a question, after all. One that he already knew the answer to at that.

She put on a cheerful manner. "So there are banns to be read and properties to apportion. When do we start?"

"We won't. When we arrive in London, I shall solicit a special license from a bishop of the church, and we can then be married immediately."

She tilted her head at him. "Men are always complicating matters. Why didn't you simply say that?"

He seemed taken aback. "I just did."

"Very well. Let me see if I have all this." She ticked off on her fingers, "You are Lord Reardon. We are not wed. You asked. I said yes. We will be wed by special license as soon as you speak to the Bishop. I must say, you have eased my mind. All of this explains why you did not want to cop—make love."

"Ah, W—"

"I suppose I am relieved. As interested as I am in natural processes, I think perhaps a bit more time to understand each other will do us both good, don't you?"

"Will—"

"There is the little matter of the jinx, however. You've managed to avoid any serious damage so far, if one does not count the knot on your temple—and I am eager to get started on little Lord Reardon—"

"*Willa!*"

"Yes, Nathaniel?"

"I have more to say."

"Oh dear. Do pardon me." She folded her hands in her lap and waited politely.

He rubbed the back of his neck, his eyes turned on the ground between them. "There won't be any little Lord Reardons. I have an heir, my cousin Basil. He isn't much of an heir, but hopefully he will marry someday and provide us all with someone a bit more . . . conscientious."

"Nonsense. You won't need Basil when I'm through with you." She clapped a hand over her mouth. "I didn't mean that quite the way it sounded."

Nathaniel didn't smile. His eyes, when he turned his gaze up to her, were sad beyond measure. "We won't be having any children, Willa, because I am never, ever, going to make love to you."

Nathaniel's vow went directly through Willa's heart like an arrow. Abruptly she held up her palm to stop his words. "Wait. Simply—simply wait."

Nathaniel nodded. He sat, his hands clasped loosely, dangling between his knees, watching her.

Willa half-turned away from him and stared into the gray sky. The clouds had gathered all through the morning. There would be rain tonight, unlike the night when she had felled a strange man, then spent the night by his side.

How stupid she was. What a stupid silly idiot. As wrapped up as she had been in her worry over *her* future, it had never once occurred to her to wonder about his plans for his own.

Add selfish to the list. Selfish and very, very stupid.

"And vain. Definitely vain."

Nathaniel frowned. "What?"

Willa gave a self-deprecating shrug. "I've had many suitors who wanted me badly enough to brave certain injury to court me. Men have been trying to marry me for years. It never crossed my mind that you weren't entirely thrilled with the match."

He reached for her hands, capturing them within his large warm ones. "No, Willa, it isn't because of you. I cannot—I will not—ever wish to have a son to carry on my name. No, no daughters, either," he said firmly, apparently sensing the thought that was even then crossing her mind.

"But why?"

Nathaniel knew he couldn't put if off any longer. She wanted to know. She had an inquisitive mind and a driving will. She was going to learn it one way or another. For the first time, it occurred to Nathaniel that he hadn't been able to say the words "I'm a traitor" because he had as yet avoided having to.

Odd. He could let others believe what they willed, and he could even play the part—but somehow he had managed never to openly admit to it.

Really, he could have used the practice, for telling Willa was going to be hard enough.

Nathaniel took a deep breath and said the words out loud for the very first time. "I plotted against the Crown. I joined a group known as the Knights of the Lily, named for Napoleon's fleur-de-lis, and plotted to have the Prince Regent dethroned."

She stared at him for a long moment; then she covered her face with her hands. She began to shake. Damn, she was crying.

Then she snorted. And snickered out loud.

"Oh dear. Really, Nathaniel, I'm loath to shatter your dreams, but your career on the stage will be deathly short."

He could only stare at her, mouth open. It only made her laugh the harder.

She put one finger beneath his chin and closed it for

him. Then she leaned her elbows on her knees and dangled her hands before her. "I told you once before. I am an excellent judge of character. You, Nathaniel Stonewell, Lord Reardon, could no more betray your country than a cobra could fly. It simply isn't in you."

Nathaniel couldn't believe it. Everyone he knew—at least, those who didn't already know the truth—had assumed the worst about him and had rejected him.

He could not deny the warmth that began to spread through some place in him that had been cold. However, Willa wasn't seeing the entire matter clearly. It was easy to disbelieve such a thing here in the country, with only the two of them about. She must be prepared for what the world would have to say about it.

"You must know what to expect. There will be unpleasantness at every turn. People have very strong feelings about traitors. The finer the person, usually, the worse the rejection. No one will talk to you. Merchants will be loath to take your money. Even your own servants will be grudging, despite that you pay them twice what their equals receive in other houses."

She'd gone quite sober as he spoke. Good. She must understand what was before her.

"There is no place where you'll be welcomed. No home, no shop, no tearoom will want you there. The reason why I could not tell you before was that I feared you would not come with me, and that you would choose to be ruined forever rather than wed me."

"Oh, Nathaniel," she breathed. "How awful it has been for you."

He blinked. "No, no, you are not listening, Willa. I told you all this because you must understand how it will be for *you*."

He gazed at her with intensity, willing her to understand. "I'm sorry that circumstances force you to wed me,

Willa. Nevertheless, one day the war will be over and my reputation may fade"—although he thought it unlikely—"but you would be disgraced forever if you did not marry me. If you wed me and then leave me, openly, you will more likely be forgiven for the mistake of not marrying well than for not marrying at all."

She gazed at him, her eyes damp. "Have you been terribly lonely, Nathaniel?"

He shook his head. He wasn't getting through to her. "Do you understand what you will be facing as my wife? I believe you will be better off in Derryton once we are wed."

Now she shook her head, as if finally awakening. "Oh. I am beginning to see. You married me, or will marry me, are taking me to London, have never touched me—well, but not really—because you thought that once I heard this silly story I would want to leave you." She sat back, shaking her head over the idea.

Nathaniel caught her hand. "Whether or not you believe in my innocence, there is a very large world out there which most emphatically does *not*. We must wed, for your sake. Then you must leave, also for your sake. You will be taking on a tarnished name. That name will do much less damage in Derryton, where you are loved." Even Reardon, filled with people who were supposed to be his own, would not welcome her.

She'd watched him throughout this speech with fascination on her face. Now she sighed and looked at the ceiling. "How more noble can one be?"

He was determined to get through to her. "Of course, you will not go back to living above the taproom. I will buy you a house and set you up with an income."

Willa bit her lip. Should she tell him there was no need of that? She had an income of her own, small but steady, from her parents' few investments. No, for the moment it was better to let him think she would need his support.

She was not yet ready to face her future according to his plan. No husband? No babies? Nothing but an eternal form of spinsterhood, only worse, for a spinster might always hope.

Unhappiness curdled the hope that she would have her own family at last.

Nathaniel watched her. She sat, bedraggled and a bit on the grimy side, her disobedient hair falling from its braid as usual. For the first time since they'd met, she seemed a little unsure of herself.

Nathaniel tilted his head to the side. With his hand he tucked away one of her unruly strands of hair. "You must be strong, wildflower. You're the fearless Willa, remember? Slingshot huntress supreme and defender of little furry things."

Willa smiled wide and happy. "You did it again."

Nathaniel took his hand away from her silky hair. "What?"

"You called me wildflower. That makes twice."

Nathaniel stiffened and stepped away. "That signifies nothing."

"Why, Nathaniel Stonewell, I do believe you are beginning to like me a little!"

"Of course I like you. I never said I didn't."

"Yes, you did. You said I was maddening, and frustrating, and you called me a chatterbox and a pest."

His jaw dropped. "I didn't." Never out loud, at any rate. "Never once."

"Silly Nathaniel. Everything you think is written on your face as plain as the nose on your . . . Oh well, you know what I mean."

Silly Nathaniel? More likely milord or Lord Treason or, among the Royal Four, the Cobra. The many epithets that Society had tagged him with, some bawdy, some vile, had never once veered near "Silly Nathaniel."

"I am *not* si—" He closed his eyes and inhaled deeply. "Never mind that. The point is, you couldn't possibly know what I'm thinking."

"Why not?"

"Because I'm thinking it. Not saying it. Not expressing it in any way."

"Humph. That's what you think."

Nathaniel put on his very worst lordly scowl. "Willa, you do *not* know what I am thinking."

"Nathaniel, it is quite all right. It is not as though I am going to tell anyone what a great marshmallow sweet you are. You go on being all aristocratic and brooding to everyone else. I won't ruin it for you."

"I. Am. Not. A. Marshmallow."

"Of course not, darling. Not a bit of it." Her voice was soothing, but her eyes sparkled with mischief. "You're Mad, Bad Nate, the scariest—by the way, darling, what is it that you do now?"

Oh yes, dear lady, did I forget to mention? I'm a spy. Then again, perhaps not. "I'm doing it."

She looked confused. Good.

"Which one, traveling or trying to get rid of me?"

"Both."

"Oh, Nathaniel, you can't get rid of me yet."

"Yes, I can. Once I finish my business and we're properly wed, I shall escort you back to Derryton."

Willa sighed. He was so adamant. She supposed she ought to do as he—

For shame, she scolded herself. Was she to let him go without a battle? She had taken an uncommon fancy to this man.

She would keep him.

"No."

"No, what?" Nathaniel frowned.

"No, this plan does not appeal to me. I want a real husband, and children, and a real home."

"This is not a possibility, Willa."

"You are my husband. It is your duty to give me this."

"I do not want a wife."

"Well, you should have thought of that before you married me."

Nathaniel opened his mouth and blinked.

She was—

She made him—

"Rrrrrr!" Leaping to his feet, Nathaniel strode away from the fire. Shoving his hands through his hair, he fought for patience.

She was just a woman. An unworldly country miss, with more brain than she had any need for and less sense. Why was she so frustrating?

Willa smiled fondly at her Nathaniel. He was such a darling when he was tearing his hair out. Gone was his aristocratic cool; gone was his ominous control. Only the real Nathaniel remained.

She watched him flexing his hands, open and shut, spread and fist. Silly man. As if she could ever be in danger from him. He was so noble, such a slave to his gentlemanly impulses. He fought it, he tried to deny it, tried to put on a hardened front, but it shone from his every action.

"There's no need to make such heavy weather about it, Nathaniel. Most everyone gets married and has children."

Nathaniel only shook his head. There was no point in arguing this with her. When they arrived in London, she would find out soon enough. By tomorrow, Willa would discover just what the world knew about Nathaniel Stonewell, Lord Treason. Then she would go gratefully on her own back to Derryton.

The harsh thoughts were somehow soothing. He should

never forget who he was and the price he must pay for duty. Funny, alluring country wife notwithstanding, he was an outcast, despised by all who knew him. The shell of that reality had become, if not comfortable, then at least accustomed, in the last months, and he wasn't about to toss that hard-won sense of peace away.

9

The town of Wakefield was a lively place of commerce and activity. Willa seemed fascinated by the bustle going on around her. "Wait until you get into London proper," warned Nathaniel. "This will seem like Derryton on Sunday afternoon."

He'd not intended to stop here, for it was unlikely that he'd be able to find anyone who'd noticed Foster among all the travelers going to and from London. It wasn't until Willa pulled her mare to a complete stop before a sign that read "Weldon's Books" that Nathaniel realized that, will-he, nill-he, Miss Willa Trent was planning to visit her very first real bookshop.

There seemed no help for it. Better here, where he was not as well known, than in Mayfair. And it would be nice to do something for Willa. Nathaniel halted the gelding and dismounted. Taking the mare's reins, he handed Willa down. As was usual in every town he had ever seen, there were a number of boys lurking about, looking equally hard for trouble or coin.

Motioning a likely lad over with a nod, Nathaniel bent to look him in the eye. "You seem an honest man. What is your name?"

"Lem, sir."

He was very dirty, but only in a daily sort of way. Young Lem no doubt had a mother who made him scrub with vigor each night before she filled his belly with warm food and his life with affection.

Lucky lad.

"Well, Lem, can you do me the great favor of looking after our mounts for an hour? Find them some water and a bit of shade for a rest?"

"Oh, yes, sir!"

After shaking the boy's hand with manful dignity, Nathaniel straightened and beckoned to Willa.

As they approached the shop, Willa looked back to see the boy walking soldier straight between the mounts. She turned back to Nathaniel.

"How do you do that?"

"Do what?"

Make people want to please you, she thought, but only shook her head.

He grinned at her. "What will you be buying, Willa?"

Slowly, she smiled, and her eyes gleamed with acquisitive desire. "How much may I spend?"

"Ah, you are human after all." Nathaniel laughed and directed her to the bookshop door. "I'll be along in a bit to pay for it. Find something new to read. Something without *vinegar* in the title."

The bookshop's distinctive aroma greeted Willa as she entered. Books had such a lovely papery smell. That combined with the shopkeeper's pipe smoke struck up longing in Willa for her father and reading with him in the evenings.

The shopkeeper had kind, curious eyes. He approached her immediately.

"And what would you be seeking on this lovely day, miss?"

Willa looked about her. There were stacks and shelves

and piles of books in the tiny shop. The plenty stunned her ability to choose.

"I don't know."

"Well, we have a large collection. Perhaps a history?"

Willa considered, then shook her head. Histories required a bit of time to delve into, being on the dry side usually.

"A novel, perhaps?" He pulled one from a stack with hardly a glance. "This one is very popular. Poor governess falls in love with her employer. Most uplifting, I'm sure."

Novels were terribly entertaining, it was true, although at the moment Willa felt rather as if she were living a novel of her own. She shook her head again.

"Do you have something . . ." She hesitated, not really sure what she was looking for.

"Yes?" His eyes were absolutely glittering with anticipation.

"Perhaps an instruction on . . ."

The man bobbed impatiently on his toes, hands clasped behind his back.

". . . marriage?"

"Do you wish a book on marriage contract law? Rather heavy reading for a child your age."

Torn between indignation and amusement, Willa shook her head once more. "No, sir. I am to be married and . . ."

"Yes, I saw you and your young man riding in. He looks well, although not as well as the last time I saw him. Bless me, I've forgotten his name. Pardon my memory, miss. It is not what it once was."

"My husband is Nathaniel Stonewell."

He shook his head. "Oh no. That doesn't sound quite right."

Willa blinked at him. "I assure you, it is entirely correct."

"Of course. You must know, mustn't you? Well, my

congratulations on your happy nuptials. A blissful union, I hope?"

Suddenly Willa knew precisely what was required. "Well . . . do you have any references on . . ." Oh, what could she call it? "On the act?"

He blinked. "The act of wedding?"

"No." Willa gave him a sunny smile. "The marital act."

The little man was scandalized. "Oh no! No, no, *no!*"

He blushed and stuttered until Willa was forced to make apologies and say that she had merely been jesting.

Eventually, she left the store without the novel about the governess, no wiser on the subject of the marriage act than she had been when she had entered.

She didn't see the man standing in the shadows who followed her with his gaze, watched her walk back to the horses, and then entered the bookshop with dark purpose in his eyes.

Nathaniel whiled away a few minutes in a dry goods shop while he waited for Willa. He purchased a bag of boiled sweets to reward young Lem but then ran out of things to occupy him. He looked around him. Sacks of flour stood in piles; barrels of corn and lamp oil hugged the corners. He had no use for any of it.

He left the merchant and walked slowly down the cobbled street. He could buy out the bookshop, but there would be no way to carry it all. Reardon had more than enough books and Reardon House in Mayfair a respectable library of its own.

Then a glimmer caught his eye. Sapphire silk and cream lace gleamed through a shadowy windowed storefront. It was a lady's gown, as fine as anything he had ever seen his mother or Daphne wear.

For the first time, Nathaniel bothered to picture Willa

in the drawing rooms of Reardon House. With her simple country muslin and her sturdy scuffed shoes Willa would be a mite underdressed.

Besides, wouldn't she look fine in blue?

He entered the shop to the tinkle of a small silver bell that hung on the door. A harried-looking woman came out from behind a curtain, then stopped short when she saw him.

Her eyes went wide and for a moment he thought she must recognize him. Then he realized it was only the natural dismay of finding a dusty, road-soiled man in her pristine establishment.

"I'm here to purchase something," he assured her.

She nodded and came forward warily. "What might I show you, sir?"

He gestured toward the blue dress, which hung on a figure by the window. "I'll buy that one."

"Yes, sir. That will be two pound sixpence." She flipped open an appointment book on the counter. "When would your wife like to come for a fitting?"

"No need," Nathaniel said. "I'll simply take it—"

His glance at the dress included a view of the window and of the street. Outside the shop stood the Blowers, man and wife, who had spoken out most virulently against Nathaniel when the thrice-damned cartoon had been made public. Now it seemed they were on their way into the shop.

Damn. He turned back to the shopkeeper. "The dress. Now." He threw three quid on the counter and turned to face the door just as it tinkled once more.

The woman blinked at him, then gasped, reaching one hand as if to pull her husband back. The man, a burly fellow with more money than political astuteness, began to color with insult when he recognized Nathaniel.

"You!" He pulled away from his wife's restraint and

stalked to Nathaniel. "You're going back to London, aren't you?"

Nathaniel lifted a brow. "I am."

The man scowled fiercely. "You've no right to stain the very air there. If you had any taste, you would take your bloody self off to hide in the country!"

Nathaniel folded his arms and leaned one hip onto the counter. "But I would miss you so."

The fellow, who truly had no imagination whatsoever, could only huff wordlessly.

The shopkeeper was busy stripping the figure of the silk gown while watching them all out of the corner of her eye. Nathaniel didn't bother listening to what else the fellow said, blustering idiot that he was, but only counted the seconds until the shopkeeper pressed the paper-wrapped parcel into his hand.

He took it and strode from the shop with a curt bow to Mr. Blowhard's wife, ignoring the shopkeeper's outstretched hand that held his change.

He wasn't fast enough. Mr. Blowhard came barreling out of the shop behind him. "How dare you offend my wife with your presence, you traitor!" The man's bellow was absolutely bullish. His words echoed down the cobbled street. "Lord Treason! Traitor!"

Up ahead, Nathaniel could see where Willa stood with Lem and the mounts. As he drew closer, walking fast, he could see the alarm growing in her wide blue eyes. "Mount up," he urged when he came close enough. He dug into his pocket for Lem's sweets, but the boy was backing away, his gaze going behind Nathaniel.

"You? You're that Lord Treason bloke?" The little boy had betrayal in his eyes. It made Nathaniel feel sick to his stomach, guilty even when he had done nothing to be guilty for. Lem looked at his offering with disdain. "I don't want nothin' from the likes of you!"

Nathaniel dropped the bag in the mud. "Of course you don't." He reached for Blunt's saddle and mounted swiftly. Turning the gelding, he looked behind him at the gathering crowd.

"I think it is time to leave," he said tightly.

"Yes, Nathaniel." Willa sounded frightened.

"Simply ride through them, wildflower. They'll move out of our way."

Blunt and the mare stepped forward as one, walking slowly but inexorably through the gathered townsfolk. Words and glares were thrown at them, but one by one the people of Wakefield stepped back from the progress of the horses. Then, when Nathaniel and Willa were in the thick of the crowd—

Splat! A handful of mud landed on the mare's white rump, startling the horse and leaving a black smear across the white hide and Willa's skirts.

"Ride!" Nathaniel urged, but the crowd pressed too closely now. The mare began to dance and rear. Nathaniel feared Willa would fall into the angry crowd. He grabbed the mare's reins.

A blob of mud struck him square in the back. Nathaniel turned to see pure hatred glaring from the eyes of little Lem. "Traitor!" the boy hissed.

That's when the mud began to fly in earnest. Black grime spattered them from all directions. Willa ducked and cried out in disgust and fear. Nathaniel clenched his jaw, swept Willa off the panicking mare with one arm to sit before him on Blunt, and kicked the giant gelding into a run, crowd or no crowd.

Blunt neighed and reared and the crowd fell back. Nathaniel kept one arm around Willa and one fist wrapped around the reins of the nearly wild mare and rode with his thighs clamped tight.

It did not take long to leave Wakefield behind them. At

last, Nathaniel allowed Blunt to slow to an easy canter. The gelding, who had never lost control, now galloped calmly down the road as if they were on a Sunday ride. The mare, who was perhaps not the brightest horse Nathaniel had ever known, still startled with wild eyes. Nathaniel held her reins tightly. He wouldn't want to make the rest of the journey with only one horse.

Willa was still pressed to his chest, her face hidden. He could feel her midriff shaking as if with sobs.

"I'm sorry you had to experience that," he murmured into her muddy hair. "It's over now. Please don't cry."

She hit her fist against his chest lightly. "I'm not cry-ing," she said. She lifted her head. Her face was red and her eyes were bright, but it was true. She was not crying. She was furious. "Oh, that *insufferable* town!"

Nathaniel couldn't help it. He wrapped his arm tightly about her and laughed his relief into her filthy hair.

The road was wide and well traveled here, and there still might be some pursuit, so Nathaniel pressed Blunt through a gap in the hedgerow to look for a likely spot to hide out. They found a river not far away where they might clean up and a sheltered bit of wood, likely kept for the master's pheasant shooting. No one would be hunting this late in the day, and as soon as they had removed the mud they would get out straightaway.

For now, it was sheltered, quiet, and, above all, safe.

Nathaniel was washing the horses in the river. The bend downstream was shallow enough to encourage them to roll once they'd been unsaddled. Willa was scraping the worst of the grime off the tack with handfuls of grass. She tried the same method on her skirts, but there was lit-tle hope her gown could be saved. Then she put the bridles and saddles out in the watery sunlight, hoping the remaining smears would dry enough to brush off later.

She wiped her hands on her ruined skirts and turned to her own toilette. She wasn't as filthy as Nathaniel, for he'd taken the worst of it when he pulled her before him. She washed her face, hands, and arms in the river. Her hair did well enough with a dunking and a quick braiding. She would change her gown after she helped Nathaniel with the horses.

She dug Blunt's currycomb from Nathaniel's bag and started downstream. Watching her feet on the damp slope, Willa didn't look up until she reached the river's edge.

When she did, her heart stopped beating, the breath left her lungs, and her mouth went dry. She saw the horses grazing beyond the bank with the pearly sunlight gleaming from their drying coats—and she saw Nathaniel.

He was beautiful.

He knelt in the shallows only a few yards away. With his back to her and her arrival masked by the chuckling water, he was entirely oblivious to her gaze.

He was also entirely wet.

And entirely naked.

The water was only to midthigh and there weren't enough bubbles in the world to cover the broad expanse of naked man that rose from the river.

Willa couldn't breathe. Her knees went weak at the sight of the sudsy water streaming down his broad back into the crease of his powerful buttocks. She had never seen anything so unbearably delicious in her life.

His back rippled with muscle as he soaped his hair, the cloudy afternoon light doing nothing to dim the sleek shine of soap and water on his male perfection.

Nathaniel bent to duck his head in the water and Willa could not control the moan that escaped her at the view.

Instantly Nathaniel whirled, one fist pulled back in instinctive defense while his other hand frantically wiped soap from his eyes.

Damn, he should have known they were too vulnerable here. He hadn't been thinking with the mind of a spy but had let thoughts of Willa's sumptuous thighs distract him.

His vision cleared and he saw her. The impulse to fight eased, only to be replaced by another equally ancient instinct.

It was her eyes. They were wide and hungry, with a shining ache in them that he knew from his own soul. She wanted him. He could see it in the way her chest swelled with heavy breaths and by the sheen of perspiration gilding her face and neck.

His own need rose in response to her hungry gaze, and he saw her gaze drop and her eyes widen in surprise. Then slowly, her gaze traveled back up him. Nathaniel stood for her perusal.

He was the most magnificent creature she had ever seen. She knew that the thrumming within her was because of his male attraction, but the ache in her heart was from his sheer lonely perfection.

He could have her. The thought ran through Nathaniel's mind like the animal it was. He could take her now, on the bank with their legs tangling in the stream edge and her hair spread across the moss. She would accept him hard and fast, he could see it in her eyes, and he could make her enjoy it.

They would be wild creatures, naked and rutting, smeared with mud and bits of grass. He could empty himself in her, here in the daylight, in the dappled green shade that smelled of peat and lust.

He was going to take her; Willa could see it in his eyes. Her knees shook from mingled desire and despair. He would plant himself within her, give her his seed and his lust, if nothing else.

But he would be hers, such as he was, and God help her if at this moment it seemed like enough. She wanted Nathaniel to show her, to feed and foster and answer the ache growing within her by the moment.

With shaking hands, Willa began to unbutton the bodice of her dress without ever taking her gaze from his. He didn't look in her eyes but followed the course of the open front of her gown as it grew.

Nathaniel began to walk toward her, wading through the water with a slow, implacable stride, his thick erection jutting mightily before him.

Her hands began to shake too much to handle the fastenings and she dropped them uselessly to her sides. The time was now, and she wasn't ready.

This wasn't what she wanted. And yet it was. The female beast within her wanted it and wanted it now. Wanted something untamed and unloving and undeniable.

The female heart wept warning, but the heat and rush of her animal blood drowned it almost beyond hearing.

Her breath coming so hard it almost sobbed, Willa closed her eyes and waited for him to overwhelm her. He stopped before her, so large she could sense him blocking the light from behind her eyelids.

She quivered in response and felt a first startling burst of pleasure between her thighs. God help her, Nathaniel hadn't even touched her yet.

He stepped closer, so close that she felt cold water drip from him onto the tops of her breasts. The drops should have hissed on her hot flesh, but they only rolled to meet one another and trickle down between her breasts.

She was hot. Hot and throbbing and aching and unbearably frightened, all at the same time.

Willa stood before Nathaniel like a pagan sacrifice, her breasts bared and her eyes shut tight, helplessly offering herself to his worst bestial impulses.

And he had them. Oh, he wanted to do terrible wicked pleasurable things to this simple country girl, this wildflower plucked from the side of the road. He could teach her such dark and sinful deeds and make her beg for more.

Slowly, Nathaniel reached out and took the shoulders of her opened gown in each hand. He could bare her in one horrific rip, tear her clothes from her sweetly offered body, and splay her on the ground for his consumption.

His aching lust pounded through him, driving him to do just that, to own and possess this ripe, willing female, and to the devil with the consequences. His hands fisted in the fabric of her gown, tugging it tight and pulling her toward him.

She swayed forward unresisting and let her head fall back, baring her throat in an ancient instinctive gesture of submission.

Nathaniel could taste her already, taste how salty and sweet she would be, the salt of her skin and the sweetness of her virginal untouched nipples in his mouth. . . .

Nathaniel pulled the neckline of Willa's gown together once more, then placed her hands upon it to hold it closed.

She opened her eyes and blinked at him, her gaze thoroughly confused. Nathaniel put his hands on her shoulders and gently turned her. Pointing her back upriver toward their belongings, he gave her a little push.

"I'll join you in a moment. I need to dress." And somehow he must cool his throbbing arousal.

As Willa stumbled out of sight, Nathaniel picked up the bucket and dumped gallon after gallon of freezing river water over his head.

10

Willa splashed her face with cold river water again and again, until the heat and blush receded and she could think again. She knelt on a large flat stone that jutted out into the water, the sort of stone that women of old would have beat their washing on. Willa only wanted to knock her own skull against the granite.

She had changed into her last clean gown, her best, for the arrival in London. Her hair was neatly rebraided, quite primly even. She was tidy, buttoned up, looking as ladylike as was possible in these conditions.

It didn't help. She wanted to do wicked, wonderful things. She wanted to strip off her clothing and be naked in the water with Nathaniel. She wanted leaves in her hair and moss beneath her buttocks and Nathaniel between her thighs. She wanted—

She plunged her hands into the chill water again, bringing up another handful of water to her face.

It would have been wrong to make love with Nathaniel on the riverbank, shocking and wrong, and she was never going to forget his magnificent form striding toward her through the shallows—

She bent to splash more cold water.

There was a motion out of the corner of her eye, and
Willa sighed. Just when she was nearly calmed down.

"Nathaniel, I—"

It wasn't Nathaniel. On the bank of the river stood
a man with a ruined face.

One side of that face was startlingly handsome, with
chiseled features beneath several weeks' growth of beard.
His eyes were flashing blue, ringed by long lashes that
Willa would have envied at any other time. One side of
his face was perfect.

The other side was all the more tragic for it. Scars ran
over the right side like branch water, one slicing into the
corner of his mouth, pulling his otherwise perfect lips up
in what must have been a perpetual twist.

His dark reddish hair was unkempt and shaggy to go
with the beard, and his clothes were rags. He took one
step forward, his hooded eyes intent upon her.

Surprised, Willa took one step back . . .

And fell into the river.

Her skirts pulled her under immediately. She was a
tolerable swimmer, but there was no fighting the way her
layers of muslin weighed like lead when soaked.

She had a bad moment, but it wasn't terribly deep next
to the flat stone. Willa managed to get the tips of her toes
under her and stand despite the current that pulled at her
heavy skirts. She flung one arm over the rock on which
she had been standing and took a deep breath and wiped
the water out of her eyes.

That's when the man on the bank jumped into the water. Quickly Willa put the boulder between them but realized almost immediately that the man was trying to swim
after her ruined dress, which must have fallen in when
she did.

He didn't do too badly at first, and Willa had hopes

that he would actually be able to help her. Then he seemed to tire abruptly. Willa watched in horror as he slid beneath the swirling waters.

"Nathaniel! *Nathaniel!*" Oh, dear God, let him hear her. The man bobbed up once, then promptly sank again. "Nathaniel!"

Nathaniel crashed through the thicket with a giant stick raised above his head. When he saw her, he threw down his cudgel and made to rush into the water to her. Willa shook her head and pointed downriver.

"Help him! There, do you see him?"

Nathaniel dived in after the briefly visible man and swam strongly into the churning current. Willa couldn't see them well anymore and struggled her sodden self up onto her rock. Ignoring the water streaming from her skirts, she stood on tiptoe. Where were they?

There was no one in the water.

"*Nathaniel!*" Willa screamed so loudly she felt something snap in her throat.

"Oh no. *No!*" Willa cried, only it came out in a desperate whisper. Oh, dear God, what if she lost him? What if her beautiful, sweet Nathaniel was gone? Black guilt washed over her. If the jinx killed Nathaniel, she wouldn't want to live.

Breathless at the prospect, Willa turned and raced recklessly back over the root-ridged path that had brought her to the flat stone in the first place. She ran down the muddy bank, skidding madly, eyes locked on the roiling river where he had disappeared. The bend was up ahead. If he could only make it to the shallows of the bend—

"Please, please, please." Unaware that her voice was nothing but an abused whisper, Willa begged any and every god ever imagined to return her Nathaniel to her.

There.

Nathaniel's water-darkened golden head broke the surface. He had the man by his shoulders and was towing him to the shallows. They were just fine.

The two men struggled near the bank, Nathaniel pulling the other man along by his arm. The fellow was quite weak and seemed to have a bad leg as well.

Willa reached them when they were a few yards from the bank. She ran into the water to take the man's other side. The two of them helped him to the grassy crest of the bank and let him collapse there and rest.

Willa immediately threw herself at Nathaniel. She wanted to tell him how worried she was, how terribly sorry she was, but all that came out was a raspy whispering sound.

He wrapped his arms about her. Willa pressed her face into his cold, wet neck and shuddered with relief. He was safe.

"Shh. We're fine, wildflower, all of us. We're just fine." Nathaniel held her close, pressing his cheek into her dripping hair. Had it only been a few moments since he had heard her cry his name?

Raw fear had coursed through him, and he had flung himself toward the river, grabbing up a chunk of deadwood on the way. When he had seen her, clinging to a rock in the rushing water, his heart had stopped beating altogether.

The presence of the strange scarred man he didn't understand at all. All he could think about was that Willa was safe.

When Willa stopped shuddering in his arms, Nathaniel pulled back to look into her face. He pushed her hair back with both hands, searching for any sign of injury, but aside from a thorough wetting she seemed in excellent shape.

She opened her mouth to speak, but the only sound she made was a harsh croak.

"What happened to your voice?"

"She screamed it away," grunted the man on the ground. "Seen it before in the hospital. Wounded soldier'll scream his voice clean gone before he dies."

Nathaniel turned to him. The fellow was a mess. Scarred face, bad arm, bad leg. He'd been in the hospital, likely a soldier himself. This veteran had paid a true price for his country. "Who are you? How did you end up in the water with Willa?"

"'Twas me that startled her in the first place. Didn't mean to, but she didn't hear me coming. I tried to help her, but I can't swim the way I once could," he said bitterly.

It briefly crossed Nathaniel's mind to wonder if the man was from Wakefield, but even if he was, he wouldn't have been present for the mudslinging.

Concern for Willa drove the thought away. Nathaniel tucked her under his arm. "Let's get you in front of a fire, wildflower." He shot a suspicious glance at the man. "You are welcome, too, if you like." If his tone was grudging, he was in no mood to apologize for it.

"Don't mind if I do."

Once Nathaniel had built a hasty fire, Willa sank gratefully down before the flames. He'd brought Blunt's blanket to drape about her shoulders, and Willa took comfort in the familiar homey smell of horse. She couldn't shake that near-escape, exhausted, sickly feeling. The water had chilled her, but it was devastating fear that had taken the strength from her knees. She was shaking in reaction to the discovery that Nathaniel Stonewell meant more to her than she'd ever realized.

Her hair dripped water down her face . . . or was that a

tear? She wasn't much of a weeper normally, but the last few days had been rather trying. She was probably due a good howl.

Only she didn't want to howl. She wanted to climb onto Nathaniel's lap and wrap her arms around his warm solidity so that she could prove to the part of herself that was still afraid that he was just fine.

Nathaniel was brushing out the horses close by, standing where he could clearly see her and the fire. She smiled, warming at his protectiveness, although she didn't think the stranger was particularly dangerous.

The fellow wasn't much improved by his wetting. With his wet hair slicked away from his face, one could see how very gaunt he was. His eyes flicked to meet hers, and the silence grew as he gazed at her unblinking.

He could be a daunting sight, she supposed, for he was a big man, as tall as Nathaniel and likely as broad when he wasn't starved.

She felt no smidgen of fear of him.

The man moved to the side of the fire where Nathaniel had put the kettle. Without taking his eyes from hers, he poured some tea into a tin traveling cup and brought it to her.

"I'll take that." Nathaniel stepped between them. The man faced Nathaniel eye to eye for a moment, then backed down, handing over the tea.

Nathaniel brought the cup to her, kneeling beside her. Without a word, he wrapped her shaking hands around its warmth. She drank it willingly enough, winced at the heat in her throat.

Never taking his eyes off them, the stranger moved silently back to his place on the other side of the fire.

Willa could almost hear Dick and Dan now.

What is he?

He was a fine and faithful wolfhound, she decided.

A splendid creature once. And through no fault of his own, he had been tossed out to fend for himself. Look at him, even now expecting a kick from her.

He was very interesting and she could have happily spent time pestering him with unwanted questions, but the sick feeling was easing at last, leaving only exhaustion and the burning desire to look at Nathaniel for long hours at a stretch.

Finally, the horses were ready and Willa was as dry as she was going to be. Even damp and wrinkled, her sprigged muslin was the best she had left. She kept Blunt's blanket about her, for the evening was not growing any warmer.

Nathaniel helped her mount the exhausted mare, then turned to the stranger. "My thanks, sir. I'm glad to see you have recovered so quickly," Nathaniel said.

The other man watched, his bearded, scarred face expressionless. There was something about him. . . .

It wasn't the scars that bothered Nathaniel, but there was something dark burning just behind the man's eyes.

Still, pity for him and respect for anyone who had sacrificed so much for his country kept Nathaniel from probing further. These days, the world was full of the battered, the armless, the legless. And the dark. This fellow wouldn't be the first veteran to walk away from the battlefield damaged within as well as without.

Nathaniel decided that the man bore watching. "Do you live near here, Mr.—?"

"Day. John Day." The man offered nothing more, simply watching Nathaniel closely. When Nathaniel nodded for him to go on, he seemed to relax a bit. "I'm on my way to London. There's a man there who owes me."

Not surprising. Most anyone traveling to London from the north would be on this road.

And the fellow had risked himself to help Willa. His

speech might be common, but the fellow definitely had the instincts of a gentleman.

Nathaniel let his suspicions go. Scarred beggars in Wakefield were not his mission. Foster was.

Mounting Blunt, Nathaniel reined the gelding around and moved back toward the road. He lifted one arm in a wave, but the man simply watched them ride on.

Willa tried to call out a farewell, but nothing came out but an airy rasp.

Her voice was gone. How annoying! Just when she needed it the most to convince Nathaniel Stonewell, Lord Reardon, that nothing in the world, certainly not a mud bath, would ever make her leave him.

It was already dusk when they entered Mayfair. The fog had risen to shield anything interesting from view. Instead, the street merely noised about them, becoming a blurred haze of gaslight and lanterns.

Eventually, they began traveling down progressively quieter streets, until the loudest noise was the dripping of the trees and the occasional squalling cat.

Sometimes Willa could hear music and laughter coming from the houses on either side of them, houses that were mere shadows punctuated by amorphous blobs of light.

A carriage came alongside them for a moment and Willa realized that the fog had thinned, for she could see the fine horses and the ornate emblem on the carriage door. The inhabitants of the vehicle could also see her now, and she heard distinct sounds of alternating indignation and snide laughter.

Nathaniel didn't seem to notice or, if he did, to care. Taking her cue from him, Willa stared straight ahead, despite her curiosity.

"I declare," a female voice drawled, "I think Lord Treason has a new mare!"

A male voice answered her. "And a white horse, too!"

This sally was met with many a tittering giggle, and then the carriage outpaced them and they were alone on the street again.

Willa was nodding a bit when the mare abruptly took a left turn, and almost slipped from the saddle. Then she spied their destination and almost fell from her perch in truth.

They were at the end of a long drive leading to a grand house. It was huge and in the hazy remnants of the fog seemed to be floating a few feet above the earth. Its windows were ablaze with light, and Willa had to wonder at the candle consumption.

As they rode closer, the house only became grander. She could see more detailed carving above every window, more intricate stonework on every corner.

Lord Reardon, indeed.

By the time Nathaniel and Willa entered the meticulously swept turnaround, the massive carved doors of the house opened slowly and a figure stood silhouetted against the light.

Nathaniel stopped and stared up at the house as if he didn't much want to enter the place he had dragged her to so vehemently.

Personally, Willa was done with riding. She managed to kick her exhausted legs free of the stirrup and pommel and slide from the saddle on her own. She pulled the small satchel that held her immediately necessary possessions from behind the saddle and limped aside as a footman stepped forward to take the mare away. Willa wearily smiled her thanks, but the footman only slid her a wary glance.

Hoping the mare was going for a rest, Willa stifled a yawn of her own and caught up with her husband. She came abreast of Blunt as the figure from the doorway came forward. From his livery and entirely arrogant expression Willa took him to be the butler.

Moira had warned her about butlers. The butler set the tone for all the servants in the house.

Nathaniel dismounted finally and absently handed Blunt's reins to the groom. He sent the gelding off with an absentminded pat on a great haunch. When the horse was past, the butler stood before them. He bowed quickly. Willa wasn't an expert on that sort of thing, but it did seem a rather forced, shallow bow.

"Welcome home, my lord. We were not expecting you."

"Hammil, the rooms are all lit." Nathaniel said quietly. "I take it that the family is still in residence?"

Family? Startled, Willa turned to look at Nathaniel, who was still gazing up at the golden light pouring from the very many windows. He looked at once grim and wistful.

Nathaniel had family? Willa was too weary—and voiceless—to question him now, but later . . .

Imagine, bringing her here, looking like she did, without a word of warning to anyone, to meet his *family.*

He was going to pay for that. Later.

She could, however, clear her throat, pointedly if somewhat raspily, to remind Nathaniel of her existence. He sent her a rueful glance. "My apologies. Hammil, this lady is my fiancée, Miss Trent. Please see that she gets the finest of attention."

The butler sent her a shocked look before his supercilious control returned. He bowed again. "Of course, my lord."

Hammil gestured sharply to one of the footmen to take Nathaniel's burden, then turned briskly away.

Any further thought on the subject of Nathaniel's preoccupation was drained from Willa's mind when the grandeur around her began to sink in.

The entrance hall was so large that Willa felt as though she were a pea in the bottom of a bowl. An imposing staircase wrapped round the room and swept upward to a domed ceiling, which was frescoed in clouds and beaming cherubs wearing scanty attire.

"Oh dear," she murmured—whispered—to herself. "All the way to heaven by stairway? No, thank you, I'd rather take the usual route."

"Madam?"

Willa pulled her eyes down to meet the gaze of the butler. The fellow was so stiffened by his own importance that he likely had trouble tying his shoes.

Where had Nathaniel gone? He had disappeared while she had been distracted by the ceiling. She was left with only the butler.

He looked at her with such heavy-handed politeness that she felt the urge to rap him with her satchel for his rudeness. She pulled herself as tall as possible and raised a questioning brow. Then she held her satchel out for him to take.

His eyes narrowed at her obvious challenge. She waited, reminding herself to project inborn aristocratic expectation.

The butler considered her stance. His gaze lingered on her ruined, wrinkled gown for a moment, then traveled to her satchel. Then he returned his gaze to hers in a staring contest of wills.

Willa nearly smiled. She always won staring contests. Something about her blue eyes always did them in. She settled in for a nice long battle, for Hammil looked as though he was quite used to his role as despot.

The butler broke almost immediately. She was almost disappointed.

He took the bag from her with only the tips of his gloved fingers and gestured ahead to the sweeping staircase.

Willa knew she looked a sight, but then she often did. Moreover, she refused to give this snide fellow the satisfaction of her acknowledging it. Raising her chin, she cast him an imperious look and swept majestically up the gilded stairs.

It would have worked marvelously if she hadn't run out of breath halfway up. Mercy, but her legs were stiff. Willa forced herself to ignore the houseman's twitching lips and pulled herself up each step by the glass-smooth railing.

At the top, she waved him on while she tried to hold in her panting. Heaven suddenly didn't seem like such an inappropriate theme for the ceiling, for the stairs were bound to kill her.

She was led down an elegantly appointed hall to one of many polished doors. The butler turned the knob with one hand as he gestured her through with the other.

It was the most beautiful room Willa had ever seen, like a golden chalice filled with cream, and she wanted nothing more than to indulge herself forever in it. Ivory draperies hung from the gilt frame of the enormous bed. Soft wheat gold carpets waited for her step, and the cream silk of the bedcovers called her to sink into them until the aches of her long journey leeched away. *Oh, yes please.*

Her knees went weak at the thought, and Willa fought the involuntary closing of her weary eyes in order to gaze at the heaven surrounding her.

A fire glowed merrily in the vast hearth. And before it, centered on the stage of the marble hearth, stood a copper tub being filled to the brim by industrious footmen.

How had they done this so quickly? She had only just

then stepped into the house. She knew a bit about hired help. The efficiency and thoroughness of the Reardon household brought Nathaniel's wealth home to her in a way that no amount of pretty furnishings ever could. She heard a faint sniff behind her and turned to catch a fleeting look of disdain on the butler's face. He was thinking she hardly dared step foot in the room for fear of dirtying the carpets, apparently.

Anger began to curl through her stomach, heating away the weariness she'd been experiencing. How unkind of him. She was a guest in this house, no matter her state, and a guest should never be made to feel inferior. She was a lady and the wife of a gentleman. She deserved to be treated as such. Any guest deserved to be treated as such.

Just then, a pretty young maid opened a vial and poured a generous amount of the contents into the bath. The delicious scent of jasmine swept the room. Willa closed her eyes and breathed it in for a moment. Her favorite scent.

She realized that she had a choice. Settle this with Hammil once and for all or dive headfirst into that divinely steaming scented bath.

No contest. Willa chose the bath.

11

Nathaniel strode through the house, his boots clicking loudly on the marble floor. Toward the back of the ground floor was a room favored by a certain someone.

Someone Nathaniel wanted answers from.

After he entered the room without knocking, Nathaniel closed the door behind him. "All right, Myrtle. What the devil is going on?"

An elderly woman looked up from her book as she read by the fire. Her chair was large. She was not.

"Thaniel, dear!" She smiled sweetly. "What a surprise."

"Myrtle, what is the family still doing in residence? You all should have been en route to the country by now." Where he wouldn't have to face them.

"Don't you even have a kiss for your own dear great-aunt?"

"Myrtle," Nathaniel warned. She was his dear and the only one of his family who had not denounced him, but at the moment Nathaniel felt nothing but impatience. He turned halfway to the door.

"I didn't want to come here like this. While I am happy to see that you are well, I would like to know why my instructions were ignored."

Myrtle regarded him for a moment. "You've become hard, Thaniel."

"Is that so surprising?" His tone was harsher than he'd intended.

"I never wanted you to leave us."

"I know, pet. I apologize."

"Oh, Thaniel, it's been awful since you left. Victoria is impossible to please, and Basil is simply impossible. And your father . . ." She shook her head mournfully.

Nathaniel didn't want to remind her that it wasn't the leaving that had shredded the fabric of their family; it was the reason for the leaving.

"Yes, thank you for reminding me. Now, would you mind explaining?"

"Thaniel, it's your father," Myrtle blurted. "He's dying."

It shouldn't have mattered. It shouldn't have glued Nathaniel's feet to the floor and kept him from tossing the lot of them off to Reardon. Yet it did.

His stepfather had been his hero. Tall and proud and infinitely demanding of his stepson, indulgent of his aunt, indifferent to the wife he'd married to gain a son.

The last Nathaniel had seen of the man had been the broad superfine-clad back he had turned on Nathaniel in disdain. Why couldn't he turn his own back now?

Helpless to deny his need to know, Nathaniel turned.

"Tell me."

Willa's thoughts were spinning. Nathaniel had brought her here and dumped her like an unwanted kitten. There was so much he wasn't telling her.

Who were the family? She could only drum up a whisper to ask the maid.

"Why, Lord Reardon's relations, o' course!" Lily said

with a puzzled frown as she scrubbed Willa's back with competent hands.

Why were they staying here?

"Well, where else would they stay?" True puzzlement from Lily this time and the beginnings of wariness, as if she wasn't sure the lady she was tending was entirely in her right mind. Willa shut up tightly before she scared the girl away entirely. Answers would be nice, but at the moment, pampering was better.

Besides, Willa didn't seem to be armed with the right questions.

After the most divine bath of her life, Willa put on her flannel nightdress after hesitating to don the clingy lawn nightdress.

Lily bustled back into the room with her arms full. Willa watched in confusion as the maid laid out a frothy construction of deep blue satin and cream lace on the bed.

Willa stroked one finger down the sleeve, then looked inquiringly at the maid.

"It is yours, isn't it, miss?" The maid looked down at the dress in confusion.

Willa shook her head.

"Well, his lordship said it was for you, and to get it ready for you to wear tomorrow evening."

Where had it come from? When had Nathaniel purchased a dress for her?

Taking her silence for disapproval, the maid hurried on. "I know it seems a bit grand for supper with the family, but there are very important guests expected tomorrow. Sir Danville is joining you."

Willa blinked. A lord and a knight. Well, she was running in exalted circles now, wasn't she? Moira would be thrilled.

Willa eyed the dress again. It was like nothing she'd

ever worn in her life. It was divine. She reached to stroke the silk again. It felt like liquid under her fingers. A girlish part of her heart longed to wear it.

So why was she hesitating?

For the first time, it occurred to her that Nathaniel might be ashamed of her. After all, he was used to women who dressed like this all the time. Women who had fine soft hands and embroidery skills and played the pianoforte charmingly. Things Willa had never had a chance to learn.

She wanted to wear the beautiful dress—but not if Nathaniel was trying to hide her in it.

Slowly, she lifted it by the bodice and held it against her. She wasn't surprised to see the hem puddle on the floor. She'd ever been less than tall.

"Oh dear, miss. 'Twill take some alteration for sure. I'd best fetch my pins." Lily scurried off.

Willa sighed. It looked as though she was in for a fitting. All she really wanted was to lie back on this luxurious bed and go to meet the sleep that beckoned her. All the days of travel seemed to catch up to her at once, and she positively ached for some rest.

She carefully laid the blue dress across an overstuffed chair and sat on the bed to wait. She sank deep into the tick and almost shuddered from the sheer temptation of it. Her eyes began to shut all of their own, and her spine dissolved with weariness.

As she slipped involuntarily to the pillow, it occurred to her that since she was a married woman, perhaps she ought to be sleeping with her husband. . . .

Nathaniel leaned silently against the bedpost and watched the only father he had ever known sleep. The face on the pillow was not the same one Nathaniel had faced over kippers every day of his childhood. This face looked like a hag-ridden caricature of that one.

His father was a giant. This man was a skeleton.

His father was powerful and opinionated. This man was weak and listless.

How could he have changed so much in a few months? What disease could have sapped the life from him so quickly?

" 'Twas his heart." The voice behind Nathaniel was all too familiar.

Nathaniel didn't turn. "Hello, Simon."

"Nathaniel."

"What are you doing here? Don't you have young minds to corrupt for that den of thieves you call the Liar's Club?"

"Actually, I think they're corrupting me. But I'm here on the request of your compatriots." Simon came abreast of him. "I was sent to wait on you, essentially. I've already sent word that you've arrived. And I came to watch over the Old Man, being a friend of the family." He folded his arms and regarded the man on the bed. "I know what you're thinking."

Nathaniel hadn't yet turned to look at the almost brother he'd never been able to live up to or to live down. "I doubt that."

"No, I do. I know because I think it every time I step into this sickroom. You are thinking that this isn't him. That this is some sort of charade, a hoax, because this couldn't possibly be the same man who was nine feet tall and could lift a dozen horses."

"Ten."

"What?"

"He was ten feet tall," Nathaniel whispered.

Simon came to stand with him. "Yes. Ten," he agreed quietly.

For the first and only time in his memory, Nathaniel looked at the man he'd long considered an interloper and shared a moment of perfect understanding.

Then Simon became Simon again. "It's good to see you, Nate, but I hope you aren't staying. You don't want to endanger your cover."

A corner of Nathaniel's mouth twisted up. Some things never changed. "You're not the spymaster of *me*, Magician."

The look that crossed Simon's face was priceless. Nathaniel could see that his old rival had forgotten to whom he was speaking. The Cobra didn't take orders from the former or current leader of the Liar's Club. The Cobra didn't even take orders from the Prince Regent.

Simon's lips twitched. "No, my lord. I am not." He bowed. "Consider me most properly put in my place, my lord."

Simon wasn't the enemy. He never had been. Nathaniel let out a gust that ended in a weary chuckle. "Consider me most properly chastised for my rudeness."

"You've got nothing to fear from me, Nate," Simon said gently. "I know the truth."

Nathaniel nodded, then stepped closer to the man lying still on the bed. "But he doesn't, does he?"

Simon ran a hand through his hair. "You know why."

Nathaniel nodded again. He had proposed this devil's bargain himself. "I know why—" His voice simply stopped working. He swallowed violently and looked away.

Simon's hand rested on Nathaniel's shoulder for a silent moment then he quietly left the room.

When Nathaniel left the sickroom a short time later, his mother awaited him in the hall outside. She was tall and fair, like him, but there the resemblance ended. In his most dapper days he'd never attained the severe, arrogant elegance that permeated Victoria. Nor did he want to. He hoped to God his eyes never took on such an icy glare.

"Have you come to cast more embarrassment upon us all?" The words were scathing, but the voice they were spoken in was so rich with studied melody that it sounded like the disdain of an angel.

Nathaniel took a deep breath, then smiled resolutely.

"Hello, Mother."

"Do not call me that."

"Of course, madam. How meticulous of you to remind me."

"If you'd stay away from your stepfather and I, as you agreed, I wouldn't have to."

"I prefer to think of him as my father."

She folded her arms. "Your father was a wastrel, like you. You are nothing like Randolph."

"And yet, he is the only father I ever had—the only one I'll never have." He didn't bother saying the same about her.

She only scoffed at his garments. "You look a proper sight. Are you performing in a mummery, perchance?"

"Sorry. I didn't want to take the time to change before I saw him." Why did he bother explaining himself to Victoria? It never got him anywhere.

"It doesn't matter, you know. You can crawl back here forever and a day, but he will never, never absolve you. Randolph never forgets betrayal."

He wanted to retreat from her bitterness. *Like a king cobra.* He smiled wryly. "Not even if I slither on my belly in penitence?"

"You are impertinent."

He clapped one hand to his cheek. "Oh no, not impertinent! Tell me it isn't so!"

Her mouth worked in silent rage for a moment. "This

is your house. I cannot make you leave it. But I pray you will take care not to cross my path if you can avoid it."

Nathaniel sketched a mocking bow. "As always, Mother, you shower me undeservedly with your maternal affection. I wish you good evening."

Turning his back on her sputtering, Nathaniel wondered where Willa was.

Alone in her great bed, Willa slept with the far-flung limbs and abandon of a child. Nathaniel sat carefully on the edge of the thick mattress and watched her sleep.

He'd bathed and changed, having had quite enough comment on his wardrobe, thank-you-very-much. With his hair clean and tied back, clad in black superfine to suit his mood, he doubted if Willa would even recognize him as the road-worn man she'd married.

He hoped she would like what she saw.

The contrast of Willa's vibrancy and health against the pallor and waste of his father revived him. Willa was riotously, passionately vital, and she affirmed that life did go on.

Sweet, enchanting Willa.

Her lashes lay thick and dark upon her cheeks, and even by candlelight Nathaniel could spy the dusting of freckles across her nose. Her lips were soft and pouting and begging to be kissed.

Even when she was completely still, Willa's hair had a life of its own. Her braid sported numerous escapees that trailed across the linens. He reached to tug a strand of hair from across her mouth. It clung for a moment, and her lips worked sleepily until it was freed. With a sigh, she butted her head more deeply into the pillow.

Nathaniel wrapped the silky outlaw around his finger. It was warm and damp from her breath. He leaned closer to catch and identify the fragrance filling the enclosed area of the bed. It was soft and flowery but spicy in its sweetness, just like Willa.

Jasmine, he thought, but did not move away, even though he had solved the puzzle.

Leaning closely above her, he could feel the warmth of her rising up to him, and it was almost more than he could resist.

Was there anything more seductive than Willa's warmth? Physically and emotionally, she was a bonfire of affection and energy. He wanted to bask his frostbitten soul in her glow, let her radiance burn away the last bone-chilling ache of war and icy pain of betrayal.

He was tired and sore, within and without. He wanted to strip away his clothing and his cares and slide between Willa's bed linens. He knew she would welcome him sleepily into her bed and he would find a fragrant haven in her arms. The heavy draperies were closed, and he and Willa would be shrouded in delightful privacy.

The pull was almost more than he could bear. *One night,* he begged himself. Just one night of loving oblivion, before he sent her away from him. One night to keep him warm forever.

But it was worse to feel a moment of warmth in the cold. It shook you, made you ache with loss and shiver even more when it was gone. It would kill him to taste of her warmth only to be forced back into his wintry isolation.

That would surely destroy him.

He had to go. He was awaited in the Chamber.

Keeping his hands quite rightly to himself, he left his wife with the merest feathery kiss on her lips.

The Chamber in the dusty depths of Westminster Palace was unchanged from the last time Nathaniel had been there—a bit mustier, perhaps. Nathaniel was fairly certain that the Lion had been smoking in there again. Hopefully, the Prime Minister's more elder nose would not pick up the scent.

Nathaniel seated himself in the Cobra's chair. The Falcon and the Lion were already there, as was Lord Liverpool, who had once been the Cobra, before stepping "down" to serve as Prime Minister of England.

Of course, Liverpool wasn't seated at the table, although Nathaniel saw him eyeing the Cobra's chair. Was that misty longing he saw in the Prime Minister's eyes, or was it the dust lining the carving that was upsetting the man?

Nathaniel was well aware he was a second-string selection for the Cobra. Dalton Montmorency, Lord Etheridge, had been Liverpool's chosen successor. The Prime Minister had still not forgiven Dalton for stepping down to lead the Liar's Club when Simon Raines had chosen to leave for his lady.

Still, second-string or no, Nathaniel was the Cobra now, with all the power and burdens the seat bestowed. The honor was stunning and the onus backbreaking, but nothing could ever convince Nathaniel that it wasn't worth every abysmal hour of disgrace. He *was* the Cobra, no doubts, no regrets.

Liverpool was addressing the Three. "Sir Foster might try to contact the Cobra on his own. He ran before the final confrontation, so he could have no way of knowing how the Knights of the Lily met their end. He may well still believe the Cobra is loyal to the French." He turned his gaze to Nathaniel exclusively. "You could act accordingly in public. It may reassure him that he can approach you."

Nathaniel only nodded respectfully at Liverpool's managing tone. Rank was a delicate matter. The Prime

Minister was only too aware that he was here only in an advisory capacity. There was nothing to be won by rubbing the man's nose in his voluntary demotion.

Not unless Nathaniel disagreed with him, at any rate.

"For the first order of business, I would like to announce that I will marry shortly."

The congratulations were warm, but Nathaniel could see the doubt his words had caused in the other two and Liverpool. "Yes, I know it is sudden. I met her upon the road to London, about the time I lost Foster. . . ." Perhaps the less said about how, the better.

"She is from the country then," stated Liverpool. "Does she know of your current position in Society?"

Thinking of the mud streaming down Willa's hair, Nathaniel nodded shortly. "She does now."

"Hmm," was all Liverpool said.

The Lion reached across the table to shake Nathaniel's hand. "My best wishes for you both."

The Falcon did as well, although perhaps a bit more soberly. "I hope you will have a smooth life together."

Nathaniel twisted his lips wryly at the Falcon's choice of words. "I don't think that's too likely, do you?"

Liverpool leaned forward. "Are you sure she's simply some country miss? The enemy knows you are in a vulnerable position for this sort of thing—"

"If you are implying that she was thrown into my path, I can assure you, it was the other way around," Nathaniel said warningly.

"I think we've a good start to the Foster matter," the Falcon interjected smoothly. "But what of this Chimera?"

"Who?" Nathaniel asked.

"The unknown master of the French espionage activities in London," the Falcon explained. When Nathaniel only blinked at him, he shrugged. "Well, the operatives had to call him something!"

. The Lion grinned. "The Liars have nicknamed the bastard, by God!"

The Three laughed at that. Out of the corner of his eye, Nathaniel saw Liverpool grow stiffer and more rigid. Well, too bloody bad. With old Lord Barrowby out of the Chamber and Liverpool out of the Four, this was a younger man's game now. He, the Lion, and the Falcon were in their prime. The Royal Four could only be expected to become livelier by nature.

Still, best not antagonize the Prime Minister over nothing. Nathaniel cleared his throat. "Tabling the Chimera for now, since we don't know goose scat about the man, I read here in this report that Denny, Simon Raines's former valet, is still missing?" The fellow had disappeared when it had been discovered he had been leaking information.

The Falcon nodded. "The Liars haven't been able to find him."

The Lion looked skeptical. "Have they really tried, do you think? After all, he was practically one of the club for years."

Nathaniel shook his head. "You don't know the Liars. When one of their own jumps the Channel, they double their hunting frenzy."

The Lion nodded thoughtfully. "So it is safe to say that this Denny has indeed joined the other side?"

The Falcon grunted in agreement. "That or he's hiding out in some far corner of Wales."

The Lion turned a page in the Liars' report before them. "But they don't believe this Ren Porter is a danger?"

Nathaniel leaned closer to peer at the page. "What is this about Ren Porter?"

The Falcon blinked. "Didn't you hear of this? Oh, that's right. You've been off on your estate since before he woke up."

"He woke up?" Nathaniel remembered Ren from their youth. He'd been a cheerful, curly-haired lad then. Later, he'd been one of the Liars betrayed by the club manager, Jackham. He was left for dead a few months earlier and no one thought he'd ever regain consciousness, but the Liars had arranged for some excellent nursing and it had apparently paid off.

"What happened to him?" Nathaniel asked.

The Falcon tapped his finger on the paper. "Shortly after he awoke, he disappeared. Apparently after a visit from Mr. Jackham."

"Co-conspirators, then?"

The Lion shook his head. "Not according to the Liars. They think Jackham may have taken advantage of Ren's muddled state to turn him away from the Liars, but they're hoping he'll find his way home."

Nathaniel rubbed his chin. "The Liars aren't beginning to leak a bit around the edges, are they?"

The Falcon shook his head quickly, frowning at Nathaniel. "The Liars are as strong as they were in your father's time as spymaster, if not stronger. The new training program is showing excellent results as well."

Nathaniel waved a hand, conceding the point. His personal feelings about the Liars had no place in the Chamber; he knew that.

"The next point of order is the Voice of Society," the Lion interjected smoothly. "The Voice still knows more than it should."

The Falcon nodded. "While the Voice is an irritant, it has never divulged enough to do real damage. Somehow, it is acquiring mangled rumor and hearsay, not facts. There is little we can do about the Voice as yet. It continues to disappear from one news sheet as soon as we begin to investigate, only to pop up somewhere else."

The Prime Minister shifted in his chair. "I say we

penalize any paper that prints that tripe! Fine them if they run the Voice, and fine them if they run that liberal propagandist Underkind as well."

The Falcon studied the arched ceiling, and the Lion made no attempt to hide his grin. Nathaniel turned to Liverpool. "Mr. Underkind's cartoons are the least of our concerns at the moment, I would say. Besides, I believe Etheridge has Underkind covered."

A strangled sound came from the Falcon, surprising Nathaniel. Was that a laugh? Impossible. The Falcon *never* laughed.

Nathaniel continued. "As for fining the news sheets, I don't think they'll concede to the pressure. They make so much money from any edition that carries the Voice that it would be difficult to make it worth their while to stop."

He turned back to the three. "No, it seems we must tackle this issue from the other end. Finding Foster—"

"And Denny," added the Falcon.

"And Denny," conceded Nathaniel, "will make finding the Chimera much simpler."

He looked at the other Two. The words went unspoken, but he knew they all thought them.

We hope.

12

Across the street from Reardon House, hidden in the shadows of Grosvenor Park, a man watched. He didn't belong
there, so he was careful not to be seen, but other cares—
hunger, chill, weariness—were of no moment to him.

All he could feel was the darkness within. Betrayal.
Vengeance. He turned the word over and over in his
mind, polishing it until it shone like a fine piece of jet.

He'd lost everything. There was nowhere left for him
to go, no life left for him to live. There was only perfect
vengeance.

Of course, this vengeance could include several indi-
viduals, but none of them had escaped the hand of the law
or of repentance. Only Reardon, the turncoat, only he had
lost nothing. Reardon had kept his rank, his wealth, his
life. And now he had the girl as well.

So much for a liar and a traitor.

Yet nothing for him. Except vengeance.

There were noises. Rustling, bustling noises. Doors opening and closing. Willa snuggled more deeply into the
profound comfort of her bed.

No.

I am not waking up. I refuse.

Finally, the sound of water being poured. It had a gal-
vanizing effect on her bladder. Now she had to wake up.

With a grumpy flounce, Willa flung back the covers
and scowled at the bright daylight peeking through the
slits in her bed draperies. Then came the fragrance of fine
tea, such as she had not had for years, and forgiveness
bloomed in her heart for the intruder.

"Miss? Will you be wantin' to rise now?" The soft
voice came from outside the drapery to Willa's right.

Willa opened her mouth to agree, but nothing came
out. Oh, she had forgotten. Her voice was gone. She rolled
over to thrust her head out between the draperies.

It was very bright in the room. She blinked at the daylight streaming through the windows at a high slant. It
must be near noon.

How astounding. The last time she had slept so late,
she had been too ill from fever to do anything else.

"Good morning, miss. I've hot tea for you if you'd
like."

Willa swiveled her head to see the pretty maid from
her bath the night before standing pertly beside a lovely
silver tea service on a table.

The girl was close to her own age, and her cheerful
smile made the last of Willa's morning grouch slip away.
She gave the girl a grin and a nod and popped back under
her covers and settled against the pillows. She'd never
had the luxury of being waited on like this, so why not
savor every moment?

After pulling aside the draperies with brisk efficiency,
the maid turned to prepare a cup of steaming tea for
Willa.

"Would you like sweetening, miss? Milk?" She appeared puzzled when Willa only shook her head.

Raising her hand to her throat, Willa reminded her of its soreness, and the girl's face brightened.

"Oh, then the tea should help considerable, miss. Let's get some in you straightaway."

The tea was poured with more elegant economy of motion, and soon Willa was rolling the lovely hot stuff over her tongue and letting it slide soothingly down her sore throat.

"Is it helping, miss? Would you like some more?"

Oh, heaven. Willa decided she could definitely become used to this. What indulgence, never even having to pour one's own tea.

After two fabulous cups, Willa couldn't deny her bladder any longer. With a careful clearing of her throat, she ventured to speak.

"May I be alone for a moment, please?" Her voice was faint, not more than a whisper really.

The maid smiled. "If you need the chamber pot, there's one beneath the bed."

The necessities taken care of, Willa contemplated the inspiring possibility of staying in bed for a while. Then her stomach growled, reminding her how long it had been since she'd had a proper hot meal. In a place this fine, surely breakfast would be a memorable experience. Time to get dressed.

In the meantime, there was no choice but to redon her muslin, which Lily had brushed and pressed as well as possible. Oh well. There was nothing to be done for it.

This was Nathaniel's family, soon to be her own. They would no doubt understand. She was quickly cheered by that thought, not a difficult thing, since nothing was likely to keep her down for long, now that she had finally come to see London.

Following the directions given by Lily, she tripped lightly down the stairs that had almost vanquished her yesterday. Passing the odious butler in the hall, she sent him a sunny smile, just because he looked so very sour.

Stopping before a set of double doors, carved from a lovely golden wood, Willa hesitated. She wished Nathaniel were with her.

But she had never feared strangers, and she'd best not start being timid now, not when she had the entire city to meet.

She thrust open the door and entered with a determined smile on her face.

There wasn't a soul in the room. There was, however, a sideboard of steaming breakfast offerings. Eggs and sausage and light white rolls. The smell drew her like it had her on a hook.

Suddenly glad that no one was there to see her gluttony, she grabbed a plate and filled it to overflowing. After days of traveling food, this was heaven. There were even some things she had never seen before, fishy things and something else swimming in a custard sauce, but Willa decided to save trying them for later.

Right now, she was more interested in making speedy inroads into her heaped plate. Plunking herself down at the table, she began busily forking it in.

Clumsy with hunger, she knocked a roll from her plate and sent it to the floor. Hurriedly she scooted her chair back and leaned for the roll, only to find that she had kicked it farther under the table.

Getting out of her chair altogether, Willa knelt to crawl after the bun. She had just reached it when she heard the opening of the door and the rustling of skirts.

"My gracious! How . . . how uncouth!"

Of course, someone would come in now. *Not* a moment ago while she had been seated quite decorously at the table. *Not* two seconds from now, when she would have been there once more.

No, they had to come in now, while Willa's rear end wriggling under the tablecloth was the first sight that would greet their eyes.

Willa sighed and clambered out from under the table, putting as cheerful a front on as possible. When she rose to her feet, she saw two very elegant ladies. One was about Moira's age, although that was about all they had in common, and one was considerably older. Older than old Pratt, even.

The lady was quite possibly the oldest person Willa had ever seen. Her face was a maze of wrinkles, as were the hands that crossed each other over the gilded top of her cane. Her costly dress of lavender silk was beaded so copiously that Willa wondered if some of her stoop were not from the weight of her gown.

But her snow-white hair was beautifully twisted atop her head, and her faded blue eyes twinkled with humor. She winked at Willa, as saucy as a jay.

Willa stared at the lady in surprise for a moment. Then, blushing, she curtsied to both ladies and waited for them to introduce themselves. The younger of the ladies drew herself up to stare haughtily down her nose at Willa. "Who are you and what are you doing in my house?"

Willa opened her mouth to answer, but her voice failed her again. She could only shake her head and raise one hand to her throat.

"What are you, some gypsy pauper? Hammil! Hammil, come dispose of this beggar trash at once. How dare you let something like this into my house!"

"Oh, put a sock in it, Victoria." The elder lady hobbled forward to beam at Willa. "Hammil wouldn't let a mouse into your house without an introduction. She must be someone." She gave a chuckle. "I hope she's as much fun as she looks. You lot are such dullards."

She came closer and peered up at Willa. "Well, how about it? Are you any fun?"

Willa had to smile. The woman looked so eager, like a little wrinkled girl about to open a Michaelmas sweet. Willa nodded at the lady and grinned back at her.

The woman nodded brightly. "Oho! How excellent! Now I have someone to play with. You may go now, Victoria, and leave me with my new toy."

"I will not! My dear Aunt Myrtle, I couldn't possibly leave you alone with such a strange creature! Hammil!"

"Get out, Victoria," Aunt Myrtle said, her voice mild, "or I'll write you out of my will."

The lady gave a sniff, and a not very nice look came into her eyes. Willa felt a bit of a chill at the gaze the lady fastened on Aunt Myrtle.

"Very well, Aunt. If you insist. I shall have Hammil set someone at the door, in case the creature attacks." She left, shutting the breakfast room door with an unlady-like slam.

"Poisonous female. Despised her from the moment my nephew Randolph brought her home."

Willa wasn't about to voice an opinion at that moment. What sort of madhouse was she in?

"So, pretty girl, who are you and why can't you speak?"

Hmm. How to answer? Charades? There was no paper or ink in the breakfast room.

Willa jumped up to pour both of them a cup of tea. She drank hers down hot and unsweetened, hoping to get a shred of her voice back.

Aunt Myrtle waited, sipping her tea, although from the jiggling of her lavender skirts Willa suspected she was hiding a toe-tapping impatience.

Willa experimented with a throat clearing. Not so bad. She actually made a sound. Aunt Myrtle sat up expectantly.

"Well, speak then, girl!"

"I am Willa Trent. I am here with my husband." Her voice was husky but seemed fine, as long as she didn't strain too hard.

"Mr. Trent? Never heard of him. Besides, this family doesn't have any friends. Excepting that tiresome Sir Danville."

"I'm sorry. I meant to say my fiancé. Nathaniel."

Aunt Myrtle's cup rattled dangerously on its saucer, and Willa jumped to rescue it from the lady's shaking hands.

"Thaniel? Thaniel is marrying?" The blue eyes filled with tears, and the shaking hands fumbled for the cane.

"Are you unwell, madam? Should I call for someone?"

"Horse apples. I'm fine. But get Hammil!"

Willa jumped up, but Hammil entered before she could even reach the door. After passing her with a scathing look, he bowed to Myrtle.

"Yes, madam?"

"Where is Lord Reardon? Never mind. Just fetch him here immediately!" Aunt Myrtle turned back to Willa. "You say you are Thaniel's affianced wife?"

Willa nodded. Aunt Myrtle stared at her with round blue eyes for a long moment. "Since when?"

"Since four days ago."

Aunt Myrtle blinked at her. "How long have you known Thaniel?"

Willa squirmed. "A little more than four days."

Aunt Myrtle's eyes grew narrow, and Willa got the feeling that this little bird of a woman could face down a raptor if necessary. She herself had seen jays fiercely drive falcons from the vicinity of their nests.

"Would you mind explaining how that came to be?" The woman's voice was suddenly cool.

"Ah, well, I shot his horse with a slingshot, or rather a hornets' nest, quite by accident of course, and there was this rock in the road, worse luck, since I doubt there was another rock within miles, and it was growing darker, and he was so terribly heavy, and I fell asleep waiting for the hornets to settle." Willa ended this recitation quite breathless and inhaled deeply. She tried not to show her nervousness but feared that her clenched hands gave her away.

"So he proposed to you? Having never touched you? Just because you slept by his unconscious body?" Aunt Myrtle nodded. "Yes, of course he did. And then he brought you home, just as he should. Well, you've had him for a while, now. What do you think of him?"

Willa smiled softly. "Oh, I've taken quite a fancy to him. He is great fun."

Aunt Myrtle blinked. "Fun? Goodness, girl, these days Thaniel is as serious as they come. For months I've tried to make that boy perk up."

"Really?" True, his eyes were sometimes sad, although not as sad as they had been. "Why, he makes me laugh all the time. Like the time he told me not to call him 'darling.' And when I made him listen to stories about my home village. He is riotously funny."

Aunt Myrtle's jaw actually hung open a bit as she regarded Willa with obvious disbelief. For a moment Willa wondered if perhaps they were not talking about the same person after all. Then a deep voice from the doorway made her jump up with a happy smile on her face.

"Myrtle, my love, how are you this morning?" Nathaniel started forward with a small smile on his face but stopped when he saw Willa. "Aha. I see you have met Willa."

"Thaniel, darling, get your manly self over here and give your old auntie a good-morning kiss."

Nathaniel looked past Willa to Aunt Myrtle once again. He knew she would never speak ill of him to anyone, and a little of the aching tension left his shoulders.

Taking Willa's hand in his, he took her with him to greet Aunt Myrtle. "Myrtle, darling, I would like to present the future Lady Reardon . . . my affianced wife."

Willa shot him such a look of surprise that Nathaniel realized he had never said the words out loud before. Strange, but they seemed natural enough at the moment.

"Your *what*?"

That indignant screech came from the doorway. They all turned to see an appalled Victoria standing with a very lovely young blond woman.

"Hello, Daphne," he said stiffly. "You look well."

"Thaniel, you—you're *engaged*?" Daphne's gaze was wide and hurt. Damn. He had not thought she would be here. Of course she felt betrayed. After all, he had insisted on breaking their own engagement.

"Victoria, take yourself and that washed-out wife of Basil's out of here this instant. You are making me lose my appetite. At my age, I dasn't skip a meal, for it may be my last." Aunt Myrtle was using that mildly bored tone, the one that the family recognized as deadly anger.

"I will not leave! I am the lady of this house, Myrtle, and I'll thank you not to forget it."

"Not anymore, according to this pretty thing, Victoria, so I'll thank you to shut your gob and leave the room."

Victoria seethed visibly and shot filthy glares at everyone in the room except the girl beside her. Nathaniel ignored Victoria, stunned as he was by what Myrtle had let slip. Daphne was married to Basil?

"You wed Basil?" His cousin had always admired Daphne and had not taken it well when Nathaniel had proposed to the girl. It made an odd sort of sense, but—"*Basil*?"

The beauty hesitated. "Well, Basil does adore me, Nathaniel."

Two sharp raps came, the sound of a cane against

the costly ebony side table, and all eyes were drawn to where Myrtle sat.

"Victoria, Daphne, leave. Now."

Daphne left slowly, with a long, desolate backward glance. Victoria, on the other hand, lingered for a parting shot. With a glare at Willa, she batted her eyes facetiously. "Poor Thaniel. Is a barefoot peasant the best you could do?"

Nathaniel felt Willa's hand tighten on his, and he realized that he had not released her during all that bitter exchange. "Watch yourself, Mother dear," he growled. "Remember, I am not a gentleman anymore."

That apparently hadn't occurred to her, and she flicked him a surprised look. Whatever she saw in his eyes made her step back. To cover it, she tossed her head and followed Daphne with a grand sweep of skirts.

"That Victoria is a harpy," muttered Myrtle.

Willa only looked at Nathaniel a little reprovingly. "That was your mother?" she asked.

Her voice was apparently returning but was still husky and low. Even with anger still roiling through him, he found it distractingly alluring.

He smiled wryly at her. "Yes, that was the ever maternal Victoria."

"You did not introduce me."

Oh hell. "Willa—"

Myrtle turned to stare at him, surprised. "He didn't?"

"No. He has barely even explained my presence to the butler."

"Oh, Thaniel." The disappointment in Myrtle's voice was obvious.

Willa remained completely expressionless. Nathaniel squirmed within. "It is not what you think, Myrtle."

She narrowed her eyes at him. "Are you ashamed of this lovely girl, Thaniel? Are you actually ashamed of what your family will think?"

"No," Nathaniel shot back quickly. "It isn't Willa I am ashamed of!"

A slow, wide smile lit up Willa's face. "I knew it. I forgive you." She planted a quick kiss on his cheek, and Nathaniel caught just a whiff of jasmine and sweet-smelling woman before she released his hand and sat down at the table once more.

She picked up her fork and set upon her eggs, only making a slight face despite the fact that the food must be quite chilled by now. Ever uncomplaining Willa.

Nathaniel picked up the service bell. When a footman immediately appeared, Nathaniel ordered fresh service for all three of them.

Willa watched Nathaniel's manner with the servants. He had been born to this. Born to his slightest wish being answered. Born to luxury and ease, to life in this vast, elegant house.

Personally, Willa couldn't look at the miles of polished floors without her knees aching in sympathy for those who must do the hours of waxing required.

Another steaming plate was brought, and Willa was astonished to see that it contained exactly what she had chosen before, in precisely the amount she had first been served, right down to the errant roll.

It was wonderful to be so attended to. Still, she couldn't help peering around her, having the rather eerie feeling that she was being closely observed.

"Willa, about taking you back to Derryton—" He pushed his food about for a moment, staring at his plate. Willa put down her fork, suddenly not so sure she was hungry after all.

"Yes, Nathaniel?"

"My father is ill." His voice was so completely without expression that Willa felt his pain all the more deeply. "After we wed, we will stay here for the time

being. If I were to leave, even just to accompany you
to—"

"Of course," Willa said softly. "Whatever you require."

"And I shall be here, too," Myrtle declared stoutly. "I
have far too little time left to waste a moment on Victoria,
but I will have fun with Willa."

Nathaniel sighed. "Myrtle, behave."

"Why?" She blinked at him pertly as she chewed.

Nathaniel shook his head. "Fine then. Don't behave.
What do I care?"

She shook her head. "Silly boy. Still trying to fix what
isn't fixable."

Nathaniel didn't reply. Instead, he turned to Willa.
"Were you given the gown?"

She looked thoughtful. "Yes . . . my lord."

Hearing his title from her lips did something odd to
Nathaniel. He was having difficulty bringing the two
worlds together in his mind.

Nathaniel and Willa on the road were an uncomplicated couple on an uncomplicated journey, where every
day was about miles covered and obstacles overcome.

Here he was Lord Reardon, burdened by wealth and
disgrace. Willa, with her worn clothing and her elemental
kindness, was wildly out of place in this tangle of convoluted debts and disloyalties that was his family.

And all he wanted was to take his sweet girl back onto
the road before the poison of this place affected her.

"It is very . . . fine." Willa looked solemn. "Thank you
for thinking of it."

"Do you not like it? I thought you would look well in
blue. Of course, you'll be needing other things. A shopping trip for both of us is probably in order, actually." He
wasn't looking forward to it. "Unless you don't wish to
go out—with me."

Willa rolled her eyes. "You had best believe I am going out with you. Those bullies do not frighten me."

Then again, if his mission was to play Lord Treason to the hilt . . . then he and Willa should be as public as possible. Lord Treason would indeed shamelessly take his bride shopping and would spend enough money to attract attention.

Spending money on Willa didn't sound so bad. And he would be sure to bring plenty of servants, in case of another Wakefield incident.

"Did you buy the blue gown because you thought I would like it?" she asked thoughtfully, her voice still no more than a breathy whisper. "Or because it would make me look as though I belonged?"

Nathaniel paused. He wasn't sure why, but the question seemed loaded with importance for her. He shrugged, knowing only to tell her the truth. "I thought the blue would suit you."

She studied him silently for a moment, then rose from her seat and rounded the table to him. Placing a hand on each side of his face, she tilted his head up and kissed him softly on the lips.

"Excellent answer." Her whisper danced over his mouth. "Thank you. I will be proud to wear the gown."

His aching need of the night before, never fully quelled, came rushing through him afresh. He leaned into her for another taste, but she was gone, settling back across the table from him once more. He blinked, then glanced warily toward Myrtle.

The little smile on her face and the sparkle in her eyes told him that she had missed nothing, neither Willa's tender nature nor his own hungry response.

"Interesting." Her smile was sly. "Very interesting."

13

Willa went in search of Lily and found her working busily on the hem of the blue silk gown in the bedchamber where Willa had spent the night.

"Hello, miss. I've nearly finished."

"Thank you. Nathaniel, I mean, Lord Reardon is taking me shopping this afternoon, but I'll likely still need it tonight. I doubt we'll be purchasing anything so grand as this."

Lily's eyes were wide. "Miss, I doubt you'll be purchasing anything but! You're going to be milady soon. You must dress the part."

"Oh, how tedious. I only wanted some underthings and a few new muslins."

"Miss—milady—don't you want to do his lordship proud?"

Willa hadn't thought about it like that. She stroked the silk, unable to resist the feel of the fine fabric on her fingers. Indeed, she would very much like to do Nathaniel proud.

A light knock came on her door. She pushed away her thoughts and rose to answer it.

A politely smiling Daphne stood there, her arms full.

"Good morning, Miss Trent."

"Willa, please."

Daphne gave her a restrained tilt of the lips. "Then I shall be Daphne, of course."

She held out her burden like an offering. "Lily told me that you were going out to the shops, and I thought you might like something a little more . . . usual to wear."

Looking down at herself, Willa had to acknowledge that she would be fortunate to be allowed in the doors wearing such a rag. She would have liked to claim that she'd never really cared about her wardrobe. She hadn't needed anything fine, not for tending the inn or tramping the fields.

Unfortunately, she had a true weakness for pretty things. She simply lacked the temperament to wear them delicately.

The items that Daphne handed over to Lily were primarily cover-ups. A redingote of lovely blue silk. A deep green taffeta mantle and one in black. A jumble of scarves and shawls and a small selection of bonnets.

"It is very damp out today, so it will be entirely expected to wear something to completely cover your gown."

It was a kind thing to say and an even kinder thing to think of. Willa had to smile at her. "Thank you. You are very generous."

Daphne nodded with polite dignity but did not truly smile. "You are most welcome. I'm . . . sorry that I reacted so badly to your betrothal. I was simply so surprised. Who could have dreamed he would ever marry?"

She glanced down to Willa's unadorned fingers. "Have you put your ring away?"

Willa wasn't prepared for the hurt the question caused. She was sure Nathaniel would remember the betrothal ring soon. In the meantime— "Nathaniel said he wished to select one here in town. There was not much to choose from in Derryton."

She was surprised at herself. Why such a shocking lie? Perhaps it was the very clumsiness of such a direct question coming from the most ladylike woman Willa had ever seen. Clumsy or snide?

"Oh dear," Daphne apologized prettily, "I have been rude. I'm sure Thaniel will find something lovely here in town."

Willa narrowed her eyes. Hmm. The apology was nicely done. Still, Willa was none too sure.

Then Lily entered with another stack of selections and the game was on.

Many things were too short and the redingote wouldn't even close over Willa's bust, but at last a mantle from last year proved to be the proper length and generous enough in the fit to cover Willa. With a quick choice of bonnet, Willa was ready to go out.

Even restrained Daphne seemed quite taken with the idea of "starting over" with entirely new things.

"Imagine never having to wear something one is so dreadfully tired of," she said wistfully. "I declare I've worn this very morning dress six times."

Willa blinked at her. She knew that ladies changed their gowns every hour upon the hour, or so Moira had claimed, but to protest a mere six wearings? That would still amount to less than a day's use altogether.

What an outlandish way to carry on.

She couldn't wait to start shopping.

After promising Myrtle final approval on everything he bought for Willa, Nathaniel left her with a quick kiss of gratitude. He had left the house and was halfway across the lawn to the mews when it occurred to him that he should have rung for someone to bring a carriage round. Odd. He had become so used to doing for himself that it seemed a bit ridiculous to tell a servant to tell another servant to tell another servant to hitch the brougham.

He was already nearly there, and it felt good to leave the house, at any rate. Rounding the wall into the cobbled stable yard, Nathaniel saw his cousin Basil leaving the stables.

His cousin was nearly as tall as he but, without any sort of regular activity, tended to be somewhat softer about the middle. Basil was by nature annoying, but Nathaniel considered him harmless. As Nathaniel's heir, Basil spent his days living off the expectation that he would someday be Lord Reardon, and so he mortgaged himself accordingly. *Debt* and *Basil* were very nearly synonymous.

"Hello, Thaniel," Basil said lazily, but without rancor. "I'd heard you rambled in last night."

"Hello, Basil." Nathaniel couldn't resist. "I hear congratulations are in order."

"Oh yes. Daphne." Basil eyed him a bit warily. "Well, you didn't want her, old man."

"I wanted her," Nathaniel replied a bit grimly. "I simply couldn't subject her to my disgrace." Although somehow it didn't sting the way it should have. Daphne was a pallid watercolor next to the vibrant oil painting that was Willa.

"Hmm, yes. About that . . ." Basil grimaced. "I hope you aren't planning on staying too long. I have guests coming in a few days. We're all to ride north together."

A corner of Nathaniel's mouth twisted up. It seemed people couldn't get rid of him fast enough. "Still the ever hospitable Basil, I see."

"Well, you know how people get around you. Spoils all the fun for the rest of us, you know."

"Really? And here I thought you rather enjoyed my exile."

"Simply trying to see the humor in a bad situation, old boy, a bad situation."

"Stop talking, Basil," Nathaniel said wearily. "You make me want to hit you when you speak."

Basil stopped talking, but Nathaniel could tell his cousin was positively bursting with more to say.

He sighed. "What is it, Basil?"

Basil shrugged. "Thought you might like to know. The grooms saw someone lurking about the house during the night. An awful scarred creature, to hear them tell it. They tried to catch him, but he was awfully fast on his feet for a crippled beggar. The grooms said he was trying to break into the kitchen window."

John Day. Blast. Apparently his assumptions about the man had been off.

At least, he'd never left Willa alone with him . . . had he?

At any rate, it was time to take measures. Nathaniel called for the closed carriage and an extra man to ride guard in front. If he was going to take Willa into the city with him, he could not take chances on putting her in danger. Shaking his head, Nathaniel called to one of the avidly curious stable boys to make sure the extra guard was armed.

It was time to face the city.

The city was more fascinating than Willa could ever have imagined. She had been so desperately weary last evening when they had ridden through it that she hadn't taken in much past the sooty smell and the fog.

Now they rode in the closed carriage through the streets, turning and twisting down this one and that, until Willa couldn't have found her way back in a lifetime.

The way was crowded with vehicles and riders and pedestrians alike, with apparently no rules in effect but for the law of get-there-first.

So many people. Intellectually, Willa had understood
how crowded the city was, but in reality, the crush of hu-
manity seemed to steal the very air from her lungs.

The noise was relentless. From the clop of horses'
hooves on the cobble, to the creak and rattle of carriage
and wagon alike, to the cries and drums of the street ven-
dors, she had never heard such a cacophony.

It was fascinating. She wanted desperately to leap
from the brougham and explore every inch.

"You become used to it," remarked Nathaniel, who
was watching her dive from one side to the other so as not
to miss a thing.

"Are you used to it?"

He looked around him. "I was once. Not anymore."

Willa thought of the fresh flood of questions hammering at the dam of her self-control but fought them back.
Now was not the time.

She needed to get Nathaniel alone, make him answer
every one with no reprieve, until the holes in their future
were all filled in. Until then, she would relish the city and
restock her lost wardrobe.

At length they turned down a much wider street, lined
with prosperous-looking shops on both sides. Above the
storefronts the buildings reached to three and four stories
high. Willa had never seen anything like it.

When they lighted from the brougham, she could
hardly keep from tilting her head all the way back to peer
at the windows so high above her, but the shops pulled
her attention as well with all their enticing and curious
merchandise.

The first one they entered was a dress shop. The selection seemed sparse until Nathaniel slipped the proprietress
a banknote. Then lovely things appeared, seemingly from
thin air.

"Oh, Nathaniel. These are very dear," Willa protested.

So she carefully chose a simple morning dress of sprigged muslin, thinking of trimming it herself, but Nathaniel promptly returned it to the proprietress and chose one more resembling the confection she had seen on Daphne today.

"It's too dear." She kept her voice to a hiss, but she was scandalized by the cost.

Nathaniel only looked at her curiously and placed another one, in a green stripe, on the counter. Then a pretty Turkish blue walking dress and a matching redingote.

"We'll start with these and we'll order more."

Three new dresses? They were so lovely. Willa very nearly had to wipe her chin. But the cost? "Nathaniel, it simply isn't—"

Don't you want to do His Lordship proud?

She smiled at Nathaniel. "It simply isn't enough," she said cheerfully.

"That's my girl." He winked at her and, after she'd been measured and he'd given direction for delivery in a few days, whisked her off to the glover.

And the milliner.

And the cobbler.

And a shop where Willa was discreetly shown behind a curtained doorway to choose from among the most decadent and fabulous underthings she could ever have imagined.

Why, some were so impractical that she couldn't imagine how one was to don or remove them without help! The thought that Nathaniel could help her remove them caused Willa several heated moments while she stared blankly at the filmy drawers in her hands and imagined. *Oh my.*

Then she realized that many women had maids like Lily to help them. Well, Willa wouldn't have Lily forever, so she was careful to choose things she could take care of herself.

There was quite an array of corsets, and Willa looked them over curiously. She'd heard all about them, but since Moira had felt they were unhealthy, Willa had never worn one. Although she would love to appear more svelte, she had to agree that they did appear rather torturous.

It took some doing, but she managed *not* to choose simple chemises and drawers of batiste, night rails of dotted muslin, and the only unclocked stockings in the place. Instead, she bought fine lawn, silk, and more stockings than any one woman would ever need.

Clocks, yet! What a vanity, she told herself, even as she bit her lip in acquisitive craving for the lacy things. She bought three pairs.

Then, blushing because she was sure that somehow Nathaniel would learn of what she had purchased, she ventured back into the waiting area where she had left him alone.

He was no longer alone. A cluster of women stood in one corner, eyeing Nathaniel and clearly discussing him. When Willa crossed the room to his side, the hushed whisper grew to a flurry. Then, as one, the group pointedly turned their backs on Nathaniel and Willa.

Willa might have been country bred, but she knew the "cut direct" when she saw it. Nathaniel's face had gone hard and his jaw was clenched. Willa quickly touched his arm.

"I didn't see a thing I needed here. Why don't we go?"

He shot her a dark look that she couldn't read. It was almost . . . fear. She gave his arm a gentle tug.

"Let's go."

Just then, the assistant came to take direction for the delivery of Willa's purchases.

"Reardon House, Grosvenor Square," Nathaniel growled, inciting a new storm of hissing from the women in the corner. Tossing the clerk a note, Nathaniel took

Willa's arm and strode from the shop. The whispers followed them all the way into the street.

"I say, it's Reardon! Lot of ballocks you've got, showing your face in town."

Nathaniel froze at the taunting call, his arm turning to iron beneath her hand. Willa looked around him to see where it had come from.

A group of gentlemen lounged about the entry, a matching set for the women inside. They appeared wealthy, bored, and very unhappy to see Nathaniel.

Nathaniel closed his eyes and breathed deeply. Willa had seen him doing it a dozen times, most often when he was exasperated. This time, he seemed more like a king cobra forced into a corner.

He turned slowly. Head up, face expressionless, he nodded to the group. "Finster. Barrow. I would appreciate you remembering there is a lady present."

The central figure snorted. He was a large man, young but already showing the signs of too much rich food and port. With a sneer in Willa's direction, he looked at his fellows.

"Can't be much of a lady if she'd be seen with Reardon, eh?" The snide laughter rose, attracting the attention of passersby.

"Too bloody right, Finster." One of the group stepped out to one side, blocking their exit that way.

Willa glanced behind them. The alleyway between the shops could be an escape route, but only if it wasn't obstructed.

This was getting dangerous. Willa didn't know these men, but she knew that when animals formed a pack, they dared things they would never do individually.

She stepped in front of Nathaniel. He put a hand on her upper arm to move her aside, but she walked right away from him, right up to face the man named Finster.

"I am a lady, but I don't expect you to believe my say-so. Perhaps you should kiss me to find out." The jinx had never let her down yet.

"Willa!"

Finster gave an evil grin and stepped closer.

"Oh, don't worry, Nathaniel." She twisted around to smile at him—and the point of Myrtle's borrowed umbrella caught Finster directly in the groin.

Willa turned back quickly—and caught him in the nose with the carved swan's head handle while he was bent over in pain.

With a wheezy little sound, Finster slipped to his knees, clutching his groin ignominiously, unable even to tend to the blood pouring from his nose.

"Oh dear." Honest pity was in her voice. "I should have warned you. Unfortunate things tend to happen to men who get too close to me."

Abruptly she was pulled backward. Nathaniel wrapped his hand around her arm and moved quickly to their carriage. After tossing her in, he stopped to look back down the walk.

Willa craned her head for a look as well. Finster still knelt, keening a high note, while his supporters gathered around him. Abruptly he vomited. At that point, even his friends deserted him and he was left with his coachman, who gingerly lifted him to his feet.

Willa looked at Nathaniel. "If you don't mind, I am feeling a bit tired. Shall we go back to the house?"

Nathaniel gazed up at her. His face was tight. "I'm sorry. I hoped—"

"Don't be sorry. I had a marvelous time."

His head came up with a jerk. "You did?"

"Of course. A day with you is worth many minutes with the pathetic Finsters of the world."

The sharp look left Nathaniel's eyes. He rubbed a hand

over his face, then removed his hat and clenched his fingers in his hair.

Willa loved it when he did that. With his hair mussed, he looked so very boyish, so . . . reachable.

"Finster isn't feeling pathetic, Willa. He is feeling superior. Very superior."

Thinking of where they had left the poor fellow, Willa wasn't any too sure.

"Shall we go home, Nathaniel?"

"I cannot accompany you now." He took her hand in his and kissed it quickly. "I shall see you at dinner." Then he shut the carriage door and stepped back, calling for the driver to take her back to Reardon House.

Without him.

Regardless of looking the goose, she thrust her head out to watch him grow smaller as the rattling carriage gained speed on the street.

Nathaniel watched Willa's carriage disappear in the traffic. As far as he could tell, she also watched him until they were out of sight.

With watching the carriage no longer a viable excuse for putting off the inevitable, Nathaniel turned to saunter down the street. He was Lord Treason, he coached himself. He was arrogant and unrepentant, just as Society had painted him. He refused to take himself off to voluntary exile in the West Indies like a good traitor should, like Sir Foster had done, in fact.

No, the thing that truly riled London about Lord Treason was that he simply continued to be wealthy and privileged and right under their bloody noses.

Nathaniel found himself taking the route to an establishment he had not seen for months, not since the night he had bowed to the necessity of taking the yoke of disgrace.

As he approached it, the stout young doorman glanced at him, blinked, then stared. Wild indecision crossed the fellow's face as he blinked rapidly at Nathaniel. Should he allow the infamous lord in or not?

Nathaniel decided to put the poor bloke out of his misery. He leaned close and whispered, "I'm here to see the Gentleman."

14

Back in the luxurious withdrawing room of Reardon House, Willa contemplated the pattern of the carpet for the hundredth time. Daphne wasn't an easy person to talk to, but Willa fought down her own tendency to fidget from boredom and made pretty conversation with the girl.

Myrtle had already given up the battle and sat bent over her cane, snoring.

"I've a gown ready, and the guests are all in town, and Basil is pressing me so." Daphne cast a stiff smile in Willa's direction. "But Father Randolph—that is what I have called him since I was a child—Father Randolph is so very ill. It quite sorrows my heart to watch him lie there day after day." She managed to make a shrug look delicate. Willa admired her skill. When she shrugged, it resembled custard jiggling in a bowl.

Daphne continued. "Mother Victoria and I have been planning the ball for weeks."

Myrtle raised her head. "Ball? With Randolph so ill? To have a ball here that he cannot even attend?" Myrtle blinked in shock.

Willa agreed with Myrtle. To hold a ball in the house of a dying man was entirely inappropriate. Willa suspected that Daphne's purpose was not so much that she could not wait to host the ball but that she dared not wait too long. If Nathaniel's father was indeed dying, as Lily had sadly claimed, then the family would soon enter mourning, and even Basil and Daphne would not defy convention so drastically as to hold a ball then, not for a year or more.

Victoria entered the withdrawing room with a swish of skirts. "Miss Trent, do sit up straight. You look like a crouching gargoyle sitting there. Examine Daphne's posture, if you please." She turned from Willa to smile at Daphne. "Darling, do come see the lovely floral settings I've ordered. Mr. LaMont has found just the thing."

Daphne rose gracefully to her feet with a faint smile in Willa's direction. "Aunt Myrtle objects to moving up the ball, Mother Victoria."

Victoria shot the older woman a withering glance. "Well, fortunately, it is not for Myrtle to decide a thing." Without waiting for a reply, Victoria motioned Daphne through the door and then swept out behind her.

"Praying mantis," Willa murmured. "*Mantis religiosa.*"

"What was that? I've no Latin at all anymore," complained Myrtle.

Willa shook her head and smiled. "Nothing. A little game I play sometimes. I compare people to animals. 'Tis silly, I know."

Myrtle shook her head. "Oh, not at all. I'm fascinated. Go on."

"Well, the mantis is a very elegant insect, quite lovely really, but a voracious predator."

"That's Victoria for you," crowed Myrtle. "Never satisfied!" She leaned closer. "What am I?"

Willa blushed. Now she'd done it. "Well, when I first met you, I thought you were rather like a jay."

"A jay?" Myrtle blinked. "Those bossy little birds? Then what do you think now?"

"Now . . ." Willa shrugged. "I am positive you are rather like a jay."

Myrtle stared at her for a long moment, lips parted. Then a sharp bark of creaky laughter escaped her. She wagged her finger at Willa as she wheezed on and on. Finally, she drew a deep breath. "You're a sharp one, you are!" she gasped. She patted herself gently on the breastbone. "Oh dear, I hope I didn't shake something loose." She blinked brightly at Willa. "Tell me, what is Daphne?"

Here Willa felt less sure. There was something about Daphne . . . Was anyone ever so completely agreeable?

"I don't know her well yet," Willa temporized. "Tell me about her."

Myrtle's eyes narrowed. "Daphne? Oh, I liked her well enough once. I thought she was a bit dull, but I didn't hold it against her." Myrtle sighed. "I suppose I've simply never forgiven her for breaking it off with Thaniel when he needed her the most."

Willa hesitated. "Has Nathaniel known her long?"

"Oh yes. Daphne has always been here. Her father is Thaniel's neighbor at Reardon, and the three of them, Thaniel, Basil, and Daphne, all grew up together. Since Daphne had no mother, Sir Danville asked Victoria to see to her feminine rearing."

"She and Nathaniel were betrothed from a young age?"

"Not officially, although Thaniel never stood a chance once Daphne decided upon him."

"Yet you say she broke it off, not him."

"Well, yes. And then turned her sights on Basil. Rather coarse of Daphne, in my opinion. Bad enough to have broken it off with Thaniel. I suppose one could hardly blame her, but . . ." She looked uncomfortable.

"Do not fret, dear. Nathaniel told me everything. I know all about his so-called disgrace." Willa gave her a reassuring smile, then changed the subject to her shopping trip. "Wait until I tell you about Mr. Finster. . . ."

Nathaniel took a chair in the quieter portion of the main room of the Liar's Club and signaled a serving boy for a brandy. It was too bloody early to be drinking, but Lord Treason wouldn't likely care about such niceties.

His drink came quickly and he tossed the lad a coin without so much as a glance. Oddly enough, playing sullen and unrepentant did not make him stand out among the other guests.

Of course, the Liar's Club did tend to attract a sullen element, at least outwardly. The place was a gambling hell, a slightly left-of-respectable home away from home for those interested in good liquor, superior tobacco, and the occasional naughty revue.

There weren't many men of his rank in sight. Mostly younger sons—"spares," as they were known in the upper classes—with their cronies and hangers-on. Most would never inherit, of course. Those elder brothers would go and breed their own heirs.

Nathaniel didn't have much sympathy for the spares, however. Like Basil, they could live out their lives on family wealth and expectations without ever having to trouble themselves with actual responsibility.

Still, the situation did tend to breed dissatisfaction. While there were several places Nathaniel could make a public appearance that might get back to Sir Foster, the Liar's Club was as good a place to start as any.

In addition, it had the rosy appeal of being a lucrative front for the Royal Four's personal band of thieves and spy operatives.

He'd only meant it for camouflage, so the level of brandy in Nathaniel's glass had not lowered by the time the serving boy returned.

The lad bowed. "My lord, your private dining room is ready, as you requested."

The only request Nathaniel had made since arriving was to see the Gentleman. Nodding, he rose and followed the boy—one of the Academy's new trainees, no doubt—to one of the doors set into the far wall of the main room.

It really was a private dining room, he saw without surprise. An intimate, masculine setting of dark green papered walls and mellow oak paneling. There was only one door, the one he'd used himself, yet at the table was seated the imposing figure of Dalton Montmorency, Lord Etheridge, the spymaster of the Liar's Club and former Cobra.

"That's a nice trick," Nathaniel said casually.

Etheridge didn't smile. "What can the Liars do for you, Cobra?" he said tonelessly.

Nathaniel settled into one of the chairs with a sigh. "Ease off, Dalton. I'm not here for the Liars. I require your assistance in another matter."

Etheridge only narrowed his eyes. "If this has something to do with Clara—"

"Clara? For pity's sake, Dalton, aren't you ever going to forgive me for kidnapping your wife?"

Etheridge folded his arms over his broad chest. "Kidnapping . . . imprisoning her on your lap . . . *kissing* . . ."

"One damned kiss! One lousy little peck!"

Etheridge raised a brow. "And things went downhill from there."

Nathaniel held up both hands in defeat. "Fine. I see I've wasted my time." He stood. "Thanks for the brandy."

Etheridge blew out a long breath, then relaxed his intimidating pose. "Oh, very well! Sit down, Cobra. Tell me what you need."

Nathaniel sat. "I need an invitation. Perhaps more than one." He leaned back. "Lord Treason is reentering Society, and I'd like it to be as public as possible. You have ties to people who can be persuaded to invite me to social events."

"Kitty Knight, Clara's niece, and her husband are holding an end-of-season ball tomorrow night." Etheridge hesitated. "I heard you are now betrothed. Will you be bringing your fiancée?"

"I will."

"Are you sure that is a good idea?"

Nathaniel smiled slightly. "No. I am also sure I could not stop her."

"Very well. I think I can arrange that invitation."

"Thank you. It is much appreciated."

"God, man, must you be so stiff? You're like a poker every time you enter this place!"

Nathaniel only stiffened further. "This club is not my favorite of places."

Etheridge shook his head. "It is time you let go of the past, Nathaniel," he said gently. "I happen to know that it will only hold you back." Etheridge softened further, compassion chasing across his features. "Speaking of, how is the Old Man?"

Hearing his father, who had once held Etheridge's place as spymaster, addressed by his Liar nickname made Nathaniel's chest twist with mingled nostalgia and bitterness. Randolph had been Liar first, father second. And now, not father at all.

"He isn't allowed visitors. He's too heavily medicated to be trusted with the information he has in his head. The pain his heart gives him can only be eased by poppy syrup. You know how easy it is for a mind to wander under the influence. He might speak to someone, thinking it was safe, and the gossip would be across the city in a heartbeat."

Etheridge frowned. "Are you sure he is not in danger of compromising us?"

Nathaniel shook his head. "I suspect that most confidential information my father knows is too out-of-date to matter, not to mention that ramblings about 'the Magician' and 'the Griffin' merely sound like fantasy."

Etheridge smiled, but it was a sad one. "I suppose that is a comfort for us, but hardly for you."

Sympathy hurt, so Nathaniel brushed it aside with a sharp gesture. "In any case, I believe that it is now very close to the end. I'm not positive he will ever rouse to full alertness again." His throat threatened to close.

Nathaniel took a long breath and met Etheridge's gaze. He was dismayed that he would reveal himself so in front of a man inclined to dislike him. But Etheridge's expression held nothing but understanding.

Nevertheless, Nathaniel pulled himself together and stood stiffly. "I must be off. I have an appointment with the Bishop. I thank you for arranging the invitation." He nodded sharply. "My greetings to your lady. Good day, Etheridge."

At Reardon House, Nathaniel was still out and Myrtle was having her customary nap. Dinner was not for hours yet.

At loose ends, Willa decided to go to her own room and see to the unpacking of her books and bride gifts. The domestic organization was soothing, although some of the things from her Derryton village made her smile damply.

Though it had all seemed like a gracious plenty then, her things seemed to disappear into the grand, lovely room. To bring a bit of home, Willa displayed Dick's carved red squirrel—*Sciurus vulgaris*—on her night table and used one of Moira's embroidered tea towels as the cloth on her washstand.

Her parents' books, a respectable library in Derryton, barely filled two shelves here. Willa told herself that only meant she would have the pleasure of finding more books to add herself.

Finally, she realized what was missing in her room. Nathaniel.

"Of course you don't share a room," she scolded herself. "You aren't wed yet!"

The problem was, she was married, according to everything she had ever known. She was a married woman, a wife, and she wanted to share a room with her husband. "Well, you can simply wait," she told herself firmly.

Since the new clothing she and Nathaniel had bought today would not be delivered until it was altered and finished, Willa dressed in the cream and blue gown for dinner with Sir Danville. Once it was on her, however, she was uncomfortable. The lace sleeves were confining and the cream net ruching that crisscrossed her bodice made her bosom look like a white hen's.

She smoothed the blue satin down her body and tried to look at the dress objectively. The fabric was really very nice, and the color did look good on her. And the dress did fit now, thanks to Lily's clever needle. Perhaps its flaws were more due to her own lack of taste, not the fault of the gown.

Lily came bustling in. When she saw that Willa was already dressed, she stood back and tapped thoughtfully on her bottom lip. "I can see you aren't pleased, my lady. I do think this was made for someone without your figure. That net there, that was put on to make a lady seem more bosomy."

"Oh, dread. I'm bosomy enough, thank you."

"And them sleeves . . . I think someone wanted to hide bony arms."

"I have no bones in my arms." Willa sighed, feeling very disappointed. She'd so wanted to impress Nathaniel tonight. "Do I look foolish?"

"No, indeed you don't! Just because a few bits don't suit you? My lady, when you get yourself out in Society, you'll see some costumes that look like a tent show has come to town!"

Lily walked around her. "Now, this'll do fine for a small dinner party—let's pull that décolletage down—" She gave the bodice a tug, making Willa's breasts swell up above the ruching. "Now, that's better. Let's let your hair fall down long in back, take the eye off them sleeves— I can fix them for next time, don't you worry."

Willa turned toward the mirror and blinked. "Oh, that is better." With a few swift motions and several pins, Lily had turned the dress from some other woman's gown to Willa's gown, showcasing her bosom and her neck. "You're very good!"

Lily smiled. "I'm glad you think so, my lady. I tried to work for Miss Daphne once, but she said I pulled her hair."

"Well, that is her loss and my gain," Willa said cheerfully. She was looking forward to dinner very much now. Wait until Nathaniel saw her in blue!

Nathaniel wasn't one to grovel, not even before a bishop of the church, but in this case was willing to make an exception. The best way to preserve what bit of reputation Willa had left was to bring about a speedy, quiet, legal ceremony.

Unfortunately—and Nathaniel was getting bloody tired of "unfortunately"—the bishop in question was having none of it, despite Nathaniel's best beginner attempts at humility.

"Why should I grant your petition?" the Bishop inquired frostily. He was leaning back in his chair with his fingers laced over his stomach, eyeing Nathaniel through disapproving eyes. "Why should I further any plan cooked up by you, knowing that it may indeed be deemed nefarious?"

Evidently the man was familiar with the story of Lord Treason. " 'Tis no plan," Nathaniel replied. " 'Tis a marriage."

"Why?" The Bishop frowned. "What have you to pass on to anyone but disgrace and infamy? Even shamed as she might be by this illegal country wedding, this young woman might do better than she would being married to you."

Nathaniel didn't bother to argue. The Cobra could force the man through other channels, if necessary. "I may legally wed if I choose. Despite Society's condemnation, I have never been formally accused."

"You may wed, indeed, by the usual means. Tell me, why do you wish to bypass the reading of the banns? Are you worried that this woman may learn of your vicious betrayal of your country?"

The Bishop was a forthright individual and a moral one. The enormous donation Nathaniel had offered to lubricate the proceedings seemed not to have affected the man's opinion at all. If Nathaniel weren't entirely weary of pleading this case, he might truly have liked the man.

He sighed. "My affianced bride knows of my history."

The Bishop blinked. "Does she? And she still wishes this union?"

"She insists on it," Nathaniel said wryly.

The Bishop regarded him for a long moment. "Is it the title and the wealth that has her blinded? It is not fair of you to distract her with grand promises when she ought to be focused on the very real fact of your disgrace."

Nathaniel hesitated. Could Willa indeed be determined not to lose the wealth and ease that being Lady Reardon would bring her? After all, she had come from so little— that shabby inn, that tiny village. . . .

Then Nathaniel remembered Willa's simple delight in all things small and inconsequential. All she needed from life was a bookshop, a ditch to explore, and perhaps a few pairs of clocked stockings. He grinned at the Bishop. "She has no interest in my wealth."

The Bishop folded his arms. "Does she fancy herself in love with you?"

The man's tone implied the veritable impossibility of any woman loving Nathaniel. At this question, Nathaniel faltered. Willa, while loyal to a fault, had never claimed any such thing. He cleared his throat. "I do not know. You would have to ask her that yourself."

The Bishop lowered his arms and leaned forward. "Ask her? Yes, I think I will." He stood abruptly. Nathaniel stood respectfully as well. "Bring this woman to see me. I shall ascertain at once if she is making this decision of her own free will."

Nathaniel realized that he must offer Willa this opportunity to be convinced. The thought that she might made his chest hurt. Defeated by his own need to be fair to her, Nathaniel could only laugh shortly. "Free will? Trust me, Your Grace, she has no other kind."

15

The footman opened the door for Nathaniel, back at Reardon House in time for dinner, and he entered the dining room. His mother sat in her customary spot at the great mahogany table, reigning over those present with queenly enjoyment.

"Sit, sit, Nathaniel. Sir Danville's supper must not be kept waiting another minute." She waved Nathaniel to a chair, smiling.

The smile must have been for the benefit of company, for Victoria hadn't given him a real one in years. He gave her a sardonic nod, then glanced to the other end of the table, where he expected to see his father's empty seat.

Basil smirked at him from his father's chair. "Do sit, Thaniel. Your little bride is quite bereft without you."

Perhaps it was the rage that coursed through him at the way Basil had preempted his father's place. Perhaps it was the way that his mother smiled at Sir Danville while her own husband lay dying. Widowed, wealthy Sir Danville, who had paid her flattering attention for years.

Or perhaps it was just as Myrtle had said, that he was the most thickheaded man in the world, but it was not until he had taken his seat at the table that Nathaniel truly took notice of Willa.

She sat across from him in voluptuous splendor, with creamy flesh spilling from her neckline and a soft waterfall of hair flowing down her back. She smiled at him, her gladness to see him unfeigned. She seemed a haven of warmth in the cold room.

Indeed, she looked wonderful in blue.

He wanted to leave this place with Willa, to ride the roads with her alone again. How could he tell her that here, surrounded as he was by people who shunned him whenever possible?

And then he knew.

She'd always claimed that she could tell what he was thinking. Maybe she would read him now.

He caught his country miss's eye and smiled slowly, until something hot began to burn behind her gaze as well. He let his gaze heat as he remembered her nude curves glazed in firelight. She responded as if reading every thought in his head.

Her eyes grew wide and dark. The flush that warmed her face now was one not of an overwarm room but of answering passion.

They sat, gazing into each other's eyes, reliving their journey and the wild places they had gone, both in nature and within themselves.

Nathaniel ignored Victoria's indignant sniff and Daphne's hurriedly changed subject and even Myrtle's gleeful little chuckle.

All he could hear was the way Willa's breath came fast between her parted lips, and all he could see was how secret knowledge thrust the curtain of insecurity from her gaze.

He wanted her, more than ever before. He dared not stand to take her from the table now. His erection was

monumental, trapped within his tight breeches, and he
had no wish to embarrass her.

And he knew that they could go no further until she
had spoken to the Bishop.

It would cost him. Oh, how it would cost him to wait
and give her the freedom to choose him or reject him. As
he sat there drinking her in, he wondered if he had any
idea how much it would hurt if she left him.

The actuality lurked just outside his reckoning, as if he
couldn't bear to truly examine the devastation and pain he
would suffer.

They should go now. His lust had subsided enough, and
there was no point in waiting any longer—

Myrtle elbowed him sharply. "Are you listening to this
at all?" Even in whisper, her voice was filled with shock
and hurt.

Jerked out of his half-passionate, half-mournful
reverie, Nathaniel turned to see the bright spots of fury on
Myrtle's papery cheeks.

"What is it?" He didn't bother to whisper.

At the head of the table, Victoria sniffed. "Oh, very
well. I shall repeat myself, although I would expect more
dutiful attention at my own table."

Nathaniel had no patience for her drama. "Are you going to repeat yourself now, *Mother,* or indulge in a bit of
theater first?"

"You are unbearable," hissed Victoria in a brief showing
of her usual colors before she remembered Sir Danville sitting at her side.

She turned to him and simpered. "Do forgive me, Sir
Danville. That boy simply brings out the worst in me."

Sir Danville roused himself enough to send a torpid
glare Nathaniel's way. "No better than he should be, I
expect. No better than he should be."

"Indeed," added Basil in a silky voice. "Thaniel, my

dear boy, Mother is announcing that we shall be holding a ball this week."

Shocked, Nathaniel leaned back in his chair and gazed at a smirking Basil with disbelief. *Now? Here? With Father dying by inches upstairs?*

Lord Treason would not care. Lord Treason would relish the chance to make a public display. The Cobra would not care, either. The Cobra would welcome the chance to further bait the trap for Sir Foster.

"That sounds agreeable to me. I assume I am invited?"

Myrtle tossed her napkin down on the table. "Thaniel, I cannot believe you would condone this! Not with your father dying!"

"Dying? What's this? You said old Randolph was a bit ill, and likely wouldn't make much of a showing, but you never said he was dying." Sir Danville wiggled bushy eyebrows at Victoria, who stammered and blinked before recovering.

"Dear Aunt Myrtle is being overly dramatic. Randolph is . . . very excited about the ball. I'm sure he'll be up to making an appearance . . . perhaps not all evening, but surely . . . for a short time."

"Oh well, then," grumped the man. He sent Victoria a mooning gaze. "I'm looking forward to one dance in particular."

She fluttered appreciatively for a moment, before turning to send a vicious don't-mess-this-up glare in Nathaniel's direction.

Myrtle began to protest again, but Nathaniel put his hand over hers. "Don't bother," he said quietly. "There is nothing we can do about it."

"Oh, Mother Victoria," Daphne spoke up with musical solicitude. "I declare you've gone utterly pale. Are you sure you are quite well, dear?"

They all turned to look at Victoria, who had indeed

gone ashen and wide-eyed. She raised a trembling hand
and pointed behind them.

"*Reardon!*"

Nathaniel turned, old instinct bringing him to his feet in
a fighting stance, his chair falling unnoticed behind him.
Willa jumped up as well, as did Sir Danville, but Basil slid
from his seat to the floor and disappeared beneath the table.

Before them all stood John Day, his ruined face con-
torted in fury. In his hands he held a pistol that Nathaniel
recognized as one of his own, taken from his study.

It was pointed at Nathaniel's heart.

Despite the trembling in his hands, Day pulled back
the hammer with the skill of long practice and sighted
down his arm.

"You are going to die now, Reardon. You ought to have
been hanged for your treason. Justice may have been
blinded by your title and your money—I, on the other
hand, see quite clearly."

The country accent was gone. In its place were the
well-pronounced vowels of the upper class. Day went on.
"How could you turn on your own that way? Your country,
your King—your own father?"

Day waved the pistol, indicating the ornate environs.
"You have everything! But you don't have him anymore,
do you?" He laughed bitterly. "I read in the gossip sheets
that the Old Man told you never to cross his sight again."
He aimed the pistol directly at Nathaniel once more. "I
wonder, did he mean sight or perhaps . . ."—he lined up
his aim carefully—"*sights.*"

The Old Man. Realization flashed in Nathaniel's mind.
This man is a Liar.

"Ren Porter." The name was nothing more than a rasp
of shock in Nathaniel's throat, but Ren heard him.

"Yes. Ren Porter at your service. Your loyal Liar." His
destroyed face twisted with agonized rage. "A Liar who

lost it *all* in the service of the Crown—then here you stand, still rich, still pretty . . ." He dipped a brief mocking bow to Willa. "And you even got the girl!"

"Ren." Nathaniel cleared his tightened throat. "I am glad to see you well."

"I am. I survived that betrayal by my fellows. James—" Emotion choked him visibly for a moment. "James got a *medal.* Did you know that? I got this face and this form. So, I thought to myself, there must be a reason." Ren's tone deepened with conviction and his aim steadied on Nathaniel's chest. "Look at you, standing there without a scratch, in your fine house with your new bride. For whatever reason, the law could not touch the likes of you and James. But I can. This is where you should die, here with all you will lose around you."

Nathaniel moved away from the table, away from Myrtle and Willa and Daphne. "Very well, then," he said quietly. "Kill me."

Willa gasped and started to run to him. Nathaniel held up a hand sharply. "Stay!" He didn't have any desire to die—but he could not explain, not even to ease Ren's pain. All he could hope for was to draw Ren's fire away from the women until he could think of something better.

Ren twitched, then looked behind him as if suspecting a trick. There was no servant sneaking up behind him. Nathaniel didn't tell Ren that he doubted any man in this house would risk such a thing for him.

Nathaniel's calm assurance only seemed to shake Ren more. His hand began to tremble anew, and he was forced to brace his pistol hand with his other one.

A single oddly clear thought went through Nathaniel's mind: *He might actually kill me now.* Nathaniel most assuredly didn't want to die. He didn't want to leave Willa. He looked over at her, standing white and motionless by the table.

He really should have made love to her, he decided. He had let the moment pass again and again. He should have accepted the sanctity of his country marriage and made her his wife in truth. Maybe she would stay with him. There was no telling with Willa.

The pistol began to fall, then came back up. "No. You cannot confound me, Lord Treason. You won't escape this."

The moment stretched, broken only by Sir Danville's appalled wheezing and Victoria's whimpers. Willa wasn't weeping, Nathaniel knew. She was too strong for that. He doubted that her eyes were even closed.

Nathaniel moved slowly, closer to the pistol. He needed to be certain that no one else would be caught with a wild shot. Closer. *Closer.*

Then he leaped forward when he saw a movement out of the corner of his eye. "No!"

A burly footman leaped out to tackle Ren, throwing him violently against the giant mahogany sideboard where his head connected with a solid thud. The pistol flew from his hand. Nathaniel rushed forward to catch Ren as he collapsed.

Nathaniel eased Ren down to the floor. Dazed and shaking, Ren still tried to fight him off weakly. "Get off me, you bastard!"

Nathaniel gripped Ren's shoulders and pulled him close. "Ren, it wasn't James," he hissed urgently into Ren's ear. "It was never James."

Ren eased his fighting to blink at Nathaniel in confusion. As the footman reached to take Ren from him, Nathaniel leaned in close once more.

"It was never James. It was Jackham."

Then he stood, allowing his men to take Ren. Pallid

and nearly unconscious now, Ren hung from their hands like a rag doll.

"Take him upstairs to a bed," ordered Nathaniel. He grabbed the largest footman by the collar. "Carefully."

The man gulped and nodded. Nathaniel watched for a moment to assure their obedience before turning to see the room packed with curious servants.

"Hammil, send for a physician for my friend." Nathaniel stopped and gave the man a significant look. "Promptly. Am I understood?"

Hammil glanced away, unable to meet the implied threat in Nathaniel's gaze. "Of course, my lord."

"Oh no. You will not allow that criminal to stay here!" Victoria strode forward, towing a red-faced Sir Danville in her wake. "I won't allow it!"

"Pipe down, Victoria." Myrtle tottered forward. "Best see to your lapdog, dearie. I do believe he's suffering a seizure. Don't want him to pop off yet, do you?"

Victoria turned to see that Sir Danville was indeed in serious trouble. His round face was dangerously flushed against his full white sideburns, and he had one hand pressed to his barrel chest.

"Oh no! Stanley? Oh dear! Hammil! Hammil, send for a physician at once! Bring some water in the parlor."

Nathaniel watched as his mother screeched orders at the absent Hammil while she propelled Sir Danville to the next room, where stood the only sofa large enough to hold the man.

Then Nathaniel was almost knocked from his feet by cannonball Willa, who flung her arms about his neck so tightly he couldn't breathe.

Shaking, she clung to him. He wrapped his arms about her and held her close. "Shh. It's over."

After a long moment, Willa shook her head and pulled

away to look into his face. "Nathaniel, what is going on? Who is this Ren Porter?"

Nathaniel froze. In the midst of it all, he had not realized that Ren had spilled out the Liars' existence. He spoke without looking at her.

"Ren is only a patriot, angry at a traitor."

"But—"

"Master Nathaniel," called a footman from the doorway. "I've sent for one doctor for Sir Danville already. The other physician has been called for . . . ah . . ."

"Mr. Lawrence Porter." Nathaniel strode to the door, then turned back, still not meeting Willa's eyes. "We shall . . . discuss this later."

Willa watched as Nathaniel practically sprinted from the room. She crossed her arms.

Nathaniel Stonewell, Lord Reardon, hadn't precisely told her everything, had he? Not about his family, not about Ren Porter, either. She wondered how many other things she was going to learn about the hard way.

Nathaniel shook the physician's hand as he showed him to the door. It had been a grueling hour assisting the man with Ren, but Nathaniel would trust no one else in this house to help. "Will he recover from the pneumonia, do you think?" Nathaniel hoped so. It would be far too much to take if Ren Porter was finally killed for the sake of Willa's laundry.

The doctor shrugged. "Time will tell. That dunking he took in the river might just have been too much for him. He isn't far gone in the infection, but he is weak and very worn."

Worn like a man who had pushed himself to follow Nathaniel to London?

"I imagine so," Nathaniel replied to the doctor. "I'll

see to it that he stays put for as long as it takes." *And put a guard outside that door as well.* Ren was ill, damaged, and misinformed. It might take a while to convince him he was among friends.

The doctor was still understandably curious. "He's a fortunate man to have such influential friends. . . ."

Nathaniel grimaced. "I'll be sure to tell him so. Thank you again, sir. Good night."

Closing the door after the doctor boarded his carriage, Nathaniel waved the driver on and watched them drive off through the dripping, tattered fog.

16

The pain was back. *Of course,* Ren Porter thought dully, *it never really left.*

His body had been broken. Hell, even his skull had been cracked! Then had come the ache of healing, of returning to use parts of him that bore no resemblance to the strong young limbs of before.

But this was a new pain, like a giant on his chest, squeezing the air from his lungs. Pneumonia, the doctor had said. Ren had taken a simple dunking in the river and now he had pneumonia.

Wasn't that just perfect? Done in by dirty laundry. He laughed shortly, only to nearly cough his lungs onto the coverlet. Finally, he caught enough breath to lie back on the pillow, gasping.

"Ow," he wheezed.

No more private jests. No blackly humorous thoughts of any kind.

No, not even sarcasm.

Only breathing allowed. He glanced sideways to look at the numerous pots set to steam on the hearth. If his lungs were full of water, why was he then set to inhaling *steam*? Bloody doctors.

Ren hated doctors. Nurses were all right. Mrs. Neely, who had cared for him when he was unconscious, had been a fine woman. If she'd been forty years younger, he would have married her.

Of course, if she were forty years younger, she would have run screaming from him like every other young lady did these days.

Willa didn't.

No, that was true. He'd startled her at first, but later, by the fire, she'd looked at him curiously but unflinchingly. He'd tested her, too, when he'd fixed her tea. She hadn't so much as blinked when he approached her.

Willa was clearly a very unusual lady.

And she belonged to Reardon, as the man had made very clear that night.

There came a sound, just a small one. A tiny shifting of fabric, perhaps, or it could have been a careful exhalation. It came from the corner of the room farthest from the candle. From the bed, nothing could be seen but shadows and shapes.

"I know you're there."

"Well, then, I suppose there's no use in being uncomfortable." The shadow stepped forward, becoming more man shaped.

"Reardon?"

"Hardly. Merely Cousin Basil, heir apparent." Basil sat down on the bed and lounged against the bedpost. He withdrew a cheroot from his jacket and, leaning forward, lit it from Ren's candle.

Basil smiled slightly, then blew a cloud of smoke that wrapped itself around Ren's throat and spiked pain into his lungs. He gasped, only to take in more tainted air as Basil leaned closer, seeming concern on his face.

"Oh, you don't mind if I smoke, do you?"

Half-choked, his sickened lungs seizing under the assault, Ren could only nod frantically.

"Pity. And you seemed like a chap who could enjoy a bit of good tobacco." Basil tossed his cigar to the fine carpet and ground it out with his heel. Then he stretched his legs out on the bed and put both hands behind his head in a pose of relaxation.

"What are you doing here?" Ren finally managed to quell the urge to cough. "Are you part of the guard?" He waved a hand to the door, where he knew at least one footman watched outside.

"I'm here to apologize for this evening, dear man. Nathaniel shouldn't have been so hard on you. That frightful family temper, you know. Quite takes hold of us sometimes."

"I notice that it didn't take hold of you while I held the pistol."

"Better part of valor, my boy, better part of valor." Basil shrugged. He cast a what-can-you-do look at Ren. "Can't just go risking myself. That's what Thaniel's for, anyway, facing down the wolf. Or the pistol. Not that it did him any harm."

Bitterly Ren had to admit to himself that it was true. His entire plan, from the moment he had seen Nathaniel Stonewell on the walk outside of that bookshop, had been to face him down and kill him.

Then he just couldn't make himself do it. Ren felt sick. It must have shown on his face, for Basil made a sympathetic noise.

"Feeling worse, old son? The physician left some laudanum for you." Leaving the bed, Basil crossed the room to pick up the bottle on the cabinet. "Quite a jug of it here. You may have all you want."

Ren shifted. "No thank you." Sleep had stolen weeks

of his life before. In the end, he'd found he preferred the sharp-minded state of unrelieved pain.

At any rate, all the laudanum in the world couldn't numb the pain away, unless he wanted to kill himself with it.

That was always a possibility, but in the weeks since he'd awoken Ren had found meaning in his wasted life. He had been left alive for one purpose, to destroy the two men who had betrayed the Liars.

And now he must contend with the fact that he had failed. He had not been able to kill Lord Treason, and it seemed there was no reason to kill James Cunnington. The story about Jackham had rung quite true to Ren. He only wondered that he'd not seen it before. His mind truly had been muddled, though he felt clear enough now.

There would be no revenge. There was only the rest of his life as half a man.

"I wonder," mused Basil. "I wonder how much laudanum it would take to kill a man? Would he taste it in his wine, do you think?"

Pulling his thoughts away from their dismal destination, Ren snorted with disdain. "Sir, the only way you could kill anyone would be to bore him to death." Nathaniel may have been a traitor, but his cousin was undeniably a fool.

Basil whirled to glare at Ren. "Fine thanks I get, after I kept my cousin from carting you off to the magistrate!"

"You did that?"

"And called a physician for you."

Ren supposed it had been kind of Basil to take him in and try to help him. Although the words *kind* and *Basil* didn't really seem to belong in the same sentence.

"So I would say you owe me," announced Basil.

Ren smiled sourly. "Ah, of course. What price kindness?"

"Oh, I want nothing for myself, you understand. It's my lovely bride. She cannot bear my cousin, you see. She feels his existence brings down the whole family's reputation. Have you ever been in love?"

Ren only looked at him.

Basil gave a gusty sigh. "Magical thing, love. Makes a man do many a mad thing to win his lady's heart."

The idea of this man being madly in love with anyone but himself was ludicrous. Furthermore, Ren felt no debt at all to him, no matter what he had done.

"Basil, I'm tired. Say your piece or go away."

Basil twitched, and Ren could see him fight down a snarl.

"Very well, then. Since you seem to have no grasp of subtleties. You want Nathaniel Stonewell to be a name carved upon the family crypt. I have come to see if you are planning on having another go."

Ren laughed, a hollow laugh. "The irony escapes you, Basil, I'm sure. I am the helpless one here, remember?"

Basil shrugged and stood. "I was only curious." He stopped at the door, only a shadow among shadows again. "Do mind the carpets next time, though, will you? They'll be mine someday." With that he was gone.

The room smelled better instantly.

Yet Basil's words lingered.

I have come to see if you are planning on having another go.

The next morning, as a curious Willa was heading to call on the newest resident of Reardon House, a strange deep voice rumbled in the front hall, causing her to halt, then backtrack to the top of the stairs out of sheer prying. Below, she saw Nathaniel talking to a tall man with dark hair.

"Of course I'm not sorry it's you, Simon," Nathaniel was saying stiffly. "Ren doesn't know Dalton at all." Nathaniel took a breath. "You should look in on Father.

He might be awake, and he'd be very glad to see you."

Simon? Willa positively burned to see him better. But
the bloody stairs were so high she could only see the top
of his head.

Then again, he was coming to see Ren Porter . . . and
she'd been on her way to see Ren anyway. . . .

"Tea," she muttered to herself. "Tea will get you in
anywhere." She made for the back stairs. "Hammil!"

Nathaniel felt like an outsider in his own home when Simon and Ren Porter greeted each other soundly. Damn,
Simon always had made him feel that way—but for the
first time, Nathaniel saw clearly that Simon did nothing
to perpetuate the old rivalry.

Simon had let it go. Why couldn't he?

*Then again, Simon is still welcome at Randolph's bed-
side, isn't he?*

Nathaniel closed his eyes in an effort to banish such
unworthy thoughts. When he opened them, he saw Willa
standing pertly before them all with a tray.

"Tea?"

Nathaniel laughed out loud, not even noticing when
Simon turned to look at him oddly. He clasped his hands
behind his back and leaned close to Willa's ear.

"Wildflower, could you be more transparent?"

She only smiled brightly and shoved the tray beneath
his nose. "Tea?"

Simon looked bemused. "Will you not introduce us,
Nathaniel?"

"Introduce us," Willa stated firmly. "Tell him I am to
be Lady Willa Reardon."

Nathaniel leaned close again. "Actually, the proper
form of address would be 'Lady Reardon.' "

That caught him an elbow in the gut and another blinding smile. "Introduce me to your handsome guest," she said through gritted teeth.

She thought Simon was handsome? "He's married," Nathaniel muttered.

"So am I—nearly," Willa muttered back. "Introduce me before I spill tea all over you, forcing you to leave the room to change, leaving me here to introduce myself."

"Heaven forfend," Nathaniel said, laughing again. He quickly swiped the tray from her grasp without spilling a drop and set it on a side table. Grinning, he turned them both to face Simon.

"Miss Willa Trent, may I present Sir Simon Raines? He is a friend of Ren's whom I have known for many years as well."

"Bother that." She stepped much closer to Simon and held out her hand. "Nathaniel's told me a great deal about you, Sir Simon." She cast a look over her shoulder at Nathaniel. "Although he left out the knighthood part." She turned her blinding smile back on Simon, who twinkled his blasted blue eyes right back at her. "How lovely for you, Sir Simon, although I have no doubt you soundly deserved it. When did His Highness bestow the honor?"

Simon took Willa's hand and bowed over it. "This past spring, Lady Reardon. Thank you for your kind words." He straightened but did not release Willa's hand. Willa didn't seem to mind too bloody much.

"You know, Miss Willa Trent soon to be Lady Reardon, I must introduce you to my wife sometime. I think you would find a great deal to talk about."

Willa brightened eagerly. "I shall call on her—if you think she would like that?"

Simon smiled again, clearly smitten. "I think she would be transported with joy."

Willa sent an arch look over her shoulder again. *There, you see?*

Nathaniel had had quite enough. He strode forward to detach Sir Stranglehold's grip on Willa, then practically shoved her from the room. "Go out and play now. The adults have to talk." It was worth riling her just to have her focused fully on him again.

She shot him a black look. "You'll pay for that one, Nathaniel Stonewell."

Nathaniel swallowed. Then again, perhaps he'd riled her a bit too much. He leaned forward to cup the back of her neck and kissed her soundly. "Gladly," he whispered huskily. She sagged toward him with a hungry, breathy sound.

He shut the door on her. Now he was *truly* going to pay. He couldn't wait.

Turning back to his guests, Nathaniel grinned without apology. "Isn't she something?"

Head tilted, Simon was watching him with assessing eyes. He glanced at Ren. "Besotted," he declared.

"Completely," Ren agreed sourly.

"None of your business," Nathaniel said brightly.

"Hmm." Simon turned back to Ren. "We were discussing what Jackham told you on that last visit."

Ren looked uncomfortable. "Simon, I was very confused. I wasn't thinking clearly."

"But he warned you to leave before you could reveal what had happened during your attack?"

"Essentially. He said there were those who had never wanted me to wake up, or something of the sort."

Simon leaned forward urgently. "What *do* you remember about that night?"

Ren shook his head, then coughed. "I don't remember— but I do. It's like a broken mirror, but none of the pieces match up. None of it *means* anything to me." His frustration was obvious. "All I knew was that I couldn't trust anyone, not even the Liars. Even before Jackham said it—but I can't remember *why!*"

Ren looked awful, gray and weak. Nathaniel stepped forward. "Simon—"

Simon sighed. "I'm sorry, Ren. I'll leave you be for now. If you remember anything, anything at all—"

Ren waved a hand in assent but seemed barely able to lift his head from the pillow.

"Do you need professional care, Ren?" Simon asked with concern. "I could send Mrs. Neely. I'm sure she'd be thrilled to see you returned."

Even sick and exhausted, Ren's eyes widened in alarm. "Please, no. She's a dear soul, but . . ." He leaned close and whispered, "She's an extreme advocate of sponge baths."

Simon grinned. "Ah. Well, perhaps someone here in Reardon's household—"

"I'll do it!" Willa's voice was muffled but clear from the other side of the door.

Horrified, Nathaniel strode to the door and yanked it open. "Were you *listening*?"

Willa huffed. "Of course not. I just came back to bring Mr. Porter his broth." She hefted the new tray in her grasp.

Nathaniel relaxed slightly. She'd clearly been down to the kitchen and back. "Oh. My apologies."

"For shame, Nate," Simon said easily. "You should know that if she'd wanted to listen, you'd never have caught her at it."

"What?" Nathaniel scoffed. "Don't be ridiculous."

But Willa sent a guileless glance to Nathaniel that didn't exactly reassure him. "We've an appointment with the Bishop shortly," she told him gaily.

Nathaniel nodded, although he was beginning to regret

his fair-minded impulse to allow the Bishop to have a shot at convincing Willa.

He waved Simon through the door. "I'll walk you down, Simon."

Simon left with a devastating smile and another invitation for Willa and a promise to return soon for Ren. Once they'd left earshot of the room, Simon stopped Nathaniel in the hall. "I have something you should see." He pulled a news sheet from his coat pocket. "Feebles brought this in this morning."

Nathaniel opened it and groaned. The Voice of Society was back, and it knew all about the incident with Finster.

Who is the mystery lady who so fiercely defends England's most hated son, Lord Treason? Sources have it that she is nothing other than Reardon's broomstick bride from the country! If she doesn't know who she married, one wonders if she can read. Do you think she is adjusting well to wearing shoes?

Fury coursed through Nathaniel. "Shoes? That self-abusing bastard!"

"Still don't think the Voice is a top priority, Cobra?" Simon's smile was very nearly vicious. "He called Agatha 'The Chimney Sweep's Doxy.' That's nearly as bad." He took the news sheet back and read it again. "No, I think I still win."

The man hiding out in the shabby room held the news sheet in hands that trembled in rage.

Lord Treason's broomstick bride.

Reardon had beaten him to the girl and likely to the item as well. How the hell had Reardon become a player in this? He was flaunting her, taking her about town, spending money on her.

Reardon wanted him to see. Wanted him to know he had the advantage, that he had his hands all over the bloody political prize of the decade!

Whatever side Reardon was on these days, he was a loose end that needed tying up.

Immediately.

17

Willa was very curious about seeing the Bishop. Nathaniel didn't speak at all on the carriage ride over, but Willa didn't allow his silence to disturb her. The Bishop believed he could talk her out of wedding Nathaniel. The man had no idea he was too late as far as Willa was concerned.

Once they were inside, the halls of the abbey were very fine. Nathaniel let her go with a squeeze of her hand. She followed her escort, trying not to crane her neck too obviously as she was led through the halls by a novitiate. The young man stopped at a large door and knocked twice before sliding the heavy oak door to one side. It disappeared into a pocket hidden within the wall. Willa coveted the design at once. Imagine doing away with the swinging of hinges entirely!

Then her attention was captured by the enormous desk that seemed anchored in the center of the grand room like a fine ship on a sea of carpet. The Bishop stood as she entered. Willa took his extended hand and bent to kiss the ring there. She'd never had occasion to greet a Bishop before, but she would not let her mother's teachings down.

The Bishop indicated a seat opposite his own. Willa

took it gingerly. It was a low sort of chair that made her feel rather small before the man looming behind the desk. To keep from sinking farther down, Willa sat primly on the front edge and sat as tall as she was able. This put her nearly on eye level with the Bishop, although she suspected his chair was much higher than hers.

He was a stout man; she could tell even through his heavy robes. His face was round and pink behind his white mustache and sideburns, and his cap did little to conceal the fact that most of his hair was on his face. He didn't seem kindly, but he did not seem frightening, either, so Willa allowed herself to relax, although not enough to sink into the chair.

"Miss Trent—" the Bishop began.

Willa raised her hand promptly, straight into the air like a good student. The Bishop raised a brow but nodded for her to go ahead.

"If you please, Your Grace, I am Lady—"

The man raised his own hand swiftly, palm forward, halting her in midsentence. "That remains to be seen, young woman," he said disapprovingly. "Pray, do not interrupt me again."

Since she herself had just been interrupted, and not very nicely, Willa thought his reprimand a bit much. Still, Nathaniel wished her to impress the Bishop with their need for his approval. She restrained herself and only nodded obediently.

The Bishop went on. "Lord Reardon tells me that you know the facts about his disgrace." He leaned forward. "Tell me, precisely what do you know?"

Willa sat forward as well, thankful to have the answer. "I know that it is believed Nathaniel joined a group called the Knights of the Lily who were supposedly trying to overthrow the throne—although they never actually did anything that I know of."

The Bishop scowled. "They planned to. That is enough."

Willa drew her own brows together. "Is it? We all *think* about doing terrible things at some point in our lives, do we not? I think about eating piles of sweets, but I don't, because gluttony is a sin." She tried not to look at the Bishop's considerable paunch as she said that, but she noticed that he sucked it in at her words.

"Young woman, you are missing the point! The very fact of Lord Reardon's association with this group is his sin. He did not *think* about joining a group of traitors and then resist temptation. He *joined.* He attended meetings in the dark of night; he plotted right along with them."

"How do you know?" Willa asked, truly curious.

"He was *seen,*" the Bishop said meaningfully. "I have the evidence right here." He opened a drawer of his desk and took out a scrap of newsprint. He handed it to Willa gravely but with a certain air of smugness that grated on her. She took the sheet slowly. She had no problem believing in Nathaniel's ultimate innocence when he stood before her, but part of her was afraid that the Bishop did have some horrible proof that would force her to face something she didn't want to face.

The scrap was folded, with only printed words on the outside, a partial column of writing that was meaningless. "Open it," the Bishop said.

Willa opened it. Printed on the news sheet was a cartoon, a caricature of three men kneeling around the figure of a woman who stood on a pedestal like a goddess statue. "Fleur and her Followers," read the words at the bottom of the drawing. "Fleur?" Willa murmured. "Oh, the Lily. I see," she said before the Bishop could answer. She didn't want him to speak just now.

"Fleur" wasn't wearing a great deal. Only bits of gossamer drapery kept the woman from complete nudity. The man to the left of the "statue" was an ordinary man of medium age and medium looks—although Willa did notice that he seemed a bit weak of chin. The man to the right was a portly figure with a menacing gleam to his eyes.

The third man, half-hidden behind a bit of flowing drapery so that only half his face showed clearly, was Nathaniel. Willa's heart turned over. She would know that jaw, that cheekbone, that particular tilt of brow—

"You see?" the Bishop asked. "That is Sir Foster there on the left—he fled England in shame when this cartoon was published—and on the right, the late Mr. Wadsworth, who died a hero after penetrating the group and exposing it forever. And there, in the center, hiding like the coward he is . . . your Lord Reardon."

"I don't believe a word of it," Willa said stoutly. She gestured to the drawing. "This could be anyone bearing the slightest resemblance to Lord Reardon."

The Bishop narrowed his eyes. He reached into his drawer once more. "Could this?"

He lay another portion of news sheet on the desk, this one unfolded to reveal the crisply drawn lines of a small and sniveling Nathaniel, along with the other man from the first drawing, cowering before the wrath of a large and handsome Mr. Wadsworth, who threatened them even while himself clearly stabbed through the heart. The line of print at the bottom read, "The cost of heroism—a mighty price indeed."

Dismayed despite herself, Willa tore her eyes away from the drawings to examine the artist's signature. "Who drew these? Who is this Sir Thorogood?"

The Bishop made a protesting noise. "Sir Thorogood is—was—a very well-known political cartoonist who made quite a splash earlier this year."

"Was?"

"Yes. He suddenly stopped submitting drawings a few months ago—some say because of pressure from your affianced groom," he finished portentously.

"Where can I find him?" insisted Willa. "I want to ask him how he knew Nath—Lord Reardon was actually part of this . . ." She waved the drawing at him. "This *company*."

The Bishop blinked. "Er, well, no one actually knows who Sir Thorogood is."

Willa tilted her head. "What do you mean?"

"Sir Thorogood is something of a mystery, I'm afraid. He came upon the scene, telling tales about all sorts of venality and corruption among the upper classes—all of which proved to be true, mind you—and then disappeared after less than a year. There was one fellow claiming to be Thorogood, a peacock dandy prancing about in high heels, yet, but I believe he was found out to be an impostor."

Willa slowly began to smile. "So this is your 'evidence'? This is everyone's 'evidence'? A drawing—a *cartoon*— done by a mysterious artist who doesn't exist?" She laughed in relief, feeling as though she'd shed a yoke of stone. "I'm afraid I'm going to need more definitive proof than that before I refuse a fine man like Nathaniel."

The Bishop leaned forward and snatched the drawing back. "Then answer this! Never, not once, has your Lord Reardon denied any of this! Why would that be, do you think?"

Willa pursed her lips. "You're saying that if he was an honest man, he would deny it. That logic is faulty, for if he were a lying man, he would also deny it. So, if we were to follow your thinking, he's an honest man for not denying it! Yet, if he were an honest man, he would not be a traitor!" She sat back, very satisfied with her argument. "I don't believe any of it."

The Bishop was looking a bit confused and more than a little angry. "Then you're a very foolish girl. Don't you realize that it doesn't matter whether or not you believe it? Everyone else does! What sort of life will you have, being ostracized by Society, having no invitations, no callers, no friends?"

Willa retained her smile. "I have friends. Nothing Society can do will change that." She shrugged. "As for the rest, I've done well enough without them all these years."

"And what of your children? What sort of life will you be giving to them?"

That was something Willa had not considered. She hesitated until she saw the Bishop's small, smug expression. He believed he had scored on her with that question.

She abruptly decided that he was an unworthy man. A judgmental blowhard, large on display, short on spirit. "A badger," she murmured to herself. "*Meles meles.*"

The Bishop glared at her suspiciously. "What was that?"

Willa took a deep breath. "That, Your Grace, was me deciding not to care for your opinion. You cannot block our marriage. You can only delay it. I will tell Lord Reardon that we must simply have the banns read like other couples do, and we shall wed when our two weeks are done." She stood, no longer caring to show her best manners. "I've had a trying day, Your Grace. I believe I shall say good-bye now."

The Bishop scowled at her. "You're making a grave mistake, child. You will soon come to regret your ill-advised love every day of your life."

"Oh dear," Willa retorted in a careless tone. "That long?" She gave a tug to her gloves and smiled at the Bishop. "When the truth comes out and you realize how wrong you were about Lord Reardon, you should not be too ashamed to call upon me then. I plan on forgiving you most sincerely." With that, she turned and left the chamber, deaf to the indignant sputters behind her.

Outside in the carriage, Nathaniel awaited her. The uncertainty was not evident in his expression, but Willa knew it was there.

"How did it go?" he asked her casually when she was settled opposite him.

Willa smiled ruefully. "I'm afraid we have some banns to post."

Nathaniel nodded, then looked away. "Did you listen to his arguments?"

"Well, I 'heard' them," Willa said virtuously. "I'm not terribly sure I 'listened' to them."

A smile broke across Nathaniel's face, a real smile, not simply a twist of his lips. "You didn't? You didn't listen?"

Willa sighed. "I simply couldn't see any logic to his stand," she said. "The evidence was unsubstantiated and flimsy, I'm afraid."

Nathaniel let his head fall back on the seat. "Flimsy, she says." He raised it to smile at her again. "The whole of England believes in that flimsy evidence."

"Well then, shame on them." She leaned her own head back on the squabs and shut her eyes.

You will soon come to regret your ill-advised love . . .

Love?

A powerful ache grew inside her at the thought of ever separating from Nathaniel. At one time she had vowed not to allow it, more from pride than anything else. That seemed like months ago. How astonishing that it had been a mere five days.

Five days was long enough, apparently. Long enough to learn to like the man he was. Long enough to know that she desired him. Long enough to miss him when he was out of sight.

Long enough to love him.

Nathaniel said something to her just then, but Willa didn't really hear or notice when the carriage turned onto Grosvenor Square.

Sunk deep into the luxurious carriage seat, Willa was really only conscious of one thing.

She loved Nathaniel. She was wildly, madly, in love with her husband. Not after twenty years, not after twenty days. Within a week, she had lost her heart.

It was miraculous. It was terrifying. Deeply, soul-chillingly terrifying.

What if he did not feel the same?

And of course he didn't. Willa knew she wasn't bad looking, if one liked dark hair and a bit extra in the bosom, but she was no beauty like Daphne. Willa came to a sobering realization as she sat there feigning sleep with her eyes closed.

If she was not mistaken, at some point Nathaniel had wanted Daphne—although Daphne had chosen Basil, something Willa couldn't visualize.

Basil, my love. Hold me, Basil. Sweep me off my feet, Basil.

No, entirely unacceptable. She could never want a man named Basil.

Daphne had wanted Basil . . . and Nathaniel had wanted Daphne.

But he had never wanted her.

She felt a little sick. She had always envisioned love as a mutual thing, even fancied herself being swept away by the devotion and desire in a man's eyes.

The danger of being the only one in love had never occurred to her.

How absolutely infuriating.

. . .

Although Willa had every intention of beginning her quest to change minds about Nathaniel immediately, she had no qualms about pausing for a good luncheon first. The table that was set in this house was one thing she had no complaints about.

So it was nearly midafternoon when she finally made her way to speak to her first subject.

He was flat on his back in the bed and was struggling to sit up when she made her own entrance. She waved him back. "Hello again, Mr. Porter. Would you like some company?"

Ren had hoped Simon had returned, but it was Willa, which was nearly as good. She had been the first one in a very long time who didn't seem to see him as anything other than an ordinary man.

Still, he answered, "No." He watched her face fall, then relented. He had spent a long night after Basil had left him, in too much pain, both physical and mental, to sleep. He was damned tired of his empty room and his empty thoughts.

"Oh, stay," he muttered. "Or go. Whatever you like."

Willa turned around and fixed him with such a smile of pleasure that he felt his pulse increase. She was a beauty, with her dark hair and those twilight eyes. He was not accustomed to being smiled at by beauties.

At least, not anymore.

The awful feeling faded, the one that had made him bark at her when she first entered. He hated the way that people looked at the scars and the broken body and turned away. Even if they tried to hide it, he could tell that inside they were turning away, unable to bear his ugliness.

He didn't blame them. He knew he'd been every bit as shallow once upon a time. But he couldn't help the fact that it hurt. Again and again, over and over, every new person who spied him brought the same shock home to him, never letting him forget that he was now a monster.

Willa picked up the tray and turned to him. He was off in his head somewhere, someplace unhappy, it appeared. She cleared her throat, waiting until he looked her way, then stepped close to the bed.

He pulled back ever so slightly as she approached, turning the scarred side of his face away. How silly. It wasn't as if she hadn't already seen it.

She plunked the tray down on his lap, but it was obvious that there was nothing he could do about it in his prone position.

"Oh, bloody hell," she muttered. He obviously wouldn't put up with her feeding him, not prickly with pride as he was. How was he supposed to eat? "Bloody doctor, had the man no sense at all?"

Ren was gazing at her with horror, she realized. Straightening, she put her hands on her hips. "Oh, perfect. You can wave a gun around the dinner table, but I cannot let loose a few little words?"

"But . . . you're a lady!"

Willa had finally gotten him to think of something else. She wasn't going to drop it now. She threw her hands high with annoyance that she didn't really feel.

"And are you not a gentleman? I think you are not one to throw stones at my black kettle, sir."

"What?" The girl was mad. That must be it. "Do they know you are running around loose?"

She stopped her railing and smiled at him. Damn, she had a lovely smile.

"No, they don't. And you aren't going to tell them, are you?"

Still, she didn't seem dangerous, and she was very decorative. Ren relaxed a bit. He needn't worry about the

good opinion of a madwoman, and he needn't hide his
face. Suddenly cheered by her company, he cocked his
head at the tray, still balanced on his lap. "If I promise not
to decry your language, will you give me a bit of assistance with lunch?"

Willa smiled again. Oh, she did like him. He was so
dear, with his shy, lopsided smile and his sad blue eyes.

She sat carefully on the edge of the bed, taking care not
to jostle him. "Well, first of all, we must get you propped
up a bit." She reached for a cushion of the nearby chair.
Placing her hand behind his neck, she pulled him toward
her carefully. Then she leaned in and placed the cushion
behind his pillow.

Ren closed his eyes and took a deep breath of girl.
Then he opened them again, for although it wasn't gentlemanly at all, he couldn't bear to pass up the exquisite
view down her neckline.

He could see the perfect mounds of her breasts, almost
to the nipples before the lace of her undergarments cut
off the view. He felt his sex stirring and promptly closed
his eyes. He didn't need that sort of torture on top of
everything else.

He had stuffed his sexual drive deep down and far away.
It was the only way to survive the lifetime of celibacy that
lay ahead.

Oh, he could pay for it, and had. But the way the
woman had turned her face away and borne his attentions
as if she could not wait to bathe afterward? That pleasure
came at too high a cost for him.

He kept his eyes shut tightly until he felt Willa move
back. Pretty girls, mad or no, married or not, had nothing
to do with his world.

Willa watched, dismayed. She had hoped to relax him.
Instead, she had sent him back to that unhappy place.
"Stay away from there," she instructed firmly.

He opened his eyes and gave her a look of confusion.

She sighed. Men. Darlings and yet so very dense. She placed a hand on each of his cheeks and looked into his eyes. "Your mind is yours to control. You can let it take you someplace sad or you can make it take you someplace pleasant."

He blinked at her. "How do I do that?"

She thought about it as she sat back, letting her hands slide gently from his cheeks.

Ren was shocked to his soul. Her touch, her easy manner, the way she looked into his eyes, made him feel as though he were not scarred at all. He could still feel her cool fingers on his face, still feel the way his own lips had parted, as if he had wanted a kiss.

Dear God, if she wasn't engaged, he would have proposed to her on the spot. Hell, so what if she was engaged? Nathaniel could get any woman he wanted—well, perhaps not.

What was he thinking? He could scarcely care for himself. It was highly unlikely that he would be considered marriage material.

"I don't care to be the plaything of a useless lady," he said gruffly.

She blinked in hurt surprise, the look on her face was one of obvious disappointment. It made him uncomfortable. He wasn't used to having to live up to any code but that of misshapen freak.

She narrowed her eyes at him. "You have very fixed opinions about people, don't you? Haven't you figured out that makes you just as bad as the ones who judge you for your scars?"

She was right. How irksome. He scowled more fiercely than usual. "What would you know about it?"

"Tsk-tsk. Judging again. You have no idea what my

life has held. You should not categorically dismiss anyone as unworthy without knowing their story."

"What about Basil?"

That got her. Ren grinned as she hesitated.

"Well, that is a poser, to be sure. I, for one, feel a bit sorry for Basil. It can't have been easy growing up in Nathaniel's shadow."

"You've got it the wrong way round. Basil is the elder. Nathaniel must have grown up in Basil's shadow."

"Nonsense. Basil doesn't cast a shadow. Not compared to Nathaniel. He is the finer man all around. Quite enough to make one bitter, I should think."

Ren wasn't convinced, and it must have shown on his face. Willa waved away his unspoken protest. "Oh, I don't imagine Nathaniel has ever meant for Basil to feel eclipsed. But he cannot help being who he is."

Ren's eyes narrowed. "Do you know who he is?"

Willa pursed her lips. She was getting a bit tired of hearing everyone spout the same lie but did not bother protesting. It would all come out in the end. At the moment, she had something she needed to know.

"I would like to hear more about this alleged act of treason. I wish you would tell me the entire story."

He didn't look happy about telling her, so she smiled a bit pleadingly, the way she had always managed to cajole John Smith.

A short time later, Willa left quietly. She was sorry she had had to press him when he was so ill, but she was not sorry for what she had learned. She was even more positive that Nathaniel could never have done such a thing.

Yet how to explain Nathaniel's lack of denial?

There was an answer in her mind, just out of her reach. There was something that she should know, something that she *did* know but could not get her mental grasp around to bring to the surface.

No matter. She knew from experience that if she left it alone, likely it would surface when she least expected it.

In the meantime, she had something else that required her attention as well. She turned the corner that would lead her back to her room. It was time to get ready for her first ball.

18

That evening, preparing for the Knights' ball, Willa was fairly sure that Lily was more nervous than she was. The maid ran in tight little circles around Willa, twirling, tucking, tinting—Willa quite ran out of words for it. Finally, Willa stepped from the circle to stand before the tall mirror.

"What d'you think, my lady?"

Willa let her gaze travel from the hem of the blue silk to the neckline, low and now devoid of the cream lace. There had been no intricate structure beneath the lace, no ruffles or ruching—only beautifully sewn silk.

Now nothing broke the solid fall of sapphire silk from the bare edge of Willa's breasts to the floor but a midnight blue velvet ribbon under her bodice that defined the high waist. Her hair was twisted high, with only a few dark ringlets allowed to fall to her neck. Paste ear bobs "borrowed" from Daphne's jewel case in a conspiracy of maids glittered from the intricate plaits that held the entire arrangement of locks together.

"There's no chance of it fallin', my lady. You could ride a lion through a thunderstorm and never get a hair out of place," Lily assured her.

"Well, there's a comfort," Willa said faintly. Hesitantly she turned sideways. Her elegant white silk evening gloves gleamed like moonlight against the blue silk.

"I look so . . . so . . ."

Lily's expectant expression began to crumble.

"I look so tall!"

Lily beamed. "Yes, my lady."

Gleefully Willa spun around to make her skirts flutter. Then she fell on Lily with a grateful hug. After a hesitant moment, Lily hugged her back with equal vigor. Willa backed away to gaze in the mirror once more.

"I," she stated proudly, "look wonderful in blue!"

Nathaniel tugged at his waistcoat and examined his cravat. The lemon yellow figured silk waistcoat shimmered against the deep blue wool of his double-breasted frock coat. Personally, he favored a more somber style—but he wanted "Lord Treason" to be noticed.

To make a showing in blue, with Willa also in blue, was an unabashed bit of attention grabbing.

He had not cut his hair, either. The mode of the day was military short, for everyone was army-mad. The symbolism of his long hair only reinforced this evening's theme of "I dare you to stare."

With his tricorn hat and gloves in hand, Nathaniel stood outside Willa's door. His knock was answered by the maid Lily.

"Yes, my lord. She's ready."

Nathaniel did not step into the room, so he didn't see Willa until she rounded the bed. Then his mouth went dry.

Striking. That was the only word in his mind for a long moment. She was all sweet curves and porcelain skin, wrapped in a severely elegant gown that served as a showcase for soft white shoulders and long, shimmering curls.

And her breasts! Plump, silken mounds pressed high—the stuff of dreams for any man!

And her eyes—they were enormous, framed by thick dark lashes. So blue . . .

The woman before him was lush, lovely, and yet elegant and flawless.

Willa? His quirky, artless, occasionally messy Willa?

She was watching him, he realized. Her gaze was cautious and hopeful. Then, as he continued to stare at her in disbelief, the blue wariness in her eyes began to spark irritation.

Finally, she plunked both fists on her hips and glared at him. "What? Do I have soot on my nose?"

She was back. Nathaniel began to breathe again. " 'Tis a great relief," he said, smiling. "For a moment, I wasn't sure it was you."

She folded her arms beneath those magnificent breasts. Nathaniel's mouth suddenly wasn't so dry. In fact, he feared he needed to wipe his chin. "That isn't precisely a compliment, you realize," she pointed out. "You're saying that I used to look terrible."

His lips curved warmly. "You used to look like Willa. Now you look like heaven."

She blushed, but the sheer surprise in her eyes made him wonder if he'd never paid her a compliment before. Unfortunately, he couldn't pull any such occasion to mind.

Lord Treason wasn't much concerned with the feelings of others. The Cobra was even less so. Nathaniel Stonewell, on the other hand, was never one to let a lady go by without praise.

One of these days, he was going to have to find that man again.

But not until this mission was over. He must remain bent on finding Foster.

So he straightened and coolly offered his arm. "Shall we go?"

As he accompanied Willa down the stairs, he kept his gaze averted so he would not see the sheen of disappointment in her eyes.

Tonight was not a time for flirtation. Tonight the Cobra was at work.

Willa forcibly cheered herself on the carriage ride to the Knights' residence. She was perfectly dressed for the occasion—something she was usually completely careless of—and she was escorted by the most handsome man in the world.

When she had seen him standing there in midnight blue evening wear, so tall and lordly and fine . . .

Well, one never knew when the urge to copulate was going to strike, did one?

There were no other vehicles pulling up before their destination. "We are very early," Nathaniel explained. "Mrs. Knight did not want her father—who is in the government—to be put in the awkward situation of having to shake hands with me in the presentation line."

Willa looked up at him in surprise. "That does not insult you?"

He gave a short, jerky shake of his head. "It would be most awkward for all. I expected nothing less. This invitation is a great favor. I'm only surprised there were no more conditions."

"Well, I am glad that there are still people in London who are willing to give you a chance. The Bishop was entirely wrong," she declared stoutly.

Nathaniel slid his gaze her way. "No, he wasn't, wildflower. You and I both know that."

She put a reassuring hand on his arm. "But that is what

this evening is all about! We *will* change their minds about you!"

He covered her hand for the merest instant, then turned away. "It matters little. What's done is done. You should leave well enough alone."

He was in no mood to be bolstered, she could tell. "Very well, Nathaniel." It would indeed be very painful for him to raise his hopes, only to have them dashed if she was not successful in her new mission. She would let him be . . . for now.

At the Knights' residence, their hostess, Katrina— "everyone calls me Kitty"—Knight, was young, blond, cheerful, and blunt.

"Oh, good, you're wearing something daring!" was her greeting to Willa. "I was hoping you wouldn't turn out to be a country mouse."

Willa blinked. "Am I daring? I had no idea."

"Oh yes. To wear that color when you are yet unmarried? Although you are engaged, so that is perhaps not quite so daring after all. Hmm. Are you by any chance known to behave outrageously?"

"Absolutely," Willa said with a straight face. "Nathaniel says I'm incredibly odd," she promised.

Kitty laughed. "So am I. Although I believe Knight's term is *quite impossible*."

Willa smiled, recognizing a kindred spirit. Kitty grinned in response. "Mind you, I was worried that our ball would not be the final destination of the evening for anyone, for we have no actual ballroom—only these large drawing rooms with the wall panels which can be removed between."

"I think it a charming arrangement," Willa assured her. "Very practical."

"Thank you, but we need not worry now that you are

here. Absolutely *everyone* will be ending the evening here, especially after word gets around the other events tonight. Oh, if you think I'm using Lord Reardon as a novelty attraction, you're absolutely right. This is my first ball and I want it to be remembered. Now it will be."

Kitty was so gleefully shameless about it that Willa could not resent the younger woman's opportunism.

"There is another reason, as well." Kitty did not seem so confident suddenly. "I was eager to help, you see. I do feel a bit responsible for ruining things for your fiancé."

"What do you mean?"

"It was I who realized that it was Na—Lord Reardon in the drawing. I—I was a bit infatuated, I'm afraid, and when I thought that he was competing for a demirep named Fleur, well, I was hurt, so I made sure that ab-solutely everyone in London knew it was him."

"How could you possibly manage that?"

Kitty gave a small, rueful laugh. "That was simple. I simply told Mama. It is not a wise thing to tangle with Mrs. Trapp!"

"Ah," Willa said. If Kitty's mother was anything like Moira . . .

"Oh yes, I almost forgot. Do not leave tonight without taking your gown," Kitty urged her.

Willa frowned slightly. "What gown would that be?"

"Why, your Court gown, of course!" At Willa's obvi-ous confusion, Kitty elaborated. "Lord Reardon asked Aunt Clara to find you a Court gown that would fit for your presentation to the Prince Regent tomorrow, for you've not weeks to have one made. I do think you and I are of a size, and very nearly the same height as well. You may wear mine!"

"Presentation? To the Prince Regent? *Tomorrow?*"

"Well, don't worry. Aunt Clara says Prinny scarcely

takes notice of the presentations. She said sometimes he sleeps right through."

"How . . . comforting."

"And Aunt Clara said your banns will be read for the first time this Sunday and then in two weeks you'll be wed." Kitty sighed. "I love weddings. I had two."

Willa almost let herself be distracted by that revelation but firmly brought her own curiosity—and Kitty's meanderings—to a halt. "Kitty, who is Clara? How does she know so much about me?"

"Clara is my aunt. Lady Etheridge." Kitty's brown eyes widened. "Didn't Nathaniel tell you about her?"

"Apparently not as much as he told her about me," Willa grumbled.

"Well, they're great friends. Of course, being married to Lord Etheridge, Clara can't be *too* public about her support, can she?"

"Of course not," Willa said drily. What lady could be public about being "great friends" with another man?

Kitty nodded vehemently. "Why, Lord Etheridge is practically the Prime Minister's right hand!"

"Hmm." Lord Etheridge was probably old and ugly. And Clara was probably young and lonely and elegant and beautiful. "Kitty, would you describe your aunt Clara to be tall?"

Kitty blinked. "Heavens, no. She's little taller than I am."

"Well, that is something, at any rate," Willa grumbled.

"Here she is now!" Kitty waved vigorously across the room.

Willa turned to see a dark-haired woman approaching them with a smile. Blast. Not much older than herself. Very nearly beautiful. Absolutely elegant. Willa felt a little ill.

"Kitty, dear," the woman cried as she neared them. "You look delicious! I do so love you in amber."

"Thank you, Aunt Clara! You look very fine as well. Is that a new gown?"

Clara smiled. "Of course. I had it especially made for your debut as a hostess." She looked around them. "You were very clever to turn this into your ballroom, dear."

"Thank you," Kitty said smugly. Then she turned to Willa. "Aunt Clara, may I introduce Miss Trent?"

Willa dipped a formal curtsy. "My lady." She might be from a Northants village, but she would not display faulty manners before this woman.

Clara lit up still further. "You're Willa! And you're lovely, just as Nathaniel said. Welcome to Mayfair."

Willa wanted to say a very vulgar word. Clara was perfectly charming and friendly. Willa was going to have a very hard time hating her properly.

Perhaps she could convince Myrtle to hate the woman for her.

Across the room, Nathaniel stood alone, feeling like an exotic menagerie animal. No one approached to speak to him, yet everyone still managed to pass by close enough for a good look. He crossed his arms and watched as yet another pair of Society dams walked slowly by him, sliding their gazes sideways to inspect him without actually turning their heads. As soon as they passed, they rushed to a seating area with their heads together. Discussing the length of his horns, no doubt.

"Damn, I forgot to polish my forked tail," he muttered to himself.

"Do be careful not to knock over any vases with that thing," said a laconic voice behind him. "We just redecorated."

Nathaniel turned to see a dark man leaning against the column behind him. Although they'd never actually met,

Nathaniel knew who he was. Alfred Theodious Knight, his host this evening.

Humor, not disdain, glinted from the man's eyes, so Nathaniel took a chance. "Nathaniel Stonewell, Lord Reardon," he said, sticking out his hand. "Infamous traitor."

The other man nodded easily, meeting his handshake. "Alfred Knight, scandalous husband of twins."

"That *is* scandalous." Nathaniel raised a brow. "Get many invitations?"

"A precious few. Kitty's hoping for more after tonight. You?"

"None at all. Thank you for tonight."

Knight shrugged. "Kitty wanted to do it."

Nathaniel smiled. "And what Kitty wants Kitty receives?"

Knight gazed across the room. "Oh yes," he said blissfully.

Nathaniel followed his gaze to where Kitty and Clara spoke to Willa. Willa did look fine tonight. The way her full breasts were pressed high and the way that one long ringlet of dark hair kept rolling into the tight valley between . . .

He pulled his gaze back. Knight was still lost in his new wife. Nathaniel snorted. "Are you always this besotted?"

Knight didn't even bother to look at him. "Every minute. You?"

Nathaniel flinched. "Me? What do you mean?"

Knight slid his gaze to Nathaniel. "I see. Well, you can answer that question later. I give you about three more days."

Nathaniel straightened. "I have no idea what you are speaking of."

Knight smiled slightly and turned his gaze back to his wife. "Make that two days."

Nathaniel cleared his throat. The man was mad, seeing love everywhere because of his own condition. He nodded shortly. "Excuse me, sir," he said, then turned on his heel and strode down the series of rooms to the other end.

Once there, he took up a similar arrogant stance near a potted palm, arms folded across his chest, eyes half-lidded, sneer faintly etched on his lips. Lord Treason was in fine form.

19

Willa watched Nathaniel walk by her and the other two ladies, feeling distressed. Clara laid a gentle hand on her arm. "He'll be fine. He wanted to come tonight."

Willa turned back to Clara with a half smile. "I knew it would be difficult for him, but . . . he isn't himself. He seems . . . hard." She toyed with her empty dance card. "I thought we were going to face everyone down together," she said softly.

"You thought he would storm the ball, daring any naysayer, and dance the night away with you?" Clara's voice was kind.

"Ouch," Willa laughed damply. "You have seen through me, I fear."

"Give him time, Miss Trent. After all, this is the first time he's appeared at a social event since his disgrace." Clara gazed down the room to where Nathaniel stood like a black mark against the wallpaper. "I, for one, am glad to see him out," she said softly. "For whatever reason."

Willa almost missed the reference in her disquiet, but then her attention caught. "What do you mean? His reason is solely to publicly brave the scorn." She looked down at Nathaniel. "For me."

Clara nodded. "Of course it is." She gave an easy smile, but Willa had the feeling that she had been talking about something else entirely.

Willa looked away. Of course Clara knew things about Nathaniel that she herself did not know. "Great friends," after all.

Friends. All jealousy aside, Willa knew that Nathaniel needed all the friends he could find. Perhaps . . . perhaps if Lady Etheridge was indeed Nathaniel's friend, she would help Willa in her quest to change minds about "Lord Treason." As far as Willa was concerned, the first step to that end was the search for that so-called artist.

Impulsively she leaned forward. "My lady, I need your help. I want Sir Thorogood!"

Clara started violently. "Wh—what?"

Willa retreated, surprised. "I suppose I was a bit abrupt, but I did not mean to startle you so, my lady."

Clara pressed a hand to her breast. "No, of course not. So sorry. I was . . . I was miles away."

"To elaborate, today I saw the cartoon that condemned Nathaniel. I want to track down this Sir Thorogood character and make him state publicly that he was wrong about Nathaniel."

Clara gazed at her for a long moment. "Oh dear."

At the other end of the room, Nathaniel was growing weary of holding up the wall. Unfortunately, sitting was out of the question. One couldn't very well loom on a floral cushion. The entire effect would be lost.

So he stood there silent and unmoving, very much like the potted palm at his side.

"Reardon," the palm said.

Nathaniel closed his eyes. If he answered, then those watching him would be validated in their opinion of him. Only a complete raving madman would talk to a potted palm.

"Reardon!" the palm hissed.

Perhaps if he tried not to move his lips? "Go away, Etheridge."

"Has anyone approached you?"

"Yes, one man."

The palm rustled with excitement. "Who?"

"His name is Alfred Theodious Knight." Damn. Now the spectators were definitely watching him oddly. There was simply no way to say "Theodious" without moving one's lips.

"Oh. It isn't Knight. He's family."

Thinking of his own family, Nathaniel didn't see that as much of a recommendation of character. Nevertheless, he didn't suspect Knight, either. The man was only being a generous host.

"I don't think anyone will approach you openly. Too visible," the palm said thoughtfully. "Perhaps you could take a stroll in the gardens?"

"Why not?" Nathaniel said drily. "There may be some plants I haven't greeted yet."

He pushed himself off the wall and tugged his waist-coat straight.

"By the way," the palm said, "how did it go with the Bishop?"

Nathaniel couldn't suppress a rueful grin. "Willa essentially told the man to take a flying leap off Saint Paul's and that we would marry in our own time."

The palm laughed softly. "I like her."

Something rich and liquid pierced Nathaniel's chest at the thought of Willa's staunch loyalty. "So do I," he whispered as he set out for the gardens. "So do I."

Willa was deep in conversation with Clara when Nathaniel passed her on his way. It was just as well. His feelings toward her were a bit chancy at the moment. Damn Knight for putting those thoughts in his head.

After all, what could be more ridiculous? Even if real love existed—and he was willing to concede the possibility, considering the example of Etheridge and Clara—it didn't exist for him. No bond could withstand a lifetime of public condemnation, not even love.

Besides, it simply wasn't possible to fall in love in—

Five days. Had it only been five days? Nathaniel pressed the latch and opened the many-paned door to the terrace. Cool evening air washed over him. Shutting the door behind him made the ball go nearly silent, with only the music audible through the glass.

So much had changed in five short days. He had changed; he could feel it. He was lighter somehow. He breathed in the evening, smelling the shorn grass of the lawn around the terrace and the climbing flowers in the garden. The scent of the flowers pulled him closer. After wandering the knot work path for a while, he found them. The tiny star-shaped flowers put out a delicate sweet scent that reminded him of something. What was it? . . .

He tracked it down to the first night he'd been back. Willa, who bathed in the stuff.

The vine's scent took him back to when he'd been leaning over her, vowing to protect her from his life and himself.

The gardens were past their prime season, but the clever twisting pathways were lined with box hedges, making the journey through seem much longer than it was. Nathaniel envied it immensely and vowed to steal away Knight's gardener at the soonest opportunity.

Provided that the man would work for "Lord Treason," of course.

Although Nathaniel walked slowly and stopped by the cherub fountain in the center for a time, he saw no one else out of doors, for good or evil.

Deciding that he needed to make another caged-creature appearance in the ballroom, Nathaniel headed back to the house.

They were waiting for him on the terrace.

Willa wandered the ballroom looking for Nathaniel in the crush that had now arrived, but could find him nowhere. She spied Kitty, dancing proudly with Knight at the head of the dance form. Waiting along the wall for the dance to end so she could enlist Kitty's assistance, Willa felt eyes upon her.

She looked to her left to see several ladies eyeing her warily, discussing something in low voices. Unfortunately, Willa had excellent hearing.

"Who is she? Does anyone know where he found her?"

"I heard that she's a tavern maid from some tiny village up north."

That was not so terrible, Willa thought. Very close to the truth. She had poured her share of ale over the years.

"Well, *I* heard that they traveled all the way to London together. *Alone.*"

Gleefully shocked whispers answered this. Willa looked away. Again, entirely true. She gripped the tiny pencil that hung from her dance card and assumed an expression of pleasant unconcern.

"There's more," said the red-haired woman who knew about the traveling. "The tale goes that she knocked him over the head with a rock and slept beside him all night to trap him into marriage."

The tiny pencil snapped in half. Willa gazed at the dancers before her with blurry eyes. How did they know so much, so soon? The only person she had told was Myrtle, whom she trusted entirely.

"Well, I for one feel sorry for her. She may have

trapped him, but she couldn't have known who he was. No woman would be that desperate."

"Nnnoo," said the entirely too knowledgeable woman, "Unless perhaps she was . . . *desperate.*"

This time the gasps were shocked indeed. "No!" "Oh, heavens, I need my vinaigrette!"

"Then they well deserve each other, don't you think?"

Enough. Willa turned to them with a sweet, deadly smile. "Why, thank you!" she said clearly. "You're so very kind."

She turned to go. Then she turned back. "When one day it is revealed that Lord Reardon is a good man, please do not be ashamed to call upon us. You'll find that while my memory is long, my nature is forgiving." She smiled again. "Usually."

When she had stalked away and rounded a column, she came face-to-face with Kitty and Knight. Kitty was smiling proudly. "Good for you, Lady Reardon."

Willa let out a breathy laugh, then curtsied deeply. "I am much obliged, Mrs. Knight."

Kitty tucked her arm through Knight's. "Darling, when next we host a ball, do let us remember who to strike off our guest list." She smiled fiercely at Willa. "My first ball is a rampaging success. And my memory is long as well."

Willa slid her gaze toward Knight. "Is her nature forgiving?"

"Ah." Knight thought for a moment. "I think the more appropriate word would be . . . *pitiless.*"

"Why, thank you, my love!" Kitty went up on tiptoe to kiss her husband's cheek. Then she turned to Willa, her gaze somber. "Are you all right, Willa?"

Willa gave a little shake. "I'm perfectly well, thank you. Except that I cannot find Nathaniel. Have you seen him?"

Kitty looked thoughtful. "Not since he went into the gardens nearly an hour ago."

. . .

Finster and his cronies stood in a youthfully belligerent, slightly drunken line, blocking Nathaniel from the ballroom.

Well, this was a conundrum. The question was not so much "Could he trounce them?" as it was "Should he trounce them?" After all, Lord Treason was a snide wastrel—the most that could be claimed was perhaps a passing interest in boxing.

Lord Treason would *not* be able to trounce six strong young fellows. The Cobra could not only trounce them but also kill them silently and have their bodies disposed of inside an hour. Nathaniel Stonewell simply wasn't in the mood to fight.

There would be no help from anyone inside, of course, nor should there be. This could be a test. Finster was probably not a conspirator, but he was stupid enough to be used by one—aimed at Nathaniel like an arrow. Calling down the cavalry now would cost the battle.

As Finster led his minions down the terrace steps to the lawn, Nathaniel decided on bluster first, to be spiced with a dash of boxing and a hint of head butting. Crude but effective, and it wouldn't alert anyone to the fact that "Lord Treason" wasn't what he seemed.

"Well, if it isn't Lady Reardon," sneered Finster. "Where is your brave defender, my lady?"

Finster really was very young if he thought accusations of girlishness were going to work. Nathaniel decided to leave out the head butting. He couldn't do it to the poor boy.

Still, if they were stooping to schoolyard insults . . .

Nathaniel straightened tall, looming over the smaller man. "Why don't you pick on someone your own size, Finny?" he drawled.

Finster blushed so hotly that it was visible even in the dim light. Good God, had he ever been that sensitive to insult?

"I think my blokes and I add up to more than enough," Finster spit. He gestured sharply to his followers, who immediately surrounded Nathaniel, pinioning his arms, although they stupidly left his legs alone.

Finster threw his first punch to Nathaniel's solar plexus. Ouch. The lad had been to the boxing gym, hadn't he? Let's see, should he stun Finster with a kick first, or should he pull his arms close and knock some sense into his brainless sycophants?

Another gut punch, harder. Nathaniel was beginning to get seriously annoyed. He was definitely going to take Finster out with a kick first—

Something whizzed through the air, caroming off Finster's skull with a *ping*.

"Ow!" Finster clapped a hand to his pate and whirled. Behind him stood Willa, smiling sweetly with her hands behind her back.

"Hello again, Mr. Finster."

Finster's face twisted into a terrific scowl. "You!" He charged toward her, fury in every movement.

Willa stepped closer as he approached, her smile softening to a thing of sexual beauty. "Me," she murmured huskily—and clocked Finster a perfect right hook.

Finster went down without a sound, splayed full out on the grassy lawn. The minions, likely out of complete shock, released Nathaniel and surrounded Willa. Nathaniel was fairly sure they were simply letting the liquor cloud their reactions. Still, he moved silently behind them, ready to kill—er, trounce—anyone who made a motion toward Willa.

In the center of the threat, Willa clapped a hand to her cheek. "Why, gentlemen! You would never strike a *lady*!"

That halted them briefly, but they did not step away from her. Nathaniel saw Willa plant a fist on each hip. "Am I going to have to tell Mrs. Trapp about this?"

That tore them down to the ground. As one, they stepped back, transforming instantly into shuffling school-boys. "No, Miss Trent." "Oh, please don't, Miss Trent!" "She plays cards with my mum!" came one panicked plea.

Willa smiled gently. "There, you see. You're good boys, all of you. Why you would follow a worthless lout like Mr. Finster I'll never know." She cast an admiring glance at the largest of the lot. "You look like a leader, sir. A true gentleman."

Nathaniel rolled his eyes as the young man stood straighter. From here it looked as though his chest swelled as well.

"Oh my. What a fine young man! I imagine there are many very attractive young ladies waiting on you gentle-men inside." She sighed dramatically, which she had to know did eye-catching things to her décolletage. "Oh, if only I were younger . . ."

The flood of courtly compliments this prompted fair to made Nathaniel toss his dinner.

"Why, Miss Trent, you are as fresh as any flower on the vine!" "Miss Trent, I must protest! There isn't a lady inside who outshines you!"

Nathaniel watched sourly as Willa herded her sheep back into the ballroom, then shut the glass-paned door on them. Only then did she falter. With her left hand cradling her right, she gazed at him mournfully. "Ouch."

In an instant, Nathaniel was by her side, stepping over the unconscious form of Finster in the process. He took her hand in his and held it to the light. Her knuckles were red and a bit swollen, but he did not think she had broken anything but Finster's masculine reputation.

"Nice hook."

She sniffled the tiniest bit. "Thank you. Dick and Dan taught me."

"Ah, that explains the professional follow-through." Gently he raised her abraded knuckles to his lips and kissed each one. "My hero," he said softly, smiling.

Willa leaned her head wearily against his chest. "Nathaniel, can we go home now?"

Nathaniel inhaled deeply. Hellfire, she smelled good. The garden could not compare. "Are you sure, wild-flower? The dancing is not yet over."

"What dancing?" she said glumly.

Her words struck him hard. What dancing indeed? For an instant, his mind began to weigh the act of dancing against the persona of Lord Treason—

To hell with that. Nathaniel Reardon wanted to dance with his bride. With a flourish, he opened the door and steered her back into the ballroom. "Have you a waltz free, Miss Trent?"

He loved watching her expression go from dejected to delighted. He resolved to cause more such transformations in the future.

"Why, yes, my lord. I do happen to have a waltz free!"

She flowed into his arms in an exquisite rustle of sapphire silk and he swept her into the swirling harmony of color and sound that was the waltz at a formal ball. Willa let her head fall back, laughing delightedly. When she looked back up at him, her eyes were glowing twilight jewels. They danced every remaining dance of the evening—always together.

And if they danced a bit too closely for propriety . . . well, decorum would be the least of Lord Treason's worries, wouldn't it?

Besides, she smelled so damned good.

20

It was very late when they returned from the ball. Willa was pleased in general by the night's events. She'd danced with Nathaniel until her feet were throbbing. She'd destroyed Finster's little gang. She'd made a friend in Kitty Knight and made inroads into public opinion of Nathaniel.

All in all, a satisfying night's work.

There was just one more thing. . . .

Nathaniel walked her to her chamber. "Good night, Willa. You ought to lie abed tomorrow morning, for we've another ball tomorrow night."

"Oh yes. Daphne and Basil's." She sighed reluctantly. "I suppose we cannot avoid it."

Nathaniel smiled slightly. "We could actually, since Basil has already asked me not to attend."

The matchless cheek of it, excluding Nathaniel when it was his house! Willa's eyes narrowed. "Then we will definitely be there."

Nathaniel shook his head admiringly. "Poor Basil."

The house was quiet around them; Nathaniel was being warm and relaxed with her—the question that had been burning in Willa ever since her meeting with the Bishop this morning burst from her.

"Why have you never denied being labeled a traitor?"

Nathaniel pulled back. "Ah. I thought something was preoccupying you today. Your chat with the Bishop was not a complete waste of his time, was it?"

"It was his strongest argument," she said reluctantly. "And you are avoiding the point."

"There is no point, Willa," he said stiffly. "It is late and we are both weary."

"Yet again, no direct answer," she mused as if to herself.

God, she was tenacious. Perhaps too much so. If he let her pursue this question, she was intelligent and obstinate enough to uncover some things that truly needed to remain buried. He tipped her chin up with one finger to look intently into her eyes.

"Willa, I have never denied the rumors because I cannot deny the rumors."

She gazed at him as if she was trying to see within him. "Cannot, or will not?"

He shook his head sadly, seriously. "Truly cannot."

It was only the truth. To deny the rumors now, with Foster on the loose, might prompt the man to reveal the secret that the Royal Four feared to become public. No one could ever know how young Prince George, caught up in youthful rebellion against his moralistic father's disapproval, had joined a group of young radicals who called themselves the Knights of the Lily. George had ever been light-minded, despite his innate intelligence, and had not realized until nearly too late that his cohorts were serious indeed.

All had been confessed and duly swept under the rug. The young insurgents had been mercifully dispersed, and all had remained quiet for thirty years.

Until Nathaniel had been recruited by the leader of the old Knights of the Lily and told of their plan to paint the Prince Regent as a patricidal maniac, hoping to prompt the people of England to depose him in the midst of war. That sort of chaos in the government was just what Napoleon needed to gain the upper hand again—and just what the Royal Four could not allow.

No matter what the cost.

Just as it was Nathaniel's mission to find the last conspirator—no matter what the cost.

None of which he could explain to Willa. Ever.

For if the Royal Four feared the revelation about the Prince Regent, they dreaded the revelation of their own secrets more. Princes and kings came and went, good ones, bad ones, mad ones. Through it all, through the chaos of all the centuries, it had been the Four who had kept England steering straight through the rocks that had ruined other larger, stronger nations. The Four were the reason that one tiny island had become a world power and had remained one for so long.

Their lack of existence was their strength—and their greatest weakness. Like the heel of Achilles, discovery was the only thing that could bring them down, leaving England without its secret armature of honor and loyalty without care for personal gain.

Willa was watching him with her blue eyes nearly swimming. Her disappointment cut him to the core.

"I'm sorry, wildflower. I know you were hoping I could deny it. I'm sorry to disillusion you." He felt the inevitability of it. He felt his brief contentment dissolving and his fiery little touchstone leaving him cold and alone.

Instead, she peered up at him as if she couldn't decide what species he was. "Are all men so stupid?"

Nathaniel blinked, then frowned. "You've been spending too much time with Myrtle."

She threw both hands in the air and turned away from him. "And you've been spending too much time running from a lie!"

Lie? The hallway seemed to shift around him for a moment. She couldn't mean what he thought she meant. Could she?

"What—what lie?"

She stopped her frustrated pacing and looked at him, head tilted, hands on her hips. "The lie about you being a traitor."

Not daring to place too much weight on what she was saying, Nathaniel moved to stand before her. He took her hands from her hips and linked his fingers in hers.

His hands weren't cold, but hers were warmer. God, even her fingers fed him warmth.

Leading her gently, he opened her chamber door and backed her up to sit her on the bed. He sat beside her, keeping her hands in his.

Abruptly she gave up her mad and leaned into him, rolling her head on his shoulder. Closing his eyes, Nathaniel tilted his head for a deep breath of warm, alive, jasmine-scented Willa.

The room was definitely shifting around him. The *world* was shifting, sliding ever so slightly from wrong into right.

Willa believed in him. She'd heard the whole grisly story, seen him refuse to deny it, and still she did not turn away.

He wanted to wrap his arms around her, to roll her back onto the coverlet and take down her hair. He ached to kiss her until she couldn't breathe and bury himself in her until she couldn't speak.

But first, he had to hear it from her very lips. Nathaniel couldn't bear the tension for another moment. "Willa, you still have faith in me?"

She smiled tenderly at him. "Oh, darling Nathaniel. Of course I have faith in you. I love you, you silly lout."

She believed. The weight upon his heart vanished like smoke, and he felt as though he very well could turn blue and fly. At this moment, he felt as if he could do anything imaginable, with Willa at his side.

Wait a moment.

"You love me?"

She tilted her head, her smile softening. "Yes, Nathaniel Stonewell. I love you."

Then he was pulling her into his arms before she could take another breath.

Willa gasped at Nathaniel's urgency, then relaxed into the strength of his arms. She had been waiting for him for so long that she gave herself up to the moment immediately, turning to instant heat at his touch.

She loved the feel of his arms wrapped tightly about her, almost lifting her from the bed. Slipping her hands around his neck for support, she let her head fall back.

Nathaniel instantly took advantage of the motion and buried his face in her neck. She felt tongue and teeth. It sent shivers down to her toes.

"Are you going to cop—" No. Wait. "Are you going to make love to me now?"

He pulled his head up to gaze down at her. "Yes, wildflower. I'm going to make love to you now. Twice. At least."

He pulled her higher and kissed the tops of her breasts above the neckline of her gown.

She shivered, anticipation making her press her thighs together. "Twice. Oh my. Is that possible?"

Pulling his head up once more, he growled, "Willa, wildflower, shut up. Please."

And then he kissed her.

He kissed her until she couldn't breathe, until her heart pounded and her knees weakened and she melted inside like warm wax.

Nathaniel couldn't get enough of the taste of his extraordinary country minx. She was everything that her one untutored kiss on the road had promised him. Sweet, hot, giving, and such a very quick learner.

Willa stroked her hands from his neck up into his hair, tangling the long silky strands in her fists as she threw everything she knew into the kiss.

The heat of his mouth, the spicy taste of him, the slick feel of his teeth and rough hot pleasure of his tongue. It was even better than the first time.

His hands began to rove over her, down her back and over her bosom. The tiny cap sleeves slipped off her shoulders, tangling her arms too tightly, so she let go of him for a moment to shrug them off.

He stepped back to look down at her, his hands sliding up her until they cradled her face. "Let me see you, wildflower. Let me see all of you."

Not sure what he wanted, she stood, reaching behind her for the top buttons of her gown until she heard his encouraging groan. The gown gaped forward, exposing more and more of her bosom. She undid the last buttons at her waist slowly, one by one, watching him watch her.

It was unbearably exciting, seeing the lust on his face, feeling the power she had over his response.

Then the button slipped from its hole and the bodice of her gown slipped down the front, hanging open but still clinging to her moist skin. He reached to pull it down the rest of the way.

Willa pulled back, suddenly too shy. She couldn't do it, not after being turned away so often.

Nathaniel looked into her eyes. "Is it my turn?"

His voice was gentle, but the look in his eyes was urgent and hungry. She shivered, and his gaze flew back to where her areolas peeked from behind blue silk. She wore almost nothing underneath, for she'd had little that would suit.

"Please?" Her voice caught on the knot of fear and heady longing in her throat. Perhaps if he were naked as well . . .

Nathaniel pulled off his open frock coat and tossed it to the chair behind her. Then he quickly undid his waistcoat and sent it flying after his coat. His stock he untied slowly, then whipped away to flutter across the room like a flag of abandon. Then, one by one, he slowly pulled the studs from his shirt, parting it teasingly so that it hung open but not off.

"That seems fair. Now you."

Willa licked her lips. His gaze riveted itself on her mouth, so she did it again. He swallowed harshly, and the hungry look in his eyes became almost tortured.

Heady stuff, this lovemaking. She felt her feminine might growing by the moment. There was only one problem. If she removed her gown, she would be naked but for her shift, while he would only be shirtless.

In the interest of fairness, then, Willa kicked off one slipper and raised her foot to the seat of the chair. Pulling up the hem of her gown, she exposed the lacy garter upon which hung her stocking.

Nathaniel thought he was going to burst on the spot at the first glimpse of creamy thigh. Oh, she was a wicked country miss. He watched as she leisurely untied the garter, letting it slide off her thigh with a satin hiss.

She tossed it onto the chair on top of his waistcoat and gave him a look of challenge.

He knew what she was doing and found it unbearably sweet that she was turning her fear and nervousness into a ribald little game for him.

Still, in the interest of moving things along, he bent and removed not one boot but two, tossing them past her to land beside the chair.

Her eyes widened, but he wasn't going to let her off easily. He smiled at her, cocking his head expectantly.

Willa swallowed. Then, bending, she rolled her stocking down with excruciating slowness, until she had to point her toe and kick it off onto the floor.

Nathaniel was going to die. The fact that she had no idea that bending over made the bodice of her gown drop open and expose her luscious breasts completely only made it more exciting. Losing that divine view when she straightened made him give a tiny groan of mourning.

Quickly he stripped off both socks and pulled his shirt over his head.

Willa froze at the sight of his bared chest. How could she have forgotten how beautiful he was? Why was she delaying the one thing she wanted in all the world?

With a sudden flurry of motion, Willa planted her other foot on the chair, stripped off the garter and stocking and tossed them aside, then stood to face Nathaniel.

He knew what she wanted, she could see it on his face, and the trace of arrogance there was not to be borne. Deciding to exert a little of her newfound power, she turned her back on him, then slipped the gown over and off and tossed it aside. Then, remaining with her back to him, as much for courage as for teasing potential, she untied the drawstring of her shift and let it slip down to hang very low at her hips.

He made a low tortured sound, and she looked over her shoulder to see his hands clenched by his sides and all arrogance gone from his face.

Good.

Then she turned to run for the bed so she could hide under the covers.

"Not so fast, wildflower!"

Nathaniel caught her in one arm and swung her around to face him, then stepped forward to kiss her—

And tripped over his own boots on the floor. With a violent twist of his body so that he would not land on Willa, he fell hard on the marble hearth.

"Oh, darling! Oh, Nathaniel, are you all right?"

He managed to pull in a deep breath but almost lost it again when he realized that Willa's heavy, soft breasts were pressed to his bare chest. He could feel her hardened nipples moving against his skin as she ran her hands over his skull looking for injuries.

Heaven. Being knocked unconscious by a nearly naked Willa was just this side of heaven.

But Nathaniel wanted to be on the other side of heaven. Better yet, the inside of heaven.

Reaching for her, he wrapped both arms about her and rolled them both to one side, away from the cold marble and onto the deep, soft rug.

"Oh, you are all right. I was so afraid the jinx—"

There was no choice at all. He had to kiss those words right out of her mouth.

Once the jolt of fear for him had passed, Willa forgot to think at all. There was nothing in the world but the taste and smell and feel of Nathaniel above her.

He kissed her deeply, braced above her on one arm while the other pulled her shift down to her ankles. Quickly she pedaled it off, then gasped into his mouth as he moved his body between her knees.

"Shh," he said into her lips. "Not yet."

She relaxed, allowing her legs to fall open fully as he lay down upon her, pressing his body into the parting of hers with his trousers still covering him. As long as he kept them on, she had nothing to worry about.

Then his hands began to travel her body with knowledge and thoroughness, and she forgot to worry at all.

21

Nathaniel couldn't believe the woman who moved and sighed and shivered beneath him. Never had someone responded to his every touch, seemingly his every thought.

He'd assumed that he had made love before, but never had it been like this. Never this generous, this achingly tender yet fantastically wild.

She was on fire beneath him, sighing and writhing, stimulating him almost beyond bearing. And taking him further by the moment were the words that kept falling from her lips.

"I love you, Nathaniel, I love you so."

He couldn't wait any longer. She hadn't come to orgasm yet, but she was swollen and wet to the touch and shuddered with every flick of his fingers. He should take her all the way, but he needed her so badly . . .

"Wildflower, I need to—" He fumbled at his trouser buttons, then gasped as her hands slid down his belly to help him. His own were shaking so badly that he took them away and let her take over.

Willa's fear was gone. All she could feel now was the blinding ache within, plus a burning need to see Nathaniel naked. Now.

She slipped the buttons quickly through their holes, taking care, at every opportunity, to stroke her knuckles against the rigid length hidden behind the fine tight wool. He quivered every time. Delicious.

Then he was free. His erection sprang into her waiting hands, but she gained not a moment to explore it. Nathaniel pulled away, frantically tore his breeches off, and rolled back between her thighs.

"I need you so, wildflower. I should make sure—"

She wrapped her arms about his neck, pulling him down for a hot, wet tender-rough kiss. Then she pulled back and gave him a deadly serious look.

"If you don't take me now, Nathaniel, I will hit you."

His reply was to thrust the head of his erection into her.

She threw her head back, gasping. "Yesss."

He withdrew, making her whimper with loss. Then he pressed in again. Every stroke rubbed against *that* place, the sensitive place that Willa herself had only touched in the bath.

It felt wicked and outrageous and very good. And it didn't hurt at all.

He did it again and again, faster and faster, until her head tossed against his forearms and she whimpered out loud.

Then he did something, lowered his body and tightened his arms about her—and thrust deep inside her.

The stretching, bursting pain was shocking. She cried out in distress, her hold on his shoulders becoming panicked, and she shook her head wildly when he bent to breathe reassurance into her ear.

"Shh," he whispered. "I'm sorry. It will pass. Shh."

He held her tightly, not moving within her any longer. She gulped once, still panting from the shock, then let her trust in him and the heat of him relax her. The searing eased as she expanded and warmed around him.

"Better?" His voice was tender.

She pulled back her head and smiled up at him, nodding, even as she drew a last shuddering breath.

Then she punched him hard on the bicep.

"Why didn't you warn me you were going to do that?"

"If I had, you would have tensed, and it would have been much worse."

"Oh." She considered that for a moment. Then she punched him again.

"Wildflower, we are really going to have to talk about your propensity for violence."

"Fine, after we talk about how you know so much about deflowering virgins."

He laughed weakly at that, and the movement of him within her made them both gasp.

"Willa," he said tightly, "if I swear to you that you are my first and only virgin, may we please continue to copulate our brains out?"

Her eyes went wide. "There's more?" The idea made her shudder beneath him, and she felt him pulse within her.

He groaned. "Oh, wildflower, there is so much more."

And he began to show her. With slow, long strokes he introduced her to her own depth and sensitivity. The pain was gone, leaving a pleasantly throbbing ache that was eased only by his deepest thrusts.

She ran her hands all over him while he thrust into her. She stroked her fingertips across his chest and she kneaded the flexing muscles in his shoulders as his speed increased.

And when the feeling within her grew from pleasant ache, to tumultuous pleasure, and then to shuddering ecstasy, she dug her nails into his buttocks and screamed her release.

His roar joined her cry as he plunged fiercely into her for the last time. Then, rolling both of them, he ended up on his back with her sprawled panting across his chest.

Nathaniel couldn't breathe. He couldn't think. Even now, he was trembling in reaction to his profound orgasm. It had never been so good. Never.

"You've killed me," she whispered, still shuddering from the aftershocks of her climax.

"Then it is mutual murder, I'm afraid." He drew a deep breath, enjoying the warm, slick weight of naked Willa on his chest.

"Mmm. I must not be quite dead yet, since I'm thirsty."

He laughed, and she lifted her head and grinned at him. She looked beautiful, with her dampened curls trailing over her flushed face, falling before her thick-lashed blue eyes.

"How could I have ever thought to resist you?" He raised a hand to cup her cheek. "My beautiful country minx."

Her eyes widened, then she blushed. Smiling shyly, Willa slipped from the circle of his arms and walked to the washbasin on the commode.

It was a view that Nathaniel had never before seen. The line of her graceful spine ended in the womanly swell of her full, rounded bottom. Erotic little dimples dotted the base of her spine, and on one buttock rode a single perfect beauty mark.

His breath left his body in a rush. Abruptly his exhausted desire rose once more.

Willa bathed herself, then pulled her shift on over her head, and the fabric fell over his view, hiding that luscious derriere from his sight.

"Take it off," he ordered.

Willa turned and placed a fist on each hip. "You presume, sir," she teased.

In one lethal motion, Nathaniel was out of the bed and standing before her. Willa's eyes widened at his monumental erection.

His gaze intense, Nathaniel repeated his command. "Take . . . it . . . off."

Shivering in response to his tone, Willa solemnly took the hem of the shift in both hands and pulled it up. When Nathaniel responded with a low animal noise, the shiver became a full-blown quiver.

He stopped her when her arms were above her head. "Don't move," he commanded. Willa couldn't see past the fine lawn of the shift over her face. The lack of knowing what came next sent a fresh tremor of excitement through her.

She felt Nathaniel move behind her, so close she sensed the heat from his naked body. Large hot hands ran over her bottom, teasingly at first, then with hard urgency.

"Oh God, wildflower. You are so beautiful." Nathaniel's voice was a breathless, reverent rasp.

He slid his hands around her to caress her breasts and pull her back against his erection. Willa stood absolutely still for as long as she could but finally couldn't resist an experimental rotation of her hips.

Nathaniel's groan was impetus enough for more experimentation. Slowly, Willa rose on her toes, letting Nathaniel's shaft slide into the cleft of her buttocks. Then she pressed back against him, rocking slightly side to side.

It was more than he could stand. With hard hands he turned her to face him, ripping the shift away to get to her lips.

He kissed her hard, plunging his tongue into her as he grasped her bottom and pulled her up to meet him. Willa wrapped her arms around his neck and her legs around his waist, kissing back with equal urgency.

Nathaniel pulled her tightly against him, groaning into her mouth as his erection slid up and down against her slick, hot center.

"The . . . bed," suggested Willa breathlessly.

Nathaniel only growled and took two steps toward the wall. Bracing her with his arms, he leaned her back against the papered wall and thrust into her clinging warmth.

Willa gave a tiny shriek of surprise. Nathaniel froze.

"Did I hurt you?"

"No. . . . I . . . simply didn't know—"

Fighting for control, Nathaniel tucked his face into her neck and breathed deeply.

"Don't stop," she said.

"I should stop. Oh, wildflower, I don't know what it is, but you wake up the animal in me."

"Well, the animal in me likes the animal in you," she said softly.

He pulled his head back to look at her, surprise in his eyes. Then he let his gaze travel down to where their bodies joined. When he met her eyes again, the heat was back. "I like the way the animal in me looks in you," he told her, his voice a heated growl.

Willa blushed at his openness but couldn't help a squirm of reaction.

Nathaniel threw his head back in response and pressed her hard to the wall. "Oh God—I want to do such things to you."

"All right."

Wrapping her back into his arms, Nathaniel held her a moment, still buried deep inside her. Then he slowly withdrew, despite her whimper of protest, and carried her back to the bed.

"Sweet Willa. I should make love to you gently, tenderly, the way you deserve."

He laid her down on the tumbled covers and sat beside her. He ran one finger from her lips to her throat and down between her breasts. Slowly, he trailed it farther, past her navel, and teased the soft curls between her thighs.

"Well, enough of that." She wriggled impatiently.

"When are you going to let the animal back out again?"

He laughed and shook his head with regret. "Oh, darling, you don't know what you speak of. You aren't a girl of the streets, to be used so harshly."

"What does that mean, 'used harshly'?"

"To take my pleasure of you, and give you none in return. To do things to you and have you do things to me, dark things that have nothing to do with caring."

"But if you . . . cared for me, as I care for you, then you wouldn't be using me, would you?"

"Willa—"

"Because there are things I would really like to do to you."

She was going to kill him. "Such as what?" he choked out.

She thought a moment. "Such as bite you."

"You want to bite me?"

"Well, not this very moment, but I did feel the urge to bite your shoulder when you picked me up like that. Not hard, of course. Lightly."

His throat threatened to close entirely. "Well, that would be nice."

"Yes, I rather thought it would." She pondered him. "Do you want to bite me, too?"

Nathaniel looked away. "The thought has crossed my mind."

"Would you bite hard enough to bleed?"

He was appalled. "Of course not!"

"Well, neither would I." She took a breath. "So that is resolved. We may bite when the moment strikes, then?"

She was a force of nature. Hurricane Willa. He could not resist her. "Yes, Willa, I think biting when the moment strikes will be all right."

"So biting is acceptable." She put her chin on her hands. "What else?"

"What else what?"

"What else would you like to do to me?"

Nathaniel felt as though he were in a dream. "This is the strangest conversation I have ever had."

"I know. It isn't my fault. I'm an orphan."

"So you've said." He peered at her. "What do you mean, exactly?"

"Don't change the subject. What else do you want to do to me?"

He laughed helplessly. "You aren't going to let this go, are you?"

"No."

"Fine then. If you must know, I want to put my mouth on you. Right here." He stroked a fingertip along her dampened slit and she shivered.

"All right. And may I put my mouth on you as well? Right here?" She grasped him in her hand and was gratified by some rapid expansion. Fascinating.

Breathless, Nathaniel agreed with a vigorous nod.

"What else?"

"I want you to ride astride me."

Willa thought about that. "That sounds agreeable. What else?"

"Dear God, Willa, have some mercy!"

"No. I like this. I feel very powerful, with you in my hand this way. Tell me what else."

He was nearly panting. "Very well. I want to take you the way a stallion takes a mare. From behind."

"Oh my." There was no saucy retort for that. "Oh *yes*."

"And up against the wall."

"From behind?"

"That, too."

"Oh yes, please."

"Oh, dear God . . ."

He was huge in her hand now. Willa could feel the beat of his heart, and her own sex pulsed in response. "Nathaniel?"

"Yes? . . ."

"I think I would like to try that stallion deed now."

"Oh, thank you, God!"

He flipped her over neatly, facedown on the pillows. He tugged her hips high. The position was almost embarrassing, until his shaft probed her slit and he bent low over her, covering her and giving her a tiny bite on her shoulder. Then nothing mattered but his animal and her animal and their undeniable primitive urge to mate.

"Are you ready for me, love?"

"Yes," moaned Willa.

His massive length drove into her slowly but implacably. New places awoke to his presence. Willa shrieked softly into the pillow.

Nathaniel stopped. "Are you all—"

Willa thrust backward, burying him deep within her. With a wild cry, she pulled away to drive herself back on him again. Hard hands grasped her hips and held her immobile.

"Let me—"

With the last of his control, Nathaniel set a rhythmic pace of thrust that was almost more than he could stand. Deeply, then deeply again. Again and again.

He felt her begin to shake and held her more tightly, not letting her go even when she began to buck wildly in his grasp.

With a quivering wail, she disintegrated in his hands. With a few last lovingly ferocious thrusts, he lost himself in her. Riding the pulsing waves of pleasure down, he eased them both down to lie on the bed, still planted within her.

He wrapped her tightly in his arms and tucked her into his body. Pressing his face into her hair, Nathaniel took a deep breath of Willa and fell asleep.

Nathaniel was walking through the air, with nothing below or above him or even around him. Gray twilight stretched forever. His first response was almost relief. There was no disgrace, no dishonor, here. He need fend off no contempt or bow to censure. Here he was not disowned, not despised.

For the first time in a long time, he felt as though he could breathe deeply without the weight of his burden.

Then the emptiness at his side became almost palpable. In the nothing, there was no Willa. There was no cold disdain, but there was no warm acceptance, either. No bright-burning woman to light his endless dusk. No softly giving lover to wrap him in her nourishing embrace.

He could not have just one, he realized. He must accept his dark if he wanted to see his light. He had made his choices; he had reached out to take on his own burdens. He wanted his burdens, for they had brought him his Willa.

Willa! He wanted to call for her joyously, expecting her to come bounding into his arms.

But his voice would not come and he could not call. He'd thought he'd come here to make a choice, but there was no choosing.

There was nothing.

On and on, only the endless nothing.

Nothing but the warmth of Willa's arms around him and her soft voice in his ear. With each shuddering breath, he took in her womanly scent, letting it cleanse his head of the dizzying eternity of loss.

"Shh. Shh."

Her small hands spread against his back and rubbed tenderly. He pulled her close, burying his sweating face in her silken neck. He was safe.

He wasn't alone.

"Do you want to tell me?" Her whisper was gentle, not pushing him. "Sometimes it helps."

"It was only a dream," he said. "It was nothing."

He could feel her disappointment in the way her fingers paused in stroking his hair and in the slight sag of her shoulders. He was so bloody tired of disappointing Willa.

"There are things I cannot speak of," he said slowly.

"I know."

She didn't sound bitter about it, but Nathaniel knew how living with a man full of secrets could erect barriers of doubt and bitterness. He never wanted her to feel the way he had felt as a boy, that his stepfather—his *father*—had held him of less importance than his work.

When Nathaniel was small, he'd tried to accept it, but as he grew and needed his father more and more, it became increasingly hard to fight the resentment. Willa could come to hate him in time, he was sure.

As Victoria had come to hate Randolph.

For the first time, Nathaniel caught a glimmer of how his mother's life must have been.

Finally, Nathaniel eased his hold on Willa to look into her eyes. Running her hand along his cheek in a tender caress, she kissed his jaw. "Your life has been difficult lately, I know. It will get better, my love. Time does take the edge off the blade."

Nathaniel pulled her close and rested his chin on her hair. He had sadly underestimated her. His Willa was no simple country miss. She was a woman, profoundly wise and generous. "You have not been sheltered but have simply not traveled much."

She sighed and snuggled closer, trailing her touch down his back. "Well, I've traveled now, haven't I?" She kissed his chest, then bit him gently.

"You've come very far indeed." He smiled at her. He only hoped he could keep up.

Just as he was nearly asleep, she started. "Oh! I almost forgot to ask you—"

"What?"

"Am I being presented to the Prince Regent tomorrow?"

Dear God, had he forgotten to tell her? "I'm sorry, Willa. It was not meant to be a surprise. It is traditional for a young lady of Society to be presented for her debut. You've had no debut as such, but I think you must do it before you wed me."

"I must?" She swallowed. "To the Prince Regent?"

He had begun to kiss her throat. He stopped to answer. "Yes. I'm sorry that you must go through this alone. If I go, it will only be worse for you. If you are with Myrtle, who has agreed to accompany you, then perhaps you will simply seem to be one of the many debutantes with a chaperone and no one will notice. If you had some family here in London, they could accompany you, of course."

"Well, I haven't been entirely honest about one point," she said slowly.

He went back to what he was doing. "What is that?" His voice was delightfully muffled.

"The folk of Derryton led you to believe that I have no family left at all . . . but I do."

He raised his head to look at her. "You do?"

She nodded. "I have a sort of uncle—rather half uncle, I suppose—here in London. Of course there are more relatives and such on his side of the family, but none of them have ever taken any notice of me. Only this one uncle, and only when I was very young, although he was fond enough of my mother. When my parents died of the fever, he sent me a letter of condolence and he asked if I wanted to come to live with him in London."

Nathaniel propped his head on his fist. "That was just what you always wanted, was it not?"

She shook her head. "No, not then. I'd lost so much—" She shrugged. "I couldn't bear the thought of leaving Moira, too. So I wrote him and asked if I could stay where I was. I told him that someday John wanted to own the inn himself and that he and Moira would be responsible parents to me. My uncle sent a man to buy the inn and give the deed to John." She lay back down. "He used to write to me. We were quite jolly correspondents for a time. Then his letters began to come less frequently, and finally not at all. Although I'm sure it isn't his fault. He's a very busy man."

"Do you think he will object to me?" Nathaniel said slowly. "I cannot ask you to go against your family's wishes."

Willa grabbed him by his open collar. "Don't you dare, Nathaniel Stonewell. You're not getting away from me that easily. It is far too late for anyone to object now. Besides, I'm sure my uncle will not object. I could have married Wesley Moss for all he cared, and Wesley was only a farmer's son."

"I'd forgotten about poor Wesley Moss." With a small laugh, Nathaniel shook his head. "Then that settles it. If your uncle was too busy to care for you properly, then I don't think much of him at all."

She blinked. "You don't?"

"No. So if you don't wish to contact him now that you're here, I'll understand completely."

She smiled. "Thank you. I do think it would only complicate things."

She curled into his arms. He held her close and the warmth grew between them. Suddenly Willa started again. "Oh! I forgot to ask you—"

Nathaniel chuckled helplessly. "What?"

"Kitty said Lord Etheridge obtained the invitation for this evening. She said he doesn't treat you badly, but he doesn't like you, either. I don't understand that."

"Dalton? He's having a little trouble forgiving me for something I did."

"What did you do?"

He shrugged, jostling her slightly. "I shot his wife."

She raised her head to look into his face, her eyes wide. "Shot?"

"I didn't mean to. I was trying to shoot him."

"Oh," she said faintly. "That makes perfect sense, of course."

"I mean, I was trying to miss him."

"Right. Because you weren't aiming at him."

"No, I was. I mean . . . Look, I can't really explain it."

"No, I don't imagine you can."

"Do you think me a villain now?"

She hesitated. Then she took a breath and smiled at him. "No," she said staunchly. "If you shot Clara, then I'm sure you had a very good reason."

"I truly did."

She nestled her head back onto his shoulder. "I'm sure."

They lay quietly for a while, wrapped in each other's arms. The night was ending around them, and the noises of a London morning were beginning to intrude. She was almost asleep when he nudged her.

"Willa?"

"Yes, love?" she murmured.

"It was an excellent reason."

"Yes, love."

"I simply wanted you to know that."

"I know, darling."

"Good night, Willa."

"Good night, Nate."

22

Nathaniel was gone when Willa awoke late that morning. Not only was he gone, but so was any evidence that he had ever been in her bedchamber. When she was dressed and on her way to find a bit of breakfast, she passed by his room. The door was open—well, unlocked anyway—so she peeked within. His chamber was vast, much larger than even her room, and composed of two rooms that she could see. Past the sitting room she could see a small portion of his heavily carved tester bed.

It had definitely been slept in. So he had not only left her before she woke, but he had also spent the remainder of the night in his own room.

He was simply being discreet, she told herself. Nothing more.

When she approached the top of the stairs, Lily rushed up to her. "Oh, my lady! Your new things! Everything is here!"

Willa gasped. New clothes! "Have it all brought up to my room. Fetch tea and toast for me, will you, Lily? And ask Myrtle if she would like to join me!" What fun! She was going to try on every single thing!

Myrtle appeared immediately, accompanied by Daphne

as well. Willa greeted the woman cheerfully enough, for this at least she and Daphne had in common.

It was a girlish whirl of mixing, matching, and trying on. Myrtle tried on every single hat, although they were all too large and slid down over her eyes. Even remote Daphne got into the spirit of it, advising Willa on which shawls and bonnets to pair with what outfits.

The tea and toast came and cooled before Willa remembered her hunger. Finally, she uncovered the tray to have a nibble while Lily sorted the hats back in their proper boxes, for Myrtle had gotten them all turned around, and Daphne decided which gown she thought Willa should wear to the ball that night. A folded news sheet accompanied the teapot and toast rack.

"Ooh, check it for the Voice of Society," caroled Myrtle. "It's spiteful. I like it."

Even Willa had heard of the tattle column by now, and she paged through the paper quickly. "Here it is!" She read the first line out loud. " 'We all know who wreaked havoc in the flock earlier this year, and last night he finally returned to the public eye—and who should be trailing behind him but a fleecy lamb, willingly headed for her slaughter.' " Willa paused, then continued more slowly. " 'Pretty lambkins cannot last long. Should we warn her that her guard dog is truly a wolf and is sure to eat her alive?' "

"Oh dear," Myrtle murmured.

Daphne shook her head sadly. "It is to be expected, I suppose."

Willa tossed the paper down with a sniff. "Awful. So inaccurate. Why do they bother?"

Myrtle patted her hand. "Don't take it so—"

"They're so wrong! Wolves travel in packs, for one thing. Nor do they eat as many sheep as people think. Sheep are very well guarded usually. Goats, now, there's a favorite meal. . . ." She went on in this vein for a moment, dwelling on a wolf pack's cooperative hunting methods. She was just getting to the moment of disembowelment when she paused, realizing that Myrtle and Daphne were watching her owlishly. She stopped, blushing. "I'm simply saying . . ." She trailed off.

"Well, you're nothing like a sheep," Myrtle said stoutly.

"Ewe," Willa said.

"What is it?" Myrtle peered down and patted her front. "Did I dribble?"

"*Ewe*." Willa shrugged. "An adult female sheep."

"Enough of that," Myrtle said sharply. "I know you're trying not to think about that awful batch of lies, so don't you try to distract me, missy!"

Slowly, Willa sank to sit among the piled boxes. "I know," she said sadly. "I didn't think it would happen overnight, but there isn't even a word in there about how fine he looked, or my gown, or anything that we worked so hard for."

"What are you talking about?" Daphne's pretty brows were pulled together. "You cannot believe that you can persuade Society to accept Nathaniel again?" She pressed a hand to her throat. "Do you even think that it could be *possible*?"

"Ha!" Myrtle crowed. "Yes, we can." She tossed the news sheet into the small fire in Willa's hearth. "Take that, you shifty creature!"

Slowly, Willa smiled at the two women. "Then I can count you in?"

The pristine white silk Court gown was pressed and donned—it fit just fine, from the wide gold-embroidered bands at the hem to the severely low beribboned bodice.

Thankfully, Kitty had chosen a tiara over a feathered turban. Willa wasn't sure she could manage a turban. As it was, she was tottering in the high-heeled slippers she needed to wear, for she could not imagine hemming Kitty's costly dress for one borrowed wearing.

Once in the Audience Chamber of St. James's Palace, Willa was reassured by the pale, pasty nervousness of the other debutantes. One girl began to weave on her feet. Her chaperone whipped out a vinaigrette and applied it like a true champion.

Willa breathed easier. She might be wobbly and unsure of her protocol, but she wasn't *that* nervous.

The wide doors at the other end of the chamber began to swing open and the crowd stirred. Willa peered through a forest of ostrich plumes, suddenly happy for her high heels. A stout, grandly dressed figure entered and everyone in the room swept into deep bows and curtsies. The Prince Regent waved a negligent hand at the audience and sat on the throne with a grunt.

"He doesn't look much like I pictured him all these years," Willa whispered to Myrtle when they straightened.

Myrtle nodded, her purple plumes bouncing. "Oh, but he was a handsome lad once. I remember watching him grow up looking like an angel half the time and a devil the other half."

Fascinating. "Really? Which one do you see now?"

Myrtle regarded the Prince, her gaze a bit sad. "I see a lonely man now, I think. Bored and lonely."

One by one, the painfully nervous girls were escorted to curtsy before the Prince Regent. Their names and antecedents were formally read aloud by a bewigged attendant, but George didn't look as though he was listening.

When it was her turn, Willa took a deep breath and moved forward, wobbling only slightly in her shoes. She curtsied so deeply that her nose nearly brushed the floor and she worried for her tiara's security.

"Miss Willa Trent," the attendant intoned, "of the . . ." There was a tiny pause. "Miss Willa Trent!" finished the man loudly, as if volume could make up for lack of information.

Willa held the pose, waiting for the Prince to respond to her name. When no response came, she broke form to glance up at His Royal Highness.

The bored royal gaze was planted firmly on her bosom. Willa straightened gracefully, but George maintained his idle perusal of her bodice. Finding him a bit more than royally rude, Willa cleared her throat sharply.

The Prince blinked and raised his gaze to her face. Willa sent him a swift wink and a "caught-you" smile. He grunted once in amused surprise, then examined her more closely.

The crowd murmured when the Prince waved away the usher who was preparing to lead Willa back to her place. Instead, the Prince motioned to the attendant who had read the presentation aloud. A brief whispered conversation took place, but Willa distinctly heard the bewigged man say "Reardon."

The Prince chuckled a bit at that and cast Willa a broad smile. Encouraged, Willa broke form once more when the usher led her away—she raised one hand to wiggle her fingers at the Prince Regent in a childish wave. The crowd's murmur increased when Prince George wiggled his plump fingers right back.

Myrtle shook her head at Willa once she'd returned to her side. "Best watch yourself around that one, dear. I don't think Thaniel would care to look aside from royal interference."

"Oh, nonsense, Myrtle. George was just being friendly."

Myrtle's brows rose nearly to her hairline. " 'George,' is it? When I told you I thought him lonely, I'd no intention of you doing anything to alleviate that loneliness!"

Willa shook her head, smiling. "Myrtle, you're being silly. The Prince Regent is old enough—old enough to be my uncle!"

Myrtle's eyes remained narrowed. "If I didn't know you were entirely mad about Nathaniel, I'd think you were flirting with His Royal Highness."

Willa laughed out loud. "Oh, Myrtle, what a notion." She smiled in the Prince's direction. "I was merely saying hello."

"Hmm. Well, it caused a storm of gossip, that's for certain. If you become a royal favorite, it will certainly be hard for people to disdain Nathaniel." Myrtle examined her closely. "Or is that your plan?"

Willa only smiled.

That evening, Nathaniel went down early to the ballroom. Basil had sent a message round to let him know that he wanted nothing to detract from Daphne's triumph. Unlike Kitty Knight, Daphne had no intention of playing on Nathaniel's notoriety. He was to arrive quietly and he was excused from his position in the family presentation line.

He did not blame her. Part of him still felt as though he owed Daphne. She had been supportive in her way, and he had rejected her only to marry another. He was willing to keep a lower profile than he had last night.

Not that that was truly possible. This was not the same crowd as had appeared last night, for this was Daphne's circle, but again, everyone was very carefully not meeting his eyes, although he knew that most of them were watching him. There were schoolmates and fellow members of the House of Lords and even a few old flames.

Nathaniel heard a familiar braying laugh and turned to look. Good lord, Finster was here, with powder apparently covering last night's damage. Thinking of Willa's none too subtle revenge, Nathaniel grinned at the man, astonishing him right out of his customary sneer.

Nathaniel heard a sudden murmur of surprise from the crowd to his left.

"I say, who is *that*?"

Idly curious, Nathaniel turned to see a stout lady whack her equally stout husband on the arm, evidently for staring at some young thing. Several people were craning their necks to see, but Nathaniel didn't bother. Whoever it was had nothing to do with him. He was simply grateful to have the spotlight taken from him.

Then the crowd parted, leaving a space right beside him. He glanced over but caught nothing but a glimpse of sea green silk and deliciously low décolletage framing a fabulous bosom. Then the crowd shut his window and he saw nothing more.

Still, that had been a lovely moment. He might be nearly married, but he most certainly was not dead, and a man would have to be cold in his grave not to notice such a delectable bustline.

In all his life, he had only seen one better, he mused. Willa's—

Wait a minute! He pushed into the crowd, following the whispers. That was *his* delectable bustline!

He caught another glimpse of green silk. Damn, if only she were taller! But then she wouldn't fit so perfectly under his chin when he held her in bed. . . .

Willa was drifting through the room, her smile fixed and her gaze sorting men as she passed. Where was Nathaniel? If he had left her in unfriendly territory again, she was going to hit him.

Suddenly she felt warm breath on her neck. Since this

was not the first time some man had come a bit too close in the last ten minutes, she was prepared for a quick toe stomp and elbowing.

"What in Hades are you wearing?"

She turned, her smile wide. "Nathaniel, you are here!"

"Of course I am. Now answer my question, damn it!"

She waggled a finger at him. "You're barking," she sang.

"Willa, go upstairs and change this instant."

She looked down. No, everything was still in place. She was as decent as any woman in the room. "Why? We just bought this dress. It was made just for me, remember?"

Willa in the blue dress had been lovely. Willa in the green . . . seductive.

He couldn't take his eyes off her. She was shown to perfection in the sea green silk. The neckline framed her bosom like the divine artwork it was. He didn't know what was keeping the silk from slipping down over her nipples, but he thought it might possibly be glue. Just beneath the bodice was a daringly wide band of black velvet, setting off the voluptuous line of her waist and hips to great advantage.

She wasn't fashionable in the slightest, but she looked devastating. Her hair was pulled up high and piled on her head. It was very proper but somehow made a man think about the sable strands spread out across his pillows.

She wore another band of black velvet around her throat punctuated by a delicate cameo. She wore nothing else in the way of jewelry, and Nathaniel realized that she had nothing else.

Not even a betrothal ring.

Dear God. He'd best step lively then. "Come. I must introduce you." He grabbed her hand and took off.

Towing her along, Nathaniel dragged her from chattering group to chattering group, introducing her so quickly that the men had no time to do anything but ogle and the women no time to do anything but wonder why they hadn't thought to wear something so dramatic.

No one cut Nathaniel and Willa, being far too curious and entirely too slow. They were there, and then they were gone. Not a whisper of the "broomstick bride" met Willa's ear; he was sure of it.

Finally, Nathaniel neared the end of the room and pulled her into a curtained alcove. "There," he said with satisfaction.

Willa was gasping for breath. "What . . . was that all about?"

"Just being as obvious as possible."

Willa wasn't sure, but she thought she might just have been insulted. She adjusted her glove carefully, then made a fist. "Explain."

He put up both hands, laughing. "No need to get violent, wildflower. I only meant that I wanted every man in that room to know that you are mine. You look entirely too delectable to go wandering about without my stamp on you."

He was jealous? He thought that other men would want her?

"Oh, Nathaniel!" She threw her arms around his neck, pulling him down for a kiss.

Before the blood left his brain entirely from the sensual rapture of her mouth, Nathaniel had only a moment to wonder what the kiss was for.

Both of their hands explored avidly, just as if they hadn't touched the same places only hours before.

"Why, Willa," gasped Nathaniel against her neck, "you're wearing a corset!"

"Mmm. Lily found it for me. It isn't . . . laced very tightly, but she said it would do a . . . marvelous job of . . . upholding things."

Nathaniel closed his eyes and groaned at the thought. "Promise me you'll wear it for me later."

She chuckled. "Just the corset?"

He shook his head. "No. How silly." He took a bite of her neck. "Stockings also, of course."

Then there were only sighs and groans and panting in the alcove.

Just when Nathaniel was learning how very skilled a seamstress the maker of the gown was, much to his frustration, he heard his name called. Pulling his hand from the breast that he had been unable to free from its iron cradle of silk and boning, he pulled away.

Willa opened slumberous eyes and blinked at him. "Did someone call you?"

"I think so." He tugged her bodice up and tucked a strand of her hair back atop her head. She was busy redoing the buttons on one side of his breeches that she had managed to get past.

Nathaniel took her hands away to finish the job for himself, or else he'd have to take her here in the alcove after all. With ruthless will, he managed to quell his monumental erection.

When they were more or less put back together, aside from her swollen lips and a slightly lopsided neckline, he took her hand.

"Shall we go see what the fuss is about?"

They didn't get far before a footman stopped them. Then Nathaniel dropped Willa's hand and ran for the stairs.

Randolph had suffered another attack.

23

Willa watched Nathaniel go, then headed for Daphne. She and Basil would want to break the news to their guests.

"No! Tell no one!" Daphne begged. "Basil has been so eager for this day. It will be absolutely ruined for him. After all, it just as easily could have happened after the ball, could it not?" Daphne raised a perfect brow.

Willa could only stare at her. Randolph fought for his life upstairs, yet all Daphne could think of was her social event? Daphne showed no worry. Her smile was as guileless as ever as she nodded genially at a pair of passing guests.

Willa watched her operate, appalled. Then she turned away. If Daphne wanted her ball that badly, then let her have it. Right now Willa should concern herself with the more sensitive members of the family.

"Hello, Willa. You are looking rather magnificent today." Myrtle smiled with satisfaction. "I'll wager that gown has Victoria in a hissing fit. Must have you consult on my next fitting."

She raised a wrinkled finger high. "Never too late to make a splash, I say. How do you think I'll look in green?"

Willa swallowed. She hated to wipe away Myrtle's good cheer. "Myrtle, it's . . . It's Randolph."

"Randolph?" The merriment was gone. "Is it—"

Willa shook her head quickly. "No, no I don't think so, not yet. But I believe it is quite serious."

Myrtle's face had fallen into its wrinkles, making her suddenly seem every bit of her years. Only her eyes were still bright, but bright with grief.

"I'll help you upstairs." With her arm around Myrtle, Willa headed for the great stairs.

"No. There's another way." Myrtle turned her in the other direction. "There's a shortcut up the servants' stairs."

In the hall outside the ballroom, Myrtle pressed upon a panel of the wall. It slid open to reveal a cramped, unadorned passage and staircase.

Willa blinked. So that was how the servants maneuvered so quietly and efficiently. This revelation made her wonder if on the occasions that she felt as if she was being watched, perhaps she had been.

The steps were a bit steep, but when they arrived on the floor where the family slept, the panel door slid back to reveal the hall immediately outside Randolph's room.

Willa was about to hurry through when Myrtle grasped her arm.

"Listen."

There was no need to listen too carefully, as the voices in the hall were very clear. Willa realized instantly that Nathaniel was speaking.

"Lord Liverpool, there is nothing to be done."

"Lord Liverpool? *The Prime Minister?*" she whispered to Myrtle, only to be hurriedly shushed.

"Myrtle, it isn't well done—"

Another voice, a dry and precise voice, speaking with more urgency. "Tell him."

"What?"

"Tell him the truth about your disgrace. It cannot matter now, so close to the end."

Willa leaned far enough to see Nathaniel. He was pale. As she watched, he closed his eyes. "I did," he said. He rubbed his hand over his face roughly and took a breath. "Months ago, after the entire affair, I told him. Not every detail, of course, but I told him that I had taken the blame for someone that needed protecting, and that I would never—" He stopped, breathing harshly.

"What did he say?" Liverpool asked quietly.

"He said he already knew everything he needed to know about me."

Willa's heart hurt for him. She had never heard him so anguished. She held very still now, listening every bit as hard as Myrtle was.

"So he will die thinking ill of me."

"Then perhaps it is for the best," Liverpool said grimly. "As a servant of the Crown, you should know that. This facade of traitor is incredibly valuable. Exposure now would waste everything."

Willa sank back, letting Myrtle have the door. She had been entirely right about her noble, brilliant Nathaniel. Thinking furiously, she sat on the top of the stairs. Why not simply tell the world what really had occurred?

There came a new voice, a man whom Willa didn't recognize.

"I'm afraid your father has worsened, Lord Reardon. He will never regain consciousness. I don't expect him to last the hour."

Too late. Willa's heart sank. It was too late now for Nathaniel to make his father understand.

Liverpool spoke. "Come, Doctor. I'll have someone show you out."

Nathaniel said not a word. Her hand pressed to her heart, Willa ached for him.

"Oh, dear Randolph, you straitlaced fool," murmured Myrtle. She climbed from the servants' passage, tears running down her face.

Willa scrambled out after her, then searched the hall for Nathaniel. He was just entering his father's rooms. She followed him through the sitting area, stopping before the bedchamber, where she could see the foot of the bed as he knelt beside it.

Willa could hardly bear the devastation on his face. She wanted to go to him.

If only she could be sure he wanted her there.

Closing the door carefully, Willa stepped back and walked slowly back into the hall, her gaze on the floor.

"You sour old gooseberry! You could have convinced Randolph!"

Willa looked up at the sharp cracking sound and registered that Myrtle had copped the Prime Minister a good one across the shins. Realizing that there was no one else in evidence, Willa hurried to Myrtle.

"Dear one, what are you doing?" She meant what was Myrtle doing attacking Lord Liverpool without reinforcements, but his lordship must have decided that Willa didn't know a thing about the recent conversation with Nathaniel.

"I'm afraid dear Mrs. Teagarden is overwrought with grief over her nephew," he said coolly. He grabbed Myrtle by the arm and swung her firmly to a point of safety before him, where the silver head of her cane could not reach. Then he reached for a bellpull.

Two footmen appeared, evidently by magic, and each took one of Myrtle's arms gently.

Pulling his dignity back together with a tug on his silk waistcoat, Lord Liverpool nodded to them sharply. "Help Mrs. Teagarden back to her room, there's the lads. I believe we may have to administer a soporific. The poor woman is quite overcome."

Willa ran to Myrtle. "Dear, are you all right?"

There were tears in the old woman's eyes, and she sagged in the grasp of the footmen. She whispered something to Willa.

Leaning close on the pretext of settling the woman's cap, Willa glanced at Lord Liverpool. He was adjusting his coat, his attention on his dignity. "What, Myrtle? I didn't hear."

"You don't know a thing. Pretend you don't know a thing."

Then the footmen helped Myrtle away, and Willa was left with the Prime Minister.

She wasn't much of a liar, but she was an excellent pretender. Willa pretended that she knew nothing before seeing Myrtle attack.

"Good heavens, my lord! What was that all about?"

She pretended not to see the way his gaze went shrewd, and she pretended not to shiver at the way he looked down the hall, ice in his gaze.

"I haven't the faintest idea."

It wasn't supposed to be this way. The estrangement was only supposed to have been temporary. But he had been so pained by his family's immediate acceptance of the story, their instantaneous belief in his cowardice. It had stung him badly that his father could turn his back the way he had.

So Nathaniel had turned away as well. Away from his father, away from Daphne, away from the glint of rabid enjoyment in Basil's eyes.

Randolph's room had taken on the stillness of an empty chamber. Before, even when he had been sleeping, he had been present. It was different now. Nathaniel sat in the chair next to his father's bedside, the same chair that he had taken at odd late hours during the last few nights.

"You don't look good, sir." Nathaniel took one of his father's wasted hands. "You don't look good at all."

His stepfather's hand was tragically unlike his own. Although Randolph was only in his sixties, his flesh had the papery look of extreme age and the bones showed through the loose-fitting skin.

Still, it was the same hand that Nathaniel had swung on when he was six, the one that had stung like the dickens on his rear when he was twelve, and the one that had shaken his like a man for the first time when he was sixteen.

He closed his eyes, trying to picture his father before him, hale as ever.

"We wasted so much time, you and I. I was too proud. You were too reserved."

He took his father's hand back between his own two. It was cool, and Nathaniel felt as if he should warm it.

"Willa is no Daphne. Thank God. She is unlike any woman I have ever known. At first, you think she is a scatty creature, the way she says the oddest things. Then when you start to listen, you realize that she has a way of looking at the world as if it is a giant gift, handed to her done up in ribbon, and she is unwrapping it one delightful layer at a time."

He shook his head. "That makes her sound like a child, but she has seen hardship, as much as any of us. She has merely chosen not to hide there in the pain but to bloom from it."

His father's hand was a little warmer now, so Nathaniel placed it gently under the covers and sat on the bed to reach the other one. Now that he was closer, he could see the bluish tinge to his father's lips and the weak way his chest scarcely moved with each breath.

"You're leaving soon, aren't you? I understand. I just didn't want you to go thinking that I had failed you." He paused. "Whether you believe me or not, I never did."

He sat for a while then in silence, watching Randolph's stillness. Nathaniel almost felt as though if he took his eyes from the slight movement of his father's chest, it would stop altogether.

And then it did stop.

Nathaniel waited a moment and watched, not wanting to believe. Then he put down his father's hand that would never be warm again and bent to kiss him on the brow.

Nathaniel could feel cool duty taking over the sorrow. In a way, it was a relief. He could do something about the mission, about Foster, but there was no way to dispel the awful knowledge that he would never hear his father's voice again, that he would never tell him something new that he had done and see the flash of humor and approval in his father's eyes.

The door opened into the chamber, and Victoria entered. Still dressed in her finery, as they all were. But her eyes were dry and her face untouched by lines of sorrow.

"Hello, Mother. He is gone. You may commence to pretend to grieve."

Her eyes glittered. "I grieve," she snapped. "Randolph has been my husband for thirty years." She turned to gaze down at the man in the bed for a long silent moment.

When she turned back to Nathaniel, there was nothing but cool composure about her. "I would appreciate your continued discretion this afternoon. Daphne and Basil are the triumph of the Season. There is no need to break it up for this."

Nathaniel nodded, his lips twisting sardonically. "Of course, Mother. Anything for Basil."

Victoria's eyes narrowed. "You should be grateful for his tolerance of you. He said that perhaps you could redeem the shame you brought down on all of us."

Nathaniel did not look at his father again. He was gone. "Why bother?" Nathaniel said without expression, then turned and left the room.

Willa waited outside Randolph's rooms, unsure of her place in all this. Should she join Nathaniel and his mother in their grief?

Although Victoria had appeared none too grief-stricken when she passed Willa in the hallway without so much as a nod of acknowledgment. Consequently, Willa had sat herself down in one of the embroidered chairs that graced the hall at frequent intervals, and waited.

When the door to the sickroom burst open and Nathaniel emerged, she jumped to her feet. "Is everything—"

He brushed past her, not seeing her at all.

"Nathaniel? Nathaniel!"

He finally paused at her call. "I need to be alone, Willa." He spoke over his shoulder, not turning in the slightest. "I will spend the evening in my study."

"Oh. I just wanted to help—"

"Help Myrtle. There is nothing you can do for me." His voice was cool. Then he was gone, his long strides and clenched fists illustration enough of his barely controlled fury.

Willa watched him go, her shoulders slumping. She wanted so much to comfort him, but she had never felt less like a wife.

"Why in the world did you marry him? I know you are only the daughter of a scholar, and shire bred to boot, but surely you could have done better." Victoria's melodious voice drawled mockingly over her shoulder as she passed Willa. She paused to look back, as if to relish the devastation caused by her remark.

There was no sting at all. What these people thought of her meant nothing. Willa shook her head, looking Victoria in the eye. "I know that you are as cold as a reptile, and shallow to boot, but surely you could have done more."

Then she turned her back on Victoria's sputtering and went to find Myrtle.

Willa slipped quietly into Myrtle's grand chambers. The carpet was thick, and she made not a sound as she crossed the luxurious sitting room to a door she thought might be that of the bedchamber.

She didn't want to wake Myrtle. She only wanted to reassure herself. Randolph's death had to upset Myrtle. She was such a saltbox that one sometimes forgot how fragile she truly was.

Willa stuck her nose into the room, then crossed to the giant curtained bed. Tiptoeing to the slit between curtains, Willa hooked one finger into them to take a peek.

She did not expect to see the intrepid little elf sitting tailor-fashion in the center of the bed, picking through a giant box of chocolates. Myrtle popped a bonbon into her mouth and cut her eyes at Willa.

"Hop on in. If you want one of these you had best hurry."

Willa sat on the edge of the mattress. "You should be ashamed. I've been so worried. Victoria thinks you are on your deathbed."

"Oh, I am. I've been on my deathbed for years. Boring as hell, deathbeds. Can never lie there very long before I get a bug in my bustle."

"Aunt Myrtle, you astound me."

"Sweet pea, when you get older, you'll stop playing their games and play your own. You shall see. Of course, you're smarter than I was. You married money young.

You'll have all the fun I didn't have until I met my Beauregard." She looked unbearably sad for a moment. Then she snickered. "Beauregard would have loved this next bit."

"What next bit?"

"The bit where I change my will. They're still dancing downstairs, you know."

"Change *your* will? I thought Basil was Nathaniel's heir?"

"Oh, he's the heir to the title and the estate. And Thaniel is certainly wealthy." Myrtle gave a small evil smile. "But I'm wealthier. Much wealthier. Without my money, and with his gambling problem, Basil will be nothing in a few years. Land-rich, cash-poor." She snickered again. "I cannot wait to see Daphne's face."

"Now, Aunt Myrtle. I don't like her, either, but if she has been counting on this inheritance, don't you think it is unfair to withhold it?"

"She has never been in my will. Only Randolph. I held Randolph on my knee when he was a baby. I loved that boy to pieces."

The faded blue eyes dimmed further behind unshed tears. "And do you know what that bitch Victoria did? She killed him. She killed him as surely as if she had tossed him from the Tower with her own hands."

"But I thought it was his heart—"

"Yes. His heart. His heart that his physician warned him about last winter. His heart that should never have made the journey to London in the spring. His doctor told him not to, that he couldn't take the strain of travel."

Myrtle narrowed her eyes. "But Victoria couldn't miss the Season, he said. Victoria insisted on coming to the balls and the soirees and salons, even if it killed her husband to do so."

She drew out her minuscule scrap of lace and dabbed

at her eyes. "And it has. It's killed him dead."

"I am so sorry."

Myrtle sighed, then shook her head. "Everyone dies, sweet pea. I have seen so many family and friends die in my lifetime. Randolph was in pain, every breath an agony. It was a mercy."

"I see."

"And all that is left is the living. And the money. With Randolph passing, I must contact my solicitor immediately. Besides, it is my money to do with as I please."

"I suppose," said Willa doubtfully.

"Well, what about you? You and Thaniel—Nathaniel. Don't you want some?"

"No," Willa said firmly.

"Not a bit of it?"

"Not one cent. Not if it means you must die first."

"Why, sweet pea, I do believe that's the nicest thing anyone's said to me in years."

"Well, don't get all slobbery on me. Can't bear sentiment," Willa snapped in a perfect parody of Myrtle herself, which sent the elder lady off in a flood of cackles.

"Oh, Willa, you do keep a body young."

"Good. Stay with me and you shall live forever."

"You know, for the first time in years, I wish I could. I truly would love to see how you turn out, pet." She peered at what Willa had in her hands. "Did you bring me something?"

"I brought a book I thought you'd like." Willa showed her the worn volume. "It's one of my favorites."

"Oh, sweeting, my eyes don't work as well as they used to."

"I was going to read it to you, anyway," Willa assured her. "It's a translation I did myself, so you likely couldn't decipher my crabbed little notes in the margins."

Myrtle tilted her head to look at it more closely. "What is it about?"

"It's a marvelous fiction, full of adventure and intrigue." Willa opened the small book and began to read.

" 'Every ruler needs a few men he can count on . . .' "

24

The fortunate thing about training to be a spy was that one learned so many useful skills.

The man outside Reardon House crept quietly to the coal chute on the side wall. A nice bit of flammable rag, a quick strike of his flint and steel, bend, lift, throw—run. He wasn't fast at all after all he'd been through recently, but it mattered little. By the time his little present caught, he'd be out of sight, poised for his next move.

He let the lid of the chute down gently, silently, and stumbled down the darkened alley behind the mews until he was lost in the shadows.

Such a handy skill.

Nathaniel had been staring into the fire in his study for hours but had found no answers in the flames. He had been prepared for Randolph's death for some time, so why was it so shocking? Obviously, he'd been unable to conceive of a world without his stepfather—

"My father, damn it!"

He would not trouble himself to use the proper address ever again. No one was left who cared, anyway. Randolph had been the only father, the only example, the only hero, Nathaniel had ever known. That was a good enough definition for him.

He rubbed his head, his mind drawn back to that day so many years ago. He'd been trying to annoy Simon into a fight—God, what a poisonous snot he had been as a young man!—but Simon had simply walked away.

So Nathaniel had followed him. Simon hadn't been much older himself then and had perhaps not been as careful about being trailed as he ought to have been. It had not been easy and Nathaniel had nearly lost him a half-dozen times, but that only made him work harder. He'd been a lazy lout. If it had been simple, he likely would have quickly become bored and gone on his way. Simon's very elusiveness inspired Nathaniel's curiosity until nothing could have stopped him.

Nathaniel had seen Simon approach a building, then pass directly past the front door. Then he'd followed the older man down an alley and watched him clamber easily up a wall and disappear through a window.

The route was much harder than it looked. Thinking back, Nathaniel was surprised he hadn't fallen to his death trying to figure out the hidden handholds and false window locks.

Then he'd been inside the club, in a storage room. His own audacity had sobered him so that he decided that he would only look around in order to find another way out. He would have gone back out the window if he dared, but he didn't.

It was when he'd been poking around the shabby hallway that he smelled it. Randolph was fond of a certain mix of tobacco that he had blended just for him. It had a distinctive sweet smell. Nathaniel followed it, realizing that he had found the place where his father spent all his time.

When Nathaniel caught a whiff of tobacco smoke coming from under a seemingly featureless wall, he knew there must be a way in.

He hadn't found it then, nor for years later. Not until last year had he found his way into the secret office of the Liars' spymaster. But he'd never forgotten the sense of frustration and betrayal that he'd felt, being locked out of that secret office.

Then he'd been forced to wander the club, hiding from footsteps, listening at doors, before he dared go further. That's when he'd made his discovery.

His father was a Crown spy. A hero. A fascinating, admirable, glittering hero.

From that point on, all Nathaniel had ever wanted to do was earn his father's respect. He'd turned his back on his peevish, wastrel ways without a moment's hesitation. His father was a hero, and he would be one, too.

So he improved himself in every way he could imagine, improving his mind, training in sports, horses, shooting— any skills that seemed useful for a spy. Then he waited to be invited into the Liar's Club—into that secret office.

It took some time before Nathaniel realized that his father had never noticed the change in him.

But Lord Liverpool had.

Weary of the past, Nathaniel took a deep breath—

Smoke?

He ran to the closed door of his study and flung it open. Thick, choking smoke was filling the hallway beyond even as he watched. "*Fire!*" he bellowed. "*Fire!*"

Then he was up the stairs and into Willa's bedchamber in a matter of seconds. He threw Willa's wrapper to her. "Quickly! Don't spare the time to dress!"

She ran after him, after swiftly throwing on her nightdress, *then* the wrapper. Burning to death tended to pale next to having a stiff breeze blow her wrapper askew!

Nathaniel ran through the house, making sure everyone was roused and making their way outside. He pushed Willa after them. "Go to the back garden and wait for me," he shouted over the confusion. "I must see that the maids in the attic are all cleared out."

As she stood in the damp yard with the other female occupants of Reardon House, she tried not to let the enormous amounts of smoke billowing from the open doors and windows worry her.

"You'd best not die, Nathaniel Stonewell," she muttered fiercely to him through the walls of the house. "I have plans for you." Without taking her eyes from the doorway through which he disappeared, she crossed the yard to join Myrtle, Victoria, and a clinging Daphne.

"Is it very hazardous in there?" Daphne asked, her eyes on the house. "Do you think he's in danger?"

Willa saw how pale the blond woman was and how her anxiety was betrayed by chewing on her lower lip. So, cool, remote Daphne cared after all. Willa could not feel jealous, for Nathaniel paid no attention to Daphne at all. Poor Daphne.

Then Willa remembered Nathaniel's cool dismissal of her earlier in the evening.

Poor Willa.

It seemed years but was likely only minutes before Nathaniel emerged from the smoky depths of the house with the female servants. They came coughing and sooty, but they all came safe.

Willa flung her arms about him. "I know it couldn't have been the jinx this time," she told him with a watery smile.

He set her on her feet without a word to her. "It was merely vandals," he told the throng. "They dirtied the wallpaper, but there was nothing irreplaceable lost."

As the relieved household made its way back inside, Willa looked around. "Where is Mr. D—Mr. Porter?"

Nathaniel looked grim. "I'd say halfway to the docks by now. He wrapped the burning linen tightly enough to keep it smoldering for hours, then tossed the lot down the coal chute. If it hadn't rolled off the coals onto the kindling, we'd still be trying to put it out."

Willa frowned. "What makes you so sure it was Ren Porter?"

Nathaniel waved a hand in the general direction of the dining room. "Well, he—"

Willa plunked her hands on her hips. "Did you even check his room, or did you just leave the poor man to burn to death?"

Abject horror turned Nathaniel white beneath his smudges. The breath left his body in a rush, and he could only stare at her in dismay.

He bolted back into the house, taking the corner so fast that the carpet buckled and slid beneath his feet.

He heard Willa calling for him to wait, but he wasn't planning on slowing down until he had proved to himself that he hadn't left a lung-sick man to die from smoke inhalation.

The rest of Nathaniel's run through the house was a blur, but he was vaguely aware that his following was growing. More voices and footsteps rose behind him at every room he passed.

He flung open the door to Ren's chamber, letting it resound with a crash against the wall.

There was no one in the bed, no one in the still-smoky room. Nathaniel sagged gratefully against the doorjamb. At least he didn't have that on his consc—

"Is it over?" A creaking voice came from the curtained window embrasure.

In two long strides, Nathaniel crossed to the window

and yanked open the draperies. Ren Porter was sprawled half on the window seat, half angled out the window. The cold night air was streaming over him, but his face and body were wet with perspiration.

"Good God, man! You'll catch your death!" Nathaniel hauled him back into the room. "You there!" He gestured to a footman. "Get those pots steaming again! Build up that fire."

"Oh no," Ren protested faintly. "Not more fire."

Nathaniel wrestled Ren gently into the bed again. "God, I'm so sorry I left you here. I thought—"

Ren coughed, then sent Nathaniel a wry, haggard grin. "You thought I'd given it another go?" He snorted. "Reardon, it's all I can do to use the chamber pot right now."

"I'm sorry. I'm so sorry." Nathaniel rubbed his face. "I could have killed you!"

"I kill you. You kill me." Ren shrugged. "I'd say we're even."

"You don't want me dead any longer?"

"Well, I wouldn't mourn you, but no, I don't think I feel quite so murderous anymore." Ren stared at him for a long moment. "To be truthful, I have my doubts about your treason."

Nathaniel straightened. "If you would keep those doubts to yourself, I would greatly appreciate it."

Ren's eyes narrowed. "Hmm. I thought as much." He glanced at the industrious footmen. Then he stroked one hand over the counterpane. "Nice *cover*," he said meaningfully. "I used to have one very much like it."

Nathaniel's lips twitched. Ren's file had revealed that on his last mission he'd been playing the disillusioned young lout ripe to be recruited for a bit of treason. "Thank you," he replied. "I can arrange for you to have another if you'd like."

Ren's gaze flew to his. He took a deep breath, then another. "Not—not yet."

Nathaniel nodded once. "I understand."

He left the room, feeling quite a bit lightened by the fact that in the entire world there was one less person who hated him.

Then again, tonight's fire was evidence that there were still some who did.

Willa stood in the doorway of her bedchamber, shocked at the state of the room.

Nathaniel came up behind her. "Your linens will be too smoky to sleep on. I have someone bringing fresh ones from the—"

He stopped, obviously as appalled as she was.

The room was a shambles. Her things were everywhere, tossed about in complete abandon. Books lay open on the floor, pages aflutter. Her lovely new clothing was strewn and trampled. Willa went to one side of the bed and knelt to pick up the shattered remains of Dick's squirrel carving. The vindictiveness in that single bit of destruction made her feel sick to her stomach.

Nathaniel moved swiftly through the room, checking any possible hiding places. Cradling the splinters of wood in her hands, Willa stood to gaze at the mess around her. "Something isn't right," she murmured.

Nathaniel began to gather some of the books from the floor. Lily came in with a fresh stack of bed linens, gasped at the madness, then swiftly began to salvage Willa's new clothes. Willa stood very still, thinking. Nathaniel examined a book he'd taken from the floor. "Why do you have Jeremy Cunnington's *Mathematical Concepts*?"

"I liked what he said about the golden mean," Willa

said absently. Then she looked down at him. "Are the books ruined?"

Nathaniel looked around him. "I don't think so. A few small tears, possibly, but nothing irreparable."

Willa turned to Lily. "Are my clothes ruined?"

Lily wrinkled her nose. "Well, I don't think I'll ever get the smoke smell out of Mrs. Knight's Court gown . . . but no, they're mostly just thrown about."

"Searched," Nathaniel corrected. "They look like they were searched."

"Precisely," Willa said, nodding. "If the intruder was simply looking for something, then why this?" She held out the remains of the carving.

"Willa," Nathaniel said sternly. "I think the more important question is . . . what were they looking for in *your* room and no one else's?" He folded his arms and stared at her as if he'd never seen her before. "Is there something I should know?"

Willa looked up at him in confusion. "I—I don't know why. . . . I don't even know what they were after!"

"No?" He stepped aside. "Why don't you go through your possessions and tell me if there is anything unaccounted for."

It didn't take long. "No," she said finally. "Nothing has been stolen. The carving is the only thing I lost."

"Are you sure?" His question was curt and detached.

"Nathaniel, I have very few possessions in the world. It isn't very hard to keep track." She looked around her at her tidied room. "Nothing is missing."

Nathaniel forced himself to relax. Willa didn't seem to be lying. There may have been something she had possession of without realizing it was important, but if nothing had been stolen, it was hard to imagine the intruder had found what they were looking for.

Lily made up the fresh sheets and Willa climbed wearily

into bed. It had been a very long day. "Was it only this morning that I was presented at Court?" she asked Lily.

"Aye, my lady. And only this evening that His Lordship's stepfather passed on."

"It seems like forever," Willa said sleepily.

Nathaniel stood just outside Willa's slightly open door, listening. He hated that he had to suspect Willa like this, but there was something going on that he was strongly beginning to suspect was connected with her.

Upon arriving in England, Foster had ridden hell-bent for leather, straight to Derryton. Then after spending the night in the inn—

"Bad enough that Dan here mucked up her packing. Made a right mess, he did."

"No, mum! Her room was already—"

"Nonsense," Moira scolded. *"Shame on you, blamin' Willie, and her bein' as neat as a pin!"*

Willa's room had been a mess before her guardian's son had packed her things. Willa's room in the inn—where Foster was staying.

Apparently Foster had not found what he wanted, for he'd then turned toward London and taken no care to cover his trail. And now Willa's room in Reardon House had been ransacked as well.

It seemed he'd attracted Foster's attention after all.

There was a public house on the docks, a place too rough for anyone not already guilty of a few major crimes. The floor was not really made of dirt. It only looked that way because of the decades of grime that carpeted it. The trestle tables had been broken in brawl after brawl until patrons had to be careful where they put their elbows, so as not to get splinters.

The ale was foul, the tavern maids fouler.

This establishment went by the unlikely name of The Red Squirrel.

Sir Foster had finally made contact, just not in the way Nathaniel had expected. Nevertheless, the message had been unmistakable. Too bad about Willa's carving.

Nathaniel swaggered into the tavern and took a seat at one of the rough tables. His manner was crude and grim, his clothing rough and dirty. He'd fouled his long hair and let it string down over his eyes.

He still looked far better than most of the clientele. After all, he still had both his eyes.

Nathaniel curled his fist, watching the way his fingers wrapped around his nearly empty tankard. He wasn't drinking so much as splashing the stuff into his face and letting it run down his stubble, then ostentatiously wiping his mouth on his arm.

He tossed his empty tankard onto the floor as was the custom here. The ale maids kept the tankards running in fast circulation. The next one he got had dirt on the rim.

Of course. Washing the tankards would have a deleterious effect on the patrons' drinking speed.

Tonight, it suited him to be in the roughest, most anonymous place one could find. Unfortunately, it was a very quiet night in this den of iniquity. Most of the patrons sat sullenly drinking and watching the barmaids bustle past.

The woman nearest Nathaniel smiled at him, and he nodded politely, although he wasn't interested. He'd sooner sleep with Blunt. He'd much sooner sleep with Willa.

He was working. There was no place in his work for thoughts of Willa. He needed to be the Cobra. Focused. Committed. Obsessed.

Someone stumbled into his bench, and Nathaniel gave him a halfhearted shove before he sent the last of

Nathaniel's ale to the floor. It hadn't been much of a push, but the fellow turned and shoved another patron, who sprawled across the laps of several other patrons, knocking at least one barmaid off someone's knee.

Someone took offense at the interruption of his negotiations, someone else took offense at his offense, and the brawl was on.

Now, there was a thought. A good fight would take the edge off the burning in Nathaniel's gut. Still, it wasn't right to make someone else pay for his troubles. It still lacked a few hours until dawn, but Nathaniel didn't think Foster was going to show.

Nathaniel stood, moving just in time to keep from being smashed by the body that was flung down onto his splintery table.

"What's the matter?" the man cried up at Nathaniel through the crimson flood from his broken nose. "Get up and fight, ye bloody *coward!*"

That tore it. With great satisfaction, Nathaniel grabbed the man by the collar and gave him a thudding blow to the belly.

"Aye, that's the way," wheezed the man. And landed a beauty of a right to Nathaniel's jaw.

As he landed blow after blow, and took a few as well, Nathaniel threw himself fully into the fray. Yes, indeed, a good fight really fit the bill.

Until one wiry bearded individual pulled a knife on him.

"There now!" Nathaniel raised both hands. "There's no need for that, good sir!"

The man said nothing, only turned his back to the brawl behind them and focused his attentions on Nathaniel. He took a hard swipe with the knife. Nathaniel sucked in his belly just enough that the blade only snagged a button off his rough workingman's jacket that he'd worn to blend in.

The next swipe caught the wool of the jacket itself. Damn! This bloke was entirely serious!

Nathaniel became serious, too. He didn't want to kill the man but would if he had to. He tried one more time to placate the fellow. "I've got some coin. You could take it all and good travels—"

The knife cut through his rough wool weskit like it was bread. He even felt a scratch on his skin. "Oh, now that is simply too much!"

Reaching behind him, he grabbed a sturdy chair and swung it at his opponent.

The fellow went down like a hammered bull. The now-unconscious man's cap was knocked off and his distinctly bald head revealed. Nathaniel blinked. *Foster.*

25

Nathaniel still had not come home. His room was waiting for his return. The fire crackled, the bed was turned back, his dressing gown was laid out, but he was nowhere to be seen.

Willa had waited in her room for hours; then she had come in here. Trailing her fingers along the mattress of the bed, she touched the dark green silk dressing gown laid across the foot of it. Picking it up, she let the silk slip through her hands until she held the lapels, then she brought it to her face.

It smelled of him, of tobacco and a hint of sandalwood, and Nathaniel. He had done no shopping for himself when they had arrived. This must be from before.

She would have liked to have known him before. Had he laughed more easily then? she wondered. Had he captivated every woman he met the way he had captivated her?

She slid the dressing gown over her nightgown, pulling the lapels up to her face again. It engulfed her, the sleeves hanging off her hands and the hem trailing on the floor, but she wore it anyway. She wanted to feel as close to him as possible.

Restless, she left his room and wandered the hall. She

ended up near Ren's room and decided to check on his fever.

Ren could not sleep. It was very late, he knew, for he could hear the chiming of a clock in some other room. His head was aching most seriously.

He had stubbornly refused a dose of laudanum before the footman who was seeing to him had retired for the night. The man had shrugged and set the bottle on a chest across the room. It might as well have been across the Channel, for all the good it did Ren.

At least, he had remembered to ask the man for a shave, and he had been surprised afterward to see in the mirror he had been given that it made him look much more civilized.

He shifted again, and the pain sent bright points of light before his vision. He held very still, not even breathing, until the pounding faded and his sight cleared. Then he blinked.

An angel stood before him. It was Willa, with only the light of a candle to illuminate her beauty. He lost his breath entirely at the vision in front of him.

Her hair was down, falling shining past her shoulders. She was fully covered by a wrapper, but simply seeing her in her nightclothes seemed exquisitely intimate.

After she had left this morning, Ren had come to the sobering realization that he didn't care if she was married. He would take whatever crumbs of herself she was willing to toss him, if only she would come to him again.

He smiled at her uncertainly and made the heedless mistake of trying to sit up the better to see her.

The pain took him by the neck and slammed him down again, making his stomach churn and his teeth clench until he thought they would shatter.

The room took a trip around his brain until the shapes

blended and smeared. He shut his eyes tightly and simply tried to bear the ride until he was allowed off again.

When the world ceased spinning and his stomach ceased churning, he was able to define the cool, soothing pressure on his brow as Willa's palm. She was speaking softly to him, calming nonsense words that one would speak to a wounded wild creature.

He opened his eyes and saw what he had longed to see all the endless day just past. She was inches above him, her sable hair falling from her shoulder to caress his cheek.

"Your fever is high," she whispered, and her breath was a gentle summer breeze across his lips.

Willa was worried. He was flushed and seemed very dazed. What should she do? He seemed to be in a great deal of pain. She glanced quickly around the room and spotted the bottle the doctor had left. Some fool had put it far out of Ren's reach.

Quickly she took it up, and the spoon beside it, and poured a bit for him. "I don't know how much to give you, but we can start with a spoonful and see if it will help you."

He swallowed it gratefully, his eyes closing.

Gently, she raised his shoulders to plump the pillows behind him. Lying flat was not helping his breathing.

The laudanum was working as well, making him float above the pain, aware of it but not affected by it.

He opened his eyes and smiled at her. "Incredible."

She smiled back. "You are feeling better?"

"No. Yes. I meant, you are incredible."

She really smiled then, a full, sweet smile that took his breath away.

"I—" He stopped himself in horror.

Good God, he'd almost said he loved her. The laudanum

was taking over his mind. He barely knew her, had scarcely spoken to her, and had spent most of that occasion being an ass.

But she was so incredible. And she was here with him again.

"Out of pity." He realized he had spoken the words out loud.

She looked at him for a moment, then shook her head. "I don't pity you. You are admirable, and intelligent, and somewhat arrogant, but you are not pitiful."

Admirable? "I tried to kill your husband."

"But you didn't. You came here to act on your convictions, even though you are mistaken. That I admire."

"I am a monster. A wreck of a man."

She tilted her head, considering his scars with disconcerting frankness. He did not turn away. Let her see what he had become.

"You do look much improved tonight. If you're more comfortable, I should probably go."

"No!" God, he sounded desperate, but he didn't care. "Stay, please."

"Very well, then, listen carefully. To me, you are not a monster, or a cripple, or any of the other things you like to call yourself. You are a fine, admirable man who has been through much, and it shows on you. That is all."

She cocked her head. "If I cut off my hair, would I stop being who I am?"

"It is hardly the same—"

Her cool fingers landed on his lips, stopping his words. "You must listen."

He wanted to kiss her fingertips but did not. She leaned close to him, placing her hand on his face once more. "You are *not* a beast."

Aching longing merged with the laudanum. He reached

for her, tugging her down with his fingers gently twined in her hair, and pressed his mouth dreamily to hers. The laudanum bottle slid from her hand to the carpet with a thump.

When she gently but firmly pulled away from him, there were tears in her eyes.

"I love Nathaniel," she said.

But she didn't look happy about it.

"Then where is he?"

She shook her head sharply and stood. "Good night, Ren Porter."

The door closed softly behind her. "Good night, Lady Reardon," he whispered.

Nathaniel delivered Sir Foster to Lord Liverpool's private residence.

Liverpool was outraged. He stood in his front hall in a russet dressing gown and nightcap. "You brought him *here*?"

Nathaniel grimaced. His face hurt and his clothing had been sliced to ribbons, letting in a distinct draft. He was in no mood. "Have you seen what I have living in *my* house?"

He passed Foster to Liverpool's men with cool indifference. He had lost so much, simply to find this man—

He pulled Foster back with a hard grip on his arm. "Foster," he shouted at the nearly unconscious man. "The fire, Foster—was that you?"

Foster blinked fuzzily at him. "Coal chute."

Nathaniel tossed him back to the footmen. "That was him. Find out what he's been looking for."

He turned to go.

"Reardon! I thought the idea was we would follow him to the Chimera?"

"He poses an immediate danger." To Willa. "I'd recommend locking him up tight and finding out what he knows about this mysterious item from Maywell's notes."

Liverpool cleared his throat. "I would speak to you for a moment."

Nathaniel turned. "You know, my lord, you still maintain a commanding manner, even in your nightshirt."

Liverpool's lips twitched, but Nathaniel defied anyone to identify a sense of humor in the Prime Minister. He followed the man into a very nicely appointed study. Liverpool sat behind a massive desk. Nathaniel declined taking a seat or even standing before him like a wayward servant. Instead, he wandered the room, poking at a globe, checking for dust on portrait frames. . . ." Your housekeeper has my compliments."

"I'm sure she'll be happy to hear it," Liverpool said drily. "I want to speak to you about this 'broomstick bride' I've been reading about."

"I wouldn't say that phrase again if I were you," Nathaniel said mildly.

"All right," Liverpool said easily. Too easily. Nathaniel watched him closely.

"I don't know precisely what happened to you on this mission, and frankly, I don't care. This could be an excellent opportunity to cement your position in Society."

Since Nathaniel's position in Society ranged somewhere between back-alley mutt and sewer scum, this did not sound promising for either Willa or himself.

"I was rather hoping we could uncement my position in Society, now that Foster is in custody."

Liverpool pursed his thin lips. "Need I remind you that I have yet to enter into negotiations with Louis Wadsworth for his information on the French Minister Talleyrand? I have not yet decided Louis's fate, but if his father's treachery becomes public, I will lose a very valuable bargaining chip."

And if Nathaniel was a hero, it would follow in the public eye that Wadsworth wasn't. "So what is this plan of yours?"

"Send that woman away. We'll tell the world that she couldn't bear you and left you to live in shame and seclusion in the country. Isn't there a cottage on Reardon land she could have?"

It was all beginning to sound a bit familiar to Nathaniel. "She won't do it." He smiled. "She's taken a fancy to me."

He folded his arms. "Besides, you once told me that the Royal Four should be married and settled. That it made them much less the object of curiosity."

"Oh no, that is indeed true. We must never be perceived to be at all mysterious. Even you. That is why it is best to have you safely off the Marriage Mart. There would always be some ambitious mama thinking that if only she could paint you in a different light, her daughter could marry a lord."

Nathaniel frowned. "Then you confuse me, Robert."

But Liverpool was thinking. "Yes, that will do nicely! To cement your reputation as Lord Treason, you should cause her to reject you—leave you quite publicly even. Send her back to her country life, Nathaniel. She'll be happier there."

"She's happy with me."

"She is now. It's the first flush of love. Anything seems possible, even surviving overpowering scandal for the rest of your life. Do you truly want that for her? If you care about the girl at all, you'll do it and do it gladly."

Nathaniel closed his eyes tightly, but he could not block out the truth of what Liverpool was saying.

The Prime Minister's voice softened slightly. "I know how you've suffered under this pretense and I commend

your sacrifice. Yet, how can you truly defend this idea of
yours to keep her? She had no conception of the future
she was tying herself to. I do not see how you can bear to
hold her to it."

Liverpool was right. There would always be another fire,
another mudslinging, another encounter with a bully like
Finster. Sooner or later, it would not be mud or harsh
words or smoky distraction. Eventually, it could be something more dangerous.

More fatal.

He knew Willa. He knew she'd never leave him. He
couldn't force her, either. He could send her to Reardon,
but he knew she would simply turn around and come
back. Derryton wouldn't hold her. Hell, they'd probably
take up a collection to pay her coach fare back. Even
if he bound and gagged her and put her on a ship for
Africa, as soon as she managed to get the gag off she'd
only cajole the captain to turn around and bring her
home.

Back in Reardon House, Nathaniel braced both damaged fists on the edge of his desk. He inhaled deeply once,
then again. Then he whirled and strode to the brandy de-
canter that always stood full and ready, despite the fact
that the servants had never seen him drink any.

He pulled a glass toward him and filled it with a great
careless splash. He gazed at it for a long moment. Not
since the day he'd realized who his father was—the day
he'd decided who he himself was going to be—not since
then had he taken a drink.

He tossed the full glass back in two swallows, then
filled it again.

The Cobra didn't take spirits. The Cobra kept his wits
about him, his emotions controlled, his hand steady.

This wasn't a job for the Cobra. This was a task for the dark man inside.

Nathaniel threw back his head and swallowed the second glass. Already he could feel the heat burning away the walls of control.

This was not a noble act—no fine, protective deed.

He was going to destroy something beautiful.

He was going to break Willa.

Upstairs, Willa still waited in Nathaniel's room. She renewed the fading fire, then clambered onto his great bed to watch the flames. It was warm in the room, but she felt cold without him. She pulled the robe over her feet, then laid her head on the pillow. She could wait for him here.

It must have been a while, for the fire had gone quite low, but it seemed as if she had only shut her eyes for an instant when she opened them at a scraping sound in the room.

Nathaniel was bending low over a chair, pulling ineffectually at his boots. Willa's heart sank. He was drunk, she could tell. When one was raised above a taproom, one learned to recognize drunkenness when one saw it.

He tottered, then sat clumsily on the floor. With both hands, he still could not remove his boots.

"Oh, for heaven's sake," muttered Willa, and slid off the bed to help him. She squatted beside him and pushed his hands away from the boot, frowning up into his face.

"Let me—"

She gasped, dropping his foot in her horror at his face. "Dear God, Nathaniel, who did this to you?"

"Won'erful brawl. Too bad you missed it. I could have used that ri' hook of yours."

She couldn't believe it. Men and their fights! She rose to light a candle, then gathered the basin and cloth from his washstand.

He was struggling to get up when she returned, but she shoved him back down. "You might as well stay on the floor. I've a feeling you'll end up there again anyway. Besides, this makes it easier to reach you."

She dabbled the cloth in the water and began cleaning his face. "I really must teach you how to guard your left. You shouldn't have let them touch you."

"S'no fun if you don't bleed a bit," he argued amiably. He blinked up at her from where he sat. "The other fellows look much worse than me."

"Don't be so proud of yourself. Dick can wade through a taproom brawl and come out with nothing but scraped knuckles."

"Well, but . . . but he's real *big*."

"So are you."

"I am?" He seemed ridiculously pleased that she thought so.

She put a bit too much pressure on the cloth.

"Ow!"

"I wish you had not gone drinking tonight. I wish you had let me be here for you."

"S'all right. You can be here for me now."

His hands moved in front of her, and she realized he had untied the dressing gown.

She backed away. "This isn't—"

He rose swiftly before her, the bumbling boy gone. In his place was a man with lust in his eyes. He stepped closer, pulling on the dressing gown. "Off."

It was so overlarge that it slid right off her. She let it go, still backing away.

"Nathaniel, I don't—"

"I do." He sprang forward, catching her by the front of her nightdress. "C'mon, Willa. I want to do it to you."

She felt a little sick at his words. He didn't sound like a husband or even a lover. He sounded like a . . . a customer, and he made her feel like a trollop. She pushed at him.

"Get off, Nathaniel. I don't like you like this."

"You said you wanted to do wicked things. You said you'd take me in your mouth."

He followed her as she backed away. Two more steps and the bed hit the backs of her legs. Then he was pressing against her and she was trapped.

He tugged at her bodice with both hands.

"I want to see your nipples."

She pushed at his hands, but he pulled at the strings tying her gown closed. The ties popped under the force of his tugs, tearing free. Then his hands were on her. They were hot and rough and she couldn't fend him off. "Stop," she blurted. "Please, *stop.*"

"I want to touch them." He put both her shielding hands over her head and held them there. Then he bent his head to take one nipple into his mouth.

Unable to struggle at all, Willa was horror-struck. Nathaniel wasn't simply drunk and clumsy. This was something else. He wasn't going to stop, no matter how she protested. This wasn't the man she knew, the man who brought respect to the most playful of bedroom games. This wasn't the man she'd defended, the man she'd sworn to stand beside—

The man she'd sworn to stand beside.

Abruptly she ceased her struggles. She let her wrists go limp in his grasp; she stopped twisting her body away from his seeking mouth. When he raised his head, she met his gaze levelly. "Let me go."

He pasted on a sickening leer. "I like you like this."

"I cannot do what you wish," she pointed out matter-of-factly. "If you want me to take you into my mouth, I can hardly do it from here."

Startled, Nathaniel released her hands and stepped

back. He half-expected her to make a run for her own room, but she calmly shed her ruined nightgown and knelt before him naked. His cock pulsed in response to her lush beauty. Her dark hair tumbled over her bare shoulders and breasts, and when she looked up at him from her position her blue eyes were like still pools.

Before he could react, she'd unbuttoned his trousers and pulled his shameful erection into her hands.

"You cannot make me leave you," she said softly. "No matter what you do to us both." Then she bent her head to take him into her mouth.

Her words hit Nathaniel like a shot to the heart. He couldn't do it.

Pulling himself free from her grip before she reached him with her mouth, he bent to sweep her into his arms. The fear he'd seen in her eyes had made him die a little inside, but the faith in her calm gaze destroyed him.

"Oh, wildflower, I'm sorry. I'm so sorry." He wrapped his arms around her and frantically pulled her close. She held very still, trembling slightly in his embrace. It tore a hole in his heart.

"Oh God, Willa. I'm sorry. I wouldn't . . . I'd never— oh, wildflower, forgive me, please."

She didn't speak. Nathaniel felt the hole in his heart grow larger, tearing even as he had torn her gown.

Then the darkness all poured from the open break in his heart.

The fear that his disgrace would endanger her. The desperation that he would never be worthy enough. The grief of watching his father dying. The pain of losing any chance to redeem himself in his father's eyes.

The emotions welled up within him, and he clung to Willa tightly. "Don't go," he whispered hoarsely. "I'm sorry. I need you. *Please don't go.*"

Very slowly, he felt her arms come around him, loosely

and carefully at first, then holding him more tightly. A vast wave of relief swept him, weakening his every fiber. He fell to his knees, sliding down her until he knelt before her with his face pressed to her bare belly.

He was gasping for air, his emotions thundering through him like a cavalry of need. Her arms wrapped tightly around him, pressing him even closer. He clung to her.

She would not leave him. No matter the man he was, no matter the things he did, she loved him even so. No one had ever loved him like that.

With Willa, he could be safe. With Willa, he was home. He let the pain free, let it burn through him, let the acid loss sear his heart.

She held him while he sobbed, stroking his hair, rocking him slowly to and fro, and saying the one thing that he could hold fast to, the one thing that would save his broken soul.

"I love you."

26

The next morning, Willa woke to find herself in her own bed, dressed in a new nightgown. Sitting up, she looked around her and tried not to feel dismissed. When she and Nathaniel had fallen asleep together, after gently making love for hours, she had felt so much a part of him.

Now, finding herself on the other side of a closed door made her feel as if last night's emotional union had never happened.

Then it occurred to her that perhaps Nathaniel didn't know any better. How could he? After all, he had never been married before. Yes, that must be it.

Well, she would take care of that lack straightaway. She dressed in one of her new gowns, which had been delivered at some point the day before, and after quickly pinning her hair up knocked on Nathaniel's door.

At his invitation, she walked inside to see him shaving himself, a frustrated manservant dancing about him.

"Master Nathaniel, please let me . . . I'm sure it would be better—oh dear, not that way—"

Nathaniel stopped to smile at Willa. He waved the razor at her. "Good morning."

Willa smiled back, her eyes widening at the poor fellow

who was having conniptions over the way Nathaniel was casually handling the razor. "Oh, sir . . . do be careful—oh my—"

Nathaniel stroked the razor one last time down his neck, then tossed it into the basin, much to the dismay of the valet, and wiped his face with a towel. He turned to Willa.

"Stinson believes I can't feed myself yet, either." He pulled her into a hug, lowering his cheek to the top of her head. "Go away, Stinson."

"Yes, sir. . . . Oh my—such a way to treat a fine instrument—" Muttering all the while, Stinson cleared the shaving debris and left the room.

"Your father is being buried today," Willa said softly.

"Yes. Since the arrangements have been made for some time, I decided it was best to act on it." He breathed deeply. "Do you think me dishonoring him with this swiftness?"

She thought about it for a moment. "Was he the sort of man to prolong matters?"

Nathaniel snorted. "Not in the slightest. He was a very decisive sort."

"Well, then, I think you've answered your question."

"You're wearing something new." He stood back, still holding one hand. "Let me look at you."

Smiling to see the dark moment ease, Willa spun once for him at the end of his arm, then laughed softly when he pulled her close again, this time her back to his chest. He folded his arms about her. "Oh, wildflower. You are so alive. You chase the darkness away."

She tilted her head back to kiss him tenderly. She felt his erection grow behind her. "I need you so," he whispered in her ear.

"I'm here," she murmured back. He knelt and then stood, pulling her hem to her waist, petticoats and all. His long fingers probed her, one of them passing through the little slit in her drawers and entering her slowly and deeply.

She gasped, and her knees began to shake. He stayed behind her, kissing the back of her bent neck, one hand holding up her skirts, the other thrusting rhythmically inside her. She felt herself becoming slippery for him, as she always did, and his finger became two fingers, thrusting ever deeper.

"Grab hold of that bedpost," he whispered, "and stand on your toes."

Made pliant by his imploring tone and his persuasive touch, Willa did as she was told. She bent to wrap both hands around the bedpost before her and rose on her toes.

"You look so amazing like that. So beautiful."

She sensed him moving more fully behind her. The weight of her skirts was laid down upon her bent back, and then Nathaniel's other hand joined the first, only this time from the front. He dipped two new fingers into her slick readiness, then used the moisture to caress the sensitive place just in front.

It was divine. It was shocking. His two hands moved more and more quickly, his fingers rubbing, stroking, thrusting in rhythm together, until she was bucking shamelessly into his hands. Until she had to wrap both arms around the bedpost and bury her face into her sleeve as she soundlessly screamed her climax.

She had scarcely begun to recover when he entered her. She was so wet and ready that he drove deeply, burying his length in her with one stroke. She cried out and quivered anew.

"Oh God!" He grasped her hips and pierced her again. Again and again, each time plunging as deeply as he could. "I can't get enough of you."

She was off again, her orgasm taking her by surprise so that she didn't think to muffle her cries.

The sound of her climax echoing through the room was more than Nathaniel could withstand. With only one more wild thrust, he groaned and ejaculated into her, his shaft throbbing intensely. The power of it shook him to his bones.

"Oh my," she whimpered. Her knees failed her suddenly, and she slipped away from him to sit on the carpet.

Thinking that the floor looked mighty inviting at the moment, Nathaniel collapsed next to her.

"Please note," he panted. "Still dressed."

"Well, yes." She breathed deeply, trying to calm the shivers that still racked her. "Although it might behoove me to don a fresh pair of drawers."

Nathaniel leaned forward and kissed her ear. "I'll tell you what," he whispered. "Don't bother with the drawers today, and I'll meet you in the library this afternoon for another romp."

"Nathaniel," she asked suddenly, "about what happened last night . . ."

His eyes darkened. "I'm so sorry, Willa. I promise that I will always listen to your wishes when I come to you."

She shook her head. "Will we share a room when we are officially married?"

He looked at her oddly. "Why would we?"

"Well, where I come from, a husband and wife sleep in the same room, in the same bed."

Nathaniel smiled and rose to his feet, seeing to his buttons as he stood above her. "Likely they simply haven't the room to spare." Holding out his hand to her, he pulled her to her feet. "Fortunately, we don't have that problem."

She stood, but she didn't smile back. "Fortunately," she said, trying to keep the hurt from her voice.

"I'll walk you down to breakfast, wildflower, but then I'll be checking on my father's funeral arrangements." His smile was gone.

Willa chided herself for her self-centeredness. Nathaniel had far more pressing things on his mind than their sleeping arrangements.

She forced herself to smile at him and took his arm as they left his room. It was silly to worry about something so trivial, anyway. No doubt she'd soon become accustomed to it.

It was only that separate rooms made her feel like an amorous convenience, not a wife.

Nathaniel wasn't quite sure what was wrong with Willa this morning. Likely she was simply tired from their second long night of lovemaking. Then he was distracted by the fine ebony casket being carried down the front stairs. The back stairs would have been too narrow, of course. He ought to have thought of that—

Nathaniel knew he had allowed no reaction to cross his face, but still Willa tucked her hand into his and squeezed.

"Give it time, my love," she murmured.

She always knew when he was hurting. He towed her a few steps away from the front hall. Pulling her close, he held her and allowed himself to be held. When the ache eased, he pulled away and smiled at her. Running a fingertip from the soft dent above her collarbone down her silken skin to the neckline of her gown, he reminded her of her promise. "Do not forget. We have an appointment in the library this afternoon."

She shivered, and her dark eyes studied him. Leaning close, she placed her palm on his neck and pulled him down to kiss him soundly.

He narrowed his eyes. "You will pay for that, you know."

"Gladly." She blew him a kiss. "Now, go manage things. I'll take care of things here."

· · ·

Nathaniel may have been disgraced, but it seemed to Willa that Randolph had been very highly esteemed. People from all classes of life were there to see him laid to rest.

She saw Clara standing next to a very handsome fellow who must have been Lord Etheridge. She saw Sir Simon with a rather smugly increasing woman who looked entirely interesting.

Lord Liverpool was there as well, although Nathaniel did not seem happy to see him.

In the back, behind the family and upper-class guests, there gathered a rather tearful band of servants. All wore the livery of one or the other of their titled guests. One coachman was a wild-haired giant whose scars made Ren Porter's dim by comparison. Another was a small, ragged man with pointy features and an elfin tilt to his ears when he removed his natty footman's hat.

Just as Nathaniel had requested, Willa stood with the family, supporting Myrtle in her grief. Nathaniel himself kept several yards back from the mourners, who left a wide space around him.

Willa was so proud of him, standing tall and straight against all the stares and vicious whispers. Proud, too, of his sensitivity, for she realized that the disturbance would have been much worse had he insisted on taking his rightful place at the graveside.

He was letting his family mourn—allowing the day to be about the ceremony of release and grief, not about him.

As the ritual drew to a close and the mourners began to leave, again they left a wide path around Nathaniel. All except for Clara. Head high, she went directly to him and put a sympathetic hand on his arm. Nathaniel covered that hand for a moment with his, then disengaged her and sent her on her way. Clara returned to her husband, who loomed nearby.

Then Willa thought she saw Lord Etheridge give Nathaniel the barest nod, hardly more than a dropping of his eyelids in sympathy. Nathaniel gave a nearly imperceptible nod in return. Curious, Willa began to watch the departing mourners more closely. It was difficult to detect at first, but she thought she saw more than one man send Nathaniel that tiny respectful nod.

How curious.

Then something else caught her eye. "Look there," Willa gasped. "Is that *him*?"

Myrtle peered at a highly decorated carriage sitting apart from the others. A stout figure was silhouetted in the window. As they watched, the figure raised a square of linen to his eyes.

"I believe it is," Myrtle breathed.

"Should I do something?" Willa was panicking. "Curtsy? Say hello? Faint?"

"If he wanted to come greet Lord Reardon, I daresay he would. I'd stay put if I were you."

Disappointed, Willa sighed. "Right. Stay put."

Finally, Willa and Myrtle were back in their own carriage, waiting for Nathaniel. Willa was watching Nathaniel, who was taking a moment at his father's graveside now that everyone else was gone, even Victoria. He made a lonely figure, tall and dark in his mourning clothes. His head was bowed.

Willa wanted to go to him. He seemed to take comfort from her presence, and she wanted to give him that. Then she saw two gentlemen approach him where he stood.

One was big and blond. The other was lean and watchful. Willa watched closely, but it seemed they only said a few words, then walked away. Nathaniel turned then and made his way to their carriage to join her.

"Well," Willa said brightly. "Those were certainly handsome gentleman. All you needed was the Fox and you would have the full Quatre Royale."

Nathaniel's gaze shot to hers. Pure horror blazed in his eyes.

"What?" Willa blinked. "What did I say?"

Failure! Again!

The man hiding in the shabby room paced to and fro. The slow-burning panic of a few days ago had blossomed into an inferno within him. He threw himself into the room's one rickety chair and dropped his face into his hands. If he failed, he would surely die. So much work, so many years of careful, brilliant planning—

He sat up slowly, a reckless madness taking over the worry within him. Perhaps it was time to change tactics. No more planning, no more careful, painstaking arrangements of events.

No more Trojan horses. No more suborning, no more manipulating, no more playing the dithering fool to cover the deadly killer inside. Only full, frontal attack would do—do or die.

Winner take all.

Lord Liverpool, the Prime Minister of England, was pacing back and forth on the parlor rug. Willa couldn't get over it. The rant went on for some time, however, long enough for the novelty to wear quite away.

"Are you telling me that you had a book, right there in Derryton, that told about the history and activities of the Royal Four? All spelled out for anyone to read?"

"Well, goodness no!" *Honestly.* "It was in Latin and in code."

Both Liverpool and Nathaniel looked vastly relieved, so Willa continued. "It took me over a year to translate it so that everyone in Derryton could read it."

"And a fine job she did, too," Myrtle chimed in stoutly.

"Well, it was a great favorite," Willa said modestly. "I used to read it aloud in the taproom in the evenings. The patrons were always so well behaved when I did."

Nathaniel sat down as if his knees had given out. "Vinegar."

Willa smiled at him. "Precisely."

"What are you blathering about, Reardon?" Liverpool snapped.

"I just realized how Foster knew just where to look for her." Nathaniel started to chuckle helplessly. "You truly were bored, weren't you, wildflower?"

Willa nodded solemnly. "I was a real trial until I could read. Into *everything*." Lord Liverpool still seemed very angry. Willa appealed to Nathaniel. "It isn't as though I kept it a secret. I told you about it. It carried on a great deal about the king cobra, remember?"

He covered her hand. "Yes, you did. I'm very sorry I didn't take you up on your offer to show it to me." Nathaniel looked up at Liverpool. "What do you think now?"

Liverpool looked sour. "I don't see any way out of it."

"What about Derryton?" Nathaniel looked worried. Willa started to worry, too. Lord Liverpool didn't look like he thought any of this was the slightest bit amusing.

"I don't really see how it matters," Willa protested. "After all, the Quatre Royale died out in my grandfather's time."

"Oh, sure," Myrtle agreed. "Everyone knows that."

"Well, then, if those are the facts generally known . . ." Nathaniel spread his hands.

Liverpool seemed more curious. "This book said the Royal Four died out. Are you sure?"

"Well, yes. The last entry read that none of the four had worthy protégés and that they had no intention of passing the burden of responsibility onto such 'weak and narrow shoulders.' " Willa's head ached. She'd been quoting to them for the past half hour. "Wouldn't you like to simply read it for yourselves?"

Nathaniel sat up. "It's here? In Reardon House?"

Willa nodded. "It's on the shelf in my room." She looked at Myrtle. "Isn't it?"

Myrtle looked thoughtful. "Have I returned it to you yet? I cannot recall."

Nathaniel shooed them off. "Both of you, go. Now."

"Wait." Liverpool turned to Willa. "Where did you get it?"

Willa blinked. "From my parents' collection of books."

"And they've passed on." Liverpool scowled. "Damn. We'll never know then."

Willa opened her mouth to speak, but Liverpool gestured sharply. "Go."

When they were gone, Liverpool let loose, as Nathanial had known he was longing to. "It has always been purely oral tradition! Those are the rules! What bloody idiot put down the whole workings of the Four on paper?"

"One with a dreadful protégé, I suppose." Nathaniel shrugged. "He was probably afraid he was going to die and it would all be lost."

Liverpool shuddered. "Go, fetch that book before I pop a blood vessel."

Nathaniel didn't laugh. He was very sure Liverpool wasn't joking. He nodded and left the room.

His and Willa's bedchambers were at the far back of the house, for he had thought she would appreciate the garden view. He ambled toward their chambers, in no hurry to face Liverpool again soon. The loss of secrecy was tragic, although Nathaniel suspected it was more containable that they realized, but his heart was on wings.

She's mine. I'm keeping—

There came a powerful *thud* and a shriek, quickly broken off.

"Willa!" He ran to the bedchamber, but the door was locked. "Willa! Are you all right?"

27

Willa gazed at the barrel of the pistol held in a stranger's hand. Myrtle lay where she had fallen when the intruder had thrown her aside. He'd rapped the woman sharply on the temple with the weapon that he now aimed at Willa's heart.

"Answer him," the man whispered. "Tell him you saw a mouse."

Willa tried to swallow, but her throat was dry as dust. She cleared her throat. "I'm fine, Nathaniel," she called out. " 'Twas only a mouse."

She heard a relieved chuckle from the other side of the door. "Really? What kind is he?"

Willa glued her eyes to the pistol, willing herself to give nothing away. "How would I know? I hate nasty little furry things!"

There was a pause. "I see."

Please, Nathaniel, please listen to me!

"If you're all right, then I'll be off to my club," Nathaniel said easily. "Don't expect me for dinner."

"All right, Nathaniel."

She heard the footsteps leaving the vicinity of the door and closed her eyes. She hadn't known how he would react to her signal. He might well have burst through the door and been taken down by a bullet.

The intruder sneered at her over his pistol. Willa decided that calling him a mouse was an insult to rodents everywhere. Yet the nasty young man would likely be considered a handsome enough fellow, were he not a bit worse for wear. His once fine clothing was stained and worn and his hair hung stringy before his eyes. Despite that, there was something familiar about him to Willa.

Perhaps if her heart were not pounding like a runaway horse she would recall where she had seen him, or someone very like him, before.

"So he loves you little, just as the gossip inferred," the fellow said with a nasty laugh. "I heard that you felled him with a stone as he rode by you."

Despite her fear, Willa was nonplussed. Even the villains knew her story? "Someone ought to shut their gob," she muttered.

"That someone is you," snapped the man. "Now tell me where the bloody book is!"

"Of course," Willa sighed. "That's all anyone wants, isn't it? The bloody book." She folded her arms to hide the trembling in her hands. "Well, I don't have it."

The man's eyes narrowed. "Oh yes, you do. I heard you and the old hen arguing about it as you came down the hall."

Drat. She had been speaking loudly, out of courtesy for Myrtle's hearing. Oh, dear. Myrtle still hadn't moved a bit. Willa felt sick. If this rotter had killed Myrtle—

"The book!" The fellow stepped closer. Willa quickly stepped back.

"I tell you, it isn't here! Not in this room." Her stomach churned with cold fear. Nathaniel had walked away from her—yet he'd said he was off to his club, even while Lord Liverpool remained downstairs. Surely that meant he'd understood, hadn't it? He would come. She merely had to keep this wicked fellow talking until—but what if something happened to Nathaniel?

Willa would rather die herself than have anything happen to Nathaniel. Yet she didn't want to die. She wanted to live. Now. Here, with Nathaniel.

Just when she was the closest to achieving that dream this . . . this *man* showed up to ruin everything! Willa was terrified beyond description, but she was infuriated even more.

He raised the pistol to aim casually at her face. Willa was certain she was due to vomit at any moment. "I have forever, you know," he said silkily. "Nowhere to go now, not unless I have that book. So why don't we pass the time while you think about it?" He leered at her in what was surely meant to be a threatening way.

Fortunately, that was the least of Willa's fears. She snorted. "Not if you value your life, you won't." She didn't bother explaining the jinx. Let the rotter find out the hard way. "Who are you?" If she was going to be killed, she wanted to know by whom.

The man only smirked. "You never saw me coming, did you?"

Willa thought about it. "Well, yes, we did, actually. You've been tracking me across England, desperately trying to obtain my grandfather's diary. I must say, you are incompetent."

"Enough!" hissed the man. He was pale and his hands were shaking. He also looked furious that she had spoiled what she assumed was to have been his moment of surprising revelation.

"You probably even put Sir Foster up to burning down Reardon House," she muttered.

"Shut up!" the man said in a restrained shriek.

Oh dear. She was getting to him. That did happen. Men

would make such open-ended statements of the obvious. She, in return, always felt compelled to point that out to them.

They didn't tend to take it well.

This gentleman was no exception. All his smug assurance was gone. Still holding the pistol on her, he began to back away from the door and the window. "Come," he said, gesturing to her.

"I most seriously doubt I will," Willa said gravely, then took two quick steps back. "I believe my chances of survival are much superior over here." She tilted her head and narrowed her eyes at him. "I'm considering banking on you missing me."

Stunned outrage passed over the man's features. "You can't do that!"

Willa smiled slightly. "Is that even your own pistol?" She folded her arms. "You haven't practiced with it at all, have you? You thought all you had to do was sashay in and wave your pistol at a couple of ladies and the day would be won?" She shook her head pityingly. "'Tisn't much of a plan, if you ask me."

"You don't know what you're talking about!" The man was nearly purple now. "You're simply Reardon's barefoot, illiterate broomstick bride!"

"Illiterate? *Illiterate?*" Willa had never been so insulted in all her days. She pulled off her right slipper and threw it at him. "I am *not* illiterate!"

He ducked slightly and the kid leather shoe slapped him harmlessly on the shoulder. Willa threw the next one much harder. This time, though he waved both arms to fend it off, it smacked him soundly on the head.

"You're mad," the man said, rubbing his head in wonder. "Stark staring mad."

"Yet you're a perfect example of sanity?" She grimaced

and held out her hand. "Give me back my shoes. I wish to throw them at you again."

The man grabbed up her shoes and held them behind his back with his unarmed hand. "Not bloody likely!"

Then he seemed to become aware that he was treating a pair of lady's soft kid slippers like a serious threat. He flung them to the floor with a growl. His eyes black with fury, he raised the pistol to aim anew at her heart. "Bugger the book! Right now I only wish to kill you!"

No, she could quite seriously say that he was not going to miss her after all. The bullet in that gun was going to pierce her beating heart and kill her.

"Bastard," she whispered weakly.

"Absolutely," the man sneered, and pulled back the hammer with a click that sounded loud in the silent room.

Nathaniel casually walked away from Willa's bedchamber door, maintaining his unworried speed for several long steps. Then he ran to his own chambers and threw open the garden window.

Willa's window was several yards away. Nathaniel eyed the wall below it. The twisted trunks of old-growth ivy had supported the intruder climbing to her window but was now torn from the wall and unstable. From the look of the tangle of broken climber, the man had scarcely survived the climb himself.

Ladders? No, it would take too long to bring them.

Breaking down the door? Good idea in theory, but the doors of Reardon House were heavy oak. It might take several tries to bring it down. In that amount of time, Willa could be made most definitely dead.

The cold fear threatened to weaken him. He would not consider the possibility. Nothing could happen to

Willa. "She's the lucky one, remember?" he whispered to himself.

Then the shadow of a decorative bit of stonework caught his eye. About three feet below Willa's and his windows ran a bit of a ledge, scarcely two inches wide. Another band ran about five feet higher, its line broken by the windows themselves.

Nathaniel ducked back into his bedchamber and tore through a drawer, looking for his creepers. As he pulled off his boots and tugged on the butter soft leather shoes with the India rubber soles that he had used for the odd break-in back in the days before he'd become the Cobra, Liverpool appeared in his doorway.

"Is there some reason why I am sitting down there with no diary in my hands?"

Nathaniel didn't bother to look at him. He moved to sit in his window embrasure. "Willa wants me to kill a mouse."

"And why is that my concern?"

"Willa loves mice." He swung his legs out into space.

"Dear God, man! What are you doing?"

"There's an intruder in Willa's room. I'm going to kill him, just as she requested."

"Why not use a key?"

"There are no keys in Reardon House. Only locks from the inside. It seemed clever at the time." Nathaniel began to drop himself out of the window.

"Wait!"

He looked up at Liverpool.

"You cannot mean to risk yourself!" Liverpool said sharply. "You know there is no Cobra candidate behind you! The Four must not be weakened now, not in wartime, especially not for the sake of some Northants tavern maid!"

Nathaniel didn't so much as frown, but Liverpool

abruptly decided to take another tack. "Why not wait until less valuable reinforcements arrive? You are the Cobra. The Cobra does not go out on a ledge to be a hero. Think, man!"

For the barest instant, Nathaniel thought. He could wait, and he probably should—just as his father had always put cool logic before any emotional attachment. He nodded at Liverpool. "You're right. The Cobra would not go out on a narrow ledge for a woman." Then he tore off his frock coat and threw it into Liverpool's hands with a grim, deadly smile.

"But Nathaniel Stonewell would. Now go get those reinforcements." With that, he dropped himself out of the window.

The little hole in the gun barrel seemed a vast black void. Willa's knees went rather dramatically weak. She quite unwillingly staggered into a side table, sending the unlit candlestick thudding to the floor. The man started violently but, fortunately, not enough to pull the trigger.

It did confuse him so that he didn't see the shadow pass the window to one side of them. Willa didn't take her gaze from the intruder's face but simply sidled away from the window, forcing him to turn his back to it.

Directly behind the man, what looked like a single finger showed briefly in the window, silhouetted against the pearly gray afternoon outside. *One?* One what?

Then, two fingers. Ah, a counting. She readied herself. *Three.*

Willa fell flat to the floor, throwing herself over Myrtle. The window burst in a shower of glass and Nathaniel leaped into the room. The door shuddered under the repeated slamming of large, determined bodies, then finally gave with a rending crash. Ren Porter rushed in

accompanied by several footmen. The intruder didn't
know who to aim at first.

Then it was too late to decide. He was down, disarmed,
and being pummeled most properly by Nathaniel. Once
the man was unconscious—oh, very well, a bit past
unconscious—Nathaniel ceased and stood up, his chest
heaving.

Willa ran to him and flung herself into his arms. He
held her closer than close. "Well played, wildflower," he
whispered, his chuckle hoarse with desperate worry. "I
particularly liked the part where you demanded your
shoes back to hurl them again."

She accepted another squeeze from him before she ran
to Myrtle. Ren Porter was kneeling next to the fallen
woman. Myrtle was rousing. "I'd say she'll have the
headache of her life, but no permanent harm done." Ren
grinned at Willa with lopsided apology. "I wouldn't recommend laudanum, however. It makes one do the damnedest
things."

Willa smiled warmly at him. "I have no idea what you
mean." He bobbed his head quickly in thanks. She pushed
him to the door. "Go back to bed, you madman. There'll
be no dying in my house, do you understand me?"

He laughed weakly and bowed. "Yes, my lady!"

Lord Liverpool appeared in the doorway. He glanced
down at the man on the floor. "Always the bedamned
Wadsworths." He glared at Nathaniel. "Louis Wadsworth
has been in the Tower for more than a week, held under
trusted guard! No one escapes from the Tower!"

Nathaniel considered Liverpool for a long moment.
"Have you actually *seen* him in the Tower yourself?"

Liverpool tilted his head thoughtfully. "No, I had not
yet visited him there. I had hoped some time in prison
would make the questioning easier."

"Ah. Then I would say that there was indeed someone put in the Tower . . . but not this man."

"Hmm. Someone close to me has failed me." Liverpool looked exceedingly dangerous. "I do not like it when I am failed."

"Hmm." Nathaniel found himself unconvinced. Liverpool had never truly adapted to the more constrained position of Prime Minister. In some ways, he behaved as if he still held all the autonomy and power of the Cobra in his hands. Power that was Nathaniel's now.

Nathaniel had difficulty believing that a man such as Liverpool would let a prisoner like Louis Wadsworth slip through his fingers. Yet what would be the purpose of aiding such an escape?

The possibility of following Louis directly to the prize—Willa's book.

"It is convenient that you are here to claim your prisoner once more, is it not?"

Liverpool looked at Nathaniel sharply, his narrow features tightening. "Your meaning, Reardon?"

Nathaniel shrugged easily. "Merely congratulating you on a happy accident. However, I do hope you realize how fortunate it is that my lady was not harmed in this incident?" His tone was light, but he knew Liverpool did not mistake his meaning.

Liverpool narrowed his eyes. "Your lady would have been far from danger, had you heeded my advice."

Nathaniel kept his own gaze level, his expression quite bland. Liverpool matched him until his gaze flicked away, apparently without volition. Satisfied, Nathaniel turned his attention to the figure on the floor.

"First Ren Porter. Then Foster. Now Wadsworth. I do feel a right target, I must say." Someone wanted him rather dead, it seemed. Had Louis Wadsworth been behind

the entire matter, only coming forward when the others
had failed? "Do you think we've our Chimera in hand
now?"

"I intend to find out." Liverpool signaled to one of his
own men. "Bind that man and take him to my carriage.
I believe I must step up my interrogation timetable."

Willa came to stand with Nathaniel again. He put his
hand on her shoulder. "Do you still have the book,
Willa?"

She blinked at him. "Goodness. I'd forgotten all about
it. You truly do want that book."

"Yes." He couldn't tell her why.

"I'll fetch it from Myrtle's room."

Liverpool glanced around at the room full of servants
tending the glass and broken door. "Shall we retire to the
library, then?"

Willa retrieved the diary from where it sat on Myrtle's
nightstand. Once in the library, she prepared to hand it
over to Lord Liverpool. Yet something in the air between
the Prime Minister and her husband compelled her to
hand it to him instead.

The appreciative glint in Nathaniel's eyes told her
she'd done the right thing.

Nathaniel tipped the book open to read the flyleaf. He
clenched his jaw mightily, then handed the book over to
Liverpool. Lord Liverpool read the flyleaf, went even more
rigid than usual—Willa would have wagered it wasn't
possible—then snapped the volume shut with a sharp *crack*.

"I'll take this, if you don't mind," he said tightly.

Nathaniel nodded silently, his jaw tensing rhythmically.

Liverpool nodded shortly to Willa. "Lady Reardon,"
he said by way of leave-taking. He strode from the library
with his expression frozen in acidity.

Taking Willa by the hand, Nathaniel followed to see him

out. In the front hall, they paused to allow two footmen to walk a groggy Louis Wadsworth out between them. "What a shame," Nathaniel muttered. "I thought I hit him harder than that."

Just then, Daphne and Basil descended the stairs, obviously dressed for travel.

Nathaniel did not seem terribly surprised. "Heading for the country already?"

Basil shrugged. "The Season is over for us, now that we are in mourning. At least at Reardon we may entertain quietly."

Daphne looked worried. "Basil, what is all this? Who is that man?"

Basil patted her hand. "It has nothing to do with us, my sweet. Let Thaniel handle his own mess. I insist that we leave now." He signaled the footman behind him to bring their trunks forward.

Nathaniel shook his head. "We are in the act of transporting a dangerous criminal from the house at the moment. I suggest you stay back until he is gone."

Daphne's eyes went wide. "Another attack? How did you survive this one?"

Nathaniel smiled at Willa. "Quick wits and a lethal pair of shoes," he said. Then he left her with Daphne and Basil to accompany the two guards to the carriage with their prisoner.

"When you get him inside," Nathaniel said to them as they nearly dragged their burden down the steps to the drive, "I suggest you bind his feet as w—"

Suddenly Louis gasped, looking over Nathaniel's shoulder at the park beyond. He began to struggle. *"No, he's—"*

A gunshot rang out, echoing against the façade of the house so that the source was masked. Willa watched in horror as Nathaniel went down in a tangle with Wadsworth and the two footmen.

"Is he dead?" shrieked Daphne. "Is Thaniel dead?"

Willa was at Nathaniel's side in an instant, down on her knees in the gravel. She pushed at the pile of men covering him. Her heart nearly stopped when she saw that his shirt was covered with blood.

The two footmen rolled aside, then pulled Louis Wadsworth up. He hung more limply than ever, the spreading stain on his shirtfront explaining why.

Nathaniel wheezed, then coughed. He took in a great lungful of air there on his back, a blissful smile crossing his face. "I truly thought they had me," he said to Willa, his voice a croak.

She laughed damply. "I think the late Mr. Wadsworth simply knocked the wind out of you, darling."

He turned to look at the prisoner. Then he rolled his head to gaze up at Liverpool, who stood by the carriage with a sour expression. "Our Chimera, do you think?"

Liverpool grimaced. "I don't doubt it."

Nathaniel sat up. "Damn."

The footman who had taken off at the shot came jogging back. "We found where they was waiting in the park, sir, but they was gone. Had a horse ready, they did."

Willa helped Nathaniel to his feet and dusted off the back of his trousers. He laughed, thinking of how long ago—had it only been little more than a week?—he'd woken by the side of the lane with a woman in his arms.

Liverpool took a seat in his carriage. "There is little point in remaining now," he said sourly.

"At least you still have Foster," Nathaniel reminded him.

Liverpool nodded. "That is a comfort. Unfortunately, I am fairly sure now that Foster was simply a minion. I suspect the Wadsworths were the leaders of their cell of espionage." His driver took off with a jerk.

Basil and Daphne stood cautiously in the doorway. Daphne had one hand pressed to her throat and her eyes were very wide. With disappointment? Indeed, Basil had nearly inherited—again.

"*Chamaeleo bitaeniatus*," Willa murmured, staring at Daphne. "The chameleon."

"Is it over?" Basil called out.

"Yes, Basil. It is now safe for you to go to the country," Nathaniel replied wearily.

Basil shuffled Daphne into their waiting carriage. Nathaniel stood on the steps with his arm around Willa and watched them load their possessions and drive off. "I hope they have not made a mistake," he said absently.

She looked surprised. "What do you mean?"

"Well, they wed so quickly after my engagement to Daphne was dissolved. You know what they say: 'Marry in haste, repent in leisure.' "

"Do they? Do they say that?" Her voice went faint, and she paled a bit.

"Wildflower, what is it?"

She shook her head and handed him back his handkerchief. "Nothing. I'm afraid I get a bit damp at shootings."

She put her arms around him and pressed her face to his shoulder. Nathaniel wasn't sure, but he didn't think it was an amorous hug. He held her close to his side, then bent to nuzzle her hair, willing to hold her as long as she needed. When she finally let go and stood back, her color was better and she was able to smile.

"Thank you. I needed that." Then she grimaced at his stained shirtfront. "I think you ought to take that off," she said, wrinkling her nose. "Shall we go upstairs?"

What a wonderful idea. Nathaniel ran for his room and a clean shirt and weskit. Wadsworth wasn't invited. When Nathaniel left his chamber, he was surprised to see Willa waiting for him in the hall. Then she waved her fingers at him, turned, and danced away down the hall.

"Where are you going?"

She turned, walking backward. "I feel the need to read." Giving him a saucy grin, she turned right way around and made for the stairs.

Nathaniel didn't catch up to her for two floors. Then he grabbed her hand and towed her through the house, passing startled servants and indifferent statuary until they reached the library.

28

Thrusting Willa into the room, Nathaniel turned to lock them in. He felt her come up from behind and press to his back. She slid her hands around his waist and down. Groaning, he let his head fall until his brow touched the door, taking her caresses for as long as he could stand it.

Then he whirled, picked her up, making her shriek slightly in surprise, and sat down in an enormous chair that stood before the fire. He settled her into his lap with her feet dangling down one side.

"I've had plans for this chair," he said.

"You have?" Then she gasped, for he had found her nipple through her bodice. "Oh!" He'd found the other nipple. "Really?"

Her voice had gone breathy, and she was beginning to squirm on him. God, he loved the way Willa could squirm.

He let go of her lovely nipples and slid his hand down her dress to the hem. Then he burrowed beneath to find her stocking-encased calves. He followed them up to her bare thighs, then continued to her naked junction. He pressed his palm to her, feeling it become kissed by her wetness.

"No drawers. Naughty Willa," he whispered in her ear. "Such a wanton thing you are."

She waited, barely breathing. He could feel her quivering already under his still hand. He rotated it a little, pressing and rubbing, until her head fell back across his other arm.

Then he stroked a fingertip over her sensitive nub, and savored the way she shuddered. His erection was pressed tightly to her hip, and every tiny movement she made against him was a caress.

He took the little button between two fingertips and rolled it gently, making sure his touch was slippery with her nectar. She was ready for him already, swollen and wet.

He took his hand away and pulled his arm from under her dress. She whimpered with loss. "Don't worry. We aren't done. But right now I want to see you."

"What?" She blinked at him, blurry with lust. She was adorable.

"I want to see my naughty wife without her drawers."

Her eyes widened, and she shook her head.

"Yes. I want you to stand before me, and pull up your dress, and show yourself to me."

She bit her lip and shook her head again.

Nathaniel wondered if he had pushed her too far.

"Show me yours first," she demanded.

He had to laugh. She was so unsinkable. "Very well. At the same time then?"

"No. You first." Then she slid her eyes to his and smirked. "I have plans for this chair, as well."

She hopped off his lap and stood before him, looking surprisingly unruffled for a woman who had just been squirming with lust. "Well, come on then. I want to see." She folded her arms and waited.

This was not going as planned. In fact, Nathaniel wasn't sure where this was going.

"Oh, very well, I'll do it myself." And she knelt between his knees and undid his buttons with staggering speed. She looked up at him. "You're not wearing any drawers, either."

"I never do."

Her eyes darkened a bit, then she finished her task and freed him into her hands. She caressed him gently, and Nathaniel gripped the arms of the chair until his knuckles whitened. "Willa, you are going to make me embarrass myself."

"How so?" Her attention was on his erection, which was growing still harder in her hands.

His teeth gritted. "If I explode in your hands, it will be embarrassing."

She grinned wickedly at him. "You did it to me this morning. Turnabout is fair play." She gripped him more tightly, and he threw his head back, clenching his eyes shut as he fought for control.

Willa liked touching him. She had not yet truly had the opportunity to explore their differences. As she knelt before him, stroking his length, she was fascinated by the hardness of steel wrapped with satin skin. The point of it was large and swiftly turning dark. She examined beneath and discovered an intriguing vein.

Impulsively she bent and kissed it. His broken gasp of pleasure echoed in the room.

Fascinating. If he responded like that to a kiss . . .

She took the head of his shaft into her mouth.

Her name came from him on a tight whisper. His hand came up to caress her hair, but she placed it back on the chair without losing her mouthful of him. She wanted no distractions right now.

With great deliberation, she rolled her tongue over him, tasting a bit of salt. The texture of him was lovely on her tongue, like the smoothness of a stick of candy. She pulled away and licked up the side of him, then down the other side.

He quivered, and she heard the snap of thread where his fingers dug into the upholstery. She laughed in gentle triumph against his shaft. How gratifying.

Perhaps if she could combine the two sensations . . .

He was very large, but if she dropped her jaw just so, and fed him into her mouth slowly . . .

Nathaniel couldn't stand it. She was performing something he had only dreamed of her doing in his darkest fantasies. The fact that she was willing to was humbling, and he would be sure to ponder that someday when he had some blood left in his brain.

At the moment, all he could feel was the hot suction of her mouth and the wicked action of her tongue. Devastating. She sucked him as deeply as she could, then released him slowly while flicking her tongue along the underside of him.

He shouldn't let it go much further, for he was fast approaching the brink. Still, just for a moment more . . .

Then he knew it must stop, and he let go of his grip on the chair to lift her away from him—

And her hands came down on top of his, pinning them to his side, and she sucked on him forcefully.

And it was too late.

With a helpless groan, he exploded into her mouth. She made a small sound of surprise but did not pull away. Instead, she wrapped her lips tightly around him and allowed him to release inside her mouth. He was so sensitized that he could feel it when she swallowed.

Then, when he was spent and shaking, she raised her head, wiped the back of her hand across her mouth, and grinned.

"Turnabout is fair play."

Oh, dear God, how he loved this woman.

. . .

Standing in the hall upstairs, Ren turned back into his room, away from the loving race that had just passed him by without notice.

She was so clearly Reardon's. Her mad love for the man hurt Ren, but he couldn't figure out why.

All he knew was that he didn't want to stay here, watching her heart fall further and further in love. He leaned against his closed door and rubbed his chest with one hand. "Heal, damn it," he ordered.

Whether he was talking to his lungs or to his heart he truly couldn't bear to say.

Nathaniel Stonewell, Lord Reardon, was in love.

And he was going to tell her so, as soon as he caught his breath—

A knock sounded on the library door. They both jumped guiltily, then laughed.

"My lord?" Hammil called. "You have a *guest!*" Hammil sounded breathless with excitement.

Probably Lord Liverpool returning, to create such a fervor in a snarky stick like Hammil. Possibly bad news from Foster's interrogation? "Thank you, Hammil," he called back. "I'll see to him in just a moment." He turned to Willa. "I'm sorry, wildflower. I have to go."

"But what about your plans for the chair?"

Nathaniel looked longingly at the chair, then pulled her close. "I'll tell you my plans, and you can enlarge upon them with your own."

Then he whispered into her ear until she gasped, then blushed, then sighed.

"Oh, you are a very wicked fellow, Nathaniel Stonewell."

He hated to leave her, but he kissed her hard, then went to face what surely was not going to be pleasant.

Then he entered the first parlor to find himself face-to-face with the Prince Regent.

Before him stood a burly figure clad head to toe in cream and peach satin. George was accompanied by a handful of Royal Guard, and Nathaniel suspected there were more currently covering all entrances to his house.

From behind him Nathaniel heard the light patter of feminine feet, rushing to the doorway. He turned around to see Victoria and Myrtle standing there gaping.

Victoria gasped and dropped into a deep curtsy, followed slowly by Myrtle, using her stick for balance. Nathaniel's bow was deep, immediate, and brief. He stepped forward then. "Your Highness, I—"

A whirlwind in charcoal silk blew past him. "Georgie!"

Prince George opened his arms wide. "Willie!"

Nathaniel stood there, eyes wide, mouth open, as His Royal Highness wrapped both arms around Nathaniel's bride-to-be and swung her gleefully off her feet.

"I think I'll sit now, if no one minds," Myrtle said faintly.

"Feel free," George said over the top of Willa's head. Then he took Willa's shoulders in both hands and held her off for his inspection. "You've grown as pretty as your mother," he said admiringly.

A bit too admiringly for Nathaniel's taste. "Your Highness—"

George slid his gaze sideways to Nathaniel. "Stand down, Reardon. I'm not poaching. Willie is practically family."

Victoria's mouth was open, and she stared at Willa. "You? You are a close friend of the Prince Regent?"

Willa smiled. "Well, my mother was."

*I have a sort of uncle—rather half uncle, I suppose—
here in London.*

And he'd arranged to have her presented at Court in a
borrowed dress? Nathaniel wasn't angry. Stunned, and a
little mystified, but not angry. Now that he saw them
standing there arm in arm, it explained so much. As in
how a simple country maid could confidently trot through
London Society without a misstep of manners, nor even a
smidgeon of intimidation by her betters. If she, in fact,
had any betters. If he was not mistaken, there was a possible family resemblance there.

The Cobra within him went cold with the implications.
Oh, dear God. Not another royal bastard?

Stiffly Nathaniel bowed again. "What is it we may do
for you, Your Highness?"

George put Willa off and seated her gallantly, then
took a chair of his own. "There has been a matter under
investigation for some time, as I know you are aware.
This was a most delicate matter, and security was a priority." He looked around at them all, but Nathaniel knew he
was the only one who realized what the Prince was talking about.

George looked at the others in the room. "I came to tell
you all the real reason why Reardon was consorting with
traitors and why he could not have done what he was accused of."

Myrtle clapped a wrinkled hand to her chest. "Please
go on, Your Highness. Tell the whole thing before I die."

"Oh dear. We mustn't have that." George smiled.
"Well, the short of the matter is, every last culprit in the
attempted treason plot has been apprehended or killed,
and we may now reveal the circumstances surrounding
the entire affair."

Victoria was white. She sat very still, staring over the

prince's head at nothing at all. It occurred to Nathaniel that no one seemed terribly thunderstruck by the revelations. He turned to Willa to find her quite calm, although she was smiling.

"I knew it wasn't true." She patted his hand. "And I knew there must be a good reason why you pretended it was."

The Prince Regent bobbed his head in agreement. "Indeed, Willie. A very good reason. But now we may all revel in the truth. It has only been a few hours since we apprehended the last of the group responsible for the plot, and things are already in the works to clear your name, Reardon.

"To speed things along, I contacted several other prominent members of Society on your behalf. The story has been passed around town all afternoon. People are quite up in arms over what was done to you, I must say."

Nathaniel watched Willa lean toward Myrtle. He thought he heard something that sounded like "Mrs. Trapp."

The world would know. According to George, half of Society already knew. Only about Nathaniel's infiltration of the spy ring—and nothing about the Royal Four. Things could go back to the way they had been before. *Lord Treason is dead. Long live Lord Reardon.*

Too late to renew his father's respect. That loss would ache inside Nathaniel all the days of his life.

Yet he had Willa and a life with her without disgrace.

"Well, I dare not stay long," George said, standing. Willa and Myrtle popped up as well. Nathaniel had never sat at all. "If I park my arse more than ten minutes in a private residence, every fool with a cause to lobby comes falling around my head."

He bowed over Willa's hand, then pulled her in for a kiss on the cheek. "Do come calling, sweeting. My Court could use a bit of life in it."

Everyone bowed and curtsied to the floor, and when they arose, the Prince had left the room. Nathaniel followed George and his entourage to the door and watched as the Prince boarded his unmarked carriage and was driven away.

29

Nathaniel reentered the first parlor, tempted to grab Willa up and carry her back to the library for a bit of private revelry in the chair. All such amorous celebration was forgotten when he saw Myrtle standing before Victoria in challenge.

"You knew all along, didn't you, Victoria? You're not the slightest bit surprised by any of this."

"Don't be silly," Victoria said shakily. "Of course, I—well, I am—well, you don't seem particularly surprised, either."

Myrtle waved a hand. "That's because I eavesdropped on Thaniel and that rook Liverpool!" Then her eyes narrowed suddenly. "Randolph knew better as well, didn't he?"

"Don't be silly. Of course he didn't." Victoria's head was high, her expression indignant, but she was lying. Nathaniel knew it. A prickle began in the vicinity of his chest.

Myrtle held up one hand. "Victoria, there is no reason anymore to tell anything but the absolute truth, unless you are determined to be purposely cruel."

Victoria snarled. "I, cruel? I? Do you know that three

weeks after I gave in to Randolph's importuning to wed,
my late husband's elder brother died and my son became
Lord Reardon? Three weeks!" She glared at them all. "I
missed finally being 'Lady Reardon' by three miserable
weeks!"

Myrtle scoffed. "And that was Randolph's fault, I
take it?"

"Of course it was," Victoria snapped. "He robbed me
of being one of the pivots of the *ton*! With that title and
Nathaniel's money, I could have had everything!"

"Poor Randolph," Willa said quietly.

"Indeed," Nathaniel said.

Myrtle raised her cane at Victoria. "Are you telling me
that you punished my poor boy for thirty years because he
wed you three weeks too soon?"

Victoria cast her gaze around the room, obviously
looking for support. Her glance fell on Willa. "You think
me shallow and ambitious. I can see it in your face. Just
you wait, Lady Reardon!" The words burst from her like
a flood held back too long. "Soon you'll realize that a
woman has nothing, no standing in the world, but what
her husband brings her and what he takes away! Once
you tie yourself to a man, you are a mere reflection of
him. You think he will give you your dreams, but he won't
care. Men—only concerned with their own interests, their
own pleasures! When the first blush of romance wears
off, you'll be nothing to him, just as I became nothing to
Thomas, and then less than nothing to Randolph."

"My nephew never mistreated you," Myrtle said
stoutly.

"Mistreated me?" Victoria laughed, a cold, jagged
noise. "No, he never beat me, never even berated me.
What he did was so much worse. What he did was declare
me *invisible*. Even when his illness struck . . . I thought,
Thank God, he needs me at last—but he didn't. He shut

me out still, keeping to himself in his study, in his rooms, keeping everyone away, muttering to himself all the time—I began to fear that he'd gone mad, but the physician said that it was an effect of the tonic Randolph took, that he spoke under his breath, that he couldn't seem to control his words."

Nathaniel went cold. Randolph hadn't dared let anyone near. God, had there ever been a man so full of secrets as the Old Man? Spymaster, privy to the inner workings of the most secret government agencies, Randolph must have lived in terror of spilling too much. Unable to trust anyone, not even himself, Randolph had made sure that no one would come close enough to know.

And what of Victoria? What sort of life must she have led, bonded to a man who cared so little for her, a man obsessed with duty he could not explain—

A man like me.

Nathaniel's gaze shot to where Willa sat, her attention fixed on Victoria, her eyes damp with sympathy for his mother's pain. Pain that Nathaniel had never seen, had never bothered to see. Pain that had made her bitter. He had blamed her for her bitterness, even while he'd felt the sting of Randolph's lack of interest himself.

Randolph, in his self-imposed isolation with his all-consuming duty, had injured them all and himself as well.

There had to be another way to unite life and duty, didn't there? Or was Willa condemned to the same bitterness that consumed Victoria? Was he himself condemned to Randolph's achingly solitary existence, removed from any contact or solace for the sake of duty?

When Myrtle began to defend her nephew vehemently, Nathaniel held up one hand. "I think being married to my father might not have been a complete joy, either," he said quietly. "His work meant more to him than any mere human being could."

Victoria sent him a stunned, oddly vulnerable glance. Apparently, she had not expected any defense from him.

"As for being cruel," Victoria tossed her head, but she also took one step away from Myrtle, "how dare you accuse me—"

"Victoria, you were not surprised by the Prince Regent's claims one little bit," Myrtle broke in. "If you cannot be truthful for your son's sake, perhaps you'll do it for your own sake. You tell the truth, all of it, right now, and I'll see to an income for you of two hundred pounds a year."

Victoria looked from one face to another, her tension obviously growing. Willa could almost see the wheels turning in her head. Reject Myrtle's offer, clinging to her cruelty, and live forever at the forbearance of Nathaniel and Willa.

Or let the darkness free, and free herself at the same time. It was money enough to live a life of certain comfort, even luxury. Willa held her breath, really not sure which way Victoria would choose.

"Very well." Victoria slumped slowly into her chair. "He knew. He suspected it was something of the sort even before the official news came. I tried to convince him it was not. He acted as if your disgrace was nothing," Victoria continued. "I expected him to despise you for what you did. Do you know what he said? He said, 'Thaniel knows his duty. He'll know that I'm only doing mine.' As if betraying us all, embarrassing us, ruining my standing in Society forever—as if it was nothing! Then he shut the door on me, like he did every day of our lives together. If I had my way, I'd burn that blasted study door!"

Thaniel knows his duty. The words went through Nathaniel like a spear. Could Randolph have *known*? All along, could he have known that Nathaniel was working for the Crown, that taking the blame for the Knights of Fleur had been an act of patriotism?

He'll know that I'm only doing mine.

Balm settled over something old and raw inside Nathaniel. Randolph had known somehow, possibly even about Nathaniel being a member of the Royal Four, and was only doing his part. Not daring to know more than his own assumptions because of himself as security risk, not willing to compromise Nathaniel's sacrifice with any public sign of forgiveness, Randolph had been *supporting* him, in the only way he'd believed available to him, by going along with the sham completely.

Nathaniel shut his eyes hard for a long moment. *Randolph, you bloody idiot. You would never—could never—have failed me.*

When he opened his eyes, Nathaniel saw Willa gazing at him with warm sympathy. She could not possibly know what was going through his mind, but it was likely she could tell something had relieved his mind, for she smiled softly, gladly, just for him.

Victoria raised her head, a spark of anger in her eyes. "But Randolph never felt the same about me then. He told me that he rejected you in part because he wanted to keep you away from me. Me! Can you imagine?"

"Do tell," drawled Myrtle.

"Randolph never truly spoke to me again." She let her shoulders fall as if she'd dropped a great load. "So, yes, when he died he knew the truth."

Willa said nothing, only gazed at Nathaniel over his mother's head. He closed his eyes for a long moment, then took a deep breath. "I wish you joy of the money promised you, Victoria," he said quietly. "I see that you have reasons for your dissatisfaction in life. I pity you and I do hope you find some. I don't blame you for your actions, but I must confess . . . I don't love you for them, either."

"Oh, Nathaniel. I—you must understand that I did my best by you—"

Nathaniel watched his mother through eyes that saw the good and the bad clearly. She was an angry woman, who had suffered many disappointments, it was true—but she had chosen to wallow in her bitterness of her own volition.

"Victoria, perhaps someday—but if you please, not now." He turned to Willa and bowed shortly. "Willa, Myrtle—if you will excuse me, I wish to be alone."

He turned and left them there without a word.

Daphne wasn't happy.

Of course, she was rarely satisfied, even at the best of times. There was always something else she wanted to acquire or someone else she wanted to best or to impress.

The drive to the country was not going well, what with the carriage wheel becoming lodged in the mud and developing a break, and they had been forced to alight only a few hours from London.

She flipped aside the simple muslin curtain that covered the single window of the inn room Basil had secured for them. She gazed down at the town in boredom. Wakefield. From here it looked like little more than a mud hole.

The dissatisfaction increased. So she turned to Basil, who was lounging in a tatty chair by the fire with his eternal brandy glued to his hand.

"Basil, I wish to go shopping."

Basil stood willingly enough. She could always count on Basil to do as she wished. Boring, but useful. In the mirror atop the chest, Daphne paused to correct her hair. The glass showed her what it always showed her. She was beautiful. Then her fingers slowed in their motion as she tucked a strand of hair away.

She was more beautiful than Willa. So why was Willa so irresistible to Thaniel and nearly everyone else who met her?

Daphne was the beauty. Daphne was the elegant one, the refined one.

Could it be that everything she'd ever been taught to be was a lie? Could it be that being the most agreeable, the most beautiful, the most fashionable woman in sight would not make her content?

So what was beauty worth, then? Daphne had always depended on her beauty. Daphne Danville, always the absolute glass of fashion. For what?

To be attractive? To marry well? She was the most attractive, she knew it, yet she'd married second-best, there was no denying it.

She gazed at her familiar, perfect, beautiful face in the mirror.

Willa wasn't actually beautiful, but she was still admired. If Daphne's beauty were gone, would anyone admire her?

Then she shook off the silly thought. She was just as she should be. She took Basil's arm and left the inn.

A couple passed them, vaguely familiar but inconsequential. Well, this was the best road north. Not surprising that they should spot a few familiar faces. The man and woman looked at them curiously, then whispered together as they made haste down the walk. Daphne smiled slightly with satisfaction. Even in mourning, even in a backwater like this, she was making a splash.

Basil belched. She cast him a reproving look. He shrugged.

"Sorry, love, but what do you expect when you drag me for miles when I've not had time to digest?"

"Do not be common," she murmured as she motioned

for him to open the door to the milliner's. "And please do not call me 'love.' You sound like a Cockney chimney sweep."

Then she swept into the shop and made her seat very prettily, arranging her gown about her with practiced grace. Not for her the standing at a counter, haggling over pennies. The milliner rushed over, her gaze admiring. Daphne preened. She knew she looked a picture.

She had better. She had spent all of Basil's quarterly allowance on this ensemble. Of course, that was if one didn't count the mink-trimmed mantle she wore. That was most of next quarter's allowance.

It scarcely mattered, anyway. When Basil's aunt Myrtle passed on, she, Daphne Danville, daughter of an upstart shipmaster who had bought himself a knighthood, would be one of the wealthiest women in England.

Posing exquisitely in the window of the shop, pouting prettily at the offerings of the milliner, Daphne dreamed of the day she would be one of the pillars of the *haute ton*. Then she heard the whispers from the two women at the counter.

"So romantic! Lord Reardon is a hero! And they say he saved his new fiancée from a pair of innkeeper's sons and she fell in love with him immediately! Willa—isn't that the most adorable name?"

Willa? Lord Reardon a hero?

"What? What is this? What are you saying?" She gazed over at the faces that now turned to her.

She, Daphne, was the acclaimed beauty of two Seasons running, who had managed to throw the fete of the year two evenings past, and was gowned like a queen— and the center of the social storm was still *Nathaniel and Willa*?

She stood, her lips parted in protest. "But . . . Nathaniel is a traitor! His wife is a . . . a tavern maid!"

"Not according to what we've heard," one of the women said archly. "Lord Reardon and the lovely Willa, who they say is a favorite of the Prince Regent's, by the way, are the most romantic tale ever! He was so brave, like a hero of legend," the woman sighed theatrically.

Daphne was scarcely able to breathe. As it was, the woven straw crackled in her fist. "Willa Trent is a common, overblown country mouse who could only attach a man by knocking him out with a rock!"

"I heard that rumor, too," said the woman. She sniffed. "But I never believed it."

"No, not for a single moment," declared the first woman. Then she peered more closely at Daphne. "I know you. You jilted Lord Reardon, abandoned him in his hour of need!" The woman sneered. "I'm terribly sorry to inform you, but your husband's cousin is by far the handsomest, most heroic gentleman London has ever seen. If you don't think so, then perhaps you are the traitor here."

The two women approached them, eyes narrowed. Even the milliner stepped forward to snatch her bonnet back. "I'll not serve the likes of you!" she hissed at Daphne and Basil.

Oh dear. Basil leaned close. "Time to go, love."

They left the shop hurriedly, then slowed to walk more normally back to the inn.

"The gall," Daphne said heatedly to Basil. "When we inherit from Aunt Myrtle, and buy our house, I am never allowing those women to step foot in it. I will cut them at every event. I will—"

"Ah, about that," Basil said breathlessly. "It seems Myrtle did not take kindly to the way you wouldn't call off the ball when Randolph went down."

Daphne turned to Basil in horror. "What?!?"

"She cut us off, I'm afraid," Basil said sadly. "But don't fret, pet. We can still live on my expectations—"

Daphne could not control her hand. It flew up and struck Basil across the cheek, right there on the street, like some sort of common . . . common tavern maid! "Basil, you don't have any expectations! Thaniel and Willa are going to have a passel of sons and you'll be last in line. Haven't you seen the way they act together? He's her willing slave, idiot male that he is!"

Basil put a hand to his cheek. "Idiot," he repeated dully.

That's when the first handful of mud struck Basil. It burst on his chest, splattering Daphne's gown and mantle and staining them forever.

Alone in his father's study, Nathaniel sank into the large chair and put his face in his hands.

To know that Randolph had even doubted the story would have been a comfort—to learn that he not only had suspected the truth but also had acted in part to assist the cover, that was a heavy weight from Nathaniel's heart.

To lighten his pain further, Nathaniel tested the depths of his other old resentment of Simon, the replacement son. Oddly, he couldn't seem to find it anywhere within him. Simon had proved to be more brother, or at least comrade, than Nathaniel could have dreamed was possible.

So much of his pain had been eased, so much of his burden lifted . . . it was going to take some time to remember the man he had been before. If that was even possible.

A short time later, Ren Porter limped into Randolph's— no, Nathaniel's study now—without knocking.

Although he'd actually been contemplating leaving to tell Willa the things he'd unraveled, Nathaniel narrowed his eyes. "I believe I left word I was not to be disturbed."

"You can brood later. I have a few things to say to you at the moment." Ren eased himself down to a chair without being invited. He looked vastly better, although he was still pale and weak. The dramatic facial scars still showed dark on his pallor, but his eyes seemed steadier, purposeful. "First, I thank you for your hospitality, but I think I should be on my way."

"You need not go. I think we would all like for you to remain until you are better. Willa especially."

"Hmm." Ren looked away. "No, I think it is best I leave."

Nathaniel spread out one hand. "As you wish. Where will you go?"

Ren smiled wryly. "Didn't you hear? Simon caught me up on my family matters. While I was sleeping, it seemed, my cousin died and left me pots of coin. There's even a tidy little estate in the Cotswolds that I've never seen. I thought I'd hire my own carriage. If I go slowly, I think I'll make it there alive."

Nathaniel refrained from commenting on the private travel. If Ren felt it necessary to hide, that was his business. Who was he to force someone to face his demons? "And the Liars?"

"I'm not ready yet." Ren looked down at his hands. "I have some things to carry out."

Nathaniel couldn't deny that the man had some healing of his own to do. "I wish you well of it, then," Nathaniel said mildly. "You know you may return to us at any time."

Ren gave a short nod. "Second, I wanted to warn you . . . Well, perhaps there is no point."

"Warn me of what?"

"It is simply that . . . Basil came to me the night of the

fire. He seemed entirely interested in my further plans for doing you in."

"Ah. I am both surprised and not surprised. Frankly, I'm stunned that Basil would actually exert himself." Nathaniel smiled wryly. "How nice to know he cares."

"Keep your eye on him, then." Ren leaned back in his chair. "How did you ever manage to survive this family, Reardon?"

Nathaniel shook his head. "It's a gift."

"No," Ren said shortly. "Willa is a gift."

Willa was a bloody divine intervention. One that Nathaniel was very worried he was going to waste. Could he balance what his father could not? Could he be the Cobra and be the man whom Willa loved?

The memory of Victoria's acrid bitterness stung his throat. If he did that to his lovely, giving Willa—if he turned her sour with his secrets and preoccupation—that would be more betrayal than Lord Treason had ever accomplished.

"A gift," Nathaniel murmured. "That she is."

Ren locked his fingers over his stomach. "One you had best appreciate. If you don't, you might find that I will."

Nathaniel's gaze locked on Ren's. "You're in love with my wife, Porter?"

Ren didn't flinch. "Can you blame me?"

Nathaniel actually felt a moment of sympathy for Ren. Willa was a force of nature. A man caught in her beams had little chance of surviving unchanged.

Then the moment of commiseration dried up and male protectiveness took over. Willa was his. "Thank you for visiting. Now, I hope you understand if I rescind my previous invitation. In fact, forgive me if I wish you far away from here."

Ren bowed his head. "Of course." He stood to leave. At the door, he turned. "Just you remember what I said. If

I ever find out you've devastated that fine woman . . . well, there's a few things I learned from the Liars. . . ."

Nathaniel shook his head. "If I destroy her, I'll be the first in line. You'll have to take your turn."

Ren nodded sharply. "Good." Then he was gone.

30

Willa had never felt less as if she belonged in a family.

Victoria was busily choosing fabrics for her mourning wardrobe and readying herself for the purchase of a small house of her own with the allowance that Myrtle had promised her.

"In Brighton, I think," she'd stated in an offhand way, as if there were no pall of awkwardness over the supper table. "London is too concerned with the Marriage Mart. I've done with all that."

The others had merely stared at her for a moment, before returning to the pushing about of food on their plates. Victoria's plans for her own stylish widowhood only made supper all the less appetizing.

Myrtle, pale yet tranquil, had declared her intention to leave immediately. "All this has worn me through," she said. She had risen and begun her slow totter to the door. "I think I may take a cure in Bath. You'll come visit, won't you?"

Willa had nodded and smiled, but next to her Nathaniel had said nothing but only muttered a good night to his aunt. Then a few moments later he had stood, tossing his napkin to the table, and left Willa with only a quick kiss on the top of her head.

Leaving Willa alone at the long, empty dining table. There was nothing to do but go to bed—in her very own room. Alone. "Which is as it should be," she reminded herself again. She was not his wife. He was not her husband.

Of course, he'd never truly wanted to be. She'd bagged him like a rabbit, just as he'd teased her. Unwilling prey.

Note his withdrawal from her today. Nathaniel was a hero now. His name had been cleared. His future was as open as it had previously been closed. He didn't need her support any longer. She was no longer the safe harbor from his isolation.

Sitting in the silent, luxurious room, Willa looked at all the opulence surrounding her. Nathaniel was going to marry her, make her his lady, mistress of all of this plenty. So why did it feel as though something was missing?

Oh yes. That's right.

"He doesn't love me." Her whisper was very loud in the silence.

He had never said so, never even suggested such a thing. She'd told him she loved him. He seemed to like hearing it, very much. He had never said it to her.

His matter-of-fact, utilitarian proposals—both of them—only proved the fact. Honor debt only. Oh, he liked making love, but Willa was aware of the fact that most men liked making love a great deal, often, with just about any woman who would hold still.

Willa planted her elbows on the table in best taproom fashion and dropped her head into her hands. "Well, this is simply bloody depressing," she muttered.

There came a great supercilious sniff. Willa looked up to see Hammil examining her distastefully, as if she'd smeared on his shoe. "If you're finished with your . . . *private conversation*, Miss Trent, the staff would like to clear."

Private conversation—translation: madhouse ramblings.

The last person Willa wished to see at that moment was Hammil. Hammil, who was always about, always sneering—

And always listening.

Willa gazed at the butler for a long, thoughtful moment. "Hammil, it is you who has been carrying tales about me," she stated with certainty.

Hammil started guiltily, then sputtered, but it seemed her accusation had caught him without a ready reply.

Willa closed her eyes briefly, then stood with a cheerful smile. If she was going to be Lady Reardon, willing slave to unrequited love, there must be a few perquisites.

"When I marry His Lordship, Hammil, you are entirely, completely, unequivocally . . . *fired.*"

The winding stair had never seemed more endless. When she approached her chamber, she heard something behind the door next to hers. Nathaniel's door. She was surprised that he would have retired this early.

In her room, she found Lily waiting, but nothing else. Her new wardrobe was gone from the room, and the books and tea towel were missing from the shelves and vanity. "Have I been moved again?"

Lily nodded. "Yes, my lady."

Willa felt hollow. "I see. Where am I now?"

"Oh, you needn't worry about it now, ma'am. I've your nightgown here. His Lordship asked for you to join him, please, my lady."

Well, at least he still wanted her. Listlessly, she allowed Lily to dress her in the wispy lawn nightgown that Moira had given her, covered by her wrapper.

When Lily had taken down her hair, Willa stood and

went down the hall to Nathaniel's room. His sitting room was dark, so Willa passed through it to the closed door of his bedchamber. *Think about a child,* she told herself. *Think about a happy life. Wish it to be so.*

Closing her eyes, she wished it, and opened the door.

When she opened her eyes, Nathaniel's room was gone. Gone was the masculine severity. Gone were the dark bed draperies and counterpane. In their place was a pagan fertility bower.

Sheer white panels fell around the bed, framing the silken ivory bedcoverings from her old room. Candles burned in ornate porcelain candlesticks, and a pretty garden-patterned rug lay before the crackling fire.

Were those—?

Willa stepped closer. Yes, those were rose petals heaped over the counterpane and sprinkled on the floor around the bed. Her eyes wide, Willa spun in disbelief. Her wardrobe stood in one corner, and Moira's tea towel brightened the washstand.

What was all this?

" 'The flowers' leaves'," Nathaniel's deep voice quoted from the shadows, " 'serve as bridal beds which the Creator has so gloriously arranged, adorned with such noble bed curtains, and perfumed with so many soft scents that the bridegroom with his bride might there celebrate their nuptials with so much the greater solemnity'."

Willa's throat closed. "Linnaeus," she whispered.

Willa searched the shadows until she spotted Nathaniel behind the door through which she had just entered. She blinked at him, and he laughed.

"Do you like it?" he asked.

"What is it?"

Nathaniel smiled. He came to her and tipped her chin up with one finger. "It's *our* new room."

Willa had to blink very fast right then. "Ours?"

"Ours."

Then he went down on one knee before her and took her hand.

"Willa, you told me that you loved me, and renewed my existence. Will you please do me the great honor of becoming my wife? A huge wedding, a ridiculously costly honeymoon—as soon as convention permits?"

Her knees began to shake. She could only nod, very fast.

"Oh, I forgot something." Nathaniel went to the other side of the bed and took an item from a drawer. Then he stood and smiled at her across the bed of rose petals.

"Willa Trent, will you, this day before God, take me to be your wedded husband?"

Willa nodded again, her throat too tight to speak.

"Will you promise to love, honor, and continue to defy me, all the days of your life?"

She nodded again. The tears were starting in earnest now.

Nathaniel stared. "Willa, you're crying. You never cry."

She sputtered through her tears, "Nathaniel, I swear to you, if you stop now . . ."

"Oh, wildflower." He started to climb across the bed to her.

She held up her hand. "Don't. Stop."

He tilted his head and smiled gently at her. "You haven't answered yet."

"Oh." She nodded vigorously, then climbed onto the bed facing him, the width of the bed still between them. "I will."

"Now, it's my turn. I, Nathaniel . . ." He walked one step forward on his knees. "I, Nathaniel Stonewell, Lord Reardon, on this day before God, will take thee, Willa, as my wedded wife." He stepped closer still, and she matched him. "I will give you my name and everything I have. I will promise to love, honor, and cherish thee, all the days of my life." He smiled. "It isn't much of a bargain but I'll do my best to make it up to you."

He opened his hand to reveal the Reardon family crest ring in his palm. The setting had been filled with a fine aquamarine, colored like the deepest twilight. "I chose it because it matches your eyes," he said softly. He slid it onto her finger. It was huge and ridiculous and meant everything to him.

Willa broke down and sobbed into her hands. Nathaniel pulled her into his arms.

"Wildflower, what is it?"

She said something, but he couldn't understand through her sobs and hiccups. "What?"

She visibly fought for a hold on her emotions, trembling in his arms. "You . . . you love me?"

"Of course I love you, wildflower. You knew that."

She shook her head. "I . . . I knew you liked me and . . . and you liked to co . . . copulate with me, but I thought it was just a . . . a passing fancy."

"Oh, wildflower." Nathaniel pulled her tightly to him and rocked her from side to side. "I should have said the words. I promise to always say the words. Every day."

"Twice," demanded Willa, her voice muffled against his shoulder.

"Thrice," promised Nathaniel. Then he pulled her down onto the rose petals and examined her in the candlelight. The glow turned her gown transparent, just as he'd hoped it would. Rosy nipples showed clearly, as did the shadow between her round thighs.

"God, I love that nightgown," he muttered fervently.

Willa smiled, her face still wet with tears. "Moira told me you would."

"You look like an angel, rolling in roses."

She snorted. "What a silly notion. I'm simply Willa."

"Precisely."

He kissed her. "I love you." He kissed her again, a bit longer this time. "I love you." Then he kissed her breathless. "I love you."

"Mmm." She nuzzled the hand that cupped her cheek. "I'm afraid I didn't hear that last one."

His lips quirked. He took both her hands and gently pressed them down on either side of her head. "To get your complete attention," he explained. Then he kissed her until she went limp and soft beneath him.

"I love you," he whispered in her ear.

"As I love you," she whispered back, and gave a blissful sigh. Then she wriggled. "You woke up my animal."

He chuckled, although his own animal was fighting the leash. "Well, then, it's a good thing I've got you trapped. We wouldn't want to ruin this pretty room by letting your animal loose in here."

"Mmm." She managed to focus on her surroundings. "Are you sure you'll be comfortable in here? Isn't it a little . . . unmanly?"

"So, you think I should bring back the boar's head?"

"Please, don't."

"Well, there's no need to worry about me. I have everything I need." He released her with a soft bite to her neck that made her shiver, then stood. He moved to the fireplace, and Willa noticed something near the hearth that was draped with a cloth.

"We have unfinished business." With a flourish, Nathaniel pulled aside the cloth and revealed . . .

The chair from the library.

"Oh no." Willa eyed the leather throne and chewed her lip.

"What is it?" Nathaniel couldn't wait to find out.

Willa crawled on all fours to the edge of the bed. It did wonders for the sheer gown. Nathaniel wondered if he needed to wipe his chin.

She sat back on her heels and tilted her head. "Do you think . . . ?" She hesitated, looking at him a little sheepishly. "Would it be too terribly depraved to . . . ?"

"Willa, you are killing me."

". . . to spend our wedding night in a chair?"

In answer, Nathaniel rushed to the bed, grabbed great handfuls of rose petals, and flung them to fall over the leather seat.

"Good enough?" God, he was panting already.

She smiled. "Perfect."

And it was.

Epilogue

"Nathaniel?" Willa snuggled deeper onto Nathaniel's lap on the bedroom chair. After weeks of planning, and cheerfully nominal chaperoning by Myrtle, the small, private wedding of their dreams was tomorrow and Willa had decided to keep custom in at least one instance, so she was going to stay at Kitty's house the night before the wedding.

Consequently, Willa and Nathaniel were making love in the afternoon, so as not to miss a day.

"Hmm?" He pulled her closer and nuzzled her ear.

"Is Lord Liverpool ever going to give me back my grandfather's diary?"

Nathaniel murmured something that told her quite clearly that he wasn't listening as his lips moved to her neck. Then he froze. "Your what?"

"My grandfather's diary. The one full of the Quatre Royale." She offered him her other ear, but he didn't take it. Leaning her head back to look into his face, she saw him gaping at her in shock.

"Willa, that diary was written by the Duke of Camberlake."

"Yes, I know."

"Your grandfather was the Duke of Camberlake?"

CELESTE BRADLEY

"And my father, too, of course. He was the last of his line." She wiggled hopefully on his lap, but things beneath her seemed distracted as well.

He leaned away from her, blinking. "You're Lady Willa Trent?"

"—the daughter of the Duke of Camberlake, yes. We've covered that. Are you going to take me now or not?"

He held up one finger. "Wait—I just realized something." He grinned. "I'm marrying up!"

She narrowed her eyes at him. "You always were," she purred. "Witness my superiority even now!" She bit his earlobe.

"Well, to be honest, it's a relief. For a time, I thought you might be a royal bastard."

She rolled her eyes. "What a ridiculous notion."

"I know. I'm sorry."

"Thank you," she said primly. "The royal bastard was my mother."

Oh, hell. Nathaniel shuddered. "Tell me it isn't true."

She blinked at him. "Very well," she said slowly. "It isn't true?"

"Good!" he said vehemently. "Let's keep it that way."

She moved to kiss him again.

"Wait!" He held up a finger again. "I just realized something else."

She sighed. "Yes?"

He threw his head back and laughed. "I'm marrying the granddaughter of the greatest Cobra in the history of the Royal Four!"

"Why is that so funny?"

He tilted his head and smiled at her. "You know, I think I just might tell you."

Tired of waiting, Willa dived her mouth down on his.

"Later," he said, the words muffled by her passion. "I'll tell you later."

*Read on for an excerpt
from Celeste Bradley's
next book*

THE ROGUE
(Book Two in the Royal Four series)

Ethan Damont left Lord Maywell's lovely ballroom with his pockets full of Lord Maywell's lovely money. Since he'd been assured by reliable sources that Lord Maywell was a very bad sort of man, Ethan had even enjoyed the evening's card game.

The refreshing thrill from a pastime that had mostly left him cold for the last year put an additional spring to his step as he crossed Maywell's expansive grounds.

Sauntering down the gravel walk leading to a rear wall that hopefully wouldn't be too high to manage, Ethan heard a sound that made him freeze in place.

Somewhere, not a dozen yards away, a woman was cursing softly and creatively.

A woman? Out in the dark alone? Ethan's lips twitched. Who said she was alone?

He began moving again. Far be it from him to interfere in someone else's mischief. He certainly wouldn't want to be disturbed at such a moment. At least, not as he recalled such moments, dimly though that was.

Then he heard it. *Sniffle.*

Oh, no, he groaned to himself. *Not that.* His spine weakened. He tried to stiffen it by sheer will.

Sniffle.

"Bloody hell," he whispered, slumping in resignation. Turning around, he retraced his silent steps until he was opposite where he believed the woman to be. The hedge was old growth and sparse between the thick gnarled trunks. Ethan wriggled through with commendable lack of noise.

The grounds here were dark, but Ethan could see the black trunks of trees silhouetted against the better lit area nearer the house. The earth was soft under his feet, so he was able to approach the ladylike sniffling.

Finally, Ethan was treated to such a sight that he simply had to pause. With a deep breath, he took a moment to appreciate it fully. Long, bestockinged, truly superior legs were wrapped firmly around a jutting tree branch. It was damned erotic, that's what it was. Ethan felt like letting go a bestial growl of his own.

He stepped closer. In the light from the house he could see the milky gleam of thigh skin peeking over the tops of the pair of rather battered stockings. The calves that were crooked over the limb looked plump and fully strong enough to hang on to him—er, the tree branch—all night long.

There was nothing else to see but yards of muslin swathing the rest of her. No problem.

Ethan had ever been a leg man.

The branch that Ethan had just been envying gave out a loud, groaning *crack!*

Ethan lunged forward, grasped the muslin bundle by what he judged to be a waist, and tugged the whole lot, legs and all, into his arms. His damsel in distress let out a yelp of surprise and sent an elbow deep into his stomach.

"Oof!" That had hurt! Just for that, Ethan put her down far more slowly than he otherwise would have. After all, one truly didn't get this sort of view every day. With his arms wrapped around her, the act of turning her over caused a few "unavoidable" liberties to be taken.

"So sorry. Do forgive me," Ethan said without much urgency. He let the luscious legs down first and watched wistfully as the muslin shifted allegiance and tumbled down to hide them. He was left with a struggling, protesting bundle of fallen hair and slapping hands.

"Get—off! Oh! *Oh!*" The woman gave him a last hearty shove, and Ethan released her.

"You're welcome," he drawled and dipped a low ironic bow, then turned to walk away. Heroism never paid. "I do hope the branch doesn't fall on your head," he called to her, his tone not terribly concerned.

Red-faced and gasping, Lady Jane Pennington, well-known Society heiress and recent rescuee, straightened and brushed her hair partially out of her eyes. The light of the house was behind her, shining on a broad back that was swiftly disappearing into the darkness.

Oh, thank heaven he was leaving! If one could catch fire from embarrassment and humiliation, she would certainly be a living torch right now. The fact that someone had seen—oh, she could die!

Still, a lifetime of taking pride in her good manners forced the words from her throat. "Thank you, sir," she said. The words choked a bit, but fair was fair.

He turned to look at her, then slowly stalked back toward her. Jane abruptly doubled her embarrassment as the light fell onto his face. He was not only tall and strong, but manly and handsome, as well. All in all, the worst possible candidate for rescuer she could imagine.

He came close, then closer still. Jane backed a step in alarm. Her hair still hung over her eyes and her face was in shadow, but it wouldn't do to be recognized.

The fellow came so near that she had to tilt her head back to look into his face. Her breath caught at the impact of his fine face and form. So near . . .

Only then did a shiver of alarm pass through her. She was alone, in the deserted garden at night with a man who had seen her drawers.

Even the most gallant of rescuers might gain the wrong impression.

His gaze was narrowed as he cast it down on her. "I'd rather an honest *get-thee-gone* than that grudging thanks, gazelle," he said, his voice low. Then he plucked a leaf from her hair and tucked it into his weskit pocket. "My token, fair maiden," he said mockingly.

Then he turned his back on her and strode away. Just as he stepped into the deeper darkness of the rear garden, the stranger sent her a flashing, wicked grin over his shoulder and pointed up to "her" tree.

"Nice limbs," he called. With an insouciant salute, he turned away again and was gone.

239   304   310   335